CIRCLE
OF
LIFE

Novels of the Joad Cycle

Join us for a discussion about America's future at WWW.Joadcycle.com

CIRCLE
OF
LIFE

BOOK III OF THE JOAD CYCLE

GARY LEVEY

iUniverse, Inc.
Bloomington

CIRCLE OF LIFE
BOOK III OF THE JOAD CYCLE

iUniverse books may be ordered through booksellers or by contacting:

iUniverse
1663 Liberty Drive
Bloomington, IN 47403
www.iuniverse.com
1-800-Authors (1-800-288-4677)

ISBN: 978-1-4620-4546-4 (sc)
ISBN: 978-1-4620-4548-8 (hc)
ISBN: 978-1-4620-4547-1 (ebk)

Printed in the United States of America

iUniverse rev. date: 08/24/2011

Circle of Life is my third self-published novel in the series, The Joad Cycle. The first two novels are The Golden Rule and Profit. In each, the words and concepts however disconcerting, they are mine and in these dysfunctional times, I stand by them. Our political leaders are fighting for every political and economic advantage and their refusal to compromise only satisfies the needs of their corporate sponsors, not the people, but I'm not naïve. That is American politics.

Every politician lauds America's Founding Fathers in great patriotic speeches. But our Founding Fathers made America great by compromising greatly, rationally, and smartly. Why has that lesson been lost? Look no further than greed and power.

Inevitably, this refusal to compromise moves America that much closer to Andy Crelli's America of 2032 and beyond. There is a circle of life and if the only thing that prevents some few from owning America is the twenty-first century American citizen, us, then our great republican experiment is truly doomed.

I have worked hard to reduce the grammatical errors and such to a minimum. If you discover any, please bear with me, I will make it better in subsequent releases.

I dedicate this novel to my wife, June, most of all, for putting up with me and helping me to develop as a person, for if I've developed at all, it is because of her and if I haven't, of course, it's my fault.

Gary Levey
7/28/2011

Chapter 1
Canada—2070

Civil disobedience—The active, professed refusal to obey laws, demands, and commands of a duly elected and legal government of the people, by the people, and for the people. Civil disobedience is commonly defined as nonviolent resistance and of civil resistance in the form of respectful disagreement.

In the Second Republic of United States, civil disobedience is the preferred method for voters to communicate their displeasure with their government between voting cycles. However, there are limits.

Due to the detrimental effects perpetrated on the U.S. economy by selfish special interest groups in the past, Circle of Life legislation was passed making it illegal to protest against the national government or its policies. The only acceptable method to air differences of opinion is to contact your appropriate government representative who is required to respond within forty-eight hours.

If it is deemed by the Secretary of the Treasury, the Federal Reserve Chairman, and the Council of Private Banks that actions by individuals or special interest groups are detrimental to the economy or to the Church, remedies within the Circle of Life begin with the suspension of Habeas Corpus. You have been warned!—**Archive**

Shivering, with wet, cold clothes clinging to her trembling body, Stacey Grant hid, terrified, in the small, dark grotto that had once been her great escape from the simple things in Angel Falls that needed avoiding, like her daily chores. That grotto was now her last sanctuary against the death that had rained down on her family and her friends and she could feel it closing in to take her, too. Over the noise of the waterfall, in her mind she could still hear the explosions that had destroyed her world and the sound of weapons fire that had murdered everyone she had ever loved. Wretched but resigned to fight to the end, even though she had no weapon, she stared through the cascading waterfall into foreboding blackness, waiting for government rangers to penetrate the insubstantial wall of water that was her only protection.

She stared at the feeble old body of Mark Rose, Gil's grandfather; the former President of the United States, as he lay curled up in a fetal position on a flat rock beside her. He wouldn't survive without her.

A willing believer that bad things happened in threes, Stacey was depressed enough to know that bad things weren't just limited to threes. She and Gil had discovered the *SurveilEagle*. She'd lied about it to the village elders and forced Gil to lie, too. They'd argued and Gil had left angry. By her calculation, that was three bad things, so to change her luck, she had wandered away from Angel Falls in search of a new trail that she and Gil could hike once he stopped being mad at her.

But if she thought something simple like that could break the string of bad, she soon realized how naïve she was. After discovering a new trail through deep ravines, she hurried home reinvigorated, but one look at her father and she had known that the rule of three was looking to expand. Her father was crying. A typically stoic New Englander, he spoke softly to modulate the grief he felt. The rabbi, Bernie, Gil's great grandfather, Bernie Rosenthal, he was dead. Instinctively, she had reached out to hug her father and they cried together.

When Stacey was younger, she had sat in the Meeting House beside her mom and dad while they and her neighbors sang the Rabbi's praises for he was their hero. He had saved Angel Falls. Her father had explained to her that the Rabbi had once worked for the huge American conglomerate, U.S. ANGS, the sole employer in Angel Falls, and how one day the company closed the production facility, ending every villagers work life and dooming the community—and ANGS did it just to save money.

It was Angel Falls' misfortune to be located a hundred miles from nowhere with no other employment opportunities anywhere close to nearby. To add insult, nary a solution had been offered by ANGS to save the community and so most of the townsfolk were forced to move on, to make a living elsewhere, leaving Angel Falls more or less a ghost town. Some, like her father, with nowhere to go, stubbornly remained, fretted, and depleted their life savings.

Seeing the wrong and the heartlessness in ANGS' draconian decision, Rabbi had vowed to help them and one cold winter day, strangers arrived, businessmen who began to hire. Soon an executive retreat was being constructed for weary professionals and jobs and money flowed in. Within two years, everyone in town was working again and many of her parent's neighbors who had moved away, returned.

Ultimately, the Executive retreat failed, but by then, it had made way for more pastoral business pursuits that flourished alongside the natural efforts of the community and it was enough to provide a good life for the remaining town folk of Angel Falls.

Years later, Rabbi returned. Rumor said he was a fugitive now, but he was accepted graciously because everyone in Angel Falls knew him as a friend and their savior. He brought a teenage boy with him, Gil, a quiet, introverted, and very good-looking boy who was close to Stacey's age. He had proved to be very different from the local boys. He was exceedingly polite but distant and hard to get to know, but she saw in him a mystery that intrigued her, a mystery that she would now never unravel because Gil was dead. No. She stiffened to fight the trembling. No, she mustn't think of that.

Her mother had insisted that she help the Rabbi, and that was better than doing chores so she spent much of her time with the old man and grew to love his gentle, kind soul. When he asked her to befriend Gil, she tried, she did. But he was so aloof that her friends made fun of him and her so she begged Rabbi to ask someone else to help. But he insisted, telling her that although Gil was difficult, someday it would be important for him to have friends he could trust. She had no idea what that meant, but she wanted to please Rabbi so she worked harder to be Gil's friend.

As the years passed, her outgoing personality and persistence slowly worked on Gil and, in his way, he began to open up to her. They began to have fun together, though he remained aloof; something rare in such a small, tight knit community like Angel Falls. Because she spent so much time with Gil, she had less time for her friends and though she complained, Rabbi had been adamant. And so with each passing day, the inability to close the distance between her and Gil frustrated her because of the widening breach with her friends. She never told Gil what she was giving up to be his friend, and he wouldn't have cared, but she blamed him for her being excluded, even hating him a little until, against all reason, she fell in love—not that he noticed.

3

Then the bad luck arrived, the discovery of the *SurveilEagle*, the lie, her argument with Gil, and Rabbi's death. She had tried to console Gil, but for no reason, he was angry and mean to her, very mean. So mean, in fact, that she had slapped him and not just once. She was sorry for that now. At the Rabbi's funeral she had watched Gil as he stood alone, dejected, a hurtful distance from her and everyone else who mourned the Rabbi's passing. She wanted to comfort him but she was angry and she needed comforting, too. Then, from out of nowhere came the roar of jets, the bombs screaming down death, the rangers parachuting from the heavens to inflict more death, and in the carnage and the hysteria, she had lost track of him. All was chaos, terrified neighbors running and screaming, so many dropping and writhing in pain, others, limp, lifeless and horrific to look at. It had been too much and she had fallen to her knees, sobbing at the horror and the loss.

Gil's grandfather, Mark, had limped by her, staggering, dazed, and in shock toward the forest trailed by a hang glider that landed near him. A ranger threw a club that hit the old man and dropped him to the ground where he remained as the ranger beat him with the butt of his rifle leaving Mark bloodied and unconscious before the ranger turned in search of his next victim.

Horrified, she stared at Mark's unconscious body until a movement caught her eye on the hill, where moments before the Rabbi had been eulogized. Someone was running into the far woods—Gil? An ATV followed—was it Gil's friend, Meat? They disappeared from view just as an explosion and an impossibly bright, billowing fireball seared the forest barren and blasted her back and onto the ground. Dazed and incredulous, she lay there staring as the part of the forest where Gil had fled became a firestorm of black smoke that plumed above blackened trees with such intense heat that she had been forced to look away.

In the frightening calm that had followed, she yelled for Gil and then buried her head in her hands in despair, sobbing until someone touched her shoulder. Expecting it to be another ranger, she flinched. The former president stood above her, blood streaming from both ears, a gash on his head, and with a wild, lost look in his eyes. She grabbed his hand and pulled herself up while searching for a way out. Everywhere, laser beams were targeting her family, her friends, and her neighbors for killing while far above, aircraft hovered like insects utilizing their own high intensity lights to aid in the massacre.

To her left there was a small rise that led off to the northeast, toward Presque Isle. She and Gil had used the trail often. Stumbling, she urged Mark up the hill. When they reached the crest, she spotted a ranger before he spotted her. She knew she and Mark couldn't outrun him so she pulled Mark down and together they rolled and crawled to a clump of high grass near the tree line. From there, she peered warily at the ranger as he continued his search for fresh targets.

Mark lay dazed as bombs continued to fall, so she reached under his shoulders and while screaming until her lungs burned, she dragged him to cover. They reached the trees before the ranger saw them and she fell, exhausted, into the woods and lay there breathing hard and whimpering as projectiles zipped past, severing leaves from branches and branches from limbs while Mark remained in place, staring up, blinking at the stars.

"Mr. Rose, crawl over here for cover," she shouted. "I can't carry you any more."

He struggled to his feet and disoriented, turned toward the rangers instead of away.

"No!" she screamed and though exhausted, she ran to him, grabbed him, turned him around, and pushed him deeper into the woods. There was an errant burst of rifle fire as they struggled through the low brush in search of the trail. The firing stopped, abruptly, replaced by the loud hum of electric motorcycles. Panicking, but unable to move very fast due to Mark's age, she prodded him along until she found the trail. Then, she quickened her pace as much as he could handle and, although worn out, they trudged away from the engine roar, sporadic rifle fire, and the screams that would never end.

She knew a place where they might be safe, at least for now, a place where she and Gil would hide when they wanted to avoid prayer meetings, the Rabbi's lessons, or her mother's chores. She tugged Mark off the trail and into a cold shallow stream, which they followed until it was too deep to walk. By the sounds around them, pursuit was closing in. She tried to move faster but Mark had nothing fast in him.

The stream widened and got shallower and Mark tripped, slipping under the water. With all her strength, she hauled him up and onto the mud bank, and though he was shivering now, she forced him to keep moving. Cold and numb, too, she coaxed him further until the stream widened again, cutting off dry land and forcing them back into the water. At a bend in the stream, she heard, and then saw the waterfall. Nearby, just over the trees, gun ships were still hovering with their blinding beacons searing the night sky in search of the last of her neighbors.

She tapped Mark, pointed to the waterfall, and dove into the stream at the point where it widened into a small lake. Out of breath when she surfaced, she looked for Mark. He stood, in plain sight, where she'd left him. Exhausted and shivering, she swam back, grabbed him again, and swam with him; her arm snaked under his ribcage, his body hoisted up to keep his head above water as her weary arm and legs paddled and kicked through the waterfall and to the other side. There was relative calm inside the slick, moss-covered, small dark cavern and together they stumbled to a ledge and sat shivering while awaiting their fate. They remained that way for an excruciatingly long time.

She moved beside a small fire pit that she and Gil had used. There was nothing to burn and she would have been too scared to start a fire if there was. Above the sound of the waterfall, she was startled to hear motorcycles roar by, and later, she heard the faint snapping sound of gunfire. Helpless, cold and desperate, she fought to keep the thought that Gil was dead out of her mind but it was driving her crazy. She awoke much later and the sounds of gunfire, explosions, and motorcycles had stopped. That's when she realized her luck had changed and that she and Mark might live through the night.

"I have to pee," Mark said, sounding wretched.

"We can't leave." She thought about it and suddenly laughed. "How pathetic are we? You can't get any wetter or more uncomfortable so just pee down your leg, sir, the warmth might help."

There was silence, then, "That feels better," he said. "And warmer." They laughed, stopping abruptly when it reverberated through the cavern.

Much later, she snuck out into the darkness to reconnoiter. No one was near the lake, nor were there lights anywhere within sight, but she still doubted they were completely safe. They couldn't stay here so she went back for Mark and together they stumbled down the trail to Presque Isle.

"If we don't see any cycles or helicopters, I can get us to the Canadian border. Gil and I hike there all the time."

"But the Elders forbid it," Mark said glumly.

"What they don't know . . ." She felt guilty so she paused. The *SurveilEagle* was her fault. She should have told the elders but she didn't.

Everything that followed, Gil, her family, and this, it was all her fault. She had to move on if only to fight through her grief.

"We'll take the trail north around Houlton about a mile from the border crossing. We . . . I have friends on the Canadian side that'll help us."

They continued to walk until shivering and moaning uncontrollably, Mark collapsed. She tried to pull him up but he offered no help. "I can't go any further." He whispered. "Go. Save yourself."

Instead, she covered them both in thick, dead branches and huddled tight to warm him. After a time, she asked, fearfully, "Did . . . did he escape?"

But Mark was asleep, so fearing the worst she sobbed quietly, and then curled closer to him to preserve as much heat as she could in the cool, Maine darkness. She fell into a restless sleep and woke with a start to a cold, quiet, sun-drenched morning. She woke Mark and they set off again. After a very slow start, Mark moved a little better than the night before trying gallantly to keep up with her as they headed for Canada.

When they reached the border, she stopped just inside the last line of trees and surveyed the area. "Can they see us, do you think?"

Mark's far-away gaze re-focused on her. "What?"

"Is it safe to cross?"

"Probably not. We haven't been on good terms with Canada for a long time, but with budgetary constraints, most of our earthbound detection systems have fallen into disrepair and spy satellites monitor the borders now. They're able to see us if we cross."

"Would it be better if we waited until dark?"

"It doesn't matter; they can detect anything that moves," he pointed to the heavens. "The only question is how long it takes them to react."

"Why didn't they use the satellites last night to track us?"

"You'd have to ask the Chairwoman."

"What should we do?"

"Surrender."

"Except that."

"There's nowhere to go. Tanya won't hurt me. I'll speak for you."

"Who is 'Tanya'?"

"Tanya Brandt. She's the Chairwoman, she runs the country."

"Oh. Why won't she hurt you if she destroyed everything else?"

"She's taken everything of value from me and she likes to gloat."

"Why did she kill my mom and dad?" Stacey asked. Mark just shrugged. She closed her eyes tightly and said a silent prayer. Then she made a decision.

"Whatever I do, I will never surrender," she said fiercely. "If they want me, they're going to have to kill me."

"That's noble, but silly . . . They kill easy enough."

"They won't get us and that's final. We'll find a way across where there's more cover." While she searched, he followed meekly. "Mr. Rose, if the Canadian police catch us, will they let us stay?"

"No, but if we're going over, we should just do it. We can't hide here forever and we're leaving a heat print anyway so the longer we delay; the better chance they have."

She started to run but before she reached the clearing, she stopped and turned. Mark was still sitting where she had left him so she returned and sagged to the ground beside him. After a few minutes of silence, she spoke.

"Mr. Rose, why'd they do it?" she asked.

"You mean back there?"

She nodded.

"They wanted Gil and my father."

"But why didn't they just capture them. They could have easily done that."

"That's not their way. A long time ago, the first time, before you were born, Tanya's predecessor, Andy Crelli, tried to kill my father by blowing up his underground hideout in Indianapolis. It was unsuccessful, of course but it made for spectacular footage and Andy made a big deal about it in the national media."

"They kill for the media attention." She covered her face. "My family and friends died for that."

"I'm sorry," he offered.

She screamed in anger and frustration. "Who are these people? They killed everyone I've ever cared about for no reason?"

"They always have a reason."

That made her more determined. "We're going over now. When I count to three, run as fast as you can."

"No, you go. I'm tired and I'll only hold you back. Let me die here."

Instead of answering, she grabbed his arm and pulled. He resisted briefly but once out in the open, with each step, she expected to be killed but she kept moving and dragging the former president along. They reached the other side, exhausted, and dropped into the Canadian woods.

"Oh, Canada," she sang, coughing hard and laughing at their small success.

"What?"

She wiped tears away. "Whenever Gil . . . ," she hesitated, telling herself not to cry. "Whenever we crossed the border, we sang *Oh, Canada*. You know, 'our home and native land.' She paused and continued, sadly. "I know it's hopeless but I hope he made it—somehow." They were quiet for a long time. Finally, she turned to Mark. "We'll visit my friends. They live about a mile from here."

They trudged through the woods until they reached a small clearing where an old beat up and rusted, silver-colored trailer was securely propped up on stacks of cinderblocks. The door was swinging open in the breeze; so warily, she dropped to her knees and pulled Mark down with her.

"What do you think?" she asked.

Mark shrugged.

"I don't see anyone," she said. Again, he shook his head. She told him to wait as she carefully stalked the perimeter until she felt it was safe to approach the trailer. She worked her way cautiously toward it, expecting with each step to have to turn and run. At the door, she peeked inside. There, lying on the floor was her friend, shot once in the head and clearly dead. She covered her mouth and screamed. When Mark arrived, she was sitting on the cot sobbing. Mark saw the dead man and shook his head. "Well that's it then. We should give up."

"No!" she yelled. "I won't quit and certainly not after they did this." She was familiar with the trailer so she crawled under the bed where she found a locker. Inside was a small two-way communicator. With it, she called another friend.

"Martin," she said, giving it the French pronunciation, "this is Stacey from Angel Falls. I need your help, right now."

Mark put his hand on the communicator to stop her. "They can trace this."

She looked up at him defiantly. "What else can we do?" She took Mark's hand off the communicator and continued, speaking rapidly. "Martin, we're at Dex's place. They killed him. They killed Dex, American agents killed him."

A voice came back, cracking with static. "Stacey . . . ? What are you talking about? What about Dex?"

"American agents killed him. I don't know why but I need help."

"Say again?"

"Stacey Grant. Angel Falls was attacked by government rangers and everyone was killed. I . . . we escaped and I need your help."

There was silence. Then, "Saw choppers. That's what it was? Is Gil with you?"

"No, he . . . ," she hesitated, unprepared to voice her fears. "There's just me and a friend. He's old and injured and can't go far. I don't know what to do. I don't have anyone. Can you help me? Martin, please."

An hour later, at the prescribed location, a car stopped to pick them up. There were ill-fitting but dry clothes to change into and Stacey was grateful to be warm and dry. They were driven north through the night. At various truck stops along the way, they transferred surreptitiously to other cars with different drivers, always heading north and west. The drivers were reticent to speak so Stacey was left to herself, staring out at the countryside worrying or cat napping. Mark slept most of the time, his mouth open, his head rolled back and propped against a window. From time to time, his snorting startled her out of her reverie.

"My shift takes us to Sudbury," the more talkative new driver explained.

"Are you with the rebels?" she asked, grateful for some conversation.

"No, Miss, we don't like what happen in America, so we help the Underground any way we can. There's no way we get involved with rebels, though, because it could start a war. The PM don't like the little help we give the Underground because of all the pressure he gets from Washington. There's a new guy who'll be our next PM and he promises to be more aggressive because he believes our Euro and Asian allies will support us."

"We really appreciate your help. What you're doing is dangerous."

"Thanks, Miss. But you're a long way from safe. If we go north far enough maybe we'll shake their surveillance, but I don't know." After another long period of silence, the driver spoke again. "Say that's a nasty bruise your sleepy friend has."

She nodded into the rearview mirror. "He'll be okay. He's been through a lot."

"Sounds like you both have. We heard there was a massacre."

"Yes." It was all she could bring herself to say.

"Was it really a rebel headquarters the government took out?"

"No, and I don't want to talk about what happened." She had no idea why they were attacked. The Rabbi, Mr. Rose and maybe even Gil were probably in the middle of it, but she never heard them say anything about being rebels. "Angel Falls is a peaceful community of Friends and it was my home. The government had no right. The people who did this are bad people."

"Yes they are, Miss, sorry."

She was too tired and stressed to sleep but it was a long car ride so she continued to nod fitfully. Even with that, time passed too slowly. Finally, they approached a town.

"What happens to us after Sudbury?"

"Someone takes you back to Toronto where you contact the Underground."

"Then what?" she asked. The driver just shrugged and wouldn't provide more information so she waited in silence.

In Sudbury, the driver stopped at a small diner for lunch. When they were done, he left and another man, wearing a bright blue Toronto Maple Leafs jersey slid into the booth to pay for the meal.

"We're going to Toronto," he said. "I'll fill you in on what happens once I know. We're trying to contact a young woman in the Underground. She's helped us before."

"Will the Underground protect us?"

"They'll do what they can," he shrugged. "We can't risk war."

"We really appreciate what you're doing."

It was another long drive but finally, in the distance, she saw the large office buildings that marked the north side of Toronto.

"We're almost there, Miss, you'd better get the old guy ready." She woke Mark who stretched and groaned as the driver explained more. "We've contacted the girl. Here's how it'll go. I'll drop you at the subway. Go down to the platform as quickly as you can and wait." He reached back and handed her some coins. "You'll need these. The girl you're meeting has short white hair with red streaks and a large spike through her left ear lobe. She should be easy to spot."

"White hair with red and a big spike," Stacey repeated.

They reached the subway stop and the driver pulled to the curb with a screech. "Get out and get down there as fast as you can." The man sounded concerned.

"Are they watching us?"

"Don't know. They have incredible surveillance capability. Our people are compromised constantly. Go and good luck."

She helped Mark out. When she turned to thank the driver, the car was gone.

They moved as quickly as Mark could handle down the steps to the subway platform. Once there, Mark sat on a bench, looking around nervously. When they didn't see anyone with funny hair and a spike, he asked, "What do we do if she doesn't come?"

"Let's not worry about that yet." She scrutinized each person who descended the steps. No white and red haired girl with an ear spike came by.

Trains came and went until one stopped and a small woman got off. She wore a cap with tuffs of white hair with the hint of red billowing out and what appeared to be a spike in her ear. Stacey stared at her when she passed by but the woman ignored her. Once Stacey was certain of the spike, she motioned Mark and they followed. The woman never looked back at them. She just walked to the end of the station platform and down the maintenance ladder to the tracks. They followed at a safe distance. Stacey was unsure whether to yell to the woman or just follow, but when she disappeared around a curve, Stacey had no choice but to run to catch up. Mark trailed, struggling.

When Stacey turned a corner, she saw a maintenance door closing so she ran and caught it just before it shut and held it open until Mark caught up. They entered and almost immediately were confronted by three men with weapons. When the woman turned, Mark saw her, groaned, and sank to the floor. Stacey just stared. The woman was compact and attractive, but had a badly scarred face.

Ginger Tucker smiled. "Mr. President, it's so good to see you again."

Confused, Stacey looked down at Mark. His hands covered his face as he rocked back and forth on the dirty floor. She bent down to comfort him but all he could do was repeat, "I'm sorry," over and over again.

The woman offered Stacey her hand. "We haven't met. I am Reverend General Ginger Tucker of HomeSec. Mr. Rose and I go back a long way, don't we, Mark? And you are Stacey Grant."

Brokenhearted, she nodded.

"Good, good, good. You're the last of that cesspool of rebels to be cleaned up." Angered, Stacey lunged at the woman who sidestepped and kicked her in the stomach. Stacey grunted and fell hard to the dirty floor.

She stared up at the woman, in pain.

"We're not rebels!" she yelled through clenched teeth. "You murdered innocent people, my family and friends." She tried to stand but another kick convinced her to stay down. Tucker grabbed her arm to immobilize her and though she twisted and turned, she couldn't break free as her captor ignored her struggles while she spoke with Mark.

"Tanya appreciates your service, Mr. President, and I wish I could be there for the reunion, but I just found out that I have other, more urgent business to attend to. Tell me, is the girl important?"

Terrified, Mark refused to meet Tucker's stare. "She's just an innocent local girl."

The Reverend General turned to one of her men. "Push her in front of the next train." Hearing that, Stacey struggled again but couldn't free herself.

"Ginger, No," Mark pleaded. "Let her go or I'll tell Tanya she was important. You don't want Tanya pissed at you again, do you?"

Ginger hesitated. "I won't kill her but she comes with us."

"Let her go. She's innocent."

"There is no such thing anymore, Mr. President and you above all know that. Besides, you know how attracted I am to this kind of sweetness when I find it wild in nature like this." Tucker grabbed Stacey by her hair and twisted it hard, forcing her to wince as she was yanked eye level with the Reverend-General. When Tucker twisted harder, Stacey screamed as some of her hair ripped out at the roots.

"Good, I love screaming. My, you're a pretty one. And feisty too. I like that in a girl—or a boy for that matter. I wish I had time for you, but maybe later. Duty calls." With her free hand, Ginger roughly explored Stacey's body making her wince and cringe at the invasion. "My, my, tight and nice titties, too, you'll be great fun. You may even be Chairwoman quality. It's quite an honor. I'd be pleased to have you as sloppy seconds." Repulsed, Stacey glowered until Tucker yanked her hair again.

Stacey screamed. "Yes, I'd love to meet the Chairwoman," she said gritting her teeth against the pain.

"Good. I'm due elsewhere so listen to these gentlemen and do precisely what they say. The Chairwoman and I much prefer our toys undamaged, but we'll play with you bruised and broken if you insist." Stacey spit at her but the Reverend General yanked her hair and pulled her close until their lips almost touched. Stacey tried to bite her but the General held her secure. "Save the foreplay for later, my sweet." With that, she flung Stacey to the ground and stepped on her on the way out. At the door, she turned to her men. "Robert, take them through customs and get them on the plane."

"Can we sedate them and send them as baggage?" the man suggested.

"You three roughnecks can't handle an old man and a girl?" She seized Stacey again. "You'll follow orders, won't you? Robert here shouldn't be concerned."

"No, ma'am," Stacey answered, sullenly.

"Good. There is paperwork at our terminal that will get them through security." Tucker turned to Mark. "You'll cooperate. We know precisely how much pain you're willing to avoid."

Mark only nodded.

Ginger grabbed Stacey once again by her hair and twisted it so she was forced, one more time, to stare into her captor's eyes. The Reverend General then leaned in and licked Stacey's lips. Seeing an opportunity, Stacey butted Tucker's head so hard she saw stars. Without checking to see if the blow had drawn blood, Ginger responded. "You're making me hot. Now that you've set the bar, my sweet, maybe I should stay. I'll be disappointed if you don't try harder when we meet again. For now, no problems, cunt, or you'll regret it." She twisted her hair again, forcing Stacey to nod as tears ran down her cheeks. The Reverend General licked the tears away and then she left.

As soon as she was gone, the men grabbed her and Mark and guided them out of the subway station and into a limousine that headed to the Toronto airport.

At the airport, Stacey prayed Canadian security would stop them but when the Canadian Police saw official HomeSec badges, they cleared them through to a small terminal.

As they waited to board, she pleaded. "I need to go to the ladies' room."

"Go on the plane or in your pants," one of her captors said, smiling.

"No, you don't understand. It's . . . my time of the month. Please. I don't want to create a scene." Robert, the leader, looked at her. "Try something and I'll beat the crap out of you."

"How will airport security react to that?"

"Fuck airport security, the leader interrupted. "Joe, you and Sam take her to the ladies room. Sam goes in first to make sure there's no other way out. Give her five minutes, that's all. Get her and bring her back. Got it?" The men nodded. He turned to Stacey. "Don't try anything?"

She nodded.

The two men walked her around the corner to the ladies' room. While one held a knife to her, the other checked out the bathroom. He returned quickly. "No problem. The windows are too high to climb out. Let her go." Then he said to her, "You got five minutes."

She entered. The man was right, there was nowhere to go. But there was a janitor's maintenance closet stocked with cleaning supplies, and there was a bucket full of dirty, soapy water on the floor but there was nowhere to escape. Frantic, she pondered her situation until she heard, "Five minutes, times up."

As soon as the guard entered Stacey hurled the soapy water at his face. He ducked but was temporarily blinded as the soapy contents splashed into his eyes. She hit him over the head with the bucket and ran for the door, avoiding his desperate grasp as he slipped to the floor. When she opened it, the other man was staring at her, dumfounded.

As he waited for his partner, she hesitated, but when his partner yelled, she ducked under his arms and ran in the only direction she could to get away. The guard turned to pursue her, but before he could give chase, his partner came crashing out of the ladies room and they collided. That was the margin Stacey needed as she bolted for the airport exit, sprinting past people and heading down a near-empty escalator. Once outside the terminal, she turned to see if she was being chased. Not seeing anyone, she continued to run, looking back fearfully from time to time. She was half way down an airport maintenance road when she saw a trash dumpster and hid behind it. Breathing hard, she waited, sniffing the sweet, cold smell of snow—the smell of home—and she cried.

She hid behind the dumpster until she was certain she wasn't followed. She tried to figure out where she was exactly, but couldn't find her bearings in this strange metropolis. She could hike the woods around home without getting lost, but here, she was helpless. Forcing the terror back and fighting tears, she carefully worked her way into and out of a few buildings while trying to get as far away from the airport as possible. Exhausted, she sat on a bench and rested while watching for her pursuers. She might be free for now, but Mark wasn't, and if she was free, for how long? And what could she really accomplish working against people who have sophisticated ways of tracking her? She cried softly as she searched the skies for *SurveilEagles.* She was on her own.

The sun set and the evening grew cold. Fighting a piercing wind, she buttoned her light yellow jacket and put her hands deep into oversized jeans pockets while she struggled toward the city lights. At every corner, she hid until she could cross unseen. Shivering, she reached a part of town with small homes and stores and began searching for a place to hide from her government and the cold.

She found an alley where wired crates were stacked high against the side of a tall building. Fearful of what might be lurking underneath, she carefully moved the boxes. When there was sufficient space, she fought a scream and crawled silently into a gap between the boxes and the wall. Once there, she re-piled the crates around her to block the wind. It wasn't great but as sanctuary, it was better than nothing. Exhausted and shivering, she used her arm as a pillow, fought for comfort, and gained a restless night's sleep in the raw, Canadian early-autumn evening.

Chapter 2
Toronto, Ontario Canada—2070

Stacey slept fitfully, dreaming of a bloody hand grasping for her, and she woke to a sudden scream, which she thought was hers but turned out to be the wind howling through the alley. At first light, trembling and sobbing silently, she brushed away tiny pellets of snow that had insinuated themselves inside her sanctuary through various incursion points. She moved the crates that cracked in the cold, now-still air, and stared out at her bleak surroundings. Depressed, she restructured the boxes to fill in the gaps and fell back into a disturbed sleep.

Sunlight made its way around the corner and down the alley and everything around her began to thaw. Cold water from a light, late night snow dripped down on her. She made a small opening in the boxes and stared through it to the end of the alley and to the street beyond. It didn't matter that she was safe; she had to move. Reluctantly, she peeled away the soggy crates, rose against the wall, and stretched.

The early sun provided little warmth and her hands were so cold that she had trouble finding the pockets of her jeans. She had to leave but had nowhere to go. This was a foreign county and she knew no one, had no food, money, or a passport or any other identification—and she wasn't dressed for the weather. She was defenseless and her situation was hopeless. All she could do was sob—except that she was out of tears.

A gentle breeze conveyed a new problem, the scent of food. Tantalized, she worked her way out of the shelter and walked cautiously to the street, looking both ways before revealing herself. It was early and few people were about, so she sniffed out the direction of the food and walked, as if in a trance, toward it.

At the street corner she saw the source, a restaurant, and hurried inside where she stood, damp and shivering, in the warm, steamy doorway, as curious customers looked up at her from their morning brews. The smell of coffee almost caused her to pass out, but she strode resolutely to the waitress at the counter. Before she got there, someone tapped her shoulder.

"You look like you're short a loony," a man said.

She was unsure. "What's a loony?"

The man laughed. "Ah, American. You seem a bit down on your luck. My name's Dwayne, Dwayne Kibbard. I'm a solicitor and my office isn't far. It's warm and safe if that'll help?"

She knew better than to accept, but she was out of ideas. "Thank you, Mr. Kibbard."

"Call me Dwayne. Let me buy you a cup."

She nodded.

It turned out to be coffee and breakfast, which she devoured. Afterward, she went to the bathroom to clean up as best she could. When she returned, she felt better.

"Wow," was all the man could say. She blushed and if she wasn't in such a predicament, she would have fled right then. But Dwayne was nice. During their short walk, she learned that besides being a solicitor, he had a wife and two teenage girls and he was planning to leave the office early to attend their hockey tournament. When they arrived at his office, he offered her a chair.

"So what happened to you?"

"You've been really nice but I don't want to talk about it. I really can use some money, I . . . I promise I'll pay you back when I get home." As soon as she said it, she knew how much of a lie it was.

"I'd love to help. What's your name?"

"Um, Renee." Another lie.

He smiled. "Well, Renee, are you in more trouble than a solicitor can help you out of?"

"I . . . I don't know." She resolved not to cry. "You probably shouldn't help me but if I can rest here for a little while that will be enough and then I'll go."

"I'd like to help. Are you a rebel or something?"

Before she could answer, he replied. "Sorry, just a silly guess."

"No, that's not it," she couldn't explain.

"I believe in your cause, I really do. Many of us are on your side. Someday, someone will do something about that fascist regime you have down there. Until then, I'll help any way I can."

Her desperation, his kindness, and the warmth of the office convinced her. "I'm really tired. I didn't sleep well last night. Could I rest on your couch? We can talk when I get up."

"Take whatever time you need. I have some clients to call. If you're up by lunchtime we'll go to the hotel buffet next door—my treat. How does that sound?"

"That sounds great, thanks." He offered her his coat as a blanket. "I'll just lie . . . ," she said and was instantly asleep.

She awoke to his voice in the next room. While securely under the man's coat and dozing off from time to time, she listened dreamily to his conversation. Finally, curiosity won out and she rose unsteadily. The solicitor had his back to her and was talking on his cell phone. She eavesdropped.

"Yes, she's tall, young, very attractive, very attractive, and American so I thought she must be the one. As soon as I was certain she was asleep, I called. She's exhausted so I think she'll sleep a bit longer. I'm sending a photo. What do you think?"

He paused, listening to the voice on the other end of the line.

"Yes, She's a real looker, what did she do?"

Stacey listened intently.

"Fine, it's none of my business," Dwayne said. "Still, I get the reward. Good, thanks, come right over and bring the check."

Horrified, she looked for a way out. The room was on the first floor but the windows wouldn't open. Cautiously, she walked back to the door and looked both ways. She couldn't leave; the solicitor was in the office between her and the front door. She grabbed his coat and sneaked across the hall to the stairs. At one point, she could see inside his office but he wasn't looking in her direction so she slipped up the stairs, unnoticed. When she reached the door to the roof, she put on his jacket and bolted out. There was no obvious escape so she huddled against a wall while she contemplated her next move. She heard the sound of brakes squealing as cars pulled up, so she bent low, ran to the roof's edge, and looked down.

Two cars were parked in front of the building and three, no four men were waiting. She quickly jerked back and ran to the other side of the building where there was an enclosed walkway maybe six feet below the roof that crossed over the street and connected to another building. She climbed over the side, jumped, and landed on the top of the covered walkway. She cautiously ran to the far side, jumping up and pulling herself over the wall and onto the next building. She tried to open the door to get inside the building but it was locked and before she could find another way down, she heard yelling from the first building. She crept to the edge of the roof and peered over the low wall. Two men were running across the roof searching. She stayed low and watched.

"It's the only way she could have gone," one of the men yelled. Then he yelled to the men on the street below. "Follow us at street level. We'll check the adjacent rooftops." The men jumped onto the same walkway she had used and ran toward her.

Desperate, she ran and jumped over the opposite side wall and ran across the top of another walkway. As she climbed over the wall of the next building and rolled onto the other side, she heard the footfalls of people running on the street below her. She cowered against the wall, worrying where to go next. She saw a fire escape and crawled onto it. The rails were cold against her bare hands as she climbed down carefully, but quickly. As soon as she reached the ground, she saw two of her pursuers on the roof above, staring down at her. Before they could react, she bolted around the corner and continued weaving through the streets until, exhausted, she backed down a long alley and hid, once again, in garbage.

To avoid being seen from the nearby roofs, she pressed against rancid food crates, not daring to come out even after vomiting from the stench. She waited there until early evening and although light-headed, she scanned nearby rooftops and up and down the street before leaving. As she made her way, she ducked into every alley and surveyed each street before moving on. It was getting dark and cold when she noticed the lights of a tiny boutique squeezed between two high-rise, glass office buildings. The small store had a blue wooden door with a large white maple leaf painted on it. She knew what she had to do, but her legs were too weak and she was too scared to try. Angrily, she removed the man's ill-fitting coat, straightened her clothing as best she could and entered.

Chimes attached to the door alerted the owner who sat behind a counter reading a magazine. The owner looked up from the magazine at her potential customer. "May I help you?"

"No, ma'am. I'm just getting out of the cold, if you don't mind." The woman gave her an odd look and then went back to reading. Stacey wandered down the uneven wooden floor of the long and very narrow center aisle, avoiding antiques and knick-knacks that were hanging everywhere. Ducking under the hanging items and dodging those sticking out from the shelves, she made her way to the back of the shop. Each time she looked for the shopkeeper, the woman was busy elsewhere so she skulked to the back door, took a breath and tried to open it.

"It's locked," the woman volunteered. "You're sure I can't help?"

Stacey turned carefully from the door. "No, ma'am. I'm just looking."

For the second time that day she heard something that made her fearful.

"You're an American?"

"Yes, ma'am," she said as pleasantly as she could. "I'm sightseeing with my family."

The woman looked questioningly at the front door.

"I'm meeting them at our hotel," she lied.

"Are you sure you don't want to talk?" The woman seemed kind, but so had the lawyer.

"No, ma'am. I don't know you."

"It looks like you could use a friend."

"I have lots of friends."

"I'm just guessing, but probably none here, right?"

"No, ma'am, just my family."

"I can help, my office is in there," she said as she pointed to a door.

"I was just leaving."

"Please, go in," the woman insisted. "I'll be there in a minute."

Reluctantly Stacey walked into the woman's office and sat. The door closed on its own and then locked. Moments later, she heard the woman talking on the phone.

Not again, she thought.

Chapter 3
Brampton, Ontario—2070

The owner's office was littered with antiques and it provided her with even fewer escape alternatives than the solicitor's office. Stacey sat quietly while frantically taking everything in. The narrow shop had doors and windows in the front and back but the windows were squares that were much too small to climb through, and the back door was locked. Too exhausted to think, she searched the office for something to defend herself with when that scary General arrived but there was precious little to use, save for stained glass and clothes hangars.

When the front door chimes announced another person had entered the shop, Stacey stood and tried to force the office door, but it was secure. Frantic, she chastised herself for not acting sooner. The chime sounded again and she slumped into an old, heavy, cracked leather chair facing the door and there she waited resigned to capture. Tears started again but she was too defeated to care. When, after a time, nothing happened, she sat nervously, her legs shaking back and forth.

"I'm closing up. Dear, that chair is creaking something fierce," the shop owner said as she entered. "You simply must stop that or the vibration will knock my lovely things from their shelves. You really can trust me." Stacey tried to control her trembling as she waited in silence.

The proprietor was almost as tall as Stacey, very thin with long, straight, gray hair. She had a thin, warm, friendly face with a ready, toothy smile set between high cheekbones and she wore a pair of round eyeglasses that framed deep brown eyes. Untamed silver eyebrows crept over her eyeglass frames.

"You're the American. Please don't be alarmed," the woman said simply. Stacey remained silent. "My name is Dorothy Bradley. My friends call me

Dot. This is my shop. Not many people come this way and rarely does a young American girl come unaccompanied. We're a bit out of the way, you see. Tourists prefer to spend their time and money in the shopping malls of Toronto, I'm afraid." She smiled and slowly walked to Stacey. "I really can help you. I have a good friend who is very well placed in the rebel community." On hearing that, Stacey perked up a little. "Dear, I don't blame you for being cautious. Canada's free but we're so perilously close to that crazy, loony bird that runs your country. She's no lady, that one, and she's made it quite clear she wishes to annex us because of our energy surplus, but like so many, I believe she wants Canada so she can make hockey a U.S. sport." When Stacey didn't laugh or smile, the woman put her hand gently on Stacey's shoulder. She flinched. "It was a joke. It's okay."

Staring at the floor, Stacey tried to understand what the woman wanted, but more, she wondered how she could escape.

"My friend says I'm not funny, either."

"I'm sorry."

"You must trust me. We're fighting the best we can. There are libertarian political groups now that Canada has given away her right to Arctic natural resources, who would like nothing better than to negotiate our freedom away to the United States, but they're clearly in the minority for now. Of course, that doesn't stop them from being loud and obnoxious as they spread blood money around in hopes of changing the vote. My friend, the one I told you about, he is bucking up our Prime Minister to insure he pushes back against that shrew south of the border and all the rest of those policy hawks who're running your country." The woman seemed sincere and was saying the right things. But after what happened earlier, Stacey wasn't ready to trust her.

"According to the media, you were with President Rose when he was captured."

Her concern got the best of her. "What will they do to him?"

"Well, sweetie, I really don't know. I should think whatever it is; he won't be looking forward to it. You have good reason to be scared, but honestly, I can help you."

"Against them?" Stacey asked. "How?"

"What do you need?"

"I need to . . ." She hadn't given that any thought. Where could she go? "Detroit."

Dot smiled. "To old Detroit? How quaint. There's a great deal of conflict there. Maybe you mean Hamilton. That's where the commerce is these days."

"I don't know. I'd heard there's a rebel community in Detroit."

"No, no, no, that won't do. That's not the right place at all. My friend would know better, of course. There's Underground activity certainly, but Detroit, it isn't a good place right now. I don't recommend going there. Besides, getting there will be extremely difficult. There are pictures of you everywhere. If you were somewhat less attractive and maybe not quite so tall, and your government didn't think you so important, Detroit would be a lovely place to visit, although waiting until late spring would be better."

"I don't want any trouble."

"That's a solid sentiment, but it's not up to you. Trouble has, most assuredly, found you. Can you tell me why they want you?"

"They don't want me. They want Mr. Rose and I was with him."

"No, no, I don't think you have that right, sweetie. My friend says they were looking for you and the former president was a bonus."

"That can't be right. It doesn't make sense."

"I know dear. But why do you suppose they want you? What did you do?"

"Nothing . . ."

Dot smiled and Stacey just shrugged. "Really, until recently, all I ever did was play and hike around my home with my friends and help my mother with chores . . ." Tears welled in her eyes at the thought. ". . . I avoided doing chores. She was . . . I should have helped her more." She wiped tears from her eyes. She was angry with herself for crying. "My Mom needed me and I wasn't there for her."

"That's a shame, dear. Was this in Angel Falls?"

"Yes, ma'am. I lived there all my life and we never did anything to anybody."

"Your government claims that Angel Falls was a rebel community."

"We aren't," she insisted. "We're a peaceful community of Friends. My neighbors were nice. There weren't any criminals."

Dot laughed. "Well, dear, without a functioning constitution, who is and who is not a criminal is rather difficult to identify. It's not real clear what a crime is down there anymore. Your government's M.O. is well known. They wouldn't have spent money destroying your community unless you had something they wanted."

"I don't know, ma'am."

"Not even under penalty of torture."

Stacey flinched causing Dot to smile as reassuringly as she could. "Sweetie, I didn't mean anything, but if the Chairwoman gets you, she'll persuade you to tell her what you know and much, much more. America's a strange place, has been for a while. They threw away such a perfectly lovely set of rules."

"I don't know anything," Stacey said tearfully, burying her face in her hands and turning her back to the woman. She felt gentle hands on her shoulders pulling her into a hug. "I'm so scared. I've been running. Have you heard anything about Angel Falls?"

"Nothing for certain. Your government is very good at what they do and we believe they killed everyone. Then you appeared and they seem desperate to have you because . . . well, what do you think?"

"I swear I don't know anything, Dot" she said. "The Chairwoman is so mean."

"My dear, you have no idea."

"I saw mom and dad . . ." Stacey couldn't voice her loss, instead bowing her head and weeping. Finally, she looked up. "I'm not like this. I never cry and now I can't seem to stop. I don't understand. Why did it happen? It doesn't make sense. We didn't deserve that, no one does."

Dot shook her head and gently reached out to touch Stacey's chin while staring intently into her eyes. "You're a lovely girl, so sweet and innocent," she said.

She pushed Dot's hand away, gently. "Not so innocent anymore."

Dot smiled. "I hesitate to explain what's going on, you seem so ill-equipped for what you have become, but you need to understand."

"Understand what?"

"You know that your former Chairman and the current Chairwoman downsized America?"

"Yes, the rabbi told us it was genocide."

"And you know what genocide is?"

"Until I saw the rockets and the rangers, no, not really, but it's something like that, isn't it?"

"I suppose. It's that hateful, certainly. Your country has a history of treating the poor badly. It's not in your text books but except for a brief period a century ago when America had a middle class and people could aspire to be something, poor people in your country were treated like property and could be eliminated if they stopped providing value. First the Crelli, and then the Brandt administrations, and your private industries for that matter pursued that policy again when President Crelli first took office some thirty years ago. All assistance to the poor was denied as wasteful and Americans became quite desperate, so desperate that many tried to come here but Canada has immigration laws we respect, and we denied them, too. Those poor folks were labeled economic criminals and security risks and they were pursued, captured and executed by HomeSec in a very grisly fashion. It was your government's way of removing economic and social risk from their economy. To avoid death, desperate Americans fled to live off the land in areas of the country that were least productive or that the reduced population couldn't fill. They're called the unincorporated territories or some such dribble. That sounds like what Angel Falls was. But mostly it was about folks being executed."

"Dot, I don't want to believe my parents died because my government kills indiscriminately."

"I'm sorry," Dot said. "But, yes, that's true. According to Crelli's law, anyone who provides no value to his economy has perpetrated an economic felony and is subject to execution—it is most effective for reducing taxes and balancing a budget, if those are the most important things in life."

"God, Dot, that's horrible."

"Yes, dear. There's an old American expression, maybe you've heard it. 'You're not in Kansas anymore.' There's a real world out there and it has most assuredly found you. It's murderous and scary, but whether you like it or not, you're part of it and it would seem a big part. In this world, mistakes cost lives."

"Dot, I'm scared. What should I do? Where can I go?"

"Sweetie, I don't know how else to say this. Americans seem to have gotten what they wished for. Survival today requires rugged individualism, there's simply nobody to count on anymore. You simply must rely on yourself. Get used to it. You have no friends, other than me and people I know who care deeply about the cause your family died for."

"My mom and dad didn't have a cause except to raise me and my brothers and sisters."

"The cause of rebellion is what I'm talking about and we need your help. My friend and I are hoping you can shed more light on what happened so that we can stop it from happening again."

"But . . ."

Frustrated, the tears came again, and that frustrated her even more.

"That's right dear, it's sad. Get it all out, now, while you can."

Stacey placed her head on Dot's shoulder. "My parents, Mrs. Singleberry, and all my neighbors, they're all dead and I have no idea why."

"We don't know for certain that everyone is gone," Dot whispered, "We only know what your government releases in Archive which is unreliable at best. Security in the States is so tight that they can prevent anyone from spying on them while they spy on everyone. It's that scary. So until our undercover contacts confirm or refute the Archive report, you and President Rose may well be it, the only survivors of Angel Falls. Until then, we can hope there are more."

Sadness deepened into anger. "Dot, I want to meet your friend. I want to do it as soon as possible."

"Certainly. He's a wonderful and sensitive man and I'm sure that he'll take care of you. We'll go tomorrow morning."

"Will he do something to the people who killed my parents?"

"That is his life's goal, but the reality is, right now, all we can do is help as many as we can. We lack the resources to oppose them more. He has virtually no weaponry and we can't compete with HomeSec technology."

"Somebody must do something," Stacey insisted.

Dot tried to comfort Stacey but she wriggled away from her embrace and asked her question again. Dot didn't respond so Stacey added, angrily, "They are horrible people and they must be punished."

"Someday, dear, but first we must unite under a strong leader and to do that, we must understand them better. That's why you are so important. For now, you're going to clean up and get a good night's sleep. Tomorrow, we'll drive to the *madrasah*."

"What's a *madrasah*?"

"It's a private school at the Prophet Omar Smith's complex. You've heard of him, certainly?"

"No, but if he can hurt these people, I want to meet him."

"And he wants to meet you too, sweetie."

Chapter 4
Smith Madrasah, Canada—2070

International Relationships—At one time in history, Canada, Britain, Australia, and a South and Central American bloc of countries were dependent upon the United States because of its wealth and might.

During the early decades of the 21st century, when the First Republic's economic power withered, these and other nations jumped ship, trying their hand on the world stage without America's influence.

Economics controls international politics, and sensing a declining America, leaders of other nations went nuts trying, but failing to sustain international free market capitalism without America's strong leadership. They lacked the savvy, the will, the guts, and the vast, dynamic, self starting entrepreneurial skills that made the United States the gold standard of global economic leadership in what was the golden age of capital appreciation.

For without American might to shield the world from its many villains, most nations could agree on nothing until, in the treaty of Guadalajara, Mexico in 2031, they decided to anchor their economies to the growth economies of China, India, and Brazil in hopes of gaining a larger share of the action from the economic vacuum that a declining America was creating. In its past, America always dealt with its recalcitrant by imposing an unrelenting program of blackmail and economic influence so the Guadalajara Accords served as protection against future American retribution. But with its economy failing, the nations of the world called America's bluff and won.

France, Germany, and the rest of the Euro market were most affected by America's decline and had the most to fear from American revenge, so they joined Russia, Turkey, and the Middle East to negotiate deals with China, Brazil, and India. These deals effectively isolated America who had little to offer. Tariff, patent wars, and economic boycotts ensued resulting in a broad and deep contraction of international commerce. This led to yet another world wide depression and that, along with famine and disease not unrelated to climate change, caused the deaths of nearly a two billion souls worldwide.

America was deemed a pariah among nations as it faced an international economic boycott which forced her crazy northern neighbor Canada to choose. While fearing American aggression along with its unquenchable thirst for energy, the Canadian government chose poorly, joining the world against America. The result was that though the American economy fell into brief irrelevance with the U.S. dollar devalued and eventually replaced as a global commercial currency, Canada was forced to defend thousands of miles of common border at great cost.

At this point, in 2032, an anxious American electorate turned to Andrew Crelli. The newly elected President seized the opportunity and further disengaged from the world in a wildly imaginative, courageous, yet daunting plan to make the America economy totally and completely self reliant.

With technological superiority and a vast nuclear arsenal, America has always been an effective negotiator, but with the world ganging up unfairly, President Crelli decided to lock down America's borders and jettison foreign entanglements, turning inward to begin the great historic, game-changing national reengineering and downsizing program (See Archive reference: *Circle of Life*) for which he would be forever lauded.

With the support of the International Monetary Fund and the World Bank, the World Court and the United Nations indicted the United States for this downsizing, but they proved to be nothing but gutless luddites and were unable to make their charges stand so instead, they enforced the isolation with an international blockade that their leaders felt, over time, would bring America to her knees. It could not. It did not.

President Crelli orchestrated a brilliant countervailing strategy, alternating military threats and commercial opportunities until the notoriously weak and vacillating nations of the world caved and they scurried once again to form the best alliances they could to mitigate the risk of America's rebirth.

These new economic confederacies continued to boycott America's economy enforcing their actions with hollow threats to use their combined economic power to implode the American economy much like what had occurred to the Soviet Union in the late twentieth century. They proved neither strong enough, nor decisive enough, and frankly, they lacked the courage to face the might of a now lean and mean America ready to reassert herself in the global corporate community and to enforce her will on the international marketplace. Stalemate continued but soon America proved dominant once again.

In the years that followed, a robust and confident America, directed by Andrew Crelli as its Chairman and his successor, the beautiful, dynamic young protégé, Chairwoman Tanya Brandt, proceeded to accomplish a dynamic revisioning of modern society with a final aggressive downsizing that eliminated the last remnants of the economically inefficient.

Though the world wants little to do with the Second Republic in America, it has no choice but to maintain intercourse now that America is, once again, an irresistible force in the global economy, one that possesses powerful economic vitality and state of the art technology far beyond anything the world will ever be able to compete against again.—**Archive**

Morning came. Rested and feeling hopeful, Stacey helped Dot load packages into her tiny, solar-powered car. She squeezed in beside Dot, and they were off.

"What are all these things?" she asked, pointing to the packages.

"Omar collects fine things. He has them shipped to me, and I deliver them."

"What kind of things?"

"I never open his packages, dear."

They drove a distance north on a two lane local road. Dot pulled off onto a winding dirt road that ran underneath a tall, formidable looking security portal. In a small parking lot, they exited the vehicle as one guard approached carrying a handgun while another guard watched, weapon at the ready, from inside the portal. Dot spoke briefly to the guard who then ordered other guards to help unload Dot's car. They carried the packages up a tree-lined hill trail with Stacey and Dot following. At the top, Stacey stared at the imposing pink wall that sliced the hilly horizon as far as she could see.

"Wow."

Dot smiled. "Incredible isn't it? He built it after he was forced to flee the states on trumped up murder charges."

"Murder?" Stacey blurted.

"Yes, dear, Omar is a dear and gentle man but he is a fugitive from the American government. When he was a congressman, he fell out of favor because he championed the poor and downtrodden. That earned him powerful political enemies like President Crelli, who was only a senator then. By their nature, organizations like Omar's attract radical members and there was an unfortunate incident. A long time ago when he was President-elect, Andrew Crelli, his wife, and their baby son visited Philadelphia to deliver a speech. A deranged, lunatic fringe member of Omar's organization strapped explosives to her person and blew herself up. It was an awful thing. Unfortunately, the only one who died was the senator's infant son—besides the girl suicide bomber, she died of course."

"That's horrible."

"It was indeed," Dot continued. "Crelli and Omar were political rivals and when Crelli insisted that Omar accept blame for the crime, Omar was forced to flee. He was innocent, of course, but it didn't matter. And though Crelli hounded him, Omar never gave up or gave in. That's why he's the leader of a great movement that helps the poor in both of our countries. Obviously, for his own safety, he relocated to Canada and though he does a great deal to help Canada, it's so unfair. He yearns to return to his country and he grieves for what it has become."

They reached a blockhouse that overlooked the valley beyond the walls where they were cleared through security. At that point, another guard directed them to a waiting powered trike. They got on and as they were driven to the palace, Stacey asked Dot more about Smith.

"Oh, you'll like him. He's unbelievably rich and quite good-looking. Stunning, actually"

"Stunning?" Stacey laughed. "Dot, nobody is that good looking."

"What can I say? You're young. You'll believe me when you see him. He's not handsome, not in any classic, movie star way. He is extremely pale with perfect, flawless skin and his hair is long, straight and white. He has large, almost root beer-colored eyes, somewhat like an albino, but so

deep and expressive. He doesn't sound like much but believe me, he's put
it all together and it's extraordinarily appealing."

"You like him, don't you?"

Dot blushed. "He's very kind and helps people in need."

"You do like him." Stacey smiled.

Dot looked away, covering her face with her hands as she whispered.
"Yes, but I assure you, there's nothing between us."

"But you wish there was?"

"Sweetie, who wouldn't? He's the real deal, but strangely he has never
been married, although I'm certain he's not interested in men." Stacey
wondered how Dot knew something so personal, but said nothing. "He
speaks with just the slightest of European accents, it's so sexy—I believe
he's from Northern Germany, originally. Another thing, although he's a
devout Muslim, he doesn't lord it over you like some. The man is a prize.
I had hoped . . ."

"You're pretty, Dot. Surely-"

"Sometimes I think . . . he can be so intimate, yet he's aloof, too. He's
a very complicated charmer, that Omar." She blushed.

"But you think he'll help me?"

"Absolutely, dear. Even if you didn't share a common enemy, he goes
out of his way to help people. He hates Brandt and he'll overthrow her
government someday. Until then, anyone who's an enemy of hers is a
friend of his, so I'm certain he'll help."

"When we meet, how do I address him? What do I say?"

Dot laughed. "Just Omar. He's fine with that."

"Are you sure? Shouldn't I show more respect?"

"He's beyond those things. Answer his questions honestly and he'll
work with you until he can find a way to help. You'll do fine."

She was excited but she didn't want to show it. It was more than she
could have hoped for—someone powerful enough to protect her from the
Chairwoman and maybe even avenge Angel Falls and help her find out
what happened to Gil.

The trike stopped beside a highly polished mosaic walkway. Her gaze
followed the path until she noticed a rippling along the top of the wall.
Her eyes followed the rippling back until it was just above her. "What's
that?" she asked as she pointed.

The driver answered without looking up. "Our Prophet must be well
protected from his enemies. What you are seeing is the reflection of the

sun off nano-wire. In the evening, it is invisible and it's incredibly sharp and impossible to cut through, undetected."

She stared, amazed at the vague rainbow effect and felt an enveloping sense of sanctuary. For the first time in many days, she relaxed as they approached a double gate with security details posted on each side. On the wall, a large brass sign read:

America the Beautiful
Mosque and Academy

"Dot, what does that mean?" Stacey asked.

"Our Prophet is one of the wealthiest men in all of Canada. He's a true asset that my government protects because, through the various schools and charities he funds, so many Canadian citizens are helped." Just then, another car approached and two men carrying pulse rifles stepped out to meet them. They scanned Dot's data card but it took another phone call to clear Stacey because she lacked identification.

When they were cleared, a guard smiled and pointed. "The Prophet awaits you in his palace office. Ms. Bradley, where are your packages?" She pointed to the back of the trike and the guard took the packages and handed her an envelope. She thanked the man and placed it in her purse.

Stacey stared curiously so Dot explained. "A girl has to eat. My commission on Omar's artistic investments pays for my little boutique; as you know, it's so far from tourist traffic."

The guards led them through the gates and onto the beautifully landscaped grounds. From a distance it appeared that the trees were decorated for Christmas. When she walked closer, she saw that on each tree were myriad small devices with red beams that reminded her of the *SurveilEagle*. She fought off a shiver and pointed. The guard responded opaquely. "Our Prophet has enemies."

They continued down a curving road past a snowboarding pipe and a glass-enclosed skating rink where children were playing ice hockey. Behind the rink was a large building topped with a minaret that came into full imposing view as they approached. A huge, ornately decorated entry, maybe twenty feet high and wide enough to drive a couple of tractors through confronted them. With each new display of power and grandeur Stacey felt both more intimidated and more reassured.

"Oh, Dot, this is so . . . overpowering. If my family and friends could only . . ." she looked down, sadly, remembering why she was here.

Dot put an arm around her shoulder. "Yes, dear, it's marvelous. Please don't be sad. This is the start of something wonderfully important for you. I just know it."

"I hope you're right."

"You've been brave and Omar will help, you'll see."

At the palace gate, two more armed men confirmed their identities. One of the guards handed them each ID necklaces—to track them better, he said—and then opened the immense doors and allowed them through. Stacey was awed and pleased to feel dwarfed to insignificance. They entered a long corridor with an elaborately decorated high-arched glass ceiling that bent the blue sky and white clouds into the shape of the glass. The corridor walls were painted with intricate designs in metallic gold with a preponderance of greens and reds. As they walked, their footsteps echoed off the dark metallic floors.

Mouth open in wonder, Stacey's legs felt weak as she coaxed herself over the threshold and down the enormous hall. In the distance, dwarfed by the hall, a man waited for them. When they reached him, he smiled.

"Dot Bradley," the man said in a deep, resounding voice, his arms reaching for her, "you don't spend enough time with us. Thank you for the delivery. Omar and the cause appreciate it." He gave Dot a formal embrace and then, turned to Stacey. "And you must be the girl from Angel Falls. Welcome. I am Warren Salaam. The Prophet is waiting for you in his suite. He will be pleased; you are far more beauteous than either the media or our friend Dot described."

He took Stacey's arm and guided her down a spiraling deep-carpeted stairway to another long corridor. As her escort pointed out and described artwork to the very attentive Dot, Stacey could only stare, open-mouthed. Finally, they paused at a large white door while their escort knocked, opened it and bowed.

"The Prophet, Omar Smith, Allah be praised," he said before leading them inside.

Entering from the brightly lit hallway into this darkened room made it difficult for Stacey to see. The room was paneled in very dark shiny wood planks that picked up a hint of the lights in the room without illuminating the room itself. In the corner, in front of a large desk, stood a man wearing worn dark jeans and a McGill University sweatshirt. His long, straight, almost-white hair framed an angular face. When she got closer, she noticed his eyes—deep, dark pools with a red cast. His stare penetrated her and she blushed. She was about to look away when he smiled, creases forming on his mature, yet youthful face. His smile changed everything. It radiated warmth and kindness that made her stomach flutter. She now understood what Dot had meant.

The Prophet bowed. "Stacey Grant. It is a great pleasure to meet you at last. I'm so sorry about Angel Falls and then what happened here in Canada. I feel responsible because I should have been there for you. My people were searching and I assure you, they will be reprimanded for not finding you. It is, however, most fortunate that fate steered you to Ms. Bradley's door. I promise you, from today forward, I will do everything in my power to set your world right."

He was beyond anything her sheltered life could have prepared her for and her mind was in turmoil. She could think of nothing to say. He laughed. It was a kind laugh.

"Ms. Grant, may I call you Stacey?" he asked. His voice was deep and melodic.

"Grant," she mumbled nervously.

"Then Grant it is," he said cheerfully.

She blushed. "No, no. I'm sorry. Of course you can call me Stacey, Mr. Prophet-uh-Mr. Smith."

He laughed again. He had incredible dimples and a cute cleft in his chin. "It will please me, greatly, if you call me Omar." His upper lip lifted above his perfect white teeth displaying the most magnetic smile she'd ever seen. Instinctively, she smiled back and relaxed.

He motioned for them to sit. "I hope you don't mind me saying this but you are most beautiful. And your smile, I simply must keep you smiling if for no other reason than to ease my burden." Then he turned to Dot. "You were right, my dear; she's lovely but you weren't nearly generous enough in your description." He took Stacey's hand and she stared at it as if it belonged to someone else. "Stacey," he said gently, "you've been through much but you're home now and you are safe. No one can hurt you now."

She nodded.

"Are you hungry? Can I provide you with anything?"

She nodded again.

"My people will prepare your heart's desire. Unfortunately, I have another matter to attend to so I must leave for a short time. Warren will see to your needs. Speak your wish; even if he's not present and he'll see to it you get it."

Smith turned to Dot. "You are looking well, my dear. Thank you again for the packages and for our beautiful heroine. The chimes of freedom are ringing brightly for us this day."

Dot blushed. "It was my pleasure, Omar."

After the Prophet took his leave, Warren helped them order food. At first, all Stacey could think of was pancakes with Vermont maple syrup, but Warren and Dot coaxed her to something more exotic. She had figs with some unknown fish in a spicy cream sauce, and there were so many varieties of cheeses and wines. Hungry, she devoured the meal, enjoying most of the new experiences. When she was done, Warren escorted them around the palace and afterwards, returned to the Prophet's suite. There, Stacey reclined on the overlarge pillows that covered the floor and promptly fell asleep.

She slept through the night and awoke in the morning well rested but disoriented. She looked at the unfamiliar wood-paneled room trying to remember where she was. Somehow she was wearing silk pajamas that felt refreshingly cool. She got up from her pillows, opened the door and peeked out. Warren immediately approached her. "Ms. Grant, I hope you had a good rest?"

"Yes, thank you. I feel better than I have in days. Where's Dot?"

"Ms. Bradley had to leave and unfortunately, so too did our Prophet. He won't return until tomorrow, but he has instructed me to give you the full tour and provide you with whatever you wish. How may I help?"

Disappointed that her protector wasn't there, she dressed, ate breakfast, and then followed Warren on another tour. Nothing in her experience, limited as it was to Angel Falls, prepared her for this. When they entered an elaborately tiled underground complex with various saunas and whirlpools and a swimming pool that contained real fish, she stopped, amazed.

"Ms. Grant, we have masseuses on call to provide for your relaxation. If you want anything, speak it. Someone will come and help. There's also a secure Canadian Archive in our all climates recreation gymnasium, if you want to play or catch up on the news."

He pointed to a private area beside the pool, paneled in opaque glass.

"Bathing suits are in the changing area, and yes, you can swim with the fishes. Leave your clothes and an attendant will replace them." When he left, she found a suit that was so small that she was embarrassed and she immediately covered up with a towel. After a swim, she walked hurriedly back to the chaise where she spent the rest of her time covered up and trying to relax and enjoy the good fortune while putting her horrible recent ordeal behind her.

After lunch, she decided on a massage and then swam and spent time in a hot tub and in the sauna drinking cold beer, her first. Totally relaxed now, she was laying languorously on a deck chair tanning under overhead lights when a well-dressed man entered the changing room and came out wearing incredibly scanty swim trunks. She blushed at his cut physique before remembering the size of her bathing suit and frantically covered herself with a towel. He smiled, waved, and walked to her.

"May I join you?" he asked in French-accented English. She nodded and he sat beside her. "My name is Jean-Paul Slattery and you . . . ?"

"Stacey Grant."

"Ah, the American. And a very beautiful American at that."

She blushed. "How do you know Omar?"

"Everyone knows Omar. I visit with him regularly. You are most fortunate to be here where you will be safe, as safe as anywhere on Earth. Where is your acquaintance?"

"You mean Dot? She left."

"Ah, so it was Ms. Bradley. Very good, the shipment has arrived. Omar must be pleased. He's back. He arrived just after me, a little over an hour ago."

Omar's return made her feel better. "How do you know him, Mr. Slattery?"

"Please call me Jean-Paul. Omar and I have common interests. I'm the leader of the minority Tory-Union party and Omar is a major contributor."

"Oh, so you're a politician."

He laughed. "Canadian politicians are not as scary as those in your country."

"I hope not. How long will you be here?"

"I was planning to swim and then head back to Ottawa, but I think now I must stay longer because I'm in love. How could I leave such a beautiful girl as you?"

"Please, Jean-Paul, don't change your plans because of me."

He frowned. "Oh, the pain. I'm wounded." He smiled.

"I appreciate your attempt at flattery, but you don't know me and you couldn't possibly care for me in such a short time."

He looked at her curiously. "Stacey, my love, you are young, yes, excitedly so. You will learn that true love isn't measured in units of time." He paused and then said, more seriously, "but, of course I'm only making conversation. If you think me rude, I apologize. I would like to get to know you better."

"That would be nice."

With that, he left to swim. He swam gracefully and when he finished, he shook off the excess water, his stomach muscles rippling as he did. And then, he sat in a nearby hot tub.

"I'm sorry about your misfortune," he told her.

She nodded glumly.

"The media is wrong. They reported it as an armed rebel encampment. It wasn't."

"No, it wasn't."

"You were fortunate. Your government isn't known for creating survivors." Tears formed in her eyes and Jean-Paul noticed. "I'm sorry, that was inconsiderate of me and I apologize. Do you play tennis or climb."

"I climb a little."

"Good. We can use Omar's climbing wall. It's one of the few real climbing walls left, the rest have been replaced by *Virtuoso,* which replaces everything that's real."

"What's *Virtuoso?*" She remembered Gil talking about it.

A big smile lit up his face. "How provincial, I love it. Sweet Stacey, *Virtuoso* is a simulator of real things. It provides us with the opportunity to satisfy our desires, gain valued experiences, or pursue our interests without risk or commitment. Real can be good too, just not so varied or as out there, you know?" She didn't. "Omar's climbing wall is very sophisticated with a number of trail choices. What's your skill level?" When she looked questioningly at him, he added, "What have you climbed?"

"Just the hills around home. They weren't high or very steep but they were challenging."

"Then we'll do a novice climb. Meet me at the gym at ten tomorrow."

"What should I wear?"

"You're adorable," he smiled. "You are in Omar's care; he supplies whatever it is you need. Tomorrow then, in the gym?"

She nodded and Jean-Paul said goodbye. She thought to reconsider but before she could, he disappeared into the men's locker room. Alone again, she spent the remainder of the day lounging and eating. Content, she napped. Later, a maid woke her and showed her to her suite.

In the morning, she was relieved when she arrived at the gym and Jean-Paul wasn't there. In case he was only late, she rushed away to the dining room for breakfast. It was there she received a message to meet Omar. She returned nervously to her room and searched her closet for the right clothes. The clothes she wore when she arrived were gone but the closet was filled with a stunning new wardrobe and everything seemed to fit. She chose a pair of tight black slacks, a long, loose fitting silver blouse and a pair of high black leather boots. She showered and dressed and headed off excitedly to see her host.

Omar was reading in a *lanai* that was nestled in a grove of trees beside a small creek and warmed by a roaring fire from a large, circular, all glass fireplace built into the floor. He put his e-book down and stood to greet her. "Good morning, Stacey. I'm sorry I wasn't available yesterday but I trust my good friend JP was fun company."

"He was very nice—for a politician."

Omar smiled. "JP will be our next Prime Minister."

"Wow, he didn't seem that important. He invited me to climb this morning."

Omar laughed. "As important as he is, he thinks himself more so. Unfortunately, he had to return to Ottawa; I'm sure he was disappointed that he couldn't make the date. You would've enjoyed the climb. I have something important to ask you.

"What is it?"

"For me to assist you and protect you, you must take an active interest in what is going on around you. You must become something more than the latest casualty of your autocratic government, or you are doomed to be their victim again. So tell me true, Stacey, are you willing to do everything in your power to prevent that?"

What he said was unsettling. "Sure, I'll do what I can. May I ask you something?"

"Certainly."

"Did anyone else survive, other than President Rose?"

"Honestly, my sweet, no one knows. If I hear, you will be the next person to know. But now it's time for you to understand certain realities.

When you crossed the Canadian border, you became a fugitive from American injustice, and your Chairwoman does not like fugitives. I know this. I experience it every day. And because of the edict that permitted the Angel Falls massacre, you are a rebel lawbreaker. But it gets worse. You may be the only survivor and witness to that massacre, excluding Mr. Rose. Attacking your own people is still frowned upon in the international community. It is an act so heinous, in fact, that the world community is debating it at the United Nations in Mexico, and that makes you a very, very important person to a great many governments."

"I'm not important," she said. His expression made her seem petulant. "I don't want to be important."

"Nevertheless. There is the genocide, of course, but the international community has waffled on that. This is new and different. You and Mark Rose are survivors of a premeditated attack and massacre by the American government on its own citizens."

"Mr. Rose . . ."

"Rose is nothing," he said dismissively. "The former president is Brandt's puppet, nothing more. Even if he had the courage to stand up, he's beyond our help."

Dismayed by that, she turned away. "Poor Mr. Rose, he's just a sick, tired old man. They won't hurt him will they?"

"I don't care."

"That's cruel."

"It is what it is. It is you I care about. Mark Rose plays no role in this."

"There must be others who escaped. I saw Meat with . . . well Meat, and there was a horrible fireball but he made it into the forest, I know it." If only she could convince herself that he had made it and she was unsure why she did it, but she stopped before mentioning Gil.

Omar pulled a communicator from his pocket and researched something. "This is difficult, my sweet, but I assure you that it's vital to our cause and to your safety." He handed the communicator to her. "Here is the official record of residents at Angel Falls, the people murdered there. It cost me one of my better teams to get it."

She was horrified. "Oh, no, not more people dead because of me."

He ignored her concern and showed her the screen. "You recognize the names."

She knew all of them. Tears welled in her eyes and to stop sobbing, she had to look away. She held the communicator out there for him to take but he gently pushed it back to her and then put his arm around her. His voice was low and soothing.

"True victories, true, true victories, my love, are forged in great pain. For some, that pain cripples, but you are strong, Stacey Grant, and you want vengeance for their crime, and that makes you stronger still. I wish it were different and someday, Allah willing, it will be, but in this world, vengeance is right thinking. It is the only way to stop the pain and destroy those who caused it so it never happens again. Tell me why this happened and together we will have our vengeance."

Why? That was a question beyond her comprehension. "I don't know," she said, sniffling.

"I understand, Stacey dear, and so then we will figure it out together. We will start with this list. Search it and tell me everything you know about everyone. Leave nothing out and I will decide what's important and who is to blame."

"Why, Omar? I know who is to blame. I am."

"Foolishness, you must get passed that so we can get to the real problem. I simply must understand why Brandt destroyed Angel Falls."

"To get Mr. Rose."

"No, she had him once and threw him out. There was never a time when Brandt didn't have that fool under her thumb. If that was all there was, you would be in Angel Falls right now, living happy and innocent as always. No, there is more and we will discover it together. Help me, Stacey love, please, and help our cause. It is difficult, I know, but please, look at these names and tell me everything."

"But they're my neighbors and family and they're all . . . dead . . . I can't . . ."

"To avenge this abominable deed, we must all be brave."

He gently released her from his embrace and she stared at the list. Her heart ached with each name, for her mind pictured good people and happy memories. "Oh no, Mrs. Almond and Uncle Bill . . ." She had watched them run . . . but not away. Tears streamed down her face blurring her vision, but not hiding the names enough or the faces she remembered as Omar relentlessly scrolled through the list. Then her parent's names scrolled into view. She lost focus, briefly and felt like she was floating, then falling as her eyes were transfixed on letters that once meant a

41

loving experience, warm and alive, but now spelled an abrupt end to her innocence. To fight against the sinking horror, she screamed and knocked the communicator from his hand. Then she turned and burrowed into the closest pillow, sobbing hard but not hard enough to make the pain in her throat lessen or for it to change reality. She felt his embrace but she wasn't comforted. The terror of that night returned and she felt queasy. Sweating, and shivering uncontrollably, she slipped to the floor and on her knees, shook as if riddled by bullets the rangers meant for her. She tried to retch but came up dry. Her eyes burned and bile seared her throat. She squeezed his arm in search of relief until finally, her head on his knee and her shoulders encased in his firm embrace, she whimpered softly.

He pulled back and allowed her no recovery time.

"My dearest, I know this is difficult, but only you can solve this riddle so we can avenge them. So we can make the world right. I insist that you stop this selfish crying and desist from feeling sorry for yourself so you can join the battle. There is a place for you. Hold onto that grief, and let it harden your resolve to destroy these monsters who plucked your life from you."

He was stern, something her father certainly never was. Sheepishly, she looked up at him. He nodded reassuringly and offered her an expensive looking handkerchief. She sat up, smoothed out her clothing and bravely wiped her tears away.

"There will be time for tears later and if we do our jobs well, they will be tears of joy and of victory and resolution. The revolution awaits you. You are the woman we need. Help us. Help us now. You spoke of 'Meat'. His name is not on the list."

She steeled herself when he handed her his communicator. She resisted scrolling directly to Meat's name because she felt she'd be dishonoring the others who died. As she got closer to his name, her hands trembled. If Meat was on this list then Gil's name would follow and he would be dead. At each name, she braced herself as a memory attacked her. She fought back tears, bit her lip, and scrolled resolutely until she saw it, Morris Mitkowski. Poor Meat. Unable to contain herself, she put her head in her hands and wept, once again.

But Omar wouldn't let go. "My poor baby, I'm so sorry." He held her and rocked her. "Is this Mitkowski, your Meat?"

She nodded.

He kissed her head and whispered. "And this other person you mentioned? Which one is he?" She didn't respond. "You said Meat was with somebody."

She wanted to answer but she found herself unwilling to voice that name. "Did I say that?" She scrolled to another friend. It hurt to lie, particularly about a friend, now dead. "Meat was with . . . Tom . . . Tom Owens. Yes, Tom and I, we played together as kids." He seemed not to believe her.

"This is very real and dangerous, Stacey. It is life and death. Is this Tom Owens the boy? Tell me true. I must know it all if we're to avenge this heinous crime." His stern look had the strength to compel her, but she was not going to voice Gil's name and so she resisted admitting that she had lied.

"Please, Omar, I'm so miserable. I thought the worst was over but what you're making me do . . . It hurts so . . ." She was having trouble breathing and struggled to speak. "Please can we stop . . . for a while?" She tried to smile through the tears, thinking it would help this end.

"If only I could. This is difficult and I'm sorry, my sweet, but to put an end to this madness and to ensure that what Brandt and Crelli did never happens again, I must know everything." He stared deeply into her eyes. She felt drawn to him and though she wavered, she stayed true to Gil and didn't mention his name. "Stacey, sweet Stacey, you are right. It is too much, too soon. Rest. I am sorry." He patted her head and then left. She watched him go, feeling equal parts ashamed and relieved.

It was still morning, yet she felt exhausted and sleep seemed so necessary that she stretched out on his sofa, covered herself with pillows, and cried herself to sleep. When she woke, he was sitting there like he'd never left. She blinked the residue of salty tears from her eyes and sat up.

"What were you doing when the attack began?" He began as if no time had passed.

"Must we . . . ?"

"We must," he said in a concerned command voice.

That's the trouble with lies. She had to be careful with her story. "One of the elders died and there was a ceremony."

"Who died?"

She lied again, knowing the name she offered was on Omar's list. "Mr. Frank."

"And what did this Mr. Frank do?"

"Are you going to ask me about everyone?" she asked.

"I'm sorry," he said, his brevity disrespectful of her upcoming ordeal.

She tried to change the subject. "Omar, you know why I hate them, why do you hate them so much?"

"They are mass murderers and that would be enough but I hate them for their politics, their economics, their lack of compassion, and the desecration that is Morgan, their warped, capitalist religion. When they celebrate success, actions like Angel Falls are the victories they claim."

"Yes, but why do *you* hate them?"

"For all of that and what they did to the poor, the elderly, the sick, and the disenfranchised—the underserved in America—in what should have been a great and compassionate nation. America had over two hundred fifty years for capitalism to prove itself and yet there were too many poor and too many dependent people and they executed every one. America's leaders are worse than animals because they kill—not out of necessity—but for lifestyle. That is Saitan's way and I was put on this earth to end it."

In the safety of this powerful man's domain, his comments caused her new concerns. "Will the Reverend-General come after you, too? Am I safe here? Are you sure you can protect me from her here?"

"My defenses are significant and what Brandt needs to breach them, Canada will never allow."

"You're certain?"

"I have invested in redundancy on redundancy because I'm sure of nothing. Canada is in a precarious position. America isn't just at her doorstep; America is making herself comfortable on Canada's entire first floor. So you see, Stacey, darling, nothing is truly safe from those vile beasts who rule America, but that also means that the most vile of the beasts, she has a great many enemies and I am only a small one right now. When I am ready, when I understand Angel falls, that will change, I promise you."

"Are you powerful enough that she will leave me alone?"

"That, she will not do. They want you because you're a witness, but there is more going on than that. You are important to Chairwoman Brandt for reasons I've yet to discover and until she has you, or is certain that you can help no one else, she will never stop pursuing you."

She was sorry she mentioned it because Omar was making her very worried.

"I'm sorry, Stacey, this is difficult and not just everyday difficult, this is life and death, freedom or slavery difficult and for that I'm truly sorry." He paused and then his voice became soothing. "I've been insensitive. This is still too soon. You need rest and relaxation before you're ready, emotionally, to help our revolution. You need to be outside your own skin, to luxuriate, but to distill also. I have just the ticket." She was curious and then a little worried when he smiled that great, confidant smile. "*Virtuoso* is what you need."

In a way it was comforting. This inquisition would end. "*Virtuoso*? Jean-Paul was explaining it . . ."

"My attendant will escort you to a chamber and instruct you on its use. I have done all that is technologically possible to ensure that my units are absolutely secure and private so you will have no concerns there. Enjoy it freely, my beautiful, sweet young angel. You deserve to feel better and you will feel better soon."

"Are . . . are you going to be there, too, Omar?"

"Alas, no, I have much work to finish. You need a diversion—some fun—and I have been a bore and a poor host. I should have recommended this sooner. Join me tomorrow morning for breakfast. I will not grill you, this I swear."

Relieved, she relaxed. "What will I do?"

"That is the beauty of *Virtuoso*. Allow your imagination to flow, and you will have what you need. Each experience is unique, as real or abstract as you wish. I have even heard people laugh in *Virtuoso*."

Still unsure, she nodded. Omar called for an attendant, kissed her on the forehead, and departed. Moments later a woman entered. "Miss Grant, the Prophet has asked me to show you to our *Virtuoso* chambers. Please follow me."

As they walked Stacey questioned the maid. "Have you ever used *Virtuoso*?"

The woman covered her mouth and giggled. "No, Miss, *Virtuoso* is a rich person's toy."

"Does Omar use it?"

She tittered again. "The Prophet? I don't know, Miss. He is devout and has little time for anything but planning and prayers."

"Is *Virtuoso* dangerous?" Again, another giggle.

"No, Miss, it's not real, so what can happen? At the Prophet's soirees, the guests who haven't been invited to use *Virtuoso* are always disappointed and those who do, they leave very, very happy."

The attendant stopped at a door. "We're here," she said opening it. On the far wall were three metallic doors. "Pick one of the pre-chambers, enter and take off your clothes."

"My . . . my clothes? I'm . . . I can't . . ."

"It is okay, Miss, the chambers are absolutely secure and private. When you enter, there will be some lockers. Put your clothes in one and open the middle drawer. Inside are small boxes that contain contact lenses. Insert the lenses. If you're unsure what to do next, just ask out loud and you'll get all the instructions you need from Dubya, our resident gaming avatar. When your lenses are in, go through the marked door to the chamber. You'll see a large circle in the middle of the room. Stand in it and close your eyes. There will be a chilling breeze and then you'll feel warm all over. That will be followed by a brief sticky sensation again, all over your body." When Stacey made a face, the attendant noticed. "It's merely a spray that allows you to participate. It's organic and safe and washes off easily. That's all there is. After that, enjoy. There are no mistakes; I'm sure you'll get the hang of it."

Reluctantly, she followed the instructions, although she hesitated briefly before removing her clothes. There were no windows and she didn't see any cameras so she carefully removed and folded them. She was nervous so it took three tries to insert the lenses but when she was ready; she entered the chamber, closed her eyes, felt the cool and then the warm spray and trembled briefly when the stuff tightened on her skin and became tacky.

A strong fragrance permeated the air and she almost coughed when she inhaled, but she resisted opening her eyes until she felt a light breeze. Dizzy, she knelt and put her hands on the ground until the waves of nausea passed. She was standing, in blue jeans and a flannel shirt on a hilltop. She looked around, trying to make out the room that she had been in, but it was now gone somehow.

She viewed her surroundings; the place was hilly like Angel Falls, but there were fewer trees and more brush. It was less green, and more brown. Unsure what to do, she turned to see a trail that led down the hill and into a grove of trees nearby. She strolled down the path and once inside the grove, she spun around marveling at the dense foliage knowing she wasn't in Maine, but it sure didn't look like Canada either.

There were turquoise and pale green, myriad yellows, and bold blue flowers on trees of orange and some even gold. As she walked and marveled, she ducked under low-hanging branches adorned with flowers and she pirouetted around trunks whose bark seemed almost plastic, yet it was real because the flowers that hung from the branches smelled like magnolias. At a creek, she paused. It was narrow, narrow enough to jump over but the banks were chocolate-colored and marshy and the water, a milky-white and there were small yellow fish darting up to the surface. She found a tree trunk that had fallen across the creek and crawled over. On the other side, she came to a gigantic tree, one so tall that she should have noticed it from the hill but she couldn't remember ever seeing a tree this tall. It was made up of one thin copper colored trunk, no wider than she was. She stared up the narrow line that it made far into the heavens where it branched out into a canopy that defied gravity, it was that enormous, with small butter cuplike flowers cascading down toward the ground, making her feel like she was cocooned. There was quiet and there were fragrances working, fragrances so wonderful that she sat at the base of the tree staring dreamily at the yellow florets as they blew in the gentle breeze.

In the distance, there were screams and then laughter that broke through her reverie. She stood and reluctantly moved out from under the magnificent tree. She heard the screams again and she walked toward the sounds. She was walking on a forest floor covered in leaves of wondrous pastels. The path narrowed until she was forced to squeeze between two narrow black tree trunks. On the other side, she caught a glimpse of heaven.

The trail ended and through a light blue-green mist, there was a pink sandy beach and at the shore line, large, jagged, iridescent rocks reflecting with intensity all the colors of the sun. The rocks jutted out through the sand, presenting themselves steadfastly to the heavens as they endured a great pounding from a mint green ocean surf. She inhaled the salty spray and sighed. No, this wasn't Maine. That was certain. Yet it felt like home—the beaches where she spent vacations as a child with waves thundering against rocks, the clean and alive scent of ocean everywhere. Kids don't forget that smell. Still, it wasn't quite right. The sun was setting; creating an impossibly bright golden ribbon across the ocean that broke into a million facets all the way to the horizon and that didn't happen in

Maine. Maine would have been perfect if it did. This felt so right that she sat mesmerized, ensorcelled by the cresting and crashing waves, watching as the spent foam washed up lazily onto the beach near where she was sitting, in beautiful lacey patterns.

She heard the screams again, closer, and she forced herself to break away from this mystical paradise and walk along the beach toward the sound at the edge of the forest. There was a small hill to climb; the voices seemed to be on the other side. At the top, the vista opened below to her.

There was an immense building, the largest she had ever seen, large enough to contain all of Angel Falls, including her lake and the little nine-hole abandoned golf course that was added when her town was briefly a resort. Protruding from the top and sides of the building at various angles were a great many large, colorful plastic tubes. Surrounding the building was an immense parking lot filled with cars, more cars than she had ever seen, even more than that day when she and . . .

No, she wouldn't think about. She paused. She was happy for the first time in days. The memories were fierce and she wanted to speak his name, but a guardian thought warned her against it.

Up ahead, outside the building, there was a picnic, she could smell the barbecue. And there were kids and teens laughing and playing. Curious, she walked to them. They stopped what they were doing and watched her approach. Nearby, an older man waved to her like a friend and smiled. When she got closer, he hugged her affectionately.

"Would you like a drink, Stacey?" the man asked. "It's only five cents."

Without considering where she would get the money, she nodded and the man handed her a cup filled with a clear liquid. It tasted of apples so sweet that she pictured baked apples like Mrs. Singleberry would make. She finished it and the man handed her another cup and though it was almost too sweet, she drank that too. Two teen girls waved and then walked over to her.

"Picnics are for old people, the shopping mall is so much more fun."

She felt dwarfed by the mile-long and wide retail space inside the mall, and though lights were flashing, and there were colorful signs everywhere, it was not as impressive as the forest. Still, it was arresting to her senses. The girls giggled at her as she stared at the myriad shops working their commercial magic. Competing to attract her attention, music played, signs blinked, and large overhead lifelike animations stunned her senses with extraordinary visions that included strategic placement of products for sale.

One of the girls grabbed Stacey's hand and dragged her into a store. She had never seen anything like it. There were exquisite fashions everywhere, in dazzling arrays of impressive materials. The place was so far beyond the general store back home that at first, she just stared as her new girlfriends began trying on clothes. They shouted for her and she was in a changing area with stacks of clothes she'd never seen before, all in her size. They tried on everything and she couldn't remember having more fun. Clothes seemed to appear magically and fit perfectly and whenever she turned to the mirror, her image was wearing something stunning, so stunning that her new girlfriends stopped laughing and whispered to each other. Then they were done shopping, and her girlfriends were laughing and smiling as they led her away wheeling packages filled with clothes in a motorized cart. She couldn't wait to wear all these magnificent clothes. The girls took her to another store and she had her nails done and then her hair. She had never felt more alive.

Laughing to themselves, the girls took her into yet another store. There were a series of pools, more grottos, and soft music playing. She was curious but the girls only giggled.

"It is time to play," one of the girls teased. "This is where we play no limit hide and seek. The usual rules apply. Your job is to find a place to hide and whoever is 'it' will try to find you. That's usually when the fun starts." Confused, Stacey just stood there as the girls took off and ran through the grotto. One of the girls turned, her voice echoing.

"Run, Stacey, and while you are running, count to one hundred. Before you get there, hide because whoever is 'it' will be coming after you." The girls counted as they ran and then split up, one running toward a cave, the other shrieking as she ran down a narrow path between the pools. When Stacey still hadn't moved, one of the girls shouted, ". . . forty-four, forty-five," and then Stacey ran.

She bolted in a different direction than the girls. Here, there were stores and booths everywhere selling grotto-consistent paraphernalia, at least that's what the signs said. As she sped past, staring at all the stuff, she struggled to keep the count. Once or twice she saw something fascinating in a store window or displayed in a booth and she thought to go in but she kept counting down until she heard a loud scream and then louder laughter. Frightened, she continued her count as she looked for a place to hide. At the end of a corridor, she turned right and headed into a dark, wet area with blue and yellow plastic tubes all around and above her. Warm water was sloshing out, trickling down to wet her hair so she moved to a drier spot just as she completed her count at one hundred. There, she hunkered down next to a bright orange tube, unsure what she was hiding from.

She listened and waited nervously. The only sound was water rushing by and dripping down. But after a short while, she heard someone running. To avoid whoever it was, she saw a door and cautiously opened it. She stepped inside. It was dark and quiet.

A hand grabbed her and she shrieked.

"Found you," she heard a teen boy's voice say.

Terrified, she tried to rip out of his hold and crawl away but his laughter made her feel foolish. He must have turned a light on because she could see him now. He was her age, tall, muscular, and very good looking, his hair dark and curly, and his dimpled smile, almost shy given the confidence that emanated from his dark and marbled green eyes that stared back knowingly under thick black eyelashes.

"Hi, Stacey, I'm Burt and I have won the right to tickle you."

She laughed at that. "How did you win that right, Burt? And I don't want to ruin your fantasy, but I'm not ticklish."

"I found you and that is the rule. As far as not being ticklish, that's both physically and mentally impossible. I am a certified master of the art. My studies have prepared me to find anyone's ticklish spots so relax, you are in good hands and it is useless to struggle." He seemed serious so Stacey stopped smiling. "Most people think tickling is, well, just tickling. That is just silly. Professional tickling requires sensitivity—an awareness, and the willingness to persist while isolating the proper combination of body region and muscles with just the right motion and intensity and just the right ambience. You are ticklish; woman, you just do not know it. I have never failed to leave a victim laughing."

"You sound proud of it."

"Immensely." He smiled proudly.

"What happens when you lose," she poked him in the ribs, "when you can't make me laugh?"

"Never happen." Then he considered it. "Is that a challenge? That will make this even better. Oh, you will laugh, you can count on that. But just for fun, what kind of wager do you have in mind?"

"I don't know. How about, if I win, you promise never ever to tickle any girl ever again for the rest of your life unless they agree to it first."

He surprised her. "I accept, but every girl wants it. Besides, how will you hold me to that promise?"

"If I can't trust you, Burt, I want no part of this or you. I'm not playing. Unless you mean it, there will be no tickling here or anywhere."

"I agree."

"You're not serious."

"What can I do to show you that I am?" he pleaded.

She thought on it. "Tell me something about yourself that nobody else knows. Trust me with a secret that you don't want anyone to know. If you break your promise, I'll squeal. Tell me and then I'll be sure you won't break your promise. But it has to be a real secret."

Burt's smile disappeared and he looked distraught. "No one has ever made me do this, but I like you even though you drive a hard bargain. If I tell you, you must promise never to tell anyone?"

She nodded.

"I mean it," he said. "No one," he begged, looking seriously alarmed in a very cute way. He leaned in and whispered in her ear.

Here it comes, she thought, he's trying to catch me off-guard. She tensed. His hot breath made her ear tingle.

"The reason," he whispered, "why I act this way," he sounded sincere, "is I have been hurt before. Tickling is not just . . . tickling. There has to be a connection made and I am too trusting. A boy, a special boy; he disappointed me, and now I feel that I have to act like this to, you know, protect myself." She wasn't buying it and that seemed to distress him. "What? So you have never acted distant to protect yourself from getting hurt."

That struck a nerve, but she tried to remain unconvinced. "Okay, okay, tell me."

"I cannot. It is too painful." She smiled and turned to go, but he grabbed her and pulled her back. "I was younger, a novice tickler, and I fell in love with a local boy who only wanted me for my tickling, for his satisfaction. He wanted me only as his plaything and I wanted more, I know I wanted more. But then he found another tickler and I promised myself I would never fall for someone again. It hurt that much." Burt looked sincere, even vulnerable, and that had a surprising affect on her. He continued. "You may not be aware of this but as professions go, master ticklers are the most vulnerable and we struggle the most to have serious long term relationships. I know that seems counterintuitive but it's true. You do not know how much I sacrifice from my craft."

"Burt, I'm sorry. If you don't want to continue . . ."

"No, I promised. There it is, and it still hurts."

"But you're a good looking guy."

"What do looks have to do with feelings? Even good-looking people have hearts that can break, don't they? But with all the hurt and disappointment, I was no longer performing at the master level, so I had to grow up or change professions. Like all professionals, I decided to give up everything for success in my chosen field so I promised myself I would be a professional first and leave love behind. It's not easy, I'm the loving kind, I guess, but I found that if I could remain aloof, I could earn enough to assure my future and then, maybe, I could retire and find someone who would love me, for me, not just my good looks or my fingers—but you know, for me.

"That is why I will never fall for another, not first I won't, anyway. I just can't, that's why the fun-loving, playboy facade. I can only hope that someday, someone will be willing to search beyond that façade but until that happens, I am unwilling to chance getting hurt again. I know it sounds silly, but I hope you are never hurt because you care more than he does. When you give what I have to give . . . when you want what I want . . ."

Burt looked down and wiped his eyes with the back of his hand. "Rejection is . . . painful. You have no idea." She put her hand on his shoulder, but before she could utter words of comfort, he continued. "Stacey, thanks, you're a great listener. When I tickle someone, in truth, it tickles me, too. It's a form of intimacy but without the exposure, but even at that it hurts." Burt blushed and looked away, embarrassed by his outburst. Stacey took a deep breath, sucking in the sweet-pungent fragrance from the nearby coastal flora. He turned to stare tenderly at her and then he said, resolutely, "Now that you know everything, you better keep your promise and not tell anyone. I have a reputation to uphold." She nodded and a smile grew on his face because of it. "Get ready; the tickle master will now create laughter from nothing."

He lunged and she yelped in surprise. Then he held her and began tickling her in all the usual places in all the usual ways. She screamed at first, then stiffened and refused to react, instead mocking him for his failure.

"Oh, you have it, Bart, that's the spot. You are the master, the tickle master. See how hard I'm laughing." She squirmed but refused to laugh; egging him on as he squeezed, gently rubbed, and pressed everywhere there might be a sensitive spot.

"Not going so good huh, champ?"

He stopped abruptly. "This is part of the tickle discipline. I am just surveying the terrain, so to speak, preparing." With that, he pushed her gently back onto—that fresh smell—they were on grass now. She took a deep breath, the smell of pine needles causing her to relax as his fingers floated and then danced gently over her chin and down her neck. She didn't laugh but she didn't resist because it felt wonderful. She sighed and relaxed as his light touch, on her ears, her eyebrows, and over her eyelids, soothed her. His fingers lightly painted her lips and then were gone. She tensed, waiting for his killer tickle.

But as the scent of lilac descended on her, he continued gently, his fingers wandering over her shoulders and working down to her waist. It felt so good. Breathing softly and rhythmically in her ear, he worked his way up, and this time, she shivered involuntarily. His deft fingers were everywhere and left regret when they departed. The buttons on her blouse were his next target. She should have stopped him. Wearing only her bra and panties, she felt warm and safe.

His tongue trailed over her breasts, the salty scent of ocean spray permeating the air along with the musky, pungent smell of the forest. His hands were everywhere and nowhere and she was naked, responding to him in unfamiliar ways, muscle groups relaxing, tensing, and trembling. His lips gently teased her skin and she endured and then surrendered to the unusual, intense sensations, so powerful that her eyes tightly closed, her stomach muscles contracted, and her body shook uncontrollably.

She was floating in a dream-like state, picturing nothing as her legs turned spastic and then to jelly. Her eyes fluttered open but saw nothing and they closed tight as rolling shivers caressed her body, coaxing responses she'd never ever felt before and wouldn't likely ever forget.

Suddenly, another exquisite fire spread until all that was left was to scream and writhe. Floating on nothingness, finally her entire body trembled into quiescence and blissfully exhausted, she was about to lose consciousness when, unbidden, she began to laugh uncontrollably.

It was morning and she lay in bed, trying in vain to recall how she'd gotten there. Fractured moments or memories flashed by and horribly embarrassed by them, she pulled a blanket over her head, hoping to hide from the world. Try as she might, she couldn't turn the pieces in her mind into a whole, but what she remembered seemed real, yet not. She felt soreness and touched herself trying to localize the tenderness but there was none. Confused and worse—mortified and unsure why—she hid under the blanket, sobbing quietly for no apparent reason.

Unspecified guilt kept her in the room while pangs of hunger were forcing her out. But it took persistent knocking by Warren Salaam to finally rouse her and it was near noon before she left the sanctuary of her room. Warren seemed oblivious to her shame as he accompanied her to lunch. On the way, she walked beside him staring down at the floor, embarrassed. When she arrived at the dining hall, Omar was already there, eating.

"Princess, it's so late, you must be famished," he said nonchalantly between chews.

She trembled. "Omar, I'm no princess," she mumbled.

He reconsidered. "No, of course not. I trust you slept well."

"Yes, I think . . . yes, thank you," she stammered.

"Good." As if there was nothing more to say about last night, he pointed to the dish on the table. "Eat. We have Angel Falls to discuss." She felt a chill. "You are refreshed, no? It is time we discuss realities. Help me to understand the puzzle and why Brandt acted as she did."

She sat beside him and though hungry, she only moved her food around. "I don't know anything, honest." He smiled back. "Omar, do we have to? It makes me sad."

"I'm sorry, but yes. I'm a patient man, but I must know the truth so I can protect you. Believe in me, Stacey, my love, and your life will be so much less stressful, happier even. I don't want to scare you, but a great many lives depend on me and you may have information that will keep them safe. We must not disappoint them and their families." His smile was warm and comforting.

"I'm sorry; you've been kind—more than kind. Of course I'll try."

"Good. You are the answer to my prayers and for this to work; you and I must traffic in honesty. You asked me why I hate them. I will explain. You must believe how evil Andrew Crelli was so that you can understand how important it is to stop his surrogate, Tanya Brandt." Omar's eyes glazed over and moments later, a servant entered and handed each of them a beer.

"I will start with the basics so that you understand all of it. I am an American citizen but I was born on the coast of Germany, north of Hamburg. I am Muslim as you know and I'm seventy-three years old."

"No, that can't be," she said. "Seventy-three? I have . . . had uncles younger who looked so much older. Surely not seventy-three."

He laughed. "You are kind. My father, Allah be praised, a man with a wretched capitalist soul, he lived to be over a hundred and twenty-five and was still active to the end—and that was before modern medical technology made long life common. My father was rich beyond belief, making billions as a sub-contractor for American security and defense interests overseas. I am the sole heir to his global empire.

"I was schooled in Geneva and came to the United States for post graduate work at Drexel University in Philadelphia. But before my father would allow me to inherit his fortune, he required that I run some of his companies. In fact, he insisted I start with his American Financial Services businesses which I ran, but it was a dirty and immoral industry. Through premiums, fees and interest, the companies were stealing from the poor and middle class and that was more than I was willing to be associated with. My father and I argued constantly. He couldn't be convinced to alter his business model and help the people he was stealing from so eventually I resigned and turned my back on his fortune. I moved to Chicago to learn in the streets where they live, how to help the poor. My dear mother, Allah blesses her, she was certain that my decision to flee my father's business caused his decline. But after he died, I didn't feel guilty, even when I was declared his one and only heir. We only have one life and one vision of ourselves and we must go where we are meant to go. Soon after Chicago, California was facing one of their perpetual financial crises and the legislature was preparing to pass a bill that would eliminate benefits for the poor and homeless. I moved to Sacramento to fight that bill.

"We lost, for it was the beginning of yet another selfish, right wing, libertarian phase in America, but because I wasn't born here, my political aspirations and ability to stop them was limited to the Congress. Still, my work was appreciated by a few who convinced me to run for a state house seat, which I won. From there, every day, I fought aggressively for the poor and disenfranchised."

"You are a good, brave man, Omar."

"It was a losing battle. The rich have already won. I mean by that, why should we all not be fighting for the poor? Most gods require it, mine and the one most Americans say they follow, those gods demand it. Alas, believing in God and doing His work are two separate things in America. Poverty became a capital offense and no American wanted to chance being poor. Two years later, I represented a district in the House at the same time that Andy Crelli was a business-oriented, security-minded moderate republican junior senator. That was his reputation. In reality, the man was deeply imbedded with very wealthy right wing entrepreneur groups that wanted total control of our government and Crelli had the plan."

"Did you ever meet Chairman Crelli?"

"Certainly. We met at the end of my only term in Congress and the best I can say about it was it was life changing." Omar paused, his eyes going blank. When he recovered, he delayed his talk. "It is time for prayers. I'll continue my tale later. Until then, you are free to relax. *Virtuoso* is available."

"No," she responded too quickly. "I'd prefer to swim or take a hike, if you don't mind?"

"My sweet, you are my honored guest. Do as you please." He hugged her gently, like her father often did on those cold, dark nights long ago when she was a child. "We'll meet in two hours and I'll explain why I loathe Crelli."

Chapter 5
Smith Madrasah, Canada—2070

While Stacey waited for Omar's prayers to end, she occupied her time by swimming and then ate in her room, by herself. The chef made her favorite, shepherd's pie—but not like her mom's, there were no peas, but it was so good she had another helping. When Omar was ready, Warren Salaam escorted her back to his study

"My sweet, before I begin, tell me about your friend. Tell me about Meat. From all you haven't said, I have grown jealous."

"Jealous of Meat?" She would have laughed except poor Meat deserved better. "You have no reason to be jealous of him, Omar."

"Then help me understand. According to our records, there were few people your age in Angel Falls. I expect this Meat desired you very much."

She blushed. "I didn't know Meat very well. He was . . . a friend. He liked to hike, that's all."

"For me to help and protect you, you must tell me the truth. You're very attractive and that affects people, boys especially. No, don't smile or blush, it is the truth. I am older and experienced and you've charmed me, so surely this teen boy was smitten." The intensity that emitted from his eyes made her feel uncomfortable. "I apologize if this embarrasses you, but you must become more aware of your charms."

"It is embarrassing," she admitted. She couldn't look at him yet she couldn't look away. "Meat was a friend, that's all, I swear."

"And a friend can mean many things."

"No it can't."

He smiled, seemingly enjoying her discomfort.

"You are a sweet, sweet girl," he said. "I understand the passions of youth—passions that are mostly gone these days. It is refreshing to find a throwback to better days. But tell me true, Stacey, it won't displease me. I must know to protect you and to further our revolution. I must know the truth." Their eyes met and she felt like she was floating. The truth was so close she trembled. Then, he reached his hand out and gently touched her below her ear and traced along her jaw to her chin, his eyes following his hands and smiling appreciatively. She trembled. "You have nothing to fear from me. This Meat . . ."

He was so kind that she began to speak more freely. "Meat was . . . Meat was my friend—kind of—but I barely knew him. Maybe . . . no, that's not possible now. You don't know what it was like back . . . It's not like here. It's nothing like here. Everyone was close, neighborly, my parents called it. But I didn't know Meat very long and no, I didn't love him, but Omar, if loving Meat would have saved his life, I think I would have loved him. I would have. But he's . . . gone and nothing can change that. I'm sad that I didn't treat him better—but we were only friends. He may have liked me, I don't know. And he visited, I guess, because he didn't have friends at home. Maybe he was bored. I don't know." Good, she could speak without thinking of Gil.

"Then tell me of your other friends?" Once again his eyes lost focus and that only added to her dread.

"That's really freaky."

After a brief pause, he responded. "What is?"

"That look you get."

"Implants, they allow me to communicate directly through my network to my staff. I couldn't function without the technology. I'm sorry it upsets you. I'll refrain in your presence."

"No, I didn't mean . . . no, it's okay." She realized she might have offended him.

"Please continue."

"I want to help but it was a small town and I was . . . friendly, only, and with everyone."

"But you loved somebody."

"I had no love life." She felt herself blushing at an intimate memory or a dream. "There was nothing, I promise you."

"I believe you, Stacey, but this is not the perverse curiosity of an old man. This is important. A strikingly beautiful young lady lives in a small town her entire life and she only has acquaintances? I will not cast aspersions on the manliness of your community that way. No, there is a love there. You are closed, Stacey dearest, closed, but I am certain of three things. You lived in Angel Falls, you were in love with somebody there, and you don't trust me enough to tell me more."

It was getting harder to avoid his eyes.

"You have only just met me so I understand why you don't trust me yet, but I am your friend, your devoted and only friend, something I am honored to be. This is a journey and we will get there. I promise you, we will get there. Let's start again with the list. When we are finished, I will explain my old friend Andrew Crelli and you will understand what you and I are fighting." He took out his communicator and accessed the list of the Angel Falls dead. He handed it to her but before she could take it, he pulled it back and smiled.

"He is not on the list," Omar whispered, sounding pleased. "That's it. You didn't see his name so you believe he's still alive. That's marvelous, princess. That is a good thing for our revolution." She turned from his stare, struggling not to share what she needed desperately to suppress. "This young man of yours, whoever he is, he is my hope too, Princess, and if I'm to help you, and possibly him, and our country I must understand who he is and what he is going through. I can help him. Don't let the embarrassment of young love get in the way of something truly crucial. This love of yours could be why Angel Falls was so important to Brandt. Tell me about him. Tell me everything."

She tried not to show the great despair she felt. How could she accept that her family, her friends, everyone in Angel Falls died because Gil was there? She pictured the *SurveilEagle*. Gil had warned her, worried her, and now, the Prophet was saying it could be true. The *SurveilEagle* had been a harbinger of doom, not some silly plaything for an immature, irresponsible girl to play with. She had killed her family as surely as the government had. She put her hands firmly on the table in front of her to keep them from shaking and remained silent fearing she would tell everything and confirm her guilt.

Omar relented. "You are distraught and I'm wrong to pressure you, sweetness. Forgive me," he said calmly. "It will all become apparent in the time that's required so we'll stop, for now. You must learn why I chose exile and dedicated my life to returning America to freedom. Perhaps you will trust me after you hear the truth."

He patted his pillow. She was so relieved and grateful for the respite that she moved quickly beside him. He wrapped his arm around her and she prayed he didn't notice she was trembling.

"In 2028, using my given name, Glen Smith, I was elected U.S. Congressman for what was once a poor district in central Los Angeles, and is now a desolate ruin where only *Wasters* can live. Like many districts back then, mine had been so grossly gerrymandered that middle and upper middle class families living in the farthest corners of the city made up the voting majority. In my primary, I was up against a rich Dutch type who campaigned from his country club bar while I campaigned on the streets, targeting the poor. No one expected me to win; yet I got out the vote and won the primary and the general election as well. That was the year President Parrington swept the national election, the first Democrat to win the presidency in over a decade and like many Democratic candidates, I surprised all the pundits and was carried into office on his coattails.

"Two years earlier, thanks to his father-in-law, Senate Majority Leader Brent Bartram, Andy Crelli was elected junior senator from Kentucky. By the time I arrived, he had convinced everyone that he was a brilliant politician, a natural leader, and a future president. In fact, though I hate him, he was all that and more and he managed it by orchestrating others to bring victory to him. Except for taking credit for defeating the e-RATS, he worked tirelessly in the background and only his closest allies knew that he was planning to run for president in the very next election."

"What are e-RATS?" she asked. She had heard Rabbi mention them.

He smiled. "Your education is sorely lacking and we must change that. e-RATS were greedy, viral predators who prowled the Mesh for economic plunder."

"Oh," she said though she didn't understand.

Chapter 6
Washington D.C.—2029

American Politics—the American Stock Market can be volatile in the short run and there is great profit to be made on the volatility index, the Vix. But there are intermediate and longer-term movements that often tell a different story, so for the patient analytic, there is profit playing the long run also. That is where politics comes into it.

Like the Stock Market, American political party fortunes vacillate from election to election, but there are longer-term trends that become apparent to the savvy investor. Since as long ago as the late 1950s, financial and conservative have been the long position in politics while communitarian and entitlement ideology based on social interest politics and bigger government that represents Progressive policy, that has been the short position.

There have been times during this period when Progressives seem to so dominate that the trend line wavers but as they say, "good money talks", and the tendency toward selfish individualism and free market capitalism continues mostly unabated. Maybe it was the aging of America, but more likely it was that Conservative thought was better taught at an earlier age and reinforced in day-to-day life, which was all business during this period. Certainly, business was better funded and thus more thoroughly inculcated into the lives of American citizens, but Conservative thought was clearly dominant.

In the winter of 2029, the freshman class of Representatives that arrived in Washington D.C., unbeknownst to the Democrats, provided the Republican Party (Soon to be the Entrepreneur Party) with complete control of Congress. But without the power of the Presidency, which was in the hands of the liberal, Vernon L. Parrington

(See: Parrington: The Last Liberal, published in 2032), its potential remained dormant. In due time, the ideologues in that famous class of 2029 came to represent the best of conservative America.

But it wasn't until President Parrington exercised executive overreach and vetoed business-savvy Congressional legislation that citizens awoke to the need for common cause in Washington in order to provide business owners with the long term consistency they needed to bring the American economy back to life. The legislation that the short-sighted Parrington vetoed would have eradicated the Federal Debt and solved immigration issues that had so haunted the country's economy for decades. This legislation would have provided the American people with the most pragmatic and effective business environment in the history of governance.

With Parrington exercising obscene veto power over every productive piece of legislation, while expanding the socialist agenda of long dead Congresses by feathering his nest in Federal Courts with old guard, bleeding heart liberal judges, the country continued to unravel.

Parrington's actions led to the great patriotic wave of Conservative victories in 2032 that brought the heroic President Andrew M. Crelli and Vice President Tanya Brandt to office and thus gave control of all three branches of government to Conservatives forever.

House Representative Glen Smith was one of the few winners from the liberal left. Though he attacked the Right with great energy and intelligence, there was no political interest within his party for his progressive programs and so he supported then Senator Crelli on most issues.—**Archive**

As it had been since he first arrived in Washington in the winter of 2029, Congressman Smith was late for yet another meeting in his endless agenda of meaningless political gatherings. He frantically searched his briefcase and the desk in his small office, but couldn't find the information he needed so he rushed to ask for help from the clerk he shared with a number of other rookie Congressmen.

"Tiffany, do you know where the file is?"

"Congressman Smith, it's in your in-box. I sent it over lunch."

"Do I have anything scheduled for tonight?"

"Yes, sir, you're playing basketball against the Junior Senators team."

He had forgotten. "Tiff, I need a favor, sweetheart. I'm late for a meeting and I left my gym bag and sneakers inside the front door of my townhouse. Can you bring it here?" She agreed, and he confirmed her access to his townhouse.

When he returned from the meeting, his gym bag and a fast food meal were waiting on his desk. He finished the meal and wrote out a thank you note for Tiffany. Then he left for the game.

He found himself matched against a young Senator who, like himself, had limited ability, but played the game aggressively. With other stars on their respective teams, he and the senator played their roles, picking, blocking out, impeding, and rebounding, rarely handling the ball except for touch passes to teammates, but because they each played the same way without the ball, they were constantly pushing, bumping, slapping, and otherwise being physical with each other in the quest to gain position. Glen's relationship with Andy Crelli began over a series of slaps, scrapes, and collisions and even a little blood. Glen's team of congressmen won.

After the game, he introduced himself to his opponent, offering a battered hand. "Senator, I'm Glen Smith, from L.A. Nice, tough way you have of playing."

The Senator was Omar's height with prematurely gray hair and an easily recognizable confidence, even on the basketball court.

"Good game," the senator said. "We'll get you next time. I'm Andy Crelli from Kentucky, the basketball capital of the world." Glen nodded and turned to shake hands with the others on Crelli's team. As he was leaving, the Senator dribbled over to him.

"A group of us are going out for drinks; care to join us, Congressman?"

"Democrats are allowed?"

"Even liberal Democrats," Crelli said, smiling.

"There can't be more than a few. Are any invited who vote repeatedly against your attempts to eliminate entitlements for the needy?"

Crelli offered a smile. "That's more reason to join us, Glen. I respect opposition; it's the best way to learn and get better."

Glen agreed to come, and quickly showered. He tossed his gym bag full of sweaty clothes into the back seat of his car and climbed in. The directions that Crelli had given him lead to a nearby Alexandria tavern. He walked through the door and looked for Crelli. In the mostly empty main room, a small group, including Senator Crelli, was seated in the bar area, eating, drinking and laughing. None were his teammates.

"Senator, thanks for inviting me," he said. "I don't see any other winners here."

Crelli smiled and shook his hand. "Thanks for coming, Glen. Beer?" They ordered and while they waited, Andy explained. "You're the only one I invited because we need to talk." Curious, Glen nodded and they took a quiet table in the corner.

"So what's this about, Senator?"

"It's good to see the Democrats finally mounting a challenge on the basketball court. You're forcing us to do a better job recruiting good ball players in time for the presidential election. You didn't play in college?"

"I didn't have time. I played some in Hamburg growing up but at Drexel, I only played in the intramural league."

"I played intramural ball, too, at Penn State, where I took my Masters. If I'd had a jump shot, well," he paused and smiled. "Who am I kidding; this is about as good as I ever got at basketball. If they called me anything, it would be a 'plucky' guard."

Glen laughed. "You earned that tonight. I have welts and scratches all over. You play hard."

"That's the only way I know how to play. Let me explain why I invited you. I've checked you out. You're a true enigma, certainly for a Congressman. You're a wealthy entrepreneur with profitable businesses all over the world, yet you speak out for the poor like you believe in it and I haven't been able to find anything in your dossier that explains why."

"Senator, that's easy. My father was as rich as he was an asshole. Should I be more impressed that I have a dossier or that you've read it?"

"Either or neither," Crelli explained. "This is what my dossier says about me. I own a large technology conglomerate and I never considered politics until I met my wife's father, Senate Majority Leader Brent Bartram. But I'm highly motivated and I have great contacts in the business community. Leadership, I'm embarrassed to say, from a purely objective perspective comes easily to me."

"Senators with ten times your seniority would kill for that dossier."

Crelli laughed. "I get things done and I'm proud of what I've been able to accomplish with the cooperation of the most powerful Senators and their wealthy lobbyists. What my dossier fails to mention is that my wife is beautiful, sexy, and politically savvy, and I have two great kids. You're not married."

"I haven't been in one place or impressed by someone enough. My life provides an abundance of companionship. Again, Senator, what's this meeting about?"

"Parrington wants to extend Social Security and other entitlements another generation and you're in favor of it."

"That can't be a great secret."

"No, but it's a waste of your vote because in four years, social welfare will disappear."

"And why's that?"

"There won't be the votes to continue it."

"Senator, we have a Democratic President so your efforts can't become law unless you can override him and according to most counts, Democrats have the voting bloc to prevent it."

"That's the short view but allow me to be gracious and do you a big favor. You hold positions in some corporations that support the elderly—hospices and other not-for-profits. For the next few years, these businesses will do quite well because of government funding."

"Senator, are you accusing me of voting to line my own pockets?"

"No, not at all. Consider this friendly advice from an insider who knows. With the next election, my demographics experts assure me there will be a significant, a cataclysmic shift in voter attitudes—so great a shift, in fact, that Republicans will be swept into power with filibuster-proof majorities, unfortunately, to face deficits that would choke even a stone-hearted politician's heart."

"Do your demographics experts explain what causes this sudden shift, Senator? Will thirty million economically-desperate immigrants suddenly decide they prefer to make it without government assistance? Or maybe there will be a change of heart among the thirty percent of the voting population who desperately needs what little the government provides to live just another day? It's hard to imagine those voter blocs supporting you or anyone who wishes to discontinue welfare even if it barely provides for subsistence living."

"This is about business, Glen. Entitlements are beyond saving because of the debt—forget about it. For decades, politicians have refused to make the tough decisions so now, everything in the budget looks vital, but we can no longer afford any of it. We have no choice but to make deep cuts. It's time to wake up the poor, the lazy, and the unfortunate and tell them that time and money have run out and they must turn their own lives around because, even if the government wanted to, we can't. By eliminating welfare and entitlements and downsizing the government, we free trillions which reduces taxes and interest rates and improves bottom lines so businessmen can once again hire from the best of the unemployed. These people need to realize that without a government check, it's time they made a difference in their own lives. It's the virtuous circle and a win for everyone."

"It's not a win for everyone, Senator. Unemployment is high and without government support these people won't have money to spend that helps their communities survive. And if we downsize, it means more people on welfare and that causes more problems if there is no welfare for them. The handouts, as your people call them, the money we give to the poor goes immediately into buying real stuff from local stores, which improves everyone's bottom line, a true virtuous circle."

"We killed Keynes decades ago, and I don't want to argue it," Crelli said, referring to the late British economist. It was Keynes in the 1920s who provided the intellectual capital that eventually became the New Deal in America that—to conservative America—led to the deep deficits that eventually undermined the country—or to the Liberals—the policy of helping the poor and downtrodden that is so critical to the humanity of the American people.

Glen smiled. "Senator, in reality, you killed Keynes after private industry had already squeezed about as much out of it as it could."

Crelli smiled. "Glen, I would love to have that discussion. It could prove interesting but tonight isn't about ideology. What I'm offering is that two years from now, if you divest those shares, your portfolio will not take a beating. It's a favor, not a discussion. In two years, those stocks will be at what history will record as their historic peak and they will be ripe for sale to the naïve, under-informed masses who we all count on to buy stocks too late. Catch the wave, Glen. There's no reason not to. Besides, the profits will offset your bitter disappointment when my party takes control for good."

"I appreciate your concerns but it makes no sense. My party believes welfare is a national security issue. If you cease to provide it, you will spend even more on security and there will be no victories for anyone."

"As I said, that's a discussion I'm willing to have, but not tonight. What you say may have been true once, but sentiment has shifted and a significant number of young voters are facing an incredibly difficult decision. Do they fund their parents, the self-absorbed generation of baby boomers, or do they use the admittedly limited funds that remain in the government coffers on their children. The old or the new, create an environment for perpetuating their DNA, or keep spoiling dying baby boomers. How do you think they'll vote in 2032?"

"I'll keep that in mind," Glen said, letting the question hang unanswered, and effectively halting the conversation.

They drank beer and talked amicably about the difficult future. Though Glen offered specific solutions, it was clear Crelli felt that he already knew the future with a precision that was more than just confidence. Still, Glen persisted, resurrecting his concern for the poor.

"Andy, when they have nothing, when welfare stops, we're all doomed because it's not just the poor that are affected. It would be different if they could find jobs but two hundred years of capitalism hasn't ended poverty so if we don't provide economic incentives to prime the economic pump, commerce compresses and everyone suffers all the way up the food chain but as always, bad times start with the poor. This is a demand-based economy and you know it, so why do we want so many struggling epically to survive when it's possible to prevent it?"

"Apparently, preventing it is your job, Glen, not mine. I'm an adult; I take responsibility for myself. If others can't-"

"But Senator, these people didn't become poor on their own. They were unskilled and unprepared in an economy ruthlessly geared to winners and they are the losers. You and I are the winners. Isn't it time we give them a chance and by doing so add more demand so the economy can grow?"

"No, I don't believe it is. As you say, there are winners and losers and isn't it up to the losers to figure out how they lost and turn it around, or remain losers? Hell, they had better be doing that because I know, without a doubt that the economic winners are busy trying to make sure they never become losers. We both know that our economy can't absorb more excess baggage carrying losers on our back. It's time you admit it."

"If we don't do something, you know what will happen. We'll spend more building walls, adding security, everywhere, and otherwise protecting ourselves and our assets from very desperate people.

"It's been said that to whom much is given, much is expected. That should be the rallying cry of the rich in America. That is what we should stand for. Like you, I prefer that forty million Americans weren't on some form of welfare but, until something changes, entitlements are more than social justice; they're a national security priority."

Crelli listened intently, nodding. "That's one way to see it. It's reasonable, but flat out wrong. I see a different world, a world where people like you and I make a great deal of money for a good reason, we earn it because of our ability and our work ethic. And because of what we do, America is better off, both relatively and absolutely. Without a motivated entrepreneur class, the poor and middle class will stop dreaming, scheming, and striving to become us. If we ever give up our star status, think of the shame. There will be no heroes to honor and nothing to show the lower classes all the benefits and the glory that make economic victory worth fighting for. Economic success must be rare enough to be valued. If success is free or easy, people won't try as hard and they'll lose the drive that's made America great. Without that drive, we may as well all be chattel or domesticated animals, for God's sake. I don't work hard to increase my wealth because I want to live better. I do it because it gives my life purpose. And if I stopped pressing ahead, or if I gave my wealth away to people who can't manage on their own, it would demoralize everyone in the system. Hell, look how far America has fallen after over a century of giving away so much of its wealth to the poor. We are failing and unless that changes, this will be a long-term disaster. Think of it. Think of our world without ideals, goals, and the drive to achieve, to make it a better place. It is because of people like you and me, Glen, that the world isn't sadder and more pathetic."

"I'll bet you've never even seen any poor people let alone been poor," Glen said.

Crelli smiled at that. "I'm guessing I've been poorer than you've ever been. My mother worked herself to exhaustion as a farmer on a small plot of nothing in central Kentucky. Every day she kept a budget, which was easy because she said no to everything. She even cried to demonstrate to me how hard her decisions were but it was always no. Even through college, I did without. But for all that, I made something of my life and improved the lives of everyone who associated with me. You do it too, Glen. That's what wealth does and what it must be allowed to continue to do."

"But Andy, for every one of us, there are millions who can't bootstrap to anything more than survival. Generation after generation, these people have been the chaff in our economy, the ones who are thrown away, doomed to live in conditions that defy their right to life and liberty, but none of them will ever get closer to something better without our help."

"Okay," Crelli said. "Tell me what you propose that's new or different? I'm all ears. How do we build your paradise where everyone is excused from effort? And how do we do it in a competitive, cutthroat world that isn't changing anytime soon because we discovered the nice god of nobility. The world wants what we have and if we ease up, just a little, if America isn't strong enough to keep our hallowed ways alive, we will lose everything and 'we' includes the poor and the rich.

"Giving wealth to poor people who don't know how to use it isn't what the world is hoping for. We've given to the incapable for generations and look where it got us. We're closer to the economic crapper than ever.

The Senator's voice grew louder and surer as he explained further. "Think, Glen, think about what is going to happen. Foreign corporations who produce in the United States, they hire lobbyists too. How many more years of failure will there be until these foreign corporations own enough lobbyists to hijack the whole damn country? And once they have it, they'll take the good parts for themselves and throw the rest—and that includes your constituency—away. It's not about me, whatever happens, I'll survive, and it might not make a difference to the abject poor, but it sure as hell will affect everyone else."

"Isn't it ironic that I'm foreign born, yet I want what's best for all Americans whereas—"

"Jesus, give me a fucking break," Crelli interrupted. "We've tried handouts for more than a century and it clearly hasn't worked. If the trillions we've already spent hasn't turned America into a paradise for the incapable and the lazy, how much more can we waste on that boondoggle, particularly in our current economic condition?"

"It's not how much; it's where and how it's spent."

"So you're saying that the best liberal minds of the past century and their fellow traveler economists couldn't figure it out, but you can? No offense, but I won't touch those odds."

"You and I disagree on approach. As a former company president, I know that the unemployed are our most abundant and least expensive resource; surely you and I can find a way to make that work for everyone. It's up to us to utilize the poor as a capitalist resource or to chase them away and gift them to terrorists. The choice we provide for them will be our legacy to America."

"Okay, maybe you and I are not that far apart. It's why I wanted to talk to you in the first place. Do me a favor, listen to my program. I haven't announced it yet so please keep it to yourself. If you like it, which I believe you will, we can work together on the details and get things going in the right direction. You can help me with your party and I know I can bring mine along. You live in Georgetown, not too far from me. Maddie's having a party next week. Why don't you come? Bring a date, and we can talk it out."

Omar was pleased by the invitation. A Crelli party wasn't an easy ticket. "Thanks, I'd love to come and continue this conversation."

They ordered another round of beers and Crelli laid out the basics of his program.

"It's simple, really. When the economy bottoms out and starts growing again, anyone who wants a job should have one. That's a given. In the short term, I can live with the government acting as the broker, if necessary. I know what you're going to say. What about those who can't find work, who can't help themselves. They're a problem, certainly. What I propose is we provide work incentives—subsidies, to employers that hire them. Large corporations, who use subcontractors to support their operations, can provide additional work support initiatives to entice their subcontractors to hire and mentor people until a strong work ethic grows so that even inferior employees can become steady economic contributors in a growing economy. Employers who don't or can't hire can kick in to help those who do, because what I am proposing will provide a more experienced and better-trained workforce. While the economy builds momentum, government projects should only accept preferred contractors who have programs to employ and mentor the previously unemployed or unemployable."

Glen was taken aback. The Senator's proposal wasn't what he expected at all so he interrupted him. "Is this a Republican proposal or are you just mocking me? If you're serious, hell yes, I'm interested."

Crelli slapped him on the shoulder. "You don't really know me, but I promise you, I'm serious about everything I do. Why shouldn't Republicans have practical answers to poverty? We're pragmatic, not heartless. For more than a century, Democrats failed using the same stale ideas. It's time for change we can all believe in. I'm as concerned as you about the poorest Americans because we are creating a fertile breeding ground for our enemies—nihilists, terrorists, and international economic predators."

"Yet you still want to end entitlements," Glen pointed out.

"We can't afford them. But I want a real dialogue on real issues with real solutions. I'm tired of the centuries of political intrigue and infighting that have only made things worse."

"Senator, I've never thought of you in this context. I'm impressed. Everyone else in your party acts like troglodytes; you see the future, differently, and I'm very interested. You're right about giveaways. They don't create better workers or lifetime contributors. Protected, nurturing environments are the answer, and rewarding employers for hiring and mentoring long term is just the thing to rebuild a good solid American work ethic."

The Senator slapped Glen on the back. "Great, I look forward to continuing this discussion." With that, Glen finished off his beer and the Senator offered his hand before leaving.

"Congressman, thanks. I hope we can work together to show that reasonable, responsible people can achieve something real when they share a common goal. I'll be president one day and I'll be looking for motivated people like you to deliver practical solutions so we can eliminate problems that generations of gutless politicians have refused to take on and solve."

"Senator, my associates won't appreciate that I'm considering something a Republican has offered, particularly now that we finally broke your party's stranglehold on the White House."

"The Democrat hold on the White House is a brief interlude, Mr. Smith," Crelli said jovially. "Once we're back in power, you can be the bridge so we can get the right things done."

"Maybe it's you that will be that bridge," Glen offered, "although Republicans are notorious bridge burners."

Crelli smiled. "You're dreaming. Democrats had this one term, but you elected the wrong man and the more exposure he receives, the more exposed he'll become. By the mid-terms, he'll have things so screwed up; I guarantee the President of the United States in '32' won't be a Democrat."

Glen returned the smile. "When we know each other better, we can wager."

"We'll do that. I'm interested in your management skills. You have run multinational corporations and you don't strike me as being doctrinaire like your fellow liberals, nor as predictable, and I like that. When I run, it won't be on a platform of old, easy solutions and you could play an essential role in my administration. Don't decide now; do your own research. If you find anything objectionable in my positions, let's talk next week at Maddie's party."

"Fair enough," Glen said. "You haven't explained what's in it for me besides a nice party."

"You are to the left of your own party, that puts you on the back benches with crappy committee assignments. I can help there and I can increase your political visibility and viability around the country, too. I'm willing to support certain of your initiatives and once elected, assuming we have an understanding, I'll provide you with access to the President, and that's no small thing. That's all I'll commit to right now. Think about it and we'll talk at the party. This will be the best decision you have ever made, as everyone who has ever backed me will attest."

"You're that sure you're going to be elected?"

"Sure, no," Crelli admitted. "But things are in motion and you could do worse than hitch your future to my star."

"If you've done your research, you know I'm not the guy who hitches rides."

"That's precisely why I want you. Besides, where can you go? You weren't born here so you can't be president. The most you can aspire to is to represent California as governor or senator. I can put you in the cabinet or provide you with other high-ranking positions where you will be able to implement your ideas—within clearly defined constraints. That is a lot better than the two tenths of a percent influence you have in the Congress."

"That's a fair pitch. I'll do the research; consider your positions, your background, and whatever else I need before we talk about this again. But I make no promises." With that, they left the bar.

On the way home, Omar considered what he'd learned. Growing up, he'd interacted with many of his father's associates, wealthy, carnivorous entrepreneurs in their own right. For all that, he'd never met anyone who impressed him so much as the Senator.

Over the next week, Glen reviewed Crelli's voting record, his company's personnel policies, his charitable contributions, and anything else that would give him insight into the man who might be president.

He even hired an investigator to dig into Crelli's past. What he found was a man with a meticulously clean background, staunch friends, and important allies, who had the financial support of the largest corporations and the popularity of a Hollywood celebrity. He even discovered and had interviewed Crelli's former business partner, a pretty, young crippled woman who spoke highly of him. But what surprised and impressed Omar most were the blueprints for his Wharton towns, Crelli's novel and private industry solution to help local communities through these difficult times.

Glen had been too busy to line up a date for the Crelli's party, so his secretary suggested an escort service. He balked at first but she convinced him that it was normal Washington style—and practical, too. The night of the party, he and his date, a beautiful, intelligent, Bolivian woman who spoke perfect, though accented English, took a limo to the party. The woman was easy to talk to and by the time they arrived at Crelli's party, he was exploring her memories of childhood in Bolivia.

The party was all that he had expected; extravagant, classy, and intimate. He spent much of the evening talking to Republican former members of the White House staff, people he would never have talked with on his own. After dinner, Senator Crelli called him into his library.

"Have you made a decision?"

"I have, Andy," Glen said. "I'm not easily impressed, but you've led an exemplary life and that is no small feat in these times. I get it that you're a staunch capitalist but the way you demonstrate your concern for the poor, your charity work, and community service they are as surprising as they are remarkable."

"But . . ."

"Yes, but. I'm not comfortable with the concept of working for someone."

"Other than your constituents."

"Yes, other than my constituents."

"Glen, we all work for someone."

"I'm a rookie Congressman but I wasn't born yesterday. Many people never work for anyone and I consider myself one of them. Your offer is appreciated, but as good as it is, and as impeccable as your record is, I know how 'right' feels to me and unfortunately, I don't get that feeling about this. You'll grease the way for me to become more effective and I'll have an easier time finding support for my bills and that's attractive, but to keep my independence, I choose to forego all of that."

Crelli's demeanor was unchanged by the rejection. "I appreciate your candor and your position. I thought you might see it that way and I have an option for you to consider. Let's form an alliance, you and me. As long as there are no surprises, going forward, I'll agree to support you publicly when I can and I'll communicate your interests to my party and do the best I can to move your issues forward—as long as I believe in them, of course."

"Of course. Keep talking."

"We're players, you and I, and it's important that we understand each other. I expect you'll come to see the benefits of my initial offer, but for now, let's shake on an alliance." Crelli held out his hand.

Glen held back. "And for this, my cost is-"

Crelli smiled. "Nothing. Nothing at all. Glen, I don't need you now. Soon, maybe, in the future, it's likely. Because of that, I'm willing to offer this one-way deal. Later on, when you're onboard, we'll see what comes up. But rest assured, I will be upfront about my requirements. It's the only way I deal."

"Fair enough." They shook hands.

Many months passed before they spoke again. Glen was working to move a poverty bill out of committee with no luck so he left a message for Crelli. Almost immediately, he received a call back.

"Glen, bad news. Your bill is stillborn. We're not going to support spending the extra millions you propose to resuscitate inner city school systems. Many of those neighborhoods are lawless and it would be better and cheaper if the schools were vacant."

"Senator, I find that a harsh position. What about the children? They have needs. If we can't find a way to reach the kids in these inner city schools when they're young, they will become far more costly and unmanageable in the future."

"If I had a silver dollar for everyone who warned me that it's either pay now or pay later, I'd be a rich man today. We're developing a bill to provide relocation incentives for anyone in the inner cities—except criminals and hoods—who are interested in getting out and can provide proof of good citizenship. Our view is that with the productive ones gone, we can cordon off the rest, coming down hard on the low-life vermin who remain. If there is to be a rebirth in these communities, we're down to it and this reboot is the last most of our larger cities will ever have. We've stopped throwing money at this problem because it doesn't go away. The time is ripe for the difficult, pragmatic decision. Get behind our bill. Call it tough love, or a progressive solution, but I need your vote. And just so you know, Glen, I am so confident that this will work that I'm certain that property values in the inner cities will soon be about as low as they are ever going to be. There's an investment credit coming in this bill that will make these relatively attractive real estate investments in a few years. So you know."

"I can't join your people in the House on this, Senator. Your bill will do nothing for the innocent children who live there. I can't give up on them."

"Our bill does everything for the good kids. Tough solutions seem harsh until they work. Look, you believe you have a good bill, fine. But given our severe budget constraints, we can't throw funds at your solution right now. Maybe when the economy improves and our bill starts doing good things, we'll see."

"You're wrong, Senator."

"Believe it or not, that happens," Crelli said. "And when it does I adapt quickly."

"Supporting my bill will enhance your reputation among the poor . . ."

"That's just what I need. It'll allow me to corner a non-voting constituency that otherwise hates me."

"Supporting my bill allows you to get in front on an issue Parrington campaigned on. He even mentioned it in his State of the Union, but dropped it from his budget and now he's in a bind because he's unwilling to give up something else for it. Support my bill, Senator, and people will identify you as the Republican leader who provided important legislative inertia against the dictates of his party and provided leadership that the sitting president couldn't or wouldn't. And you benefit while my bill helps our most precious resource, the children."

Crelli considered it. "That could work. But you're proposing we redirect funds from schools in our wealthiest districts. Not exactly a voter friendly issue for me."

"What I'm proposing will have little effect on wealthy schools. At worst, they won't be able to repaint the lines in their parking lots as frequently.

Certainly you have perks for the wealthy sitting in some goodie bag, somewhere, that you can offer up to appease those who object, because the reward will be worth it. We both know that smaller and more responsive schools can save these kids and give them a better future. With your name associated with this bill, goodwill will ripple through voting constituencies all over the country. It gives you broader appeal, particularly with those you're only a good cause away from winning over. My bill is right and with your help, there are votes in it to make it a win for everyone."

Crelli considered it. "I won't give up the relocation program, but this I will do. I'll give it some thought. I'm giving a speech in Newark next week. If I agree, I'll mention your bill in that speech."

"Thanks, Senator."

Glen's first piece of legislation passed with Crelli's support. Months later, he was working on another issue and contacted Crelli again. "Senator, I need a favor. But first, is there anything I can do for you?"

"Yes, Glen, there is. I want a photo opportunity at the ground breaking for the first new inner city mini-school that's built using funds from your bill. Now what can I do for you?"

"Thank you, Senator, for your help on that bill. Consider the photo op done. Here's my problem. I've uncovered something troubling. I've been trying to find out why the increased funding to cover hardship pay for inner city teachers that was in my legislation, is not available. It seems to have been . . . redirected. I investigated and discovered that the funding in my bill has been tampered with. The bill that was approved isn't the bill that was recorded. It's been turned into more of an unfunded mandate because, somehow, the agreed to funding got decoupled. When the bill was approved, everything was copasetic, so in digging further, I found that it wasn't just my bill. Funding from many other bills have been redirected also. When my people researched it, it turns out there's an illegal operation somewhere in the system that is removing funding from certain bills and diverting that funding to some off-budget project, a sophisticated surveillance project that I have never heard of and one that is on no record or budget. I've been digging into it, but I can't discover who's doing it and how the funds are being diverted. Needless to say, I'm very concerned. This is a national security issue."

"If that is going on, my e-RAT subcommittee would be aware of it."

"Nonetheless, Senator, I'm certain the subterfuge exists. We deal in trillions, so billions is merely skimming off the top, but I need those funds. And what can you tell me about this illegal surveillance project that's being funded? I contacted a number of agencies, but no one has responded back. I even talked to the Government Accountability Office and they have no knowledge of the program or any interest in getting involved."

"If the GAO doesn't know, that should tell you that you have bad information."

"This is real, Senator," Smith argued. "Just last week, a financial services company of mine lost a bid totaling more than fifty billion dollars on a top secret, surveillance project. They were informed they had lost to Hagiburton, the Saudi defense contractor. Two things, you can't award a surveillance contract to a company incorporated in a foreign country, and Hagiburton never received notification that they had won that contract. This must be investigated, Andy. My chief Information Officer insists it was bid on, the project exists, but I can't find any government record of the program. I asked for a copy of the RFI to be sent over but I have yet to see it."

There was brief silence. When the Senator spoke again, he was subdued. "There is nothing to be concerned about. This is your first term. We always have a shadow project or two in the budget—well not exactly in the budget, its off-budget, but that's the way things are done. The projects are usually in support of efforts necessary to keep America safe where we must remain a step ahead of the terrorists and our other enemies around the world. Because of the delicacy of that issue, these expenditures are too secretive to handle through normal channels. To win our 'War on Terror', it's critical that assets be developed covertly, so I'm not troubled by this and neither should you be."

"Fine, I can understand that," Glen said. "But the odd thing is when I asked my CEOs to get more information; none of them returned my calls. Finally, one told me that he couldn't discuss it further—even with me. I have clearance, so I put some of my more industrious workers on it."

"And what did they find."

"That's why I'm calling. Nothing, less information than before. What information was available to me once, has since evaporated. I'm talking billions and there are no details anywhere to support it."

"You must be wrong. There are so many places to look."

"Senator, I'm thorough and I'm concerned."

"What can I do to help?"

"Have your e-task force check it out. If it's normal—as you say—and there's nothing illegal, I understand. I just need to know. If it's something more, well, you know what that means. Please let me know as soon as possible. If its fraud or, I don't even know what could be worse than fraud, but the only way it could happen is if it reaches to the highest levels in our government. You could make a case that Parrington is involved or the Majority Leaders and the Speaker. We need to understand this yesterday."

That seemed to interest Andy. "I think you are worrying unnecessarily but if you think Parrington is funding something illegal, I am concerned. I'll put my people on it. Good work, Glen. I'll get back to you."

More weeks passed and he heard nothing so he contacted Crelli again. The junior senator from Kentucky was apologetic.

"Of course I remember the discussion," Crelli admitted. "My bad. I should have had one of my people call you. If I could pin something on Parrington, you know I would, but I'm not permitted to tell you much except to assure you that the programs you uncovered are in fact active, productive, and necessary for the defense of the United States of America. It's a relief to know with all the other problems we're facing that there is no plot, and nothing is being done illegally."

"Is that what you found? I've done some homework on my end and from what I was able to piece together—and it wasn't easy to find pieces—the funding is being diverted to support something bizarre and quite large. Have you ever heard of omniscient, omnipresent surveillance, whatever the hell that is? I know it hasn't been discussed on the Hill, at least since I arrived on the Hill."

"That project. I feel better already. Ever since the last terror attacks, the revised Patriot Act provides funding for new, state-of-the-art surveillance technologies and they are being funded under the radar. I know. It seems crazy, but I assure you everything is being done the way it has to be done."

"Senator, according to my experts—"

"I said everything is okay," Crelli interrupted. "Is this going to be a problem?"

"I don't know if it's going to be a problem. One of my best men has conjectured that this technology could link global surveillance with artificial intelligence and electronic stealth infiltration capability. That is espionage at a level never before considered possible. He's concerned about it and frankly, Senator, if he is concerned, so am I. He believes that once something like this is perfected, every previous security protocol will be obsolete and he warned me that, with software like this, every terabyte of data in my companies can be extracted or acted upon without our knowledge. He's very concerned that, from what he's been able to put together, this could be the tip of an enormous security breach iceberg.

"Andy, if Parrington is pursuing this solution, covertly, everyone should be very concerned. From what my guy says, this could provide functionality way beyond terrorist surveillance into industrial and political espionage, and even into the private lives of our citizens. That makes it illegal, unconstitutional, and possibly treasonous. I'm talking treason, Andy."

"You're not serious."

"I trust my guy. This isn't the raving of a liberal fear monger. Believe me, if I weren't deeply troubled, I wouldn't have called. I need to know as much as you can discover. If you think it best, you take the lead, you break the story; it's my gift to you for all your help, but you should definitely direct your e-task force to get to the bottom of it."

"Glen, I assure you your concerns are duly noted but I think you're overreacting. We've eliminated most e-RAT hazards, but we're always concerned they may try to bring down our financial and military networks. My task force receives funding to develop sophisticated technologies to prevent it. That may be what your man is talking about, but you're right, it's too important to ignore. I'm impressed with your diligence, and though I think you and your experts are taking this a bit too far, you've convinced me it needs my attention. Get me the name of your expert and anyone else you've discussed this with and I'll have my best people work with yours on it."

"Thanks, Andy, I appreciate it."

"One more thing, I'd appreciate it if you wouldn't say anything until we know what your people believe is happening. I'll await the names. Thanks."

"I'll send them right over. Get back to me as soon as you can."

"My people will check it out immediately."

"Thanks, Andy. I'll keep digging."

There was brief silence. "Do that. We'll talk." With that, Crelli disconnected.

Glen sent the names of his technology experts to Crelli but not only did he not receive a reply, far more troubling, the people whose names he provided seemed to disappear. And during that time, the Senate version of his inner city education bill got hung up in committee and seemed likely to die after all. He left messages, but he never received a response from Andy.

On the day before Congress was scheduled to adjourn, frustrated and angry, he headed to the Crelli office suite at the Capital where he was greeted by a plain, young intern with extraordinary violet eyes, who guarded the entrance to Crelli's inner sanctum.

"Congressman Smith, this is a surprise. The Senator isn't expecting you. I can set up an appointment."

"It's Tanya, right?"

She nodded.

"Tanya, tell Senator Crelli it's important. I'll wait."

If the Senator got the message, he didn't react quickly. It was late in the day when he was ushered into the inner sanctum to find Crelli sitting at his desk.

"Glen, it's good to see you. What was so important that you had to run over?"

"My bill, the one that you said you'd support, it is being held up and tomorrow we recess. What's going on?"

Crelli pulled out a box of Havana cigars and offered him one. "Horse trading, can't be helped. I'm coming up a bit short. It may have to be rescheduled."

"I don't understand. What's changed since we last talked?"

"Why would anything change? I never promised you that the Senate would speed the bill through. Things like that take time. There are deals to construct, trade-offs to be made, adjustments needed to bring on others to support it. You know that."

"After all the promises you made, I'm getting the feeling you're letting it die."

Crelli stood. "Do you trust me, Congressman?"

He hesitated. "What kind of question is that? We're politicians and businessmen."

"Still, do you trust me? If we're going to move forward, I need to know."

"That I trust you?"

"Yes."

"No, Senator, of course I don't trust you."

Crelli slowly, carefully began to clear his desk of papers. "Why, Congressman?"

"Among other things, you know more about that surveillance project than you told me."

"And that surprises you?" Crelli asked. "A great deal goes on behind the scenes here, things first term congressmen never know. If we went paranoid with each new discovery, the media would rule the country and nobody wants that. I'm displeased that you went extracurricular to find out about surveillance funding, but your tone tells me you think there's something wrong and that demonstrates a lack of trust."

"I'm trying to get to the bottom of it."

"There you go again. Why does there have to be a bottom? When you first mentioned it to me, you withheld pertinent information and now you're withholding more. I had hoped you and I could have a mutually productive relationship, but without trust, I don't see how that's possible. I'm sorry; Congressman but you and I are no longer doing business in the public's interest."

"How the hell do you know what I know and what I don't know?"

"It's my job."

"No it's not. I've been working on this with people I trust and some of them have gone missing. Missing? Do you know anything about that?"

Crelli laughed. "I don't know what that even means."

"They aren't at work or at home and I can't contact them. Their secretaries and their wives don't know where they are and they are worried. Missing! They work for my companies and I'm much more than concerned. Until you and I talked about surveillance funding, these people were readily available. Now, they are not. This is America, Senator and I'm very concerned, Senator, because what I suspect is occurring is very un-American." Glen paused before asking the question he came here for. "Senator, have you done something to my people?"

Crelli didn't flinch. "Now you're paranoid. It is standard procedure to debrief people on security issues but that doesn't take long and I wouldn't think that would cause them to disappear unless they've done something very, very wrong. But I'll check. I'm certain they haven't been detained but maybe they were ordered not to speak with you until our investigation is over. I'm sure they're fine but I expect an apology."

"What investigation?"

"Those were serious charges you laid out for me. An investigation was in order."

"Senator, since none of my people has done anything illegal, the only way you could learn anything is if you forced them to talk and that's unlikely. I know my people."

"Certainly, the attempt, alone, would be clumsy of me. You'd discover it and think we have a bigger issue than we do. It's difficult keeping secrets in business; in politics, it's impossible."

Angrily, Glen turned and headed for the door.

"Leaving so soon, Congressman?"

"Senator, I've learned two things. Coming in, I knew that you are the one responsible for diverting funds to develop sophisticated artificial intelligence. I'm certain now that what you're doing is criminal and treasonous."

Crelli seemed indifferent to the accusation, but curious. "And the second thing?"

"That the artificial intelligence project that you are funding illegally is functional. You couldn't know what my people were doing unless you broke through our firewalls without detection."

"You are paranoid, Congressman. Surveillance is legal and indispensable if we are to protect our American way of life. The game is stacked against us and the only way we can win is to change the rules. That's what I'm doing. This new functionality isn't treasonous, as you say, it's patriotic and it will make Americans safe and allow our return to greatness. There is nothing illegal or sinister about possessing the most sophisticated state-of-the-art information analytics protocol in the world. Businesses, like my former corporation and the ones you own, they have been gathering and analyzing information for years to determine what customers want or need. Until now, the government has been negligent in taking advantage of these technologies. What you stumbled on is, in reality, a new government infrastructure service that will bring more information to bear to improve how we govern and how we protect our citizens."

"If that were true, you would have made a public announcement. You're running for president and if you can guarantee safety there is no way you can lose. Your e-task force provides credibility; this intelligence is your victory margin. The specifications my people extrapolated from the RFIs they were able to obtain shows a technology capable of extensive and universal espionage that will set back international relations for decades and could start wars. Information analytics is just a euphemism, but whatever you call it, it's illegal."

"A president must to do everything in his power to keep America safe," Crelli declared.

"But you're not the president right now."

"I will be, and soon. Liberals, progressive thinkers like you; you know nothing about what we're fighting and how to truly defeat it. The positions you've taken, the 'holier than thou' moral and ethical argument about what we should and shouldn't do is irrelevant to our survival in an ultra-competitive, dog-eat-dog world where everyone is our enemy. The American people expect leadership that protects them in a world where modern warfare is commercial, never ending, and unremitting and in order to achieve victory, those who have limited themselves, lose. It's my responsibility to make certain America is always the strongest, whatever that takes and we don't have time to amend laws that I'll break anyway to save my country. And I can't worry about offending people like you because I take my responsibility very seriously and failure is not an option.

"You should be comforted that someone like me is here to ensure our survival while everyone else argues petty differences and self-serving agendas. I have their back, and yours, too, because I'll do what most won't—everything in my power to keep us alive and free and ready to fight for victory every day. Everything and everyone—and I include you, Congressman—are at risk if I waver or fail. True patriots don't have the luxury of hesitating to assess the proper moral and ethical response. Our enemies hope for that, because it means we're weak and weakness ensures their victory and our defeat. If I vacillate, even for a moment, we become a footnote in history."

"You can't convince me, Senator," Glen said. "In my marrow, I know what you're doing is wrong. The people need to be protected from terrorists of course, but it seems now they need to be protected from you. Americans need a . . . a beacon, I don't know, something to help them identify the patriotic good guys from the devout wrong-thinkers like you.

They desperately want to believe in us—just a little—maybe less every day given our record. The world needs heroes they can emulate and it can't be allowed to worship you because you will destroy everything America stands for."

Crelli's face turned red with rage. "Rubbish! The barbarians are at the gates of Rome and it is up to me to keep them out."

"So you're emperor now? Hail Crelli and all of that?" Glen asked, sarcastically.

"This is my democracy. I love it and there's nothing I won't do to save it. And if I fail, we all fail. Accept it, Congressman, and shut up and get the fuck out of my office." Crelli's face was purple as he leaned forward, his fists pressed hard against his desk.

"Calm down, Senator," Smith said, trying to diffuse the situation before it redlined into something neither man wanted.

"Calm down, my ass. I was fighting e-RATS while self-proclaimed patriot pussies like you were pissing in your pants. I doubt your patriotism and if you try to stop me, if you try to destroy my country, the land I love, I will do anything, anything to stop you. Give me any more shit and you will be public enemy number one, plain and simple. I'm not wasting more time with you. Get the fuck out, Congressman before I call my guards."

Smith refused to leave, trying one last time to make this misguided lunatic in front of him see reason.

"Can't you see that what you're doing will be the end of us. You can't save democracy by destroying it. You can't protect everyone by spying on them or declaring everyone who's not with you is the enemy. If you do and you succeed, what you say you're fighting for dies. You're a patriot, I believe that. But if you believe in America, have faith that our system is strong enough to overcome difficult problems, even if the solutions aren't evident right away, or take longer than you'd like to resolve. If you do this, you'll tear America apart because I'll fight you. With the technology you've developed, you give me no choice because the world will be too small for me or anyone else who opposes you."

"I'm done debating," Crelli reiterated. "Join me, oppose me, I don't give a fuck. What you believe won't survive, so what good is it? And frankly, what the hell good are you? My America will always be prosperous and free, but it's time to change what it is free to be."

"Are you insane? Listen to yourself. Listen to reason. Let's air our differences in public and let the people decide."

"Fuck the people," Crelli shouted, spittle flying from his mouth. "You heard me, fuck the people. If they want to survive, I'm all they have. Don't look so shocked, Congressman. Since the Republic began, Americans have always blindly relied on their leaders. If it was good enough for our forefathers, it is good enough today." Crelli leaned in and brought his tone down to a harsh whisper. "More to the point, Smith, if I hear that any part of this fucking conversation has been repeated to anyone, you'll be silenced. I'm not fucking around. You have no idea who you're fucking with."

Glen wasn't cowed. "Get out of my face, Senator. You don't know me as well as you think you do. I'm leaving; I have a revolution to prepare for." With that, he turned his back and stormed out of the office.

In the lobby, Glen considered his options. For something this despicable, a great many powerful people had to be involved so he had to be wary. Crelli's father-in-law was Senate Majority leader so he couldn't travel that path. Friendless in Washington, he needed to disappear until he could decide what his next move should be.

He stopped by his office to download his most important documents. Then he called his chef to have a meal prepared so he could eat and run. When he didn't get a response, he headed home and went directly to the kitchen. Neither his chef, nor his staff was there. It wasn't until he tried to leave the kitchen that he realized what kind of enemy Crelli was.

The door wouldn't budge. He peered through the small window in the kitchen door in time to see three men fleeing from the house. Hurriedly, he checked the other kitchen door and all of the other windows, but they too were locked. He ran back to the main door to try to force it open but it was bolted closed from the outside. He was trapped. He reached for his personal communicator but there was no signal.

Concerned now, he considered his options. That's when he smelled the smoke. He tried to locate the source but nothing in the kitchen was burning. When he put his hand to the tile floor, it felt warm. The fire was in the basement! He waited briefly for alarms to sound but when all remained quiet, he turned on a burner, lit some paper and held it under a smoke detector. It too failed to go off.

Smoke billowed from the dumb waiter door as he looked anxiously for another way out. He ran to the nearest window and tried to force it. Unable to open it, he fumbled in a drawer for something to break it. All he had was a meat tenderizer and a food processor. He whacked the window with the processor but that only managed to crack the thick glass, the imbedded chicken wire continued to hold the glass in place. Realizing he needed something more substantial, he searched until he found a large metal trashcan among all the plastic ones. He lifted it and pummeled the wire-reinforced glass, succeeding mostly in denting the trashcan. He turned to see the first flames and smoke appear in the heat registers. Sweating now and coughing, he ran back to the kitchen door and tried harder to force it open again but the metal door simply wouldn't budge. Perspiring freely and hacking from the fumes and smoke, he climbed onto a steel counter to avoid the hot and darkening floor. He was rarely in the kitchen for more than a snack, so he searched frantically for salvation.

An icemaker sat alongside a long, sturdy, steel preparation table. He made one last check around the room. Certain nothing else was of use, he bent down to lift the icemaker onto the table so it would be level with the window but it was too heavy. He ran to another steel topped table, the heat rising from the floor beginning to scorch his feet, and he kicked two of the table legs hard until they bent and finally broke off. Then he dragged it to the table near the window and propped the legs to form a ramp. His throat burned as he squatted down, put his shoulder against the icemaker and pushed it up the ramp. Sweat dripped from his suit as, with labored breath, he forced the icemaker partway up the ramp. With his muscles cramping, he paused to catch his breath, but with the room filled with smoke, his coughing intensified and the icemaker slid back to the floor. Time was running out. The fire was finding access points all around the kitchen now. He covered his mouth with a wet cloth and began pushing the icemaker back up the ramp. He thought he heard the faint sound of sirens but he couldn't wait. His leg muscles and his throat were on fire as he used his last bit of strength to lunge and push the icemaker onto the table. Dizzy and with eyes burning from sweat, he jumped onto the table and repeatedly rolled the icemaker hard into the window, bending the cracked glass further and further out.

Seeing the billowing smoke being sucked out renewed his hope but the fresh air also increased the intensity of the flames. He put his head close to the opening and drew in some life-sustaining fresh air. The opening widened as he continued to slam his body against the icemaker and the icemaker against the window, until it finally fell through taking him with it. The icemaker landed on the ground with a jolt and with Glen fortunately on top. His lungs filled with fresh air and he coughed hard and deep, the pain in his chest so severe that each cough was unbearable. Certain that his ribs were broken; he lay in the alley coughing and fighting to stay alert.

He heard a siren and awoke in an ambulance receiving oxygen from a paramedic as the ambulance headed, siren blasting, toward a hospital emergency room. The oxygen helped clear his head and everything seemed to slow down. He knew that if he entered the hospital, Crelli would make sure he'd never leave. Holding his sides to alleviate the pain, he considered his options. But it was when the ambulance rushed by a hospital that he knew it was time to act. He bowled over the surprised paramedic and lurched for the door but the other paramedic tried to restrain him. He hit the man hard and wobbled to the back door of the speeding ambulance, forcing it open as someone tackled him from behind. Together, they rolled out onto the street. Fortunately there were no cars following and the paramedic hit the ground first. For the second time that night, Glen landed on top. When they stopped rolling, he disengaged from the now unconscious man and searched him. He found the man's HomeSec ID and then he staggered unsteadily onto the sidewalk, the ambulance continuing on, oblivious that it had just lost its victim. He needed to get away fast so he hailed a cab. He hid for a few days in an inner city motel and then slowly worked his way south before heading out of the country, to sanctuary from Crelli's America.

Chapter 7
Smith Madrasah, Canada—2070

Stacey sat transfixed by Omar's story. When she said nothing, he coaxed a response from her.

"Why did Senator Crelli try to kill you?"

"Crelli was four years from the White House and couldn't have a scandal, particularly this scandal. It would come between him and his destiny. He tried to kill me because he's one of those forever successful people who must ramp everything up to an emergency in order to have complete control over it so he can deliver the results he wants. I was a fool. I should have seen it coming."

"And that technology stuff, the surveillance, it was real, just like the *SurveilEagles* in Maine?" she asked.

"Yes, like the *SurveilEagles*. He spent trillions perfecting the technology that allowed him to lord over us like a dictator, or Chairman as he eventually called himself. What his research team developed, there's no way to fight. Even today, years later, after spending billions of my own funds, I can't be one hundred percent certain we've kept the United States out of my networks."

"Then . . . then we're not safe."

"Fear not, Stacey, love, you are quite safe. Even if they were to break through my firewall, they can't attack me without the Canadian government getting very much involved and America has need of Canadian water and fuel so they won't risk it. You are safe, I assure you."

"What did you do after you escaped?" she asked.

"I went to Europe, and then on a *hajj* to Mecca. I stayed in Tehran where the Mullahs were quite supportive. After a few years of intense planning, I slipped back into the states, hired local protection, and spent my time helping to organize the poor on the streets of Chicago, Philadelphia, New York and L.A. While I was gone, Crelli eliminated all of his opponents, clearing the way for his rule."

"Why didn't the President arrest you when you returned?"

"As I said, I had protection but also, Crelli saw that he could take advantage of the unrest I was creating so he gave me space. I knew I didn't have long and many of my friends and supporters, people who helped me to discover Crelli's diabolical plan, they met horrible deaths. Everything was ready. He was elected president, but you never know about destiny. One day, if the fates hadn't got involved, it would all have turned out right. As President-elect, Crelli was scheduled to speak in Philadelphia and during his speech, a brave, patriotic, local college girl decided to rid the world of this monster. I don't know why she did it but God bless her, she wrapped herself in a vest of explosives, walked onto the stage and blew herself up."

"Oh, no, the poor girl. Did she die?" Stacey asked, shocked.

"Explosives, my sweet. Yes, she most certainly died. But that poor, idealistic young woman, whom Allah has surely blessed, she was a true patriot. She was young and innocent, much like you, I think, but she understood like few do today that it's only when you're willing to give your life for a just cause that you're truly free. She is truly free."

Saddened, Stacey covered her face but didn't cry. "She blew herself up? That's horrible."

"Horrible, sad, and wonderful, well almost wonderful, it was. Crelli was an implacable enemy of the people and he had to be stopped. If only she had walked those few extra steps behind the podium, what a gloriously rewarding afterlife she would have discovered. Think of the tens of millions of poor souls she would have saved, souls including those of your beloved at Angel Falls."

"But you said Tanya Brandt made the decision to attack Angel Falls."

"Of course," he said it dismissively, "but she is Crelli's creature. You will have your vengeance on her." He hugged her close. "Stacey, Stacey, my sweet, sweet darling, now that you know how evil Crelli was, I beg you, join me—truly join me and I promise that everyone responsible for Angel Falls will be punished severely."

"And you will free Mr. Rose, too?"

"Yes, if that's what you want, you can help me to free President Rose. But Brandt is first, and if Chairman Crelli is still alive, he must be punished as well. But Brandt is the head that must be severed from this evil snake. Trust me, vengeance will heal you."

"You . . . you won't ask me to blow myself up, will you?" It sounded strange and she felt embarrassed for asking.

He laughed. "Never, my sweet. Maybe someday you will feel such joy about our revolution that to ensure our victory, you will do things that you think are unlikely today. But I would never want you to blow yourself up; you are too precious to me and to our cause. We need you for a far more important task and your role in this is vital. Together, we will unite the rebels and build a glorious army to defeat the Chairwoman."

"It sounds . . . dangerous."

He squeezed her tight. "You are young and youth feeds off danger. After all, you survived an attack designed to have no survivors. I will never ask you to do anything you are uncomfortable doing, but remember, those who need me, need you. You will help me and them in places I can't be seen. But I vow, on my life, I will make certain you are well protected, always. You must be safe so you can gain your vengeance. This I promise."

"But-"

"My love, I am desperately in need of your trust, your belief in me. You are special to me and you have my word, nothing that I ask you to do will be dangerous. On the contrary, you'll dress in fine clothes, travel comfortably, and meet with good, interesting people. Everyone will like you and come to love you as I do. And with your help we will grow our legions and avenge those who murdered your family and friends in Angel Falls."

"But the Chairwoman—"

"She's been trying to kill me for years and I'm still around."

"Will I really wear fine clothes? And can I . . . can I stay here?"

"Stacey, darling, you will have the most fashionable wardrobe possible, I will send to Paris for the best designers and you will have jewelry, too. And this is your home; you will always be safe here. Please say you'll help me."

What else could she do? If he sent her away where could she go? She needed him to need her here. She needed him to need her. She needed him. "Of course I'll help."

"Then it's settled. You will perform a great service for our cause." With that, he leaned in and kissed her cheek. Feeling his warm lips on her skin, she smiled and leaned into his expected embrace, her anxieties lifting. But he pulled away before she could take pleasure in his comfort. Still, he smiled warmly and she forgave him. Then, he finished his story.

"Obviously Crelli didn't die in that explosion. That poor sweet girl was too nervous. She detonated the bomb too soon, too soon. It's understandable; you can't practice in front of a live audience. Crelli's infant son and the nanny died but Crelli was unhurt. At least he tasted what he was doling out."

"The poor baby, that's so sad," Stacey said.

"Yes, it's an evil world where babies are casualties."

"I remember when my Aunt Dora lost her baby. She didn't eat or talk to anyone for so long. But then she got pregnant again and was better though she was never really the same." The fact that Aunt Dora and her baby were on Omar's list saddened her more.

"That's good to know, Princess. It is time. Tell me all about your boyfriend."

She stiffened. "But I don't have a boyfriend."

"Then tell me of the one you're not telling me about. It's crucial."

"Please don't be angry with me, Omar."

"I can never be angry with you, sweetie." He paused. "I am disappointed that after opening up to you, you still don't trust me you have been through so much that I understand your reluctance. We'll discuss this again." Relieved, she nodded reluctantly. "My attendant will show you to *Virtuoso*."

She blushed at that. "Please, I don't feel up to it. Please."

"*Virtuoso* is precisely what you need. You are sad and tense. Do it, for me."

"I just need a good night's sleep."

But he was already walking away and soon a maid entered. Reluctantly but obediently, she followed the maid to the *Virtuoso* chambers. Naked and fearful, she stepped inside.

It was a bright, hot sunny day and she was standing in the middle of a narrow street that was lined on both sides by tall dead trees. The street was empty except for urban tumbleweed slowly being blown along in a light breeze. There was no shade so she walked down the center of the street until she came to a cluster of one-story shops whose windows were obscured with whitewash. There were *for sale* or *for lease* signs in every window. She fought off a chill. The buildings were lifeless perversions of the small town center of her home.

Before she reached the luncheonette, she heard someone shout her name. The voice seemed to be coming from the adjacent building so she walked to it. There was someone inside but she couldn't see through the windows so she stepped back and was surprised when someone lifted a window.

Burt stuck his head out. "Stacey, hi, it's Burt, you remember me don't you?"

"I . . . I . . ." Unsure, she blurted, "Burt, yes, of course." A strong musky scent seemed to billow through the window, almost overwhelming her.

"It's great to see you again, Stacey. Can I show you around town?"

She hesitated, troubled by something vaguely ominous. "Ah . . . no, Burt, I . . . I don't think so. I'm sorry, not today."

"That is perfectly fine. You can say no." He laughed pleasantly. "We are a town of good solid republican values and no, means no. You cannot create value by forcing people to do things they are uncomfortable doing. Individuals must be free to do what they prefer, that is the American way. Don't you think?"

She didn't know what she thought about that, but nodded anyway. He was kind of cute, no, really cute, but for some reason, she wanted to dislike him even though his smile was so infectious. Without thinking, her eyes trailed down from his smile to the open front of his shirt where the cut of his chest and stomach muscles, particularly the way they tightened when he laughed, made her feel oddly warm and tingly. She blushed and, suddenly frightened, she backed away from the window.

"Please don't be that way. You are just unfamiliar with our ways. We are good people. I promise." He smiled that nice smile again and continued. "There is nothing we want more than to see you happy. We live for it. Stacey, more than anyone I know, you deserve to be happy and if I ever do anything to make you sad, I will be eternally sorry." He sounded contrite for some reason and it made her feel better as did a whiff of the incense he was burning.

She felt like flirting a little. "Tell me, Burt, why do I deserve to be happy?"

"Everyone deserves to be happy, but you, I really care about you and if you care about someone, you want to see them happy. Surely you feel that way too."

She did and nodded.

"You matter to me, Stacey. You are a kind, sweet, and a very thoughtful young woman, and what more can one be. You deserve happiness. Every nanosecond I spend trying to make you happy is worth it to me and when you are not around, each nanosecond feels like a lifetime."

She laughed, inhaling more of the incense and coughing a little. Burt was so over the top, like no one she had ever met. She was still a bit anxious but after a series of incense induced coughs, her apprehension evaporated as she wiped away the tears that formed from her coughs and began to relax. "That's some line you have there, Burt. But if you think it will get you somewhere with me, you can forget it. I'm not that gullible."

"I live to prove you wrong. Now don't get me wrong, I don't love you. If I did, I would assuredly hurt you and I will never do that."

"So loving means hurting to you?"

"It's rarely intentional, of course, but when you love too much, how can you avoid hurting and being hurt? No one has ever explained to me in any significant way that I can believe, where love goes, but it always goes. You can trust me because I will never love you and that means I will never hurt you."

"Do you really believe that? You can hurt someone without loving them."

"Sure you can hurt people but not as deeply and permanently as love hurts. I say that in the most loving way," he smiled impishly.

"You're so sweet."

"I have to get back to work at the therapy spa." He invited her inside. As the window closed, she caught the briefest of whiffs of vanilla.

She was standing beside him on a wooden floor inside a low ceilinged, narrow room with elaborate massage tables lining the walls on both sides. The room was dim except for the faint glow of sunlight that came through a whitewashed window on the far wall.

"This is what we do," he explained pointing to the various stations where fully clothed attendants worked on fully clothed clients. "I am a certified Ice Blue Kimono—that's one step from green Executive class service—and I am fully accredited to work on all types of angst with all levels of positive net worth individuals. It is my job to remove accumulated stress and make everyone super comfortable. I can provide references."

She shook her head.

"To my professional eye, you seem uptight and anxious and that just happens to be my specialty. In fact, without bragging, I have never had an unsatisfied customer. Once I apply the exotic Eastern American subtle science of manipulation, you will feel like you are drifting on a cloud without a care in the world and when I'm done, you will be so focused and ready that you will leave here and improve your worth immediately. I guarantee it. How does that sound?"

He reached gently for her hand but the hint from some forgotten recollection caused her to pull away from him. He tried to reassure her. "You definitely need some stress relief. Look around you at these clients taking therapies. What is there to be afraid of with them around—and there are professionals at every station, each one licensed by the board; certified professionals proud to contribute to the economy."

She smelled cucumber, like those in Mrs. Zeman's garden back home and in the dim parlor light, she saw that he was right. Each of the six beds in six separate alcoves, were occupied by fully-clothed clients receiving treatments from fully-clothed professionals.

"You do massages fully clothed?" she asked.

He laughed. "How else? If you are not sure, ask any client, if you can get their attention." He smiled that smile again and it warmed her.

She walked beside one massage station to speak to an older gentleman. His eyes were closed and there was a smile on his face. As the masseuse worked different muscle groups, the old man grunted but continued to smile.

"He does look pleased."

"Hop up." Burt pointed to an empty table. "I promise you will be as pleased, too."

Laying face down on the table, she shivered involuntarily when she first felt his hands working her back through her blouse. When his hands felt her back muscles ripple, he laughed and coaxed her to relax. He worked carefully and gently, massaging her back and neck. It felt good, but she remained tense, resisting the urge to give in to it. It wasn't long before she began to enjoy the feeling and without thinking about it, she relaxed. He shifted his attention to her legs, working warm oils into her muscles.

The scent of nutmeg and wax were stimulating as his fingers worked their magic and her mind drifted.

"It is a joy to work on someone like you, you are so athletic, long, tight muscled, you even have nice biceps. But your neck muscles are too tight. Too tight, way too tight . . . tight . . . tight."

His oily hands felt hot on her skin. Her skin? His hands were . . . they were . . . her mind formed a protest but it escaped her lips as a moan and her body shuddered out a last tense burst of energy and she felt like she was floating—as if in a dream populated by erotic spirits—as he plied his science, this time with the assistance of the scent of citrus until she felt a sweet intensity build.

"Stacey, sweetheart, you have the stomach of a runner or maybe a beauty queen and those thighs, they are so firm, so firm, firm, firm. If that smile of yours had never drawn me to you, my life would have been so sad, sad, sad. And I will suffer the rest of my existence if I never share another moment like this with you. I am so glad you came . . . came . . . came."

Her eyelids were pressed tight and suddenly she was blinded by white light, her body spasmed, and she was trembling and twitching, trying to avoid his touch yet seeking for more. Her hands grabbed for and ripped at the sheets and she screamed. She allowed her eyelids to separate and there, above her was Burt with his comforting smile. Then it was dark and she went slack with only the feel of warm soft caressing hands gliding over her body, lightly mapping her skin and wherever Gil's fingers went, tiny tremors trailed after. Her body constricted and she contorted into a fetal position, undulating gently. With each shiver, she reveled in Gil's touch as the joy he delivered consumed her. Totally sapped of energy, she closed her eyes and smiled just a little to herself—picturing Gil satisfied, loving face above her. This was how she had imagined it would be; what his caring touch would be like. But before her mind disappeared into oblivion she reached up to Gil only to find a stranger there to receive her.

When she awoke, it was morning and she was in her own bed with no memory of how she got there or of the previous evening. In clouded horror, she lay under the covers, afraid to think, to remember, and unable to move. She sobbed, not knowing why, with only the vaguest ephemeral recollection of what assuredly must have been a dream, a perverse dream. For this sweet, innocent teenaged girl from the wild, reality was never so far away.

Chapter 8
Canada—2071

The American Automobile Industry—America is the once and future capital of the automobile industry. In the twentieth century, three out of four cars produced came from facilities in and around Detroit, Michigan and the supply chain that fed the assembly lines employed the Midwest and the greater part of a great nation.

Everyone drove a new car every year or two and the auto industry thrived from the top to the bottom of the supply chain. Managements and stockholders became wealthier, employees lived better, cities and towns prospered and the government, now flush with tax revenues, broadened and deepened its responsibilities to the underserved and spent oodles on research and development for the future.

Statistics confirm that three quarters of all American small businesses depended on large businesses, like automotive, and government spending for their survival and America was the small business capital of the world.

The American automobile industry drove American exceptionalism and that exceptionalism created an economic paradise.

It was a time when American labor out-competed the world, risking their lives to generate profits and to make better products. This they did until socialists in the guise of unions took advantage and formed hard-working yet naïve workers into counterproductive cooperatives. The battle against socialism raged on in the automobile industry producing decades of strife which provided the unrest and inefficiency that allowed the world to catch up and pass the American auto industry until too late, unions realized their mistake, ceased to blackmail industry with short-term, blind, destructive programs and agreed to rest on their ill-gotten gains. For an ever so brief period, America had their middle class, not rich, not poor, but with few worries and a great future to invest in.

But the genie had been let out of the bottle and the world restored, now competed, and that was the beginning of the end of the First American Republic.

The rich never think of their children living better lives, only different lives. But the poor and the middle class dream dreams of a better life for their children and those dreams work against entrepreneurs and the economy. That is why the great American automotive industry declined and in so doing, bankrupted the country. Like all Socialists, America's labor unions were greedy and selfish, and they stand guilty of destroying opportunity in the *Land of Opportunity.*

It was decades of creeping socialism later, during the reign of President Crelli—with the passing of his ground breaking *Circle of Life* laws—that the automotive industry, indeed the country's entire capitalist economy was reincarnated. The rich, of course, continued to be rich, though there were fewer of them to build the required entrepreneurial solutions that America needed to thrive in the more robust and competitive global marketplace of the twenty first century.

In this economic battle for global dominance, the greatest part of the American population was pitched into third world poverty by foreign competitors who, unburdened by the higher wages unions demanded for their muscle, used their poor as laborers and under priced America in pursuit of the hearts of the world's consumers. Though destitute, poor was something new to loyal union members and so, unfamiliar with desperation they refused to cost enough less to make American products competitive.

Free markets work, as does supply and demand and thus the great American economy reverted back to late nineteenth century character with enduring, regular, and frequent recessions and depressions followed by brief and inadequate economic recoveries. America desperately needed to make things that consumers wanted at a cost they could afford, but no one knew how and so the economy refused to jump start—that is until Mark Rose, the Chairman of Crelli Enterprises proposed the solution.

Soon to be President, Mr. Rose proposed a methodology that would create sustainable profits that jump started the economy and kept it humming for generations. Lacking demand and with excess capacity everywhere and with business losses rampant, Mr. Rose's entrepreneurial breakthrough involved ruthless cost containment and the elimination of all taxes on corporations. It succeeded, brilliantly, and the flow of profits became a torrent though, by design, it reached the masses as a trickle.

What Mark Rose did was modify a system that was no longer in favor in America's economy, one every American businessmen had discounted or forgotten long ago. To save Detroit and America, the poor unemployed were gathered up from around the Great Lakes region, tested for capability, and the best qualified and shipped to Detroit along with their families to build cars at the cost of merely food and shelter. Those disqualified for work, were eliminated as the *Circle of Life* law required.

A new company, a car manufacturing corporation, Make America Great, LLC or MAG, was formed and with it, Mark Rose joined the hallowed line of great American entrepreneurial geniuses from Whitney to Bonsack to Edison to Jobs and he saved American manufacturing and returned the American economy to greatness. His efforts seeded the rebirth of the great American automotive supply chain that had been destroyed generations ago by self-serving unions.—**Archive**

When she was very young, all Stacey had ever dreamed of was to be treated like a princess in a palace of her own with her very own handsome prince to do her bidding. She was living that dream now, but other dreams—nightmares, really—that she couldn't escape or clearly identify, were ruining it. What was she to do? Her choices were few. She could remain and ignore them, or face the world outside alone, a fugitive pursued by a relentless, malicious, and proficient government.

Winter melted into a cold Canadian spring and she felt as conflicted as the weather. Alternately content yet confused, satisfied yet shamed, free yet forbidden, she struggled to make sense of her new world. Omar, her devoted prince, constantly avowed his love for her, but he treated her more like a daughter than a consort, while providing all the material things she asked for. He complimented her endlessly and flirted charmingly, but always with a peculiar detachment as if not wanting to want her.

In the mornings, and again after extravagant dinners attended by his high-powered and connected friends, with sumptuous wines and liqueurs flowing freely, they would sit amidst the ornate pillows strewn in his office complex and he would grill her relentlessly on the finest details of life in Angel Falls, and of her friends and relatives. Though she answered every question, he would dissect each response, rearticulate it, and drill deeper, like he was endeavoring to exhume her truth. He never raised his voice or threatened her, but invariably, by evening's end, she was anxious and depressed because his questions led to horrifying visions of the brutal deaths of her family and friends.

Some nights, as punishment or reward, she never knew which, he'd send her off to *Virtuoso*, and she went begrudgingly, to experience things that, for all the compelling shame and dread that greeted her in the morning, she was unable to recall. The worst were the nights of restless need when he withheld *Virtuoso* from her.

On those nights, feeling nervous and edgy, she woke early and often. He was always near and ready, so weary and anxious, she endured his questioning until she lost her bearings and was unsure of her responses. Sometimes, something in his line of questioning exposed what he considered a revelation, an as-yet-unrevealed kernel of some truth that she'd held onto with hopeless devotion. Though she felt the loss, his triumph gave her comfort. And every day, in the most secure part of her heart, she held onto Gil's existence whether it was true or not, and that thought alone allowed her to brazen out yet another day in paradise. Protecting Gil's presence from some unknown outcome wasn't without great risk because only Omar could protect her and only he could help her to avenge the horror of the Angel Falls massacre. And yet she flirted with that disaster by withholding Gil's name from Omar's questing.

As difficult as the inquisitions were, as frustrating as living with and without *Virtuoso* were, they weren't the most difficult part of her existence. In spite of everything—Omar's relentless pursuit of truth, the haunting *Virtuoso* experiences he bestowed on her, even the significant difference in their ages—she loved him. He was her only and best friend, his generosity and affection were reassuring, and his charm was a bridge over her despair. The way he regaled her with stories of his youthful worldly adventures and his noble calling to rid America of tyranny and to protect America's underserved, he was so much more than anyone she'd ever known. And sometimes, in spite of his relentless inquisitions, he'd smile that wonderful smile that made her forget, if ever so briefly.

One evening she asked him about Dot's artwork.

"Dot provides us with so much more than what you saw in her store."

"I wondered about that. Her taste is nothing like yours."

He laughed. "You mean not so opulent." Hoping she hadn't offended him, she began to apologize. He smiled. "No, no, you're right. My taste runs to German Gothic or Byzantine extravagance while hers is sturdy early-American and maybe Shaker. But it's not for art that I value Dot. She disseminates information for my revolution. She is my connection to the ferret network throughout the States."

"What are ferrets?"

"Before Dot and the ferrets, I knew what Crelli had, what I was up against, but my people were being compromised and my networks destroyed, sometimes before, but most times immediately after they transmitted information to me. The government knew everything and HomeSec was always where we didn't want them to be. With Crelli's perfected surveillance my forces for good were helpless. So fearing the death of my revolution, I made an alliance with necessary people uniquely placed in America's economic system, yet transparent to it—people like repairmen, cab drivers, trash collectors, teachers, and even golf caddies—expendable workers in indispensable jobs. Today, they form a strategic human network throughout the country that acquires critical information for me, directly from the source. It is priceless espionage and oftentimes more timely and accurate than any I received before.

"All this I attribute to Dot. I was shopping in her boutique, not finding anything I liked, as you can imagine, when I overheard her talking with a purchasing agent for a company doing business with the American government. She said she had a network of ferrets who could sneak almost anything out of the States illegally. I approached her on it and she explained. Her ferrets are American economic survivors who traffic in goods and information. Dot wasn't a rebel back then; she acquired contraband American goods from her ferrets and resold it for a tidy profit. After the great downsizing, there were a great many personal items that had neither owner nor a prospective buyer.

"I saw the possibilities immediately, and asked her to join me for dinner so we could discuss a business deal. At first, she refused, she insisted she was just a simple hockey mom trying to earn enough to get by and all she wanted to do with her spare time was participate in pay-to-play virtual ice hockey tournaments. Dot loves hockey. She can afford to be anyone on her teams but she chooses every time to be the quick, undersized, chippy third line center. I so adore my Dot! Anyway, she was involved with her ferrets to earn money so she could bring her grandchildren here from America. We struck a deal. I help her support her children and her store and she brings me useful packets of information and gear from America. Dot is one of our valued patriots."

"I had no idea."

His smile faded. "Of course not, until the attack on your village, you gave little thought to what survival in America means. You were raised in a safe, out-of-the-way place and if you're to serve the revolution, it is time that you learn the hard realities."

He was always so certain. "Teach me, please Omar."

"I will, my precious, and you will learn to feel as we do. Close your eyes. Picture what it will be like to live free again, without me to protect you, though I will, gladly. Freedom is what we fight for and that fear, that dread you feel, hold onto it, agonize over it and never, ever forget it because without that dread we will never overcome their terror. Passion drives our victory, Princess, and we need your passion, desperately."

She feared the government, which meant she feared being put out of Omar's palace. "Are you mad at me? Please don't send me away."

"Mad? How can I be mad? I will never send you away. Not ever. But my revolution can't succeed until you commit, and to do that you must believe your life here could end at any moment because until we win, you will never be comfortable. Tanya Brandt's government preys on the lazy mind and the weak of spirit. You are beautiful, Stacey, sweetheart, you will always be that, but you can no longer be innocent because you no longer live in some primitive, out-of-the-way village where you can survive that malady. This is the real world, and you must hate it with all your heart."

"Isn't it enough that I believe in you?"

Instead of answering, he stood up and grabbed her hand. "Come."

When she realized where he was taking her, she resisted and he was forced to pull her along. When she dug her heals in, he let go of her hand and she slipped to the ground. "Get up and stop this at once," he yelled, indignantly. "You're not a child and this is important."

"It's just that I . . . I'd prefer not to, Omar, please, don't force me."

He hugged her to him in a tight embrace. She strained to look up at him. He was so close. She raised her mouth seeking his but inexplicably, his mouth eluded hers even though her lips continued to pursue his. "Stop this. Stop acting like a child. We have important things to accomplish."

Humiliated, she slumped into his arms and whimpered. "But I want you," she said, not grasping what that meant or why she said it.

He disengaged from her. "My beautiful Princess, you will be a fine consort someday, but this is not a game and your passions must be focused on the right things. You have much to learn and if you continue to act this way, then you are too immature for me."

Hurt by this rejection, she covered her face with her hands and whispered in a small voice as though she didn't want to hear what she was saying. "I don't need *Virtuoso*, Omar, it . . . it scares me. I need you. You care and I love that. Don't make me go. It makes me feel so . . ." She couldn't name the dirty feelings that surfaced with just the thought of *Virtuoso*. "Please, it makes me think things . . . and I'm going crazy thinking them about you."

He seemed to understand and he embraced her again, but again she misread his intent and her lips sought his. This time, he hugged her so tight that her face was trapped against his neck. Frustrated, she struggled to lift her head so she could kiss him but his embrace restricted her. His fingers gently traced her lips and she shuddered. She ached for him but what he said made her fearful. "Stacey, my darling, I would be so happy if you truly meant what you say. But you lie and that saddens me."

"No!" She couldn't stop her tears. How could he know? "No, that's not fair." He pulled back and gave her that stern look that her dad could never quite pull off. She took a step back and cowered. "You've been so good to me, Omar. I . . . I need you. I want you . . ." She couldn't voice what she wanted.

"I care about you, too. I care very much. But I am from the old world and I'm old fashioned. For love to be right there must be trust and yet every day I show you how important you are to me and you say you love me, but you say things, or don't say things, and I can't trust. If you are to be good to me and to yourself, it is time you learn that adults, responsible people are judged by what they do when it counts. Everything else is frivolous noise. You withhold from me or lie and it devalues our relationship. That is the curse of lies. Why should your fear of another's reaction—particularly one you say you love—why should it keep you from speaking the truth? When you lie, you devalue yourself, but you devalue me, as well and it is too much. The way you act, it will destroy love. That is no way to live and it is certainly no way to love. Someone else has your heart, someone you trust more than you trust me. What else can I believe? You are an extraordinarily brave, sexy, and attractive young woman, but I have no chance if someone else has the most important part of you."

"But I don't . . ."

He put his finger to her lips. "Shhh," he said gently. "It doesn't surprise me that you fear *Virtuoso*, it is a way to truth."

She slumped along beside him, worrying her way to the *Virtuoso* complex. Once there, he pointed to the door, opened it, and held her hand until she was inside. She entered, dutifully and waited as he offered instructions.

"Today, there is something totally new. Learn, my sweet, and tell me about it when it is done. This is critical and I still hold out hope that when you come to understand the great task of my life, truly understand, you will trust me and commit to me so that I can love you like you deserve to be loved. If you earn the right, there is great security in my love." Before she could respond, he closed the door and she was alone. Despondent, she undressed slowly.

A warm breeze was blowing down the empty street in what seemed a familiar town. In all of the store windows on the street, the glass was shattered, while ripped, bent and water stained *For Sale* and *For Lease* signs flapped in the breeze. Inside each buildings, the floors were littered with cracked ceiling slabs and other debris.

Fearful of what she would find, she walked down the center of the street searching for danger in every corner and shadow, for though oddly familiar, she had never seen a place so grim and desolate as this. As she walked, she noticed exposed windows on the floor above the shops, and there were thick, heavy bars on those windows with drapes so thin, cheap, and insubstantial that the light barely noticed them as they flapped against the security bars in the breeze.

At the far end of the street she saw a chain link fence, maybe twenty feet high, with foreboding-looking sharpened shiny wire on top that glinted in the sunlight. She approached, her neck craning to see the wire.

Who would climb so high, she wondered, *with that wire on top to thwart them?*

Then she shuddered when she realized that the fence was designed to keep people in, not out. She was inside the fence, now, standing in an immense parking lot whose cracks had become a perverse growing field for persistent flora. In the ripples of heat that emanated from the surface, the bent, grotesque looking scrub pines stood, slight and insubstantial in so many types of weeds and brush that the parking lot appeared to be a great battle front of a colossal war between nature seeking to surmount man and man steamrolling nature away.

There was silence. Even the wind made no sound here as it blew into wisps the light coating of sand that seemed to portend that nature was giving up and committing suicide. She heard a soft hiss and walked toward a gigantic building where the noise seemed to emanate from. As she approached, the hiss went from barely discernable, yet steady, to a high tension growl. She touched the building wall and felt it vibrating. She came to a metal door that was smooth and dull from the sandblasting wind but when she opened it, the inside was severely dented. She stepped inside and a hot blast of air followed her to be answered by the roar of mechanical sounds that forced her to cringe and cover her ears.

She had entered on the second floor of the building. Below, there were winding row after winding row of automobiles, all greater or lesser works in progress, depending where they were on the assembly line. The oppressive brightness of the overhead lighting system illuminated an assembly line that continued on as far as she could see and everywhere, there was machinery and filth and an orchestrated cacophony of loud harsh industrial noise that made the ground shudder, her teeth vibrate, and her ears hurt.

Because of the blinding lights, it was warmer inside than out, so she removed her coat without wondering how she came to be wearing it. She smelled the sweetly foul odor of vintage sweat as men, women, and children labored on the lines, their heads wrapped in cloth as they concentrated on the screws and bolts, the upholstery, the trim and electronics, all the details that turn parts into finished goods and effort into profit. The workers wore ripped and filthy clothes, their gaunt, weary bodies lacquered in dirty sweat and dried blood as they toiled in repetitive moves, up and down, back and forth, twist and turn, side to side, over and over, moves designed to build a convenience but break down people.

In the recesses of the factory where the extraordinary lighting didn't reach, fully depreciated elderly watched naked young children who wore miner's hats with lamps to illuminate the nooks and crannies in the vehicles where only they could fit to do the job. Some of the workers were mothers, Stacey guessed, their newborns strapped to their backs as they bent to help children perform the simple, repetitive tasks that were in their purview to accomplish. Those too old and feeble to be productive sat crammed into dark areas watching, some, almost feral, others offering advice by shouting over the din.

The adults on the main line worked with a dour concentration, their eyes riveted on their work, their mouths tightly shut knowing that opening them would only make their life worse. Confused and concerned, Stacey continued on until a large, husky, tough-looking man carrying a three-foot section of thick, metal pipe stopped her.

"Ma'am, you shouldn't be here. The *Circle of Life* expressly prohibits anyone other than union workers in here. Please be respectful and move before it's too late."

She walked away but turned to ask the man what he meant by too late, and union.

"This is Detroit, the auto capital of the world," the man shouted, as if that answered her question.

Along one massive wall, there were long rows of lockers that disappeared into the darkness of a tunnel. In front of the lockers were narrow metal benches and on them, at various points, men, women and children huddled, waiting for their shifts to begin or their lives to end.

Troughs ran between the rows of lockers and some were using them to wash and others to eat from or drink. Each trough was covered in a greenish-brown nauseating muck. The troughs were fed from above by large black plastic tubes that extended through the roof. Down the center there were other troughs, built nearer to the ground for septic purposes, but they were too revolting to look at so she turned away but not before noticing the flies. These weren't the tiny, annoying small flies of Angel Falls. These were big, fat, and courageous flies that were everywhere.

She felt queasy at the thought of families sharing these ghastly facilities and the even more sickening food and the brownish, oily drinking water and she staggered against a cinder block wall to vomit only to see a small boy of no more than five years old, who smiled sadly at her. Queasy and enduring a clammy sweat, she smiled back and he ran to her and hugged her tight. And then he began to cry.

Before she could comfort the boy, the man with the pipe came by. He swung hard, hitting the child in the head, the pipe creating a sound like that of an organ. It vibrated to silence as the boy's arms spasmed and he sank to the ground, limp like a doll. Ever so briefly, the boy shook with a terrible seizure and then it ceased as did he. Stacey stared and screamed.

Paying no attention to the now dead child at his feet, the man with the pipe became insistent that she leave. "Ma'am, I won't ask you again. I don't know how you got in here, but if you want to be someone who can walk out, please, do so now."

Frightened, she backed away, and then dashed toward an exit. Along the way, she noticed long rows of wheeled dumpsters piled high with waste. At first she thought it was old clothing, but as she got closer, she realized the dumpsters were filled with the bodies of workers who hadn't outlived their productivity, some wearing clothing not needed elsewhere. She screamed again and fled through the first door she could find, hitting it so hard on the way out that she hurt her wrists as she blasted through. Outside, heaving in the still air of the parking lot, she fell to the ground and vomited again.

Though the air was hot, it revived her somewhat and when she looked up, it was evening and there were bright headlights everywhere. She was in a large and rapidly filling parking lot, with crowds of couples and groups moving past her heading toward a huge lighted outdoor amphitheater in the distance. Unsure what to do, she stood and was pushed along by the crowd until she saw the marquee. It read: Dr. Milton Cavanaugh Speaks Tonight. And though it meant nothing to her, the sign indicated there was a full house. Security guards with pulse rifles directed her along with the crowd into the long lines of a corral that was patrolled by other guards carrying even nastier looking rifles equipped with night scopes. Far above, helicopters shined bright beams that scanned the crowd. It reminded her of that night in Angel Falls when her world ended and it made her sad and uneasy.

When she reached the front of the line, she entered an individual scanning booth. When the light turned green, she was instructed to insert her ticket so she reached into her pockets, but came up empty so an armed guard angrily motioned for her to get out of line. As she left the booth, she caught the scent of popcorn from a nearby refreshment stand.

A man not much older than her was waving at her and shouting, "Officer, she is with me." He seemed familiar but she couldn't place him.

When the officer allowed him by, he ran to her waving two tickets. That's when she noticed his exceedingly pale, narrow face and dimpled chin, and his glorious smile. Glorious was the only word she could think of as his lips widened to reveal perfect white teeth to the gums. Bright white hair draped long and straight reached to his collar and he had oddly familiar, large, profound, root beer-colored eyes. The young man seemed truly magical because he managed those unusual features into gorgeous. She blushed, realizing he was next to her, and she was staring.

She was tall, he was taller.

"Hi, I'm Glen Smith," he said, his voice musical, "your date for the evening."

There was something about that name. She smiled. "Hi, I'm Stacey."

He inserted his tickets into the reader and the gate opened to allow them to pass inside. He put his arm around her and guided her into the venue.

"I'm really looking forward to this." He said as they fought through the large crowd in search of their seats. He leaned toward her and continued in a whisper. "You can't tell anyone, but I'm rich and I help the poor. When I heard that Reverend Cavanaugh was speaking, I couldn't resist, I had to attend. The man is a genius, an amazing, angry, bigoted genius. I mean look at this crowd! The Reverend preaches hatred of the poor to the poor and somehow they eat it right up. America is sick." She smiled at him, too taken aback by his ardor to respond. "My father has great business contacts so after some calls—well here we are. This is so ironic, that it's funny. There's no way I could attend safely if they knew I helped the poor—who are the Reverend's victims and his supporters, but having money, anything is possible." He spoke with a slight accent but his voice was clear and even melodic. "If they find out about me, run like hell, because, like most Christians today, these people are decidedly unChrist-like."

"I . . . I won't say anything," Stacey stammered. Even the carnival atmosphere of this event couldn't wipe from her mind what she had just seen in that factory earlier, but it helped. Everything was coming at her so quickly. "Why . . . why would they do something to you for helping the poor? And who is Reverend Cavanaugh?"

He laughed. "You never heard of Reverend Milton Cavanaugh? This is 2030, where have you been, girl? The Reverend would be disappointed to learn that somebody doesn't know who he is because he believes he's a bona fide legend, a gift to the people from God himself."

"I don't get out much," she shared.

He laughed. "That's hard to believe of a beautiful young lady like you." She blushed. "Reverend Cavanaugh is the leading and most profitable Libertarian Evangelical Minister in America. As religion goes, he's Fortune Ten stuff and high on that list. The Reverend preaches free market capitalism as the endgame of God's holy order and he does it in an exciting new way. Well actually, it's a very old way, updated to take advantage of the lack of sensitivity and intelligence of his perverse flock. He appeared on the religious scene just as all hell was breaking loose in the country economically, and because of his, I guess you could call it his unmitigated gall; he's been able to attract a great many angry and fearful middle and lower middle class idiots to his version of the truth. Before the Rev, most every media evangelist had exhausted their repugnant power to excite the pathetic and needy Christian hopefuls with their extreme xenophobia and their thirst for lies and empty promises. Until Dr. Cavanaugh, that is.

"With technology, any evangelist worth his weight in gold or even gold contracts could pinpoint the devil down to his GPS location. But said evangelist can call for the end of times in clear and certain terms just so many times before even the dimmest Christian bulb gets enough of a glow to realize he's being sold something that he is confusing with a benefit, and maybe even God almighty is embarrassed because he's falling for it. Anyway, it was only a matter of time before those evangelists failed."

Glen was so good looking, charming, and intense that she could only smile and nod as he continued to whisper his privileged perspective to her.

"It's been preached for too long and people have grown tired of theologies based on some undefined time determinant for prophecy to be fulfilled, with rewards to be redistributed to the faithful at some celestial socialist weenie roast that precedes a poorly conceived vision of forever in some nebulous paradise for the virtuous victorious. Yep, old time religion had lost its cachet before Cavanaugh. He's on top because he owns the most enterprising and entertaining of the new faith ministries. The Reverend hit it perfectly. Today, with all the medical breakthroughs, the desperate and aging Christian faithful are far more comfortable with forever as an out more than a concept. Cavanaugh understands and he rallies his flock to a far more experiential and marketable vision—everlasting life on earth as we've been told it will be in heaven, and he goads his flock to action with real-time computer generated effects. If you're absolutely sold on mortgaging your future, Cavanaugh is the man to take advantage of you. And he can really pick his targets, too. He's waging a holy blood feud against the abject poor who you would think have more to worry about than having Cavanaugh as an opponent, particularly after the Republican Supreme Court expanded the Second Amendment and further broadened the Fourteenth to allow corporations to fund and arm militia, rioters really, who do God's more brutal work in the streets. Other than giving in to corporations, anymore, the government does nothing, a stance they seem to be very comfortable with come election time."

Glen was so intense and handsome but what he was saying was beyond Stacey's ability to comprehend. "That doesn't sound good."

"You have no idea how not good it is. Hey, we need to find our seats and get ready for the show. What you will witness here tonight, I promise, you will never forget."

"Glen, how did you know I was going to be here?"

He answered a different question. "Do you know how expensive these tickets are?"

She shook her head.

"To get them, I had to promise my father's purchasing manager that I would stop quarrelling with my father's politics, at least for a while. You don't know my father. Anyway, once I got the tickets, I promised myself I would find the best looking woman among the true believers in attendance and ask her to accompany me." He pointed to Stacey. "You are the best looking woman here, and at least for tonight, we are meant for each other."

She laughed at that. "Really?"

"My rationale is sound. Check it out. You are a true believer and once you discover that I'm not, you will try very, very hard to convert me, and when you try hard enough," he smiled that incredible smile, "you will succeed." She laughed again and slowly his smile faded. "But you're not a true believer, are you?"

She shook her head. "I'm sorry to disappoint you in so many ways."

He shrugged and stared at her. "One thing I am not is disappointed. You are a very pretty girl."

"Stop it. Where are we sitting?"

"Up front, where else?"

As they walked, it grew more crowded, louder, and more belligerent and as he was pushing back, she asked. "Tell me again, who this Reverend Cavanaugh is?"

"He's dubbed himself the Prime Minister of the Capitalist Fundamentalist Church, Bar and Grill, just kidding about the bar and grill. He also answers to the Beacon Believer or the Deacon Deliverer, or some such crap, but he is nothing so much as a pretentious opportunist clown with a gift for entrepreneurial undertakings and a wicked love for God; pretty much like all rich evangelicals, although Cavanaugh is more dangerous by half than those who preceded him." As they got closer to the more expensive seats, the crowd thinned and quieted and he lowered his voice accordingly.

"When the good doctor begins, do what the crowd does," he advised, "because the only ones who get past this point are the tongue-swallowing, true believers"

"Believers of what?"

"Unless you sleep through it, you will know the answer soon enough. Cavanaugh preaches an unforgiving form of anti-communitarianism and non-inclusive capitalism and he teaches it to people who aren't bright but are easily stirred, people who have little chance of ever achieving the benefits they admire in the wealthy, but are self-righteous enough to do their dirty work. Cavanaugh attracts the lightly educated and the generally uncurious, traditional loyalist capitalist cannon fodder that the rich have taken advantage of and abused for generations to move their football closer toward their goal of truly unbridled capitalism and the wealth redistribution that favors them immensely."

Understanding little of what he was saying, she leaned into him and whispered, "Why do these people allow themselves to be taken advantage of?"

"Duh, it's a religion. Why else? In a strange way, it's a win-win. These people live dull, drab lives and have no one to blame for it but themselves—and what right mind would want to blame themselves. Cavanaugh shows them a good time, produces a readily available and not particularly elusive scapegoat for bludgeoning, a visceral mechanism to discharge overwrought anger and frustration. It's a well run enterprise and a mutually beneficial—excuse the term—cluster fuck."

Stacey blushed.

"Sorry. I didn't mean to embarrass you. According to the Reverend, the only way for America to become great again is for her to cleanse herself of her sins and her sinners—quite a bit more extreme than their Lord, Jesus Christ himself would approve of, but in reality, sin and sinner is code for the entitled poor and any funding the government provides that business doesn't benefit from directly. Cavanaugh believes with a great many others the farcical concept that libertarians who hate government can run government, particularly in a country with a significant poor population. Cavanaugh's preference, if you read his monosyllabic writings, truth be told, is to run a libertarian government WITHOUT a poor population and he pursues it with vigor to a point where his philosophy seems redemptive to these clowns." Glen pointed to the crowds. "Oh, and it's a musical. You are in for a real treat.

"Cavanaugh names names, the destroyers of America, the people who deliver entitlements to the pathetic poor and he holds a special place in his hell for anyone who supplies the poor with alms of any kind and preaches a decidedly Christian doctrine. It is abhorrent to him that anyone could need the government, except the rich, and that anyone who uses the government, other than the rich, should be persecuted if prosecution proves too cost prohibitive."

She didn't know how to react to him and he noticed.

"I take it that you're not political. In these times, that's a dangerous position but you're young yet. We're close. I have to be quieter. From here on, maybe it's best that you watch and learn."

"What you say sounds serious but I don't know anything about it."

"You will soon enough. There's a choir, pyrotechnics, a mega-screen media presentation and, if we're lucky, Cavanaugh will perform economic healings and even exorcisms on a few lazy poor who were bussed in and paid to brave the crowd."

"What are economic healings and exorcisms?"

"Anyone whose career is not progressing as he'd hoped comes forward, has the word of God injected into his brain, or at least Cavanaugh's best impression of the word of God, and then they go all silly and beg for an opportunity to help a capitalist get rich. It's silly. Exorcisms are different, meaner. Some lazy poor guy gets a beating and a good scolding after which he fills out job applications, and declares that he's willing to work for less. It's something like that. Anyway, the crowd eats it up because they believe they're watching the healed become the well-healed. In a way, it's kind of cool. Everyone leaves the stage vowing to go forth and appreciate, or something, and the audience goes ballistic. Then, it's all Wagner and Souza but you should mouth the words because the rancor in the crowd really ramps up because their credit is being tapped because the audience is required to invest in the newly healed with Cavanaugh taking his cut off the top. It's another lucrative peripheral industry for our great Cleric of Capitalism and the people sure do seem to get their money's worth. He stirs them up and up and then closes with a riot, literally, a riot."

"Is it safe?"

"We're sitting in the expensive seats so for insiders like us it should be safe enough. Cavanaugh is smart. If too many of his faithful are injured during the riots, his fund raising rate goes way down. He requires some injuries because he needs martyrs to spur his flock on and sometimes, the poor fight back. In the end, he's a good capitalist who has the fiduciary interests of his stockholders at heart so there shouldn't be too many issues until the riot and there, if it's good theatre the deaths are sustainable financially. Don't you worry, though; I'm here to protect you. The key is to anticipate the good Reverend. He understands that masses in motion are easier to direct. In the end, this is America and with the good seats everything is less dangerous. Besides, the easiest people for the Reverend to manipulate can only afford the cheap seats." He waved his tickets. "The Lord may say that vengeance is his, but wrath he has cleverly assigned to the irrational."

He took her hand and together they finished their walk down the main aisle toward a glass enclosure that protected their seats from the remainder of the crowd. As they entered each new section, their tickets were re-scanned by security guards who seemed to get bigger, better armed, and more cautious as they got closer to the stage. Stacey walked with Glen but her eyes wandered to the outlying aisles where religious performance artists in green and gold church robes were trying to coax a buck from the audience with heady displays of prestidigitation while in other places, men in tuxedoes and women in nano-stringed bikinis, sang and danced to songs about one socio-economic issue or another while soliciting donations.

When they got closer, a group of teenagers, each wearing necklaces with the large gold, silver and green Almighty Dollar icons, offered strange, street gang hand signs, but when neither of them responded, the gang made some obscene gesture and moved on.

Glen's tickets provided access to the nano-glass enclosed box seats in an area just below and in front of the stage where an orchestra might be placed. Once through the nano-glass doors, the outside din quieted, deadened by the nano-glass technology. All that remained were the sophisticated, conversational sounds of the wealthy guests within softened by a woman in white robes playing an electronic harp. Stacey stared at the incongruity of this cultured crowd, everyone well-dressed, well-coiffed, and reserved, so close and yet so far removed from the crazies outside. When she stared out at the people beyond the glass, folks were screaming, cheering, and stomping in anticipation.

As the maitre de showed them to their table, she caught a whiff of eucalyptus from the plants decorating the box. And while they sipped the complimentary champagne, outside, the choir began singing patriotic songs and everyone joined in, the people outside, guzzling beer and rowdy, the people inside, demure, sipping champagne or fine wine.

Excited, she shouted to Glen, "Is this how it starts?" He just pointed to the stage and nodded.

The choir stopped and the lights dimmed. Soon silence fell over the crowd and even the rowdies knew to cease. In the darkness, she smelled a different scent, magnolia? There was a murmur of anticipation, which quickly turned into a cheer and then the crowd stood and roared at the show's opening.

Beams from thousands of tiny lights appeared throughout the crowd followed by booming music that caused the arena to pulsate. Excited, Stacey squeezed Glen's hand and he hugged her close.

The rousing music stopped abruptly creating a dizzying silence that drove the crowd silent and went on and on long past when the ringing in her ears stopped. Then, a loud and deep, God-like voice bellowed from above. She searched in the dim light, but no source of the voice was visible.

"American Natural Grains Stuffs, Incorporated, makers of *DaGrosse Brand Pancake Mix and Syrup*, along with Studebaker, '*What a car; What a future*,' present the Holiest Capitalist the world has ever seen, a great and selfish dude who maximizes his god-given talents to make the world a better, richer place. Everyone, praise Jesus, here he is, the one, the only, the Most Reverend Morton Cavanaugh our great and glorious Deliverer. Give it up for God's great hero on earth!"

Though the sophisticates inside the glass box remained calm, through the glass, there was frenzy in the general admission crowd and she couldn't decide which group to watch. She had decided to watch the crowd outside when Glen touched her arm.

"The real action is up there," he said, pointing high above the stage. She stared where he pointed until the last few lights went out and the entire arena was pitched into darkness once again. Nothing happened for a long time, too long because the outside crowd was becoming restive. Inside the glass, when anyone talked or even coughed, a loud shushing by others swept that sound into oblivion.

She lost track of time and except for Glen's warm hand holding hers, her mind was blank with anticipation. Then, through transparent speakers imbedded into the nano-glass, she heard a low, deep rumble that she was soon able to recognize as words.

"The . . . Lord . . . is . . . my Business Partner," the voice intoned solemnly and the crowd beyond the box seats immediately joined in the prayer, even as the insiders declined. The lights flickered but remained dim as the voice continued. "And I have a fiduciary responsibility to my Lord as I strive for everlasting wealth accretion. The Lord endows me with opportunity and stimulates my passion for excellence so that I will fear not his business cycles, for though my value may diminish, my desire to satisfy his requirements will remain with me. The beauty and balance of His Free Market comforts me and I will create such wealth as to do God's work on earth, forever."

More extended silence followed until the voice began anew, but this time enormous 3D images were projected onto the front curtain for all to see. Glen explained that the scenes were of famous business transactions, important inventions and technological breakthroughs, great financiers, and truly great brand names, and they were displayed in concert with music and the crowd oohed and ahhed at their favorites.

The voice continued. "Passion is the Lord's special and favorite force for good in the world. Believe in Him with all of your soul and wring the passion from your heart and use its great power to propel your career forward to accumulate your forever fortune. By so doing, you will have made holy the consecrated ooze within yourself, ooze that is powerful like our good Lord God's very essence, much like his body and his blood.

"Passion," the voice shouted and then calmed for the rest, "Passion, along with the positive forces of merciless greed will enable you to achieve the great wealth that compels forever to bend to your way. Passion provides the drive and greed the ingenuity and necessity. Together, they will drive you to expend the greatest of effort, incur the most intense risk and from which the greatest reward, that of a funded forever will be bestowed. Do this with diligence and perspicacity and you will, using God's special building blocks, construct your everlasting and fully depreciated domain. Do all this, but it is through passion alone, that the wealth of Christ's true greed congeals into great and everlasting goo, the true goo that makes each and every building block steadfast and prolific evermore.

"As has been foretold by the most devout liturgical economists since the birth of our Lord, Jesus Christ, God has made a covenant with his subjects. In that covenant, he has promised that every resource that will ever be needed will be supplied so that every person of faith can construct the best limited liability, ongoing concern personhood that a person can be. Be a person who will never die and live in grace with our Lord forever.

"This the Lord provides especially in these times when most human life has caused itself to be valued as a commodity and while the twin reapers, foreclosure and divestiture, relentlessly stalk our assets. And with that grim duo skulking America, the followers of the Lord and his agent and son, Jesus Christ, they will survive because of their faith in holy economics. And when the Rapture comes, it will not be to heaven that they ascend. No, Jesus will not allow that. In chapter seven, verse three of the Book of Rand it states that a great communist lord will ascend from hell and he will offer sloth and entitlements to his followers and they will be enticed and go with him to hell and the Lord God will seal the entrance to hell forever and thus the time will come when Jesus will walk with his followers on earth untainted by the sins of socialism. On that Day, when the true followers of God's Capitalism walk with Jesus, his self, immortal, it will be clear which religion has won and which religions have lost. For those among you who have worked religiously and have always made the devout decision to continuously accrete your wealth and have installed a value structure in your lives that generate a stress free, everlasting annuity, your reward will be cocktails with Jesus, forever."

There were cheers and screams and a great many followers pumped chests and high-fived.

"Even though some will be confronted by the daunting demons and naysayers of Socialist Christianity, beware. Those misguided over-thinkers value caring and kindness above financial matters. These unfortunates will discover the reward for their sins in a brutal and painful near term death and you must not give in to them. You will be challenged by non-believers who quest not for our Lord, but for nothing and thus they will achieve that less lofty goal and join the Social Christians in a merciless death.

"Beware of liberal, cynical people, the sons and daughters of sloth and of death, for in spite for our Holy mission, these negative nincompoops will entice you with the Devil's mantra. Ignore their siren calls to go easy, to have fun, to rest on your laurels, and to do good things so that you can reward others in this life and find your just reward in some other. Beware of Satan's smooth falsetto because it will turn Christ's words to honey and those words will be used against you and against Jesus, his self, if you let them. Heed not these usurpers of forever and be one with the true Savior, Christ the Deliverer, Christ the Redeemer, Christ the Investment Broker of our souls. Praise Jesus."

The voice-over the pictures stopped just as the most poignant business portrait in mankind's storied economic-theological history was projected onto the curtain. The crowd went wild. It was the famous Renaissance painting by Pope Simony II, "Jesus Making Change." The arena went dark, and the crowd went silent. Confused, Stacey stared at the painting while Glen just smiled and shook his head in wonderment while the audience communed with the fine art from the great capitalist painter-pontiff.

The painting was gone and the arena went dark. From on high, a narrow beam of light shined down to create a small, impossibly bright white dot on the center of the stage. Slowly, the beam began to climb the indigo blue curtain until it halted high above the stage and the audience. Outside the glass, there was hysteria, while inside, it was mostly fine dining. Stacey had been too absorbed to notice but a waitress had served up a very rare and expensive fresh water fish cooked to perfection and presented on exquisite American-made Chinette. She looked to Glen, who had already started eating. He pointed with his fork to the spotlight high above where an almost invisible nano-glass walkway extended from beyond the curtain.

"Is it . . . ?" she asked.

He nodded. The walkway seemed to be floating beyond the curtain. The curtain opened just enough to allow a heavy-set, blond, curly haired but balding man with thick dark glasses and a shiny emerald and gold robe strode out, seemingly hovering in the light above the crowd. Floating beside him was an immense whiteboard.

While the crowd roared, and Stacey and Glen ate, Reverend Cavanaugh, the Prime Minister of the Capitalist Fundamentalist Church, raised his hands above his head and held them there, slowly bringing them down as the crowd dutifully quieted until, finally, hands at his side, there was silence.

Hi, y'all," The Reverend shouted and the crowd roared back. "So that you know, I've done my part. With gold prices where they are, GoldBrick Inc. the place to buy precious metals before precious metals become precious, GoldBrick Inc., thank the Lord, has provided me with forever funding. Now, I'm here for you. It is your time to prove that you believe and are willing to bankroll a capitalist heaven on earth for all time. Are you with me?" The crowd shouted their assent. "Then prove it. In the coming election, everyone in this room, your family, your friends, your business partners, anyone you employ or who employs you, all of you must vote for the Republican for president and you must vote for every candidate running on the Entrepreneur party platform. You must do this or kill every Democrat you can find. I will have more about that later. If you fail to act, there will be such an iniquitous redistribution of wealth that you will, most assuredly, have voted for your own death and the death of everyone you love and everything you hold dear. Am I clear?" The crowd roared again. Stacey was taken aback, unsure, and Glen just shrugged his response.

"As God-fearing Americans, it is for each of us here in this arena to use all of our God-given power to prevent Democrat President Parrington and his Congressional ring of culture whores from stealing from us and ending our lives by taking from us the forever we justly deserve. Make no mistake; the coming election may appear to be about many things. It is not. The coming election is purely about life and death, their life, your death. Your vote could not be more important because it may be your last. But America is a free country so it is up to you to defend your life or to just throw it away. It is your choice, your birthright, vote Republican and Entrepreneur Party and never die, or die too young and too Democrat."

After a soft musical interlude, while the Reverend drew some arcane diagrams on his whiteboard, he led the assembly in prayer. "Oh God, our Supreme Market Maker, call us to judgment in this ever fair, yet cruel free market world you built for us to thrive in. Allow us, Oh Lord, to serve *your* divine entrepreneurial purpose here in America, the land of true believers; for *you, Lord,* are the ultimate *customer* and everyday, we live to satisfy each and every one of *your* requirements as we seek glorious productivity in *your* every free market business process. Bless us, Oh Lord, and fill our hearts and souls with faith in the divine dollar so that through our boundless passion and properly directed greed, we will invest, not just in *you*, but with *you* someday. Sanctify us, Oh Lord, and fulfill *your* part of this glorious business contract so that we may live forever in *your* presence in an ever-appreciating world of continuous improvement. This we humbly beseech thee, Oh Lord. Amen."

Stacey was startled to see a thick mist descend from the rafters. The mist coalesced on the glass roof above her and obscured the masses outside. Then, through a beam of light, she saw a gigantic rainbow form across the great expanse of the amphitheater from just above the Reverend and his whiteboard all the way to the refreshment stands in the back. This time, those inside the enclosed box seats as well as those outside, screamed their hallelujahs, but it took a few moments for Stacey to add her voice, a delay duly noted by some pious patrons seated facing her at nearby tables, sipping champagne.

In time, a velvet silence spread throughout until the band began to play while Cavanaugh remained motionless above. Stacey coughed at the smell of camphor, and sighed contentedly. Below the rainbow and the Reverend's station, the curtain opened and a troop of young gymnasts and ballerinas dressed in revealing and form fitting Civil War garb leapt across the stage displaying unusual agility as, between leaps, they posed in inspiring patriotic positions. Stacey put her head on Glen's shoulder and just stared. Soon the soaring voices of the choir echoed through the arena, singing.

I have read a fiery gospel writ in burnish`d rows of steel,
As ye deal with my contemnors, So with you my grace shall deal;
Let the Hero, born of woman, crush the serpent with his heel
Since God is marching on.

Glory! Glory! Hallelujah!
Glory! Glory! Hallelujah!
Glory! Glory! Hallelujah!
His truth is marching on.

He has sounded forth the trumpet that shall never call retreat
He is sifting out the hearts of men before His judgment-seat
Oh, be swift, my soul, to answer Him! Be jubilant, my feet!

Our God is marching on.

Glory! Glory! Hallelujah!
Glory! Glory! Hallelujah!
Glory! Glory! Hallelujah!
His truth is marching on

As one, the choir and the crowd sang together as the gymnasts and ballerinas danced a gavotte. It was so compelling; Stacey found herself mouthing the words and swaying with the dance. Bemused, Glen sang along, too. The song ended in a blaze of fireworks, pulsating lasers and strobes whose throbbing beams diffracted in the smoke above, lighting up the pavilion. She closed her eyes to the sensory overload and caught a whiff of sulfur. She gagged again. Glen leaned over and hugged her tight and then he touched her chin, drawing her mouth up, and he kissed her. And he kissed her again. Thunderous noise became ethereal calm until he broke the kiss and the bedlam returned. She stared up at him as he laughed at the lost expression on her face. The Reverend shouted, snapping the wonder from her eyes.

"The path to forever is a perilous journey through the evil, besotted lands of communists and socialists, communitarians, liberals and feared progressives, atheists and agnostics, Hindus, Sikhs, Moslems, and so many more fellow travelers who will be long dead and forgotten while you and I reign here on earth, with God. Beware of these sinful people who believe with all their heart that profit motive is a curse to be expunged from our world because it dooms mankind. I say to you, if you heed them, mankind is certainly mortal and you will die, bound as you are to short term thinking. Rise up! Rise up to extinguish their short run souls! Rise up to lesson their profits! Rise up to arouse their suppressed unquenchable lust and greed! Rise up to save your enemy. Make him your low wage employee, your vendor, your customer, and yes, your stockholder. And maybe someday even your partner. Rise up; there is room in Forever for everyone but only if they believe with the passion of Christ."

Stacey was staring so intently at the Reverend that when Glen whispered to her, she jumped. He smiled and pointed back to the crowd. The people in the cheap seats were tearing at their clothes and scourging themselves with small whips.

119

She turned away in concern and buried her head in Glen's chest. He patted her and whispered. "It's not as bad as it looks. They sell special Reverend Cavanaugh brand scourging whips in the booths just outside the arena. I tried one." Stacey looked up, both surprised and disgusted. "I tried one because they're pretty cheap construction. They don't hurt, but its great theatre. When he smiled, she smiled and returned to listening to the Reverend's rant.

"For those who refuse the Word, you must oppose them and their aberrant artifices with every fiber of your soul because when you are one with God's free markets, you will be certain of all things including life everlasting. Oppose the false way, the Devil's way of State Capitalism or just plain gulag style socialism. Fear it for the devil wears many guises and just because it's called capitalism, it doesn't have to be good or right. God only holds dear the truth of free markets and he wants to partner with you forever. Your effort to create wealth and value is not solely a noble endeavor. It is more, much more. It is a perpetual blessing. Paradise exists for the faithful. It is said that it is harder for a poor man to enter heaven on earth than it is for someone who can afford the 2030 Mesh-enabled *Buick DXL 4 Autocruiser®* equipped with all wheel drive and a set of *Forever™* brand all-weather radials that lists for thirty-ninety five, but through the Cavanaugh church membership discount program it can be yours for much less and it will cruise easily through the eye of a needle, just in case you're into metaphors."

With that, the Reverend Cavanaugh stopped. There was no sound inside or out and Stacey realized she hadn't taken a breath in a while, so she slowly exhaled. The Reverend faced his whiteboard. In the squares he'd drawn earlier, names appeared. Unfamiliar with most of the names, Stacey asked Glen for help. He explained that President Parrington, various members of the Presidential Cabinet and certain of his financial supporters, some financial heretics like the Chairman of the Federal Reserve, and some celebrities who were enemies of the Reverend's church, along with well placed moderate Republican leaders and, for some reason, in a block in a remote corner of his whiteboard, Cavanaugh added presidents from antiquity, Woodrow Wilson, William Clinton, and in the largest block, Barack Obama.

Reverend Cavanaugh gesticulated wildly and suddenly the squares were connected with long squiggly lines. Arrows appeared and there was underlining and highlighting that thoroughly confused Stacey but the crowd seemed to eat it up. The Reverend explained.

"You see here, the intertwined conspiracy that we Capitalist Christians face. We can concede nothing to these unholy rascals or it will mean our literal death just at that perfectly divine moment when God has shown us the light of living truth forever."

The colors on the white board began to run. They swirled together and became as brilliant as the sun. Stacey had to look away. Then the board began to melt and liquid gold dripped from the platform, descending to the stage, cool, where as currency, they bounced off the stage and into the eager hands of the frenzied crowd.

Reverend Cavanaugh waited as the crowd put away their coins and quiet was restored. "God promises us the great reward of everlasting life but the sinners in America's bureaucracy have been won over by the votes the poor offer them. These bureaucrats show only contempt for our religion by stealing, as taxes and regulations, our hard earned wealth so they can salve their finite existences by giving it to the undeserving, slothful poor. This is Satan's doing and it must stop. It is profane and they deserve the doom they seek, hideous, short, derisory lives followed by death, the perfect censure for their denial of God's existence and their ridiculous lack of faith that has them fantasize about walking with Him in heaven, not on earth. Their death will come as it comes to all nonbelievers and redistributors; death waits in all of its horrible forms. Today, I say unto them, reject the Lord God at your peril." Throughout the crowd, true believers screamed their endorsements.

"And what of these zombie legions of idiot poor who have been nurtured to sloth by our politician enemies? There are too many of them and too few of us for if there is one thing the slothful do well, it's to procreate and not slowly. And though they procreate, they do not parent while the sloth in their DNA multiplies exponentially to infect our world until it strangles us to death."

Cavanaugh stopped to let that sink in before continuing in a whisper that quickly built to a scream. "Free markets are cruel, but they are fair. Free markets are color blind; sexually, racially, and geopolitically unbiased. And because free markets are of God, they are perfect and constant. You, my people, are the only variable and that makes free markets the ultimate test of one's faith and oneself. Free markets reward and punish based on immutable laws and for individuals, failure in a free market is cold and uncompromising, but it is also necessary and proper in that it guarantees the survival of the holiest and thus the ultimate transmogrification of humankind into Gods themselves. All of you, work assured in the knowledge that material success is not evidence of God's grace, material success IS God's grace."

Reverend Cavanaugh lifted his arms and the crowd stood in unison. The band played, and she smelled peppermint. She felt buoyant and along with the choir, he sang, *God Bless America* and she and Glen joined in, he hugging her close. She stared into his strange, dark eyes and they kissed once again and as the Reverend sang, so enraptured was she by the kiss that her interest in Capitalism waned until Glen finally broke the kiss.

She continued to stare at him as Cavanaugh wrapped up his sermon. "I say unto you here tonight, as I have said to others throughout the country, we, the devout, we will do what forever—what never dying—requires." There were cheers throughout the crowd and some in the general admission seats nearby began pounding in unison on the glass, while others stomped their feet so hard that the arena shook and the nano-glass rippled. Stacey looked out at the frenzied crowd in wonder and fright.

"As you know, not far from here," the Reverend continued, "tens of thousands of cursed non-believers, Detroit's homeless poor, the pagans and the slothful, progressives all, they huddle under bridges and in alleyways plotting to drain God's Free Markets with the support of the satanic socialist ruling class whose only hope of victory is to starve out God's true believers and deny us life, liberty and the pursuit of happiness. Yes, not far from here, these evil minions lurk in their food distribution lines taking sustenance that they have not earned—that has been diverted from the Lord's Free Marketplace, destroying these markets with false shortages. This is just as it happened in God's Holiest Temple in the Jerusalem of antiquity.

"These evil, idle sinners have earned no rights or privileges; they have schemed to take from us what our devout endeavors have rightfully earned. These detestable, savage degenerates are a plague of locusts spawned by Satan, his self, to create inflationary pressure that erodes our God-given abundance in a mortal struggle to pitch our economy into hellish depths and thus deny us our holy quest for eternity. These impoverished fiends want our wealth to decline while they deplete our natural resources, resources that are ours and that we will need forever. These hounds of hell waste our forever for their selfish needs today and by allowing them to freeload; we permit them to destroy all the resources we have worked so hard to accumulate. This great and mortal sin must be rectified, now."

The impossibly bright white light reappeared, shining out into the poor districts of Detroit. "God shows you where our enemies lurk, where they waste our valuable resources. Their existence," the Reverend pointed again, "here and here, mocks God and sullies His Markets and it must not be allowed to continue. They must not be allowed to drain infinite possibilities from our world and from our lives. They must not be allowed to desecrate God's valued Commandment, *'Thou shall not waste'.*

"Out there," he shouted, "out there is evil," he screamed. "Out there is corruption, out there is the death of life. Out there are the warrens of hell where we must do battle to cleanse and prove our faith."

Reverend Cavanaugh swept his hands over the crowd. "Arise, my faithful, the time has come to rid the world of evil's spawn and preserve life everlasting. Look! Look under your seats. Do it now."

Stacey questioned Glen who nodded and pointed to her chair. She leaned forward and placed her hand under the seat where she felt something cold. Concerned, she pulled her hand back, but Glen just smiled and nodded. She grabbed a hold of whatever it was and pulled. Out came a plastic bag containing a foot of steel chain with the word 'God' etched into every other link and a dollar sign on the others.

"What?" she questioned. He nodded, pointed to the Reverend, and whispered. "Unfortunately, I think that he's going to end without the healings. That's a shame."

From the ceiling above the arena, once again, a gentle mist drifted down. When it reached her, it smelled like burnt rubber and that made her angry.

"Take this implement from God." The Reverend implored. "Take your sacred scourging tool to the devil's own and cleanse our world, cleanse our economy with their blood. Go and together, we will wipe out the poor, the lifeblood of the ruling class; we will wipe them from God's great earth, for ever and all time. Do it for you are needed for God's holy work on earth to make ready for his return."

Stacey looked around. Inside the glass walls, the well-dressed were idly surveying their instruments of mayhem for some had nunchuks; others had bolas, short swords, blow guns and other assorted hand weapons of the Lord. Outside the glass, crazed devotees were practicing with their relics, screaming and banging on the nano-glass creating ripples that distorted her view of the stage.

"Live forever, lift your weapons and destroy the *Wasters* who prey upon us."

The crowd screamed as a blood red haze descended over the arena. Stacey inhaled this acrid smell and joined the crowd in screaming blood-curdling epithets. Glen turned and embraced her, tilting her head and kissing her lightly on the lips and she felt the fervor drain from her. She put her arms around his neck and returned his kiss as her passion intensified.

When he broke the embrace, she felt angry and empty. Couples were staring at them, some shouting, angrily. At first, she thought to shout back but one man made an obscene gesture and threatened her with his scythe so she backed into Glen's arms for protection. He hugged her close and defiantly kissed her again, making the couples even angrier. Immersed in his kiss, his tongue played on hers, soothing her. He put his lips to her ear and whispered over the din.

"Let's go." The rhythmic foot stomping of the crowd got louder and her body shook. They joined in the stomping before leaving their table.

With a wave of the Reverend's hand, the noise ceased and he continued. "The poor have failed and they serve no purpose in our future. To allow them more is to reward waste and that, we can never allow. Eradicate them before it's too late."

"Yes!" the crowd roared. She reached for Glen's hand and held it to her lips for reassurance. He took her hand and they moved toward the exit.

"What will we do?" Cavanaugh roared. From the audience, depraved voices screamed. "Waste the *Wasters*!"

"Gut the filthy bastards!"

"Fuck Islam!"

"Maim the cretin Jew lovers, kill them, kill them, kill . . ."

People kicked their seats until they broke and then they used their weapons to pummel anything in sight, the girders, trash cans, even the concrete floors. A deafening cacophony of hate choked the arena. Inside the glass, couples smashed their plates and wine glasses against the glass walls while those outside hurled their bodies against the glass as if the people inside were the enemy.

She and Glen huddled together and joined the rant, shouting, "kill them, kill then, kill them, and kill them all . . ."

They quickly left their seats and went outside the glass box. She yelled to him, "Is it safe?" He just grabbed her hand and quickened his pace, dragging her along until they reached the gate where one of the security guards offered her a bat with screws protruding from it. Another offered her a machete decorated with a painted island scene.

"No, thank you," she said politely showing the guard the chain she carried as if to explain her decision. The guards allowed her to pass.

"Hurry," Glen yelled, taking her hand as they ran from the amphitheater gates and out into the vast parking lot. In full battle armor, armed men stood in battle formation facing the approaching crowd. She hesitated but Glen pulled her forward and they ran through the ranks of the police without incident and headed into the empty street where he took her chain and tossed it into a dumpster, along with his nightstick.

"Can the police stop this?"

"Detroit can't afford police. What you see here is a private army that's here to provide plausible deniability. The mayor will say his forces couldn't handle it and he will be right."

"What do we do?"

"We run."

Crowds from another exit cut them off and briefly they were driven along with the fury of the mob. She lost her hold on Glen's hand and started to panic as the crowd relentlessly pushed her forward, their blood curdling screams scaring her even more now that Glen was gone. Everyone was moving so fast that it was all she could do to stay on her feet and keep from getting trampled.

At the first intersection, a group in front of her discovered a very old man in a tight-fitting fedora hiding ineffectively with an old woman behind some trashcans. As the couple frantically searched for a way out, the crowd surrounded them. Unable to move in the crowd, Stacey watched, horrified as the old couple wet themselves in fear before the crowd made fast work of them, their screams brief and ineffective as pipes and whips pummeled them into a pulp before a knife ended their lives. There was blood everywhere and all Stacey wanted was to faint away.

She started to swoon, but Glen caught her in time and dragged her away from the crowd. "I have an apartment nearby; you will be safe there until this is over."

She looked over her shoulder. There was mayhem everywhere and to avoid it, Glen pulled her along the buildings until they were standing at a glass door to a large apartment building. Two men approached, menacing them with *shafras*, small curved blades that they held at the ready. Glen threw his nightstick at them and when they ducked, he leaned into the door and pulled her inside. The door locked automatically and the frustrated men briefly beat on the door but then quickly searched for easier victims.

It was calm and quiet inside, but feeling decidedly unsafe, Stacey stared mesmerized at the mob as it went by. Some stared angrily through the glass at them as if they were the enemy; others threw things at the glass. Glen pulled her away and they raced up the steps to the top floor where he unlocked the security door and then an apartment door and they entered. He closed and locked the door and they were alone. In the surreal quiet, she sank, listless, onto a couch and sobbed at what she'd witnessed. She was grateful for his embrace and began to finally calm. Then she noticed how beautifully appointed his furnished apartment was and she smiled. The extravagance somehow made her feel safer. When he was sure she had calmed enough, he pointed to the balcony and reluctantly she nodded and allowed him to guide her outside. She was scared to look down at first, for below, spread out for blocks; the angry crowd was surging through the streets leaving behind the dead and dying poor in pools of blood.

The crowd was being urged on by various preachers dressed in the emerald and gold of Cavanaugh's church. The incensed masses chased behind them, catching and slaughtering every poor local they could find as Stacey watched from above in horror. She covered her ears to drown out the screams and futile pleas of the victims and she tried closing her eyes to the terror but it played relentlessly in her mind and she felt physically sick. Glen's hold on her provided the only comfort and though frightened and revolted, she gamely kept her eyes open and stared as, without a means of defense, the poor suffered their fated righteous fate. *Was this,* she thought, *like Angel Falls, truly God's work?* Certainly it was a visceral reminder of the massacre at Angel Falls. No matter how fast or far she ran or how far she fled, she would never outdistance the wails of the wounded and dying. She couldn't take it any longer and put her head on his chest and sobbed.

Glen led her to a lounge chair where they sat together and watched as a priest, not Cavanaugh, raised his staff to urge the attackers on. The battle was further away now, and the maimed poor, unable to escape, mounted a feeble defense. Those able to crawl or stagger inflicted what harm they could but Cavanaugh's army relentlessly purged on. Some of the incapacitated poor, the wounded and maimed, exacted what little revenge their mutilated bodies could mete out, biting, tearing, and kicking their assailants.

The air smelled of death.

At the far end of the street, some of the poor fled into a warehouse, securing the doors just as Cavanaugh's army arrived. It was a standoff until smoke and then flames billowed up from the warehouse roof. As the warehouse burned, the mob outside cheered while inside there were hideous screams. Once again, Stacey tried to look away but Glen insisted that she watch. Just then, the warehouse doors opened and the poor streamed out—but now they were armed with rifles and pistols. They fired on their attackers killing those in the lead, finally slowing the advancing army and causing them to turn and flee in the face of a now armed adversary. From a distance, the priests rallied the crowd forward as the now-fortified poor exacted their revenge. The rioters wavered, and then broke and fled back toward the amphitheater, back below the balcony where Stacey cuddled with Glen. One gallant man led the poor. He was handing out weapons, directing the counter attack, and killing anyone near him.

"Who is he, Glen?" Stacey asked, marveling at the man's heroics.

"He is a true hero of the revolution. His name is Rachman Turner and I found the poor fellow on the streets of Philadelphia when I was searching for an army to fight against these capitalist, religious zealots. Allah be praised, Rocky was a good one. He had no fear and we needed more like him. He was my faithful servant and I miss him."

As it always does, the tide of battle suddenly turned. In the distance, near the amphitheater, Stacey heard a loud hum and she pointed toward it. From inside the arena, armored helicopters rose, and through the gates, armored vehicles burst forth lead by Reverend Cavanaugh himself, in his religious garb and wearing a battle helmet with his Almighty Dollar emblazoned on it. He stood atop an armored personnel carrier protected within a nano-glass bubble and he was holding aloft his symbol, the Almighty Dollar, on a great golden staff for all to see. As rockets, bullets, and flames ripped into the poor, the Deacon Deliverer directed the assault and backed now by armored support, the righteous renewed their attack until *Waster* and righteous alike lay dying on the Detroit streets, but, as God surely intended, only the righteous lived to tell their story.

The sounds of battle slowly faded until all that remained were the unrequited pleas for mercy and Stacey stared down at the carnage in disbelief. She hadn't seen the end of Angel Falls and prayed without belief that this was not how it ended there. Burned and mutilated corpses were everywhere. The wails of the survivors mounted, turning into a ghoulish symphony of heart-rending proportion.

"I don't understand." She asked. "He told them they could live forever." Once again, she buried her head on Glen's chest and sobbed. He kissed her forehead and hugged her close. She cried herself to exhaustion yet still couldn't block out the scenes of death, so she moved away and vomited until tears blinded her. He lifted her gently and carried her inside where the coolness and the aroma of fresh cut flowers helped to soothe her. Sitting on his lap, she cuddled desperate for any comfort his embrace might offer and he stroked her hair and kissed her until slowly she stopped trembling. With a cool, silk handkerchief, he smiled and wiped her eyes and she smiled back, shyly. Then, he carried her into his bedroom, offered her a large bath towel and pointed to the bathroom. She bathed in a large hot tub, relaxing in a scented mist, while sobbing quietly from time to time, but by the end of her bath, she had calmed. Wearing his pajamas, she crawled into bed and fell asleep to the sound of him showering.

In the morning, she awoke to the strong smell of coffee. Glen was spooned against her, asleep. Depressed by the events of the previous evening, she lay quietly trying not to stir until the warmth of his breathing against her neck began to excite her. She smiled but stopped, haunted by the memories of the previous evening. When he stirred, finally, desperate for his attention and any way to forget that horrible experience, she allowed his hands to slowly work their way under her pajama top and he gently rubbed her stomach. She turned to him and they kissed. His hands found buttons and entry and he massaged her breasts. His mouth replaced his hands and need drove her to hold him close.

His tender and loving touch helped her forget and staring into his reddish eyes, they made love. He came first and then took his time pleasuring her until she too was sated. He continued to embrace her long after her trembling stopped. Wrapped in his loving arms, she stared at the slow moving clouds floating outside the open window and smiled. Her eyes half-closed, she luxuriated in this most perfect morning. She closed her eyes and sighed but a moan soon followed as his hands began to wander once again.

She awoke feeling wonder and satisfaction. She stretched and then rubbed her body as her mind recalibrated. Fearfully, she opened one eye expecting his apartment. One eye might have been wrong so she opened both for confirmation. She was in her own bed, safely nestled in Omar's compound. But last night was real, it had to be. And the early morning love making after a good night's sleep, how could that not be real? But her eyes, unlike her dreams, wouldn't lie.

She dove under a pillow and screamed until her throat was raw. In her palace with her prince, everything wrong felt so horribly right while right so hauntingly wrong. With all her might she forced herself to consider where that happy-go-lucky tomboy from Angel Falls had gone, but her mind resisted the insanity of it and refused to cooperate. She felt wicked and used. What was to become of her?

Chapter 9
Canada—2071

Advertising—A form of communication aimed at influencing the attitude of a community toward some cause or position. It is the most intense form of proselytizing with the ability to acquire and keep consumers for any brand. A perfect market, not to be confused with a free market, requires perfect information for both the buyer and seller. The avoidance of perfect information makes advertising in a competitive free market both necessary and proper and though it is subject to deceit, advertising is always the difference between a deal and failure and death.

In our super competitive economy, accurate, effective information is essential to corporations in order for them to produce the most effective, profitable products and services. This knowledge is essential to attracting consumers, as well. Where a product or service has benefits, these benefits must be properly played out and where they do not have benefits, well-crafted lies are necessary and proper. When effective lies are aimed at interested communities with the sole purpose of selling products or services for profit, changing beliefs, preferences, and actions, oftentimes without the awareness of the target audience and often toward some cause or position the target audience may not agree with or might not want to support or would never consider otherwise without advertising, this is effective marketing and truly God's work.

Effectively packaged for resale as information, advertising, in its most basic sense, entices its audience with fantasy. To the discerning, carefully concocted advertising selectively presents facts and manufactured realities in order to move the consumer closer to the seller's chosen goal. Advertising uses message to produce an emotional rather than a rational response with the desired result, attitude change, the more complete, the more productive the advertising, the more it furthers some targeted product, service, or agenda.

To the less discerning, advertising must be entertaining where satisfaction coerces the consumer's impulse. If a product or service clearly cannot be peddled on its own merit, advertising must adapt aggressively, or the product or service must retreat from that market space.

Without concern for truth, a commercial outcome must produce a proper return or go begging. For the seller/advertiser, to acquire the wealth necessary to live forever, deluding the public for commercial gain is both necessary and proper. It is God's will. Caveat Emptor!—**Archive**

The first real warmth of spring fought through the defenses of the Canadian winter and the change was exciting. Distance and time had worked their magic. The morning after her last *Virtuoso* adventure, Stacey reconsidered her situation and her feelings for Omar. She had good reason. That morning, he had left without seeing her or even saying goodbye. At first she had been relieved, but as time passed, she had worried that something in her behavior had caused him to go. When he didn't return soon enough, worry became anxiety and she convinced herself she'd acted badly to a good man who had saved her life and treated her like a fairy tale princess. As more time passed, she became more fearful that he would send her away so she promised herself that when he returned, she would be different. She would be better.

When an aide announced at dinner that Omar would finally return late that night, Stacey was excited. She went to bed but was too excited to sleep so she rose at dawn. Dressed in an outfit he favored, she scurried down to the dining hall to meet him. As usual, the servants had started a fire in the pit, but today, due to the warmth of the season, the fire was more for aesthetics. She waited nervously for him, but hunger finally overtook her and she was eating when he finally appeared.

"You're late, sleepy head," she ran to him and embraced him. He seemed startled and leaned away, managing to kiss her forehead while softly stroking her hair. She tried to kiss him on the lips, but he pulled back.

"I missed you, Princess," he said, simply.

"I missed you, too. How was your trip?"

"I received some intriguing news from Cleveland. Things are falling into place."

She was puzzled. "What things?"

"Just things. How have you been?"

"I really, really missed you," she said shyly, hoping he wouldn't be angry.

"I missed you, too," he said, adding, "I didn't realize how much until now."

She beamed.

"Some facts have come to light and there is something more we must explore in Virtual . . . that is if you want to."

Was this a test? She tried not to look concerned or disappointed, but he sensed her reluctance.

"Stacey, dearest, I understand your concern, but there is no cause. I promise you, this is merely another history lesson. You'll find it . . . fascinating."

She nodded, gamely. She loved him and the sooner she showed him that she would do anything for him, the more certain she would be that he loved her too, regardless of how he chose to demonstrate it. What she remembered of that night, she was certain of. They had consummated their love, hadn't they? So what if he preferred to express it virtually, she could accept that, for now. She tried to sound eager.

"For you, Omar, I will do anything. When do we start?"

"My, aren't you enthusiastic," he said. "Not so fast. We never discussed your last trip in *Virtuoso*. Not sure if he was speaking of their love-making, she didn't respond, hoping he'd offer a clue. "About the Reverend . . ." he added.

"The Reverend yes, he was okay, I guess, I mean some of what I remember was horrible, the rioting, but afterward with you was nice. If you want to . . ."

Omar blushed. "Ah, so you do remember?"

Had she said something wrong? "I'm being silly, Omar. You're always so serious. I thought I would joke."

He seemed less pleased by that. "I am an adult with serious responsibilities. May we discuss Cavanaugh?

She had made him angry. "Of course, Omar. He, Cavanaugh, was really mean for a religious person. The Rabbi wasn't religious really, but he was kind. And the murder in the streets and the working conditions, that was horrible. Did that stuff really happen?" When he began to explain, she relaxed, knowing she had responded adequately.

"Yes, they happened and a great many of the scenarios like the one with Dr. Cavanaugh were made available as early *Virtuoso* gaming experiences so people could train to hate without the physical commitment. By the mid-twenty twenties, both middle and low income workers were equally fearful of underemployment and unemployment because their families starved and died either way. It was particularly infuriating because so many others lived so well and refused to offer even subsistence wages. Some of the poor fought. They were angry and frightened and their government did nothing but talk about solving economic problems, while continuing to pass legislation that favored the wealthy. A great many did nothing but remain stoic until they were murdered.

"The few times that liberal politicians tried to expand entitlements or to seed neighborhoods with funds so more jobs could be created where they were most needed, conservative politicians, Libertarians and Republicans, funded by business interests and supported by media-savvy fellow travelers, they rallied to prevent it on capitalist—certainly not humanitarian—grounds. To the wealthy, the poor were always lazy and good for nothing, so nothing done for them could ever provide enough economic payback to justify it on economic grounds; and economic grounds are the sole determinant for conservatives. Humanitarian efforts were needed, but for conservatives, charity meant private citizens responding through tax exempt churches, certainly charity wasn't for politicians and the government to offer. So the poor and middle class became the object of fear and derision by the mostly Christian capitalists who didn't want their money going to help others. But any good capitalist will jump at a money making opportunity, and Cavanaugh was no exception. He developed his religious franchise and it soon attracted others. His brand of vitriol launched a crusade that demanded death to economic non-contributors and panic spread throughout the country propagating riots everywhere. People who thought of themselves as good people, good Americans, even good Christians, were afraid also and most were easily convinced of the rightness of Cavanaugh's jihad. They allowed the poor to be enslaved, and then slowly, the worst of them hunted down and finally eradicated the poor with the assistance of private businesses that were subsidized by the government."

"Why didn't the government stop it?"

"Think, Princess, think. Like it or not, everything that requires money is owned by someone. The government requires money and the rich in business were tired of wasting money on the poor so the rich funded and the government subcontracted for the assault on Angel Falls just like it subcontracted for the elimination of *Wasters* like what you saw in Detroit.

"When you own power, violence is more efficacious than negotiations. For Capitalism to prosper it needs adversaries and with our power in the world declining, it was getting easier and easier to find adversaries. Still, leaders are bullies and they needed foes that couldn't fight back, the poor. Once I saw the form of American pain that Cavanaugh's rioters were inflicting on the poor, I took to the streets to organize the victims and supply them with weapons. We were gaining strength and would have stopped the insanity but for Crelli, who was omniscient, and HomeSec who was invincible."

"That must have been dangerous."

Omar shrugged. "That is of no matter. Danger must never prevent you from doing what is right. When they linked me to the attempted assassination of Crelli, I realized I would have to leave the country that I love. I used my wealth and business connections to avoid prosecution, and I escaped into exile before Crelli bludgeoned our beloved Constitution into submission."

"I hate our government, Omar."

"That is a very good start. I tried but I failed to stop him. I tried to expose him for the murderer he is, but he had better technology. The other reason that I failed was because Americans are selfish and wealthy Americans are the most selfish. They actually wanted what Crelli believed more than the equality that I fought for and so I failed. I lost.

"But there was one who seemed to have an advantage over Crelli. His name was Berne Thau. Berne was an old man when I met him but he came from nowhere to talk truth to power. I don't know how he did the good things he did and how he managed to avoid capture, but he was an inspiration."

The name Berne Thau sounded oddly familiar and Omar noticed her reaction.

"Did you know Mr. Thau?"

She shook her head.

"Think on it. He was old, not quite my height, pudgy, and with blue eyes." Omar was probing again, but she couldn't allow him to see that she was troubled.

"His name is familiar, Omar, but I can't place it," she answered truthfully.

His eyes narrowed, forming creases at the bridge of his nose and across his forehead. "You've only lived in Angel Falls. How would you know that name?"

"I don't know." She didn't want to make him angry. "I'm thinking."

"Then think out loud."

"It must have been something Rabbi said." She pictured the old man's cabin, him in bed and Gil sitting on a chair beside the bed.

"And . . . ?"

"The Rabbi talked about stuff that happened in the past, just like you do."

"According to the records, Angel Falls was a Quaker community. It didn't have Jews. What was a rabbi doing there?"

She knew that voice. She was in trouble. "I don't know."

"No Jews, no need for a rabbi."

"I didn't know you needed Jewish people to have a rabbi? What are they like? I don't think we had any. The Rabbi helped us and that's all I know about him."

"Your community had a rabbi, yet no temple, and this rabbi helped, even though everyone was a Quaker?"

She nodded.

"Did your rabbi travel much?"

"He was very old and I don't think he ever left town. He had visitors, deliveries, mail, you know, stuff like that. Rabbi wasn't from home. He settled there."

"Did he have a wife and family?"

The direction of this discussion was troubling. "No, I believe his wife died, but Mark Rose was his son, he was there sometimes."

Omar reached across the table, grasped and opened her tightly clenched fist. "Of course he was." Excitedly, his fingers traced each of her fingers down to her wrist and back. It tickled.

"Forgive me, my sweet, I've been rude. Have I mentioned how much I missed you when I was gone?" His face was so close that she could feel his warm breath. "Tell me about your rabbi."

"The Rabbi's name was Bernie Rosenthal and he was very old, of course. I don't know much more about him."

He pulled back and stared at her. "Yes, it makes sense. Rose's father was a rebel!" he was almost shouting. "Why wasn't his name on the list, and why haven't you told me this before?" Stunned by his intensity, she looked down; her chin trembling as it almost touched her chest and she felt like crying. "I'm sorry, Omar, I . . . I just didn't think. I should have . . ."

"If Rosenthal isn't on their list, then he's still alive."

Caught in a lie that she was desperate to extricate herself from, she replied meekly, "No, Rabbi died. He was the one we were having a funeral service for when we were attacked." She felt like crying as she anticipated Omar's retribution.

She mistook his excitement for anger and her tears flowed. He moved to her and she pulled back defensively. His hand sought her chin and she was helpless as he tilted her head to wipe away the tears with his handkerchief. He stared into her eyes and she felt powerless to resist. And then he kissed her, ever so softly on her lips. Fearful he would somehow disappear if she didn't try harder to keep him, she opened her mouth but as soon as she did, he broke off the kiss.

Embarrassed and afraid of what he was about to say, she apologized but he held his hand up to stop her.

"Stacey, my beautiful, beautiful princess, the precious love of my life, this is wonderful, a breakthrough. I'm sorry that I've been insensitive and have pushed you so hard, but discovering the riddle of Angel Falls is absolutely critical to our success. I was too caught up in the details. I see it now. It was foolish of me not to be more sensitive. I'm sorry. Will you forgive me?"

He leaned in cautiously, and kissed her again, his hands resting on her shoulders and this time he sustained the kiss and allowed her some latitude, but as soon as the kiss ended, he asked her about the Rabbi. Relieved and pleased that he wasn't angry, she told him what little she knew about him and Mark.

"Did Mark Rose live there or did he arrive before the attack?"

"That's an odd question. I don't remember. Let me think. He arrived the day before. Why?"

"Continue and tell me everything. You mustn't lie."

Once again, she felt like crying. Her deceit was ruining her only chance at a wonderful salvation. "Oh, Omar, I'm sorry that I lied. When we first met, I was confused and scared. I didn't know you like I do now. I didn't . . . I didn't trust you or anyone. I'm sorry. Please forgive me. I trust you now and I promise I won't lie anymore."

"That is not a good thing to hear at the start of a loving relationship but no matter." He waved his hand dismissively. "You're forgiven. It's understandable. We all learn to trust in our own time. Today is a momentous day." He pulled her close and kissed her on her forehead. She grabbed him around the waist and held on tight.

"Now, tell me about Rosenthal."

"I don't know, truly. He helped the town so much, that's all. He was very old and he died the night before the attack. You know the rest."

"Yes, yes, you were very brave saving the life of Mark Rose, a man who didn't deserve saving. Do you think it was a coincidence that Rose was there before the attack?

"Mr. Rose is a nice old man. He and the Rabbi have more reason to hate the government than anyone."

"Why is that, Princess?"

"They murdered the Rabbi's wife and daughter, Mr. Rose's mother and sister."

Omar nodded. "Unimportant. Did Rosenthal ever mention Berne Thau?"

"Maybe, I don't remember. It is similar to his name but I don't remember."

Omar's face took on that distant look she found so unsettling. Soon he refocused. "Well, that's interesting. Official records claim Rose's father was killed in that other HomeSec attack on a domestic rebel headquarters, the one in Indianapolis in the early thirties. The only reason I've ever found official records to be incorrect is when the truth is somehow unproductive to someone important.

"What you've told me will help a great deal. I knew about Mark Rose, but his father in Angel Falls is most intriguing. I'll have to think on it. His presence might have been why Brandt needed to destroy the town but if Rose visited there before, why wasn't Angel Falls attacked sooner? I must know more. Was there anything special that day?"

She made a show of concentrating. "No, I don't think so."

"Do you remember anything Rosenthal said before he died?"

She tried to look like she was recalling something. "I took care of him sometimes but we rarely talked and I don't remember much of what he said."

"Try harder. This is critical, Stacey."

She had nothing.

"There must be something. I can't protect you unless I know everything. Was this 'Meat' friend of yours involved in some way?"

She laughed. "Meat, no, he was scared of Rabbi. I remember once, Gil-"

She stopped.

Omar's eyes widened with interest, and frightened by that and appalled by what she had just let slip, she shrank back into her chair. What had she done?

"Gil?" he replied back to her. She was surprised and saddened by the fear she felt when he spoke Gil's name after so long. Omar opened his arms and she crawled submissively into them, crushing her face against his chest, wrapping her arms around his shoulders, hoping for forgiveness.

With her head buried in his chest and her tears wetting his shirt, she pictured being sent out into the night to face armed rangers waiting to take her to that horrid scar-faced general who had tried to hurt her at the Toronto train station. "Don't send me away, please," she wailed. Omar was silent. She sobbed as she babbled her concerns, but she couldn't make herself understood. He rubbed her back and then made her repeat it.

"I'm so . . . so stupid, Omar. Please, I beg you, forgive me. I love you. I do. It won't happen again, I promise. I'll never lie to you, ever, ever." He remained silent. "Gil, he was just a boy, nothing for you to worry about. I had a silly crush on him, but nothing happened. Absolutely nothing, nothing, I promise. That's the honest-to-God truth. Don't be mad at me. I liked him, sure, but we were young, too young and I, I . . . I'm not saying I would . . . we were friends, no more." She felt sick to her stomach.

"It is okay."

But she was frantic. "No, please, don't be mad. I missed you so much and I love you, I really do. I've been so stupid. Ask me. Go ahead; ask me anything, anything at all. I told you about the Rabbi and now . . ." she lowered her voice, "about Gil. I'll tell you everything but it isn't much, I promise. And I'll never lie again." Her head dropped and she pouted. "I'm so bad at it, anyway."

He smiled and placed a finger to her lips, quieting her.

"My, what a gusher we have here," he said soothingly. "I'm not mad. I could never be mad at you. Sometimes we lock something up so tight inside our hearts that it begs for release and if we ignore its plea to tell the right person, it explodes out on its own. But that is good because if you stifle it and it stays inside, it changes you in bad ways you'll never know until it's too late and you will hate yourself for it. You believed you were doing the right thing. That's commendable. There is honor in that and we need honor in our revolution. No one's hurt. I'm not some young boy easily offended. These things happen. Tell me now. Tell me all of it."

She had been foolish, even childish to trifle with his affections. If he pointed her toward the door and sent her away, she truly had no where else to go. But he didn't do that. He was nice; he was always nice to her. But she still feared that she'd ruined everything and couldn't stop trembling. His compassion made her feel both better and worse. She reached up to him, hoping. He kissed the back of her hands and she grabbed his hands and mirrored his kiss. He turned her palms up and kissed them again, tickling her with his tongue. She laughed her tears away.

"We've been through much, you and I," he said quietly, tenderly. "This will be our new beginning. Tell me of Gil."

She was beyond the point of withholding and didn't. She tried to be honest, but it was difficult to describe what she didn't understand herself.

"We were like best friends. It wasn't romantic. We didn't do anything you would be angry or jealous about. We hiked and swam together. We did all kinds of things because the town was boring and we wanted to get away." It felt so wrong to say that after what had happened there. When she mentioned the *SurveilEagle*, Omar probed.

"Why would a surveillance craft operate so deep into the unincorporated land of northern Maine? Stacey, honey, who is Gil?"

It was the question she hoped wouldn't be asked but she responded truthfully. "He is Mr. Rose's grandson and Rabbi's great-grandson."

For a man who never betrayed his emotions, Omar registered shock and she feared that look most of all. To absolve herself, she would have willingly embellished the story if she had known what he wanted, but after his initial astonishment, he just sat there, his brow furrowed, thinking, but without that distant look that so annoyed her. While she waited, she tried to think of something, anything to say that would please him. Before she could, his eyes took on that far away look. After a few moments, his eyes refocused. He rubbed his temples and smiled.

When he finally spoke, she felt he wasn't speaking to her.

"So the child lived. It makes sense now. Odd that it was kept secret. I wonder from whom?" He paused again. "Records show that the girlfriend of Mark Rose's son had an illegitimate boy while Rose was president. The boy, Gil, his death was officially recorded, but you say he's alive. That's distressing because it's the second aberration in Archive today. Inconsistencies are quite rare and since both concern the Rose family, this needs special attention. Do you know who this Gil is?"

Confused, she shrugged. "He's Gil," she said simply.

"And you know nothing about Berne Thau in Angel Falls?"

"No." She was worried that she was in more trouble now, somehow.

"You did well. I'm grateful." He rewarded her with an embrace and a kiss. She was so relieved she squealed in delight. When he reasserted his desire that she visit *Virtuoso*, she agreed willingly.

"You're right, Omar, I have so much work to do to be of help to the revolution."

"I am glad to see the change in you. Tomorrow, we will do this tomorrow. It will be an important lesson and when you're done, you will be ready." She stood and leaned against him. He hugged her close, massaging her neck.

"Omar, my love, when you left, I thought you were going to return and send me away. I wouldn't have blamed you and I should have trusted you. I'm so sorry."

"I will never allow you to leave my side. Not now or ever." He ran his fingers through her hair long, silken hair and then he sniffed it. Giddy, she giggled.

On her way back to her room, she remembered Rabbi once telling Gil how people needed to be necessary to someone with power in order to survive. She was heeding Rabbi's advice and though she had nothing to offer Omar other than her love and devotion, she would offer that and become irreplaceable in his eyes. She could only hope it was enough. No, she would make it enough. Still, she was fortunate, today could have been another horrible experience, maybe her worst. She shuddered to think that.

The next morning, he came for her and like lovers; they walked to the *Virtuoso* chambers hand in hand. Before she entered, Omar turned her to face him.

"I first heard of him from the street people I was forming into my rebel army. Berne Thau was a legend among them before he became a business partner of mine. Then, suddenly, he disappeared, but before he left, Berne told me about the coming Messiah. It wasn't what I wanted to hear, Berne wasn't a religious man but he was quite insistent about it. He said that the troubles of the poor would get worse and worse until a leader, he specifically used the word messiah, a leader would arise to overcome the wicked and remove the yoke from the oppressed. I never thought of Berne as a fanatic but he said this messiah would be good and kind, and lead America to a better place. At first, I was certain he was talking about me but when he insisted that the child hadn't been born as yet, I was more than skeptical, as you can imagine."

"I don't understand, Omar, who is the messiah."

"Apparently it is this Gil Rose."

She was speechless.

"Tanya Brandt has identified him as this messiah. He is why Angel Falls is gone. And failing to destroy him, I suspect she is sparing no resources to capture him, turn him, and then use him to her advantage. You have seen what she is capable of and she will do all that she can to find him. And once she has him, she will launch her propaganda arm to convince *Wasters* to unite behind her messiah and that will be the undoing of my glorious revolution. Your friend, in Tanya's clutches, will cause the deaths of so many more innocents, just like at Angel Falls. The Chairwoman is devious, mean and relentless and she will use him to eliminate all resistance. If Gil Rose is still alive, I must find him before she does, or my revolution, the people's last hope, it will fail. Omar stared at her intently. "Is he still alive?"

It was the one question she had asked herself ever since the attack. At first, she only shrugged. Then she explained what she saw, the attack, the great explosion and the certainty of Meat's death in close proximity to Gil.

"Brandt wants you for a reason so he must still be alive. I can make the world a better place, but this messiah, this Gil Rose; he is the one thing I can't account for. For us to win, for you to be completely and totally safe, and for us to make a happy life together, we must do everything in our power to be certain that your friend doesn't fall into Chairwoman Brandt's wicked hands."

She heard the words, 'a life together,' and she liked the sound of it. But Gil as the messiah, she thought it preposterous.

"Do you believe he's alive, Omar?" she asked hopefully.

"Berne Thau, who was your Rabbi Rosenthal, he is dead and they have Mark Rose. Rose's son is nothing, but I'm having him watched, just in case. Now I understand why you are important to them. They know that you two are friends and they believe you know how to find him."

It made no sense. "How could they know that?"

"Mark Rose, of course. They know everything because of him. You must help me to find this false messiah before Brandt has him."

"But I don't know where he is or if he is even still alive?" At least now she had reason to hope. "What will you do with him when you find him?"

"I will help him, of course, and keep him safe from Brandt. Because she wants him so desperately, he will be useful to my cause and if I have him then I am certain Brandt does not. Your friend and I, we will free America from that accursed woman."

She smiled at that.

"I need you to help so that together, we will save the world and avenge what they did to the people of Angel Falls."

Today was an unexpected godsend. He needed her and that made all the difference. "But there was a terrible explosion and . . . and he was . . . gone."

"His name isn't on my list. That is everything! Your friend stands on the fulcrum of our victory or the cruelty of Tanya Brandt and more massacres like Angel Falls."

It hurt to think of Gil, alive and in harm's way, but it hurt worse to think of him dead. She stared at Omar; her protector, her mature and handsome lover. She couldn't deny him. "Omar, I love you. I'll do whatever you ask."

He grinned, happily. "And we must marry."

At first it didn't register and she became confused. Then, she screamed with joy.

He dropped to his knee. "Marry me," he repeated. "I love you, Stacey Grant; I love you more than life. I beg you, please marry me. My life will be nothing without you at my side as my consort." He took a small box from his pocket and presented her with a diamond ring that was so large that when he slid it on her finger, she couldn't bend it.

The fear of losing him and being sent out to face Brandt's minions evaporated and a hopeful life sprung into view. For the first time in her life, she was where she needed to be and she was truly elated. Omar Smith wanted to be hers ever after. Her face glowed and tears flowed glistening her happiest smile.

"Tell me, my beautiful Princess, will you honor me and become my bride?"

She hugged him fiercely, releasing all the energy she had been unable to express in words in these anxious months. Her lips sought his and they kissed passionately. She tried to coax him into a small degree of intimacy, real intimacy in this real world, but he resisted her advance ever so slightly and she accommodated him.

"Yes, yes, of course I'll marry you," she said. He held her in a tight embrace, resisting anything more physical than a peck.

"We will consummate our love when the time is right, when you're officially Mrs. Glen Smith."

Mrs. Glen Smith. A feeling of contentment swept over her as she warmed in the depth of his root beer eyes. She sighed, closed her own eyes, and hugged him as tightly as she could. She was to be a princess, evermore. She was safe, she was loved, and her future was assured. She took a deep breath, smiled, entered *Virtuoso*, and shed her clothes.

Chapter 10
Ohio—2070

The blinding light of a winter sun reflecting off the snow-covered highway, made Gil's eyes tear as he squinted into the emptiness at the horizon where Bree's truck had disappeared.

He reconsidered his options. He hadn't gone with her because he intended to go to Aeden to visit his father, Howard. Ever since Mark told him about his father's life, Gil felt the need to see him again. Now that he was so close, he had to go. He admired Bree's steadfast devotion to finding her own father and he felt guilty, too, for not searching out his. After her truck was out of sight, he reconsidered. Aeden would be too dangerous for him. He needed to disappear and allow time to pass, and so with one more look south toward home, he turned north, reluctantly walking in Bree's fresh tire tracks, following signs that directed him to the production town of Hamilton near Detroit.

When he walked up the first rise in the otherwise flat highway, he fantasized finding Bree waiting on the other side, and he smiling at her grand surprise. But there was only barren road ahead to the horizon, a reality check to keep what little hope he had safely caged. Life was tough enough without self-delusion, and its accompanying disappointment. He had made the right decision by separating from Bree, if only for her protection. The sharp pain in his throat and dull ache in his chest were his only travel companions as he tramped onward down the snow-covered, desolate highway.

If the terrain and occasional traffic permitted, he walked on the hardtop surface, but whenever something moved on, or near the highway, he scurried to find a hiding place. Sometimes he hid in nearby abandoned homes, other times he hid behind weather-beaten and broken advertising signs or even frozen brush and tumbleweeds, but he always stayed within view of the highway as he headed relentlessly north.

The unchanging road provided little diversion and memories of Profit were his only distraction where he dwelt on times when he and Bree had enjoyed each other's company and had needed each other. When his thoughts drifted to the time she'd been attacked on the road, he felt uneasy. He wouldn't be there for her now and that worried him. Finally, unable to free his mind to focus on anything but her, he screamed, but the returning echo proved empty company. Depressed and listless, he flopped by the side of the road and stared off into the distance. He wouldn't allow himself to cry, so he forced himself to think of something else.

First, he considered Laurence Hilliard, the strange, good man who had died so he and Bree could escape. It was beyond him how anyone with the opportunity to live forever could give that life away. He imagined what Bernie might say to explain it, but that also provided no solace. With no frame of reference for Hilly's selfless act, Gil became more depressed, so he explored other thoughts. His mind targeted his father, Howard, first, then he thought of Bernie, Joad, Mark, Bree, Profit, Doris, and even Rachman, but there was no relief for his sorrow from those memories so, once again, he screamed out his frustration into a cold, empty and uncaring world.

With comfort out of reach, his thoughts drifted to his other great failure, Annie. By now, he was a father or could be. The thought of Annie and their baby depressed him further. Poor Annie. Was it possible to be a father to a child he'd never know? He wanted to pray that Rachman would treat her and the baby well but without knowing a prayer, he merely watched his frozen breath dissipate in the wind and his thoughts drifted back to his youth, to Howard and his garden. Was that ever real?

Frustrated, he stood and continued his journey but as he walked, Gil's mood darkened with the day until the frigid night wind forced him to act. He huddled behind a sign, curling against the chill, hoping for sleep and blessed release, but there were no prayers to be answered easily this bleak night. When he finally fell asleep, his dreams were of Andrea and he woke to something screeching that was carried by the wind. Nothing moved but blowing snow, so he closed his eyes again and tried to concentrate on nothing but that wasn't possible.

He smiled at his thoughts of Bernie and their long trek from Aeden to Angel Falls. It was amazing that such an old guy had known so many people who could help in their journey. He pictured Bernie, bedridden now and teaching, desperately teaching things that Gil had fervently tried to avoid learning and a chill ran through him. As desperate as he was now, how much more desperate must Bernie have been, persevering long after his family had been murdered by the President of the United States? Poor Bernie, he had lived such a hard, sad life and when he died, he had nothing to show for his troubles but an inconsiderate teenager. Would Gil share Bernie's fate? He deserved to. Why had he refused Bernie? What had he been thinking?

He closed his eyes once again, listened to the few night sounds, and tried to think happy thoughts. He was hiking the rolling hills of the Presque Isle trail, laughing at the challenge, joyful at the freedom. He pictured green eyes and blond hair and she was laughing right along with him. His eyes shot open and he screamed and all around him it was suddenly silent.

Eventually, he drifted into a fitful, all too brief sleep, but the wind-driven snow burrowed into every crack and crevice and soon he woke again with enough discomfort to convince him to find true shelter. He backtracked to a building that he'd passed earlier, one that hadn't seemed inviting in the cold light of day and he forced his way inside through a broken segment of what was once a door, suspended precariously on a single bent and rusted hinge. Inside, the floor was filled with hay and farm debris, punctuated by fallen, rotted timbers. In the light of the moon, he grabbed a shard of wood that had broken from a large beam, and though choking from the pungent odor, even in this cold, he cautiously poked under the hay for critters. Nothing moved but still uncertain, he worked his way into the hay and fell into another fitful sleep.

He was atop a mountain on an island surrounded by islands with far higher peaks, peaks that dwarfed the one he was on and he was standing in a torrential downpour.

Then he was soaring above the island, surveying the land below when movement caught his eye. A child was running, hands flapping like a bird, toward a sheer rock formation that jutted out from clear, calm water and continued up the shoreline. He soared closer. A little girl was being chased by a pack of snarling, mewling, four-legged things and instinctively, he dove to protect her. A piercing, authoritative screech caused him to veer away and he landed facing a tall, thin, grinning woman with long dark hair. The child had vanished but the woman tilted her head and smiled.

"The thing about family members," she said matter-of-factly as if continuing a conversation, "is they can never truly understand each other in a lifetime together. It's a perspective thing and death seems to help." It seemed right to him so he nodded to the woman. Her smile began to stretch into a comical caricature of a grin and her lips slowly distorted forward into a beak as she grew into a menacing predator that towered over him, her beak open and threatening to consume him. He froze in panic, inhaling her moist, fetid breath. Her beak was so close and from her dark, cavernous gullet, a deafening shriek emanated and he screamed.

He woke shivering to the sun's early morning rays and another shriek. He jumped to his feet and looked around nervously. Above, on a burned out beam, feathers rippling, sat an owl. One final screech separated him from his dream and into the cold morning reality. He ducked under the door and ran from the building, through the piled snow to the highway. He ran until fatigue overcame his fear and then, he just walked, walked until, in the gathering twilight of another day he saw plumes rising in the distance. He was approaching the town of Hamilton. Maybe here his luck would change.

Exhausted and too afraid to sleep, he pressed on, walking trancelike through the dark. On the highway at the outskirts of the town, he was startled by a, distorted voice that came from his pocket.

"Can . . . hear me?"

He searched the skies, which were empty, before reaching for the glove that had been stashed in his back pocket.

"Joad, Joad, is that you? Can we talk?" he asked, excitedly.

"Secure. No danger . . . present."

Her voice should have been reassuring to him but it wasn't. "Is it you?" he asked knowing there was no good answer to that question.

"Gecko . . . broke . . . patched . . . More . . . careful.

"How do I know this is you?" he repeated.

" . . . say?"

"How do I know it's you?"

"Bernie . . . but Gecko could . . ."

"Unless you can prove you're not Gecko, I'm throwing this glove away." During the silence, he picked up his pace while searching the heavens for signs of the enemy.

There was more crackling static and words he couldn't process. When the static cleared, he heard the words he dreaded. "I'm sorry."

He stared at his glove. "I know." He squeezed the glove into his fist. "I'm done with you!" he shouted, but in an act that proved his weakness, he stuffed the glove into his back pocket. Hopelessly alone, he fought tears and trudged on blindly in the newly falling snow. With desperate determination, he leaned into the cold, biting, wind-driven snow and trudged slowly and with a dull ache in his heart toward Hamilton.

The snow got heavier so he concentrated on the road ahead, walking cautiously so as not to fall or lose his bearings. He was concentrating so intently that he jumped when a loud horn blasted from behind him and bright light like daylight extended his stark shadow far into the distance. Startled and scared, he jumped off the road and turned, putting his hands up to shield his eyes from the intense light. Based on the size of its lights, it was the largest truck he'd ever seen. It moved slowly closer, but when it stopped, he was too far below the cab to see its driver.

On the side of the truck was painted, *Red Wing Toller Services, Inc. Irvine Primeau, Owner.* A cab window opened and a smiling face appeared. The driver waved and Gil returned the wave. Then the driver yelled for him to get in so he climbed the long, metal ladder and entered the cab to a comforting blast of warm air and loud music.

He sat beside the driver who turned the music lower before offering his hand. "Looks like you could use a ride, bub. I'm Irvine Primeau of Hamilton Proper."

The cab was warm and drew the chill from his body. "Thanks, Mr. Primeau, I'm glad to meet you."

The man smiled. "I'm a pretty good guesser. I guess you're heading to Hamilton."

"Yes, sir. Are we close?"

"I have a few more runs and then I have to dump the snow into the recycler. If you can wait, you'll get there faster and we're far more comfortable than walking."

"Thanks, I appreciate the lift."

Irvine drove a bit further and then turned onto a road that needed plowing. He pressed a button on his joystick and the massive V-shaped plow dropped to the street with a thud. Fascinated, Gil stared through the windshield monitor as great mounds of snow funneled into the plow and were then transferred into a vast storage tank in the back of the truck.

"Because of the severe water shortage, the mayor extended the funding for my truck. Once we get to Hamilton, I'll pump the melted snow into storage tanks and receive credit for the delivery, less a fuel and a maintenance surcharge, of course, and then I'll go back out and do it again. By morning, me and the misses will be able to afford groceries; hopefully until the next snow. With the cost of water rising, this here truck's going to pay for itself ten times over."

Gil felt the water sloshing in the huge tank in back as they drove. "Do you live in Hamilton?"

"Nope. Can't make ends meet there so me and the missus live in a *Toller* annex community outside town where it's less pricey and there are fewer rules. In the heart of winter, we earn our keep with snow removal. The rest of the time it's hauling, road maintenance, and collecting tolls from travelers. 'Cause of the weather, I'll wave the traveler charges, but don't forget this kindness once you're settled."

"Thanks, I won't."

"Say, I'd ask you where you're from, but generally speaking, people out in weather like this don't offer a name or won't say much you can believe."

Gil shrugged. "Sorry. I'm from back east. I'm traveling to Hamilton to see someone a friend of mine said can help me."

"Who? Maybe I know him."

"Dan Burghe?"

The man laughed and slapped the seat. "Good old Dan Burghe? Hearty ho. Carny Dan? He's the founder and mayor of this fine town and a great person to know. Tell you what, forget the toll charge entirely just don't forget my name when you meet Carny Dan."

The driver's description of the mayor sounded like that of Mayor Doris in Profit and he wasn't sure if he should worry. "I don't know the mayor. I know someone who knows him, that's all."

"It's close enough in my book. From what I hear, you'll like Carny Dan. He's a great guy and Hamilton's America's most productive city because of him."

"It sounds like he'll be too busy to see me."

"Can't say, never actually met the man. I find the best way to see anybody is to have something they want. If you don't, network until you do. This is his town and I'm sure he'll help once you have what he wants. Like everyone, he's about getting richer. It was his team that evaluated my profit plan. Next year, production ramps up on some new trucks and we'll sell these beauties into Canada and other North American Production towns. My piece of the action is to train *Tollers* how to use them. Things are looking up for me and the missus so if you should get to know Carny Dan, tell him I said thanks. He's a miracle worker when it comes to turning stuff into profit. The very first thing you'll need is a job. Like all of them, this is a cash and carry town but people don't come here much in the winter and they're always looking for good workers."

"That's great to hear."

Irvine steered the truck down a ramp and onto a long wide street near the river. "With the size of this baby, the regulations say I'm to stay on major roads and I'm forbidden from entering the city street complex so I'll drop you here; it's a short walk to city hall. You should be able to schedule an appointment with the mayor there."

"Thanks, I appreciate this, Mr. Primeau. Do you know a place where I can stay?"

"It's best to apply for work first. Do it in the city hall basement, its open all the time. You'll complete some forms and they'll get your PID updated. It's late so my guess is they'll get you a temporary residence, but you'll be charged for it, including interest." The truck stopped with a groan from the load pneumatics and the driver pointed. "Down that road and left at the river, can't go right or you'll fall in and break your neck. City hall's lit up; can't miss it, even in a blizzard."

"Thanks, Mr. Primeau."

"Give my regards to Carny Dan."

The snow was letting up as Gil climbed down from the cab. He trudged through the snow until he reached the river but as he turned toward the lights that marked city hall, three men carrying rifles at the ready confronted him. He smiled and started to wave when one of them fired.

Chapter 11
Hamilton, MI.—2070

Gil awoke in a brightly lit room shivering uncontrollably. The room was so bright, and his head hurt so much that he had to shield his eyes and keep them tightly closed. He groped for anything that would provide warmth, eventually finding a thin blanket lying bunched at his feet. He wrapped himself in it, covering his head so his breath could help warm him and he lay there. From time to time he would open his eyes, cautiously using the blanket to block the light, but the pain was too severe. He caught glimpses of shiny steel bars before the tears and the pain forced him to close his eyes again. Cocooned under the blanket, he tried to focus on the fabric pattern until his eyes adjusted and the pain ceased. Finally, he opened the blanket just enough to stare out on so many rows of parallel bars that they formed *moiré* patterns that made him dizzy and he vomited on the shiny white tile floor.

He shut his eyes and returned to relative comfort under the blanket. Still trembling but now sweating profusely, he hid from the acrid smell and waited for the waves of nausea to subside. When he became aware of noise, he opened his eyes again, shading them with his hands. Fighting the return of nausea, he stared at a specific floor tile, slowly becoming more venturesome until he was able to stare out to the bars again. After a time, he began to feel better and uncovered his head to look around. In the next cell, a man lay moaning on a small cot. Gil yelled out, but the man didn't respond. He sat up carefully, keeping the blanket wrapped around him, and the nausea returned. He stared at the floor and remained perfectly still while looking for a pail.

"You'll get the hang of it," someone yelled, laughing. "It's the fucking tranquilizers they use. You have to just wait out the damn tremors. Sometimes it takes a whole day to reorient."

Without seeking the source of the advice, he muttered, weakly, "Thanks," then taking the advice, covered himself as best he could and fell back asleep. When he awoke, he felt better. He noticed a small tray on the floor by the bars with a tiny water bottle and some capsules on it. Expecting to fell dizzy again, he sat up, but all he felt was weakness. He slid off the cot and crawled to the tray where he shielded his eyes from the light and read the instructions. He took the capsules with the fluid. Soon he was feeling better.

With nothing to do but sleep and take the pills when they were offered, he slept often, waking up far too exhausted for the amount of sleep he'd had. Days passed slowly until one day he decided to stop taking the pills and almost immediately, he began feeling alert. What time he spent awake, he spent as a contortionist trying to keep warm under a blanket too thin and too small.

A large woman in a yellow and black uniform appeared at his cell. She pointed to him with what seemed to be a sixth finger but was some sort of molded plastic, flesh colored handgun.

"Mr. Cooper," she said authoritatively, "you will leave your blanket on the bed and come to me." At first he thought he was dreaming and just closed his eyes. When she repeated it, he struggled up and managed to stagger to the bars. "Good, Mr. Cooper, now put your hands through the bars." Unsure why she was calling him that, he did as he was told and she handcuffed him, then opened the cell, and led him to a windowless room with a single metal chair secured in the center of it. She pointed and he sat shivering on the cold metal.

"Mr. Cooper," when Gil didn't respond, she demanded. "Ron Cooper, you must pay attention. You should be feeling better. You have stopped taking our meds so you are obviously alert enough. According to Archive, you're from Pittsburgh and you are a rocket scientist. Is that right? You're kind of young to be a scientist." He wasn't sure he was hearing her correctly so he remained silent. "Mr. Cooper, it's been days without moderatives. Are you acting dense on purpose or is this how Pittsburgh rocket scientists act with strangers?"

"Yes, no, I'm sorry, excuse me, yes; I'd like to meet with your mayor, Dan Burghe."

"Yes, Mr. Cooper, Carny Dan is certainly our mayor. And while your credentials are impressive, it is particularly beneficial that you are a Fiscal Deacon in our Morgan Church, as you can imagine, we don't have much need for rocket scientists here in Hamilton right now and there are no contracts pending that require such skills. So as impressive as your credentials are, they're nowhere near enough to warrant the wasted time and expense of a meeting with the mayor.

"Unfortunately, we won't be able to offer you whatever work rocket scientists in Pittsburgh are privileged to accept, however if an opportunity for a rocket scientist presents itself, you will be at the top of the list for consideration."

He was confused. "Yes, thanks. Any work is fine, but I'd really like to meet the mayor."

"We have little work to offer in our basic metals or technology sectors, but our bio-recreation sector has accommodative housing available so I strongly recommend you begin your career with us there. The work will not be as challenging as rocket science but a career is a career, as they say. Here, take this." She handed him a slip of plastic. "This has directions to your apartment and the name and location of your work supervisor. We've taken the liberty of updating your PID and our accounting avatar has initialized your ledger so you can earn and spend, in that order. You know how it works."

He nodded.

"So you know, you've incurred charges while in jail, including not just the jail time, food and lodging but the prorated cost of the three officers and the pellet that took you down. There's more, it will be itemized on your wealth ledger and you should be able to pay the balance along with accrued interest quickly because *Chrisnukkah* is fast approaching and that means hard work and profit for all, ho, ho, ho."

When Gil didn't laugh, the woman made a face and continued.

"Once you're debriefed, you'll be issued a standard wireless handheld that's connected to your PID. You can use it to familiarize yourself with our protocols while awaiting a work assignment. You should be aware that Hamilton is a right-to-work community. That means if you are inefficient or wasteful, your employment contract will be summarily terminated and your permanent file will reflect that you are economically undesirable. You take that record with you until you turn it around or . . . well, that's a discussion hopefully you won't need but if you do, we'll save it for another day. By accepting employment with us, Mr. Cooper, you have agreed to give us the right to prosecute, if necessary, to recover any expenses owed to us plus interest and fees. We're like most other towns, the greater your inefficiency, the harsher the penalties, yadda-yadda-yadda, you know all this. While you're waiting for assignment, you should study our production laws and the underlying ethical and moral standards we use to apply them, precedents, etc . . . you're a Deacon in the Church so you know this. The estimate for your wait for work is currently two days and six hours so please don't check with your supervisor until a personnel avatar contacts you. Do you understand?"

"I think so. But help me out; wasn't *Chrisnukkah* last month?"

She laughed. "Unless Pittsburgh has seceded from the Union, that's a surprisingly naïve and unproductive question, Mr. Cooper. Of course *Chrisnukkah* was last month. Surely Pittsburgh, even with its rocket scientists, celebrates the High Holy Commercial Days quarterly, like everyone else."

Not wanting to sound ignorant, or to focus attention on his bogus Pittsburgh background, he sputtered through a response. "That's true, ma'am. As a rocket scientist, I work extended projects and never got much involved in day-to-day things."

She gave him an odd look. "Remind me never to relocate to Pittsburgh."

"Or become a rocket scientist," he joked.

She laughed, uncomfortably. "Yes, well, good luck, Mr. Cooper. You should be aware that while you've been unproductive, our actuarial avatar has prepared an initial assessment of your long term professional expectations. She believes you should have a modestly successful career here, but that assessment will be fine-tuned based on performance over time. Until we discover a compelling need for rocket scientists of your ilk if not caliber, you likely won't qualify for elite status unless you find a career sweet spot and produce wealth in some breakthrough capacity. By the way, when you check into your apartment, you'll be issued a life-planning guide along with a questionnaire. See that it is complete before your first performance review."

"When will that be?"

"Pittsburgh," she said with a hint of disgust. "I didn't realize our country had such backward towns. Your first performance review of course is immediately following your first day of work so assume three days from today. Good effort to you." She stood up and offered Gil her hand. He absently took it and gave it a weak shake, and with that, the door slid open and he walked out. Along the corridor, he passed three armed men clad in bright yellow overalls dragging a man into another room. Stenciled on the men's overalls was their department name, *HWD—Hamilton Waste Disposal, LLC.*

His small apartment was on the third floor of one of the many large high-rises that were clustered nearby. It was small and as sparse as the one he and Bree had shared in Profit but at least he had a bed. His view from the one small window in his living room was of other windows. With nothing to do, he waited the allotted three days until, at the prearranged time; an avatar's image appeared on his apartment wall.

"Mr. Cooper, hello, I am Joe, your supervisory avatar. Our shared primary purpose is to ensure our department's work queue meets requirements. We will be evaluated and compensated based on how well we satisfy that one requirement. I don't know about you but I am excited for this opportunity. Now for someone with your superior education, the initial work will not be difficult and we should be able to take advantage of your accelerated learning curve and parlay it into something much, much more financially rewarding. But don't get cocky; intelligence without enthusiasm, and performance without inclination, they are a sure map to financial hell. It is my job to supply you with great advice as well as a financial perspective second to none but I expect efficiency, enthusiasm, and continuous improvement. I do not like disappointment, and will not tolerate whining or blame of any kind. Give me what I require and promotions and financial well-being are just a defined number of 'I am on it, sirs away. Got it?"

And so Gil was working again. As impressed as everyone seemed with his credentials, his first job was entry level, a clerk in a receiving facility. It was his job to ensure the conveyers were properly distributing an unending flow of inbound uniform small green boxes. It was boring work with no mental challenge and though he had barely anything to do, he couldn't forget his employment difficulties in Profit, and so he worked diligently to build value quickly in order to request a meeting with the mayor as soon as possible.

Unchallenging weeks passed before he asked Joe for that meeting. Joe assured him the mayor would be made aware of his request. Besides being easy and boring, his job was lonely because he was the only person assigned to the vast automated warehouse located in a section of Hamilton with a great many other vast automated warehouses. Occasionally, a *Toller* would enter the facility searching for a lavatory and Gil would direct him, but that was the extent of his human contact. At the end of his shift, that first step outside the warehouse amplified his reality. The view from his warehouse door was of an unbroken string of similarly immense warehouses in all directions for as far as he could see. Sometimes, when he left, he'd notice in the distance another tiny solitary figure leaving through an identical door of an identical building.

Time passed slowly until one day Joe informed him he had earned the following day off and if he wanted, Joe would forego waking him. He agreed and woke the next day on his own. He was free for the first time since he'd arrived so he dressed quickly. Before he left, he contacted Joe.

"Mr. Cooper, how may I assist you to exercise your hard-earned wealth on your off day?"

"I requested a meeting with the mayor months ago. Has a meeting been set up?"

"Let me check . . . A person with your status . . . let me see . . . yes, here it is, a person with your status will . . . never be allowed to see the mayor. Sorry."

"But you promised me a meeting."

"Let me check . . . no, there are no promises in your account. According to our records, the only promise made was by you, and that was to work hard, spend your wealth wisely to help the Hamilton economy, and build your worth for forever."

"But that's not . . . I mean sure, I'll work, but I need to see Mayor Burghe."

"Mr. Cooper, I cannot help you there. My responsibility is limited to Joe jobs only. This is on you. Your efforts have not been sufficient to lift me to a position where I may petition the mayor's avatar. I am sorry for any misunderstanding and I am certain that when you become more productive, an opportunity will present itself."

"But you promised . . ."

"A promise, which I did not make, is not a contract; there was no consideration, no quid pro quo. If you wish such a meeting with our mayor, work harder, get promoted, and do whatever you must do to make yourself a priority. Only then will I be able to petition for our mayor's valuable time and he will find it worthwhile to fit you in."

"But that wasn't . . . how do I do that? I had an agreement."

"Oh, an agreement. Why didn't you say so? That is a completely different story. Tell me who agreed, when and where, and what proof you have and what consideration was offered so we can evaluate who benefited most and then I will have it taken care of. Even at that, it is not likely you will be speaking to the mayor, probably just one of his stuck up legal avatars. Still, if you wish me to research it, I will. I must alert you that time is money and my time outside of supporting your warehousemen efforts must be purchased and on your off hours, I'm not cheap."

"There has to be another way."

"As your trusted advisor, I provide you with only the best choices. I must warn you, people who persist when the mayor has been declared unavailable; they are generally put on a watch list. It is ironic, really, because getting your name added to a watch list will be of interest to the mayor, but inclusion on said list makes it impossible for you to ever see him. Such things as these are the ironies of bureaucracy. As a rocket scientist, I am certain that you understand."

"But a friend of mine is a friend of Mayor Burghe. I'm certain the mayor will want to know that I'm here."

"Why did you not say that in the first place? Now I can build a case. All you have to do is commission me to develop said case and pay for the interface time with the mayor's security avatars who work on these requests. If it's approved, your chances of seeing the mayor will improve substantially."

"That's great, Joe, thank you."

"Yes, it is great. However, you should be aware that such inclusive research, out of necessity, might uncover information that could cause the mayor to avoid you or worse, there could be issues in your past that require expensive professional resolution and barring that, could lead to dismissal and the hinterlands, *Wasterville.*"

"What kind of issues?"

"That is hard to say. Some who took the route you're considering were executed."

"What? Why?"

"The law is the law. It doesn't matter where or when you break it or how productively you've lived your life since, retribution is an assurance to our society that we play by rules. Let us say you have an unpaid debt. Before you see our mayor, you will be required to pay said debt, including interest and fees, but additional penalties could increase that debt far beyond your ability to pay and thus, indenture, slavery, or death could result depending on the ruling by our Financial Court. I am just saying . . ."

"What? That's crazy." He was beginning to understand. "You're making it impossible . . ."

"Nothing is impossible to a true entrepreneur, Mr. Cooper, so do not get theatrical on me. The rules are clear and you have no room to negotiate. At current, your balance sheet has little value to our mayor so I would say you lack even a puncher's chance of paying off any debts or fines if financial aberrations are discovered. Still, this is a free country and it is your choice though I would advise against it if there is anything in your past you could come to regret. You might try to set your balance sheet right before you incur the additional expense of intensive research."

"But . . ."

"I will initiate contact at your request. I estimate two hours at one thousand credits per hour should provide me with the incentive to make said request. Who is this friend you speak of?"

Gil made a quick calculation. Was this worth three days wages and could they uncover his past, something Rachman and Doris couldn't? He started to agree but hesitated. Suppose they have someone like Laurence Hilliard on their side. It was a large city. Fearfully, he offered the name. "The mayor's friend was Laurence Hilliard."

"Was?"

"Do your research and get me the interview. This is my day off. Can you suggest a place to go or something to do?"

"You will be charged for my research and the only free advice I can give you is spend time with friends."

"Friends? How can I have friends? I've been secluded in your warehouse since I started and I haven't met anyone in my apartment building yet. The few I've seen aren't very friendly."

"My, you are a whiner. If your friendship was worth something, you'd have more friends. Maybe you should consider that it is your whining that keeps you from making friends. That's just a suggestion; there is no charge for it. You seem like a potentially productive citizen, improving net worth is something everyone here has in common. Use that. Perhaps you have other interests. Your records show gambling, property flipping, and pyramid scheming, Those are all very impressive interests that should give you a great deal in common with local *Conducers*. Use your interests as conversation starters; particularly because it opens dialogue toward cooperation in financial ventures, or it could provide you with the enjoyable opportunity to jew your new friends out of something of value. Mr. Cooper, stop not having friends and get into the game. Really, if I am to progress in my career, you must progress in yours. Hone your skills, learn to lie, cheat, and steal, develop your greedy side, you'll get the hang of it, every *Conducer* does, everyone who is as interested in creating wealth as you are, and friendship is the best way to meet competitors you will need to get the measure of."

"I didn't know . . ."

"Mr. Cooper, your birth town of Mellon is a great financial center, but it is similar to Hamilton in many ways. I am certain people here will be interested in the economically expedient things you learned there."

"Rocket science is very demanding," he lied. "I never had much time for social stuff." This was his first day off and time was passing. "Please, I need some ideas?"

"There are always parties at the cusps."

"Thank you. What are cusps?"

"I thought you would ask what a party is. Before you were hired, you were instructed to research our community. You must take our requirements seriously. There is a cost to explaining things, Mr. Cooper."

"I'm sorry. I don't know what a cusp is."

"Here's one last piece of information before the meter starts running. Hamilton is divided into market sectors. Each is further divided into support segments. You, for example, are in the bio-recreational technology market sector of the *Pharma* group and you work in the logistics-warehouse support segment. At the cusp, or intersection of each segment, there are retail and entertainment operations. The cusps between each market sector are larger than those between the support segments. At these market cusps, along with retail commerce, of course, there are nightclubs and other entertainment venues. That is where the *Conducer* cognoscenti go to stimulate the economy and recharge their batteries. Go and party hearty."

"Party hearty?"

"Use your imagination. It can be as productive a good time as any *Conducer* should want."

"You mention *Conducer*. What is it?"

"I am trying to be tolerant here. You are a consumer-producer. A *Conducer* is you. You will give rocket science a bad name if you keep up this naiveté."

"I'm sorry. At these cusps, is there a cost?"

"Morgan tells us that there are no stupid questions, but it is merely an aphorism as the Great One has never met you. What you have asked is a classic stupid question. What purpose would anything have if it was free? You have accumulated a limited amount since you've been here, but spend it and enjoy so you can return to work invigorated and ready to earn so much more."

"And the cusp is open now?"

"Unlike you, Mr. Cooper, commerce never sleeps. As the infomercial says, 'Cusps are the one place to go when you only have one place to go.'"

"And that's where I'll go. Tell me when the mayor wants to meet with me."

"You will know when I know. I am adding your request to my to-do list and once complete, I will transfer your file to the mayor's security avatar."

"Thank you."

"Enjoy the parties, Mr. Cooper, and remember that while everything is technically legal, anything that adversely affects the economics of our community will come home to roost, so be prudent. If you're not sure about something, reconsider. If no one else is doing it, it is probably something you should avoid also. If you do not feel you have the self-control necessary, there are insurance kiosks throughout the entertainment district that will help you mitigate risk."

"I don't understand."

"You're quite the simple fellow for a rocket scientist. Say you and a small group are drinking and someone in the group does something foolish like, say, break a window. You and your friends will be charged for it immediately prorated by cause and relative irresponsibility. Your worth is reduced by a pro rata share of the cost of the window replacement and any ancillary charges. If you lack the wealth, you will feel enough unpleasant heat to mobilize you to work harder, but if it continues, it becomes immobilizing. At that point, when the crews get around to it, you will be picked up and processed for indenture, slavery, or if our actuarial avatars determine that you are unrecoverable from the debt, you will be worked for organ redistribution. It couldn't be more efficient. It's why our legal system is the wonder of the world. To prevent or delay any of those outcomes is where risk mitigation insurance comes in. The cost of said insurance is based on ground-breaking algorithms developed by PhD financial types and is designed to protect your worth and your quest for forever from a momentary lapse of reason."

"I'll be careful to avoid trouble. I'm going now. Get me that appointment, Joe."

"Working . . ." Joe said.

Gil grabbed his communicator and headed for a day out on his own.

As he left his apartment building, he walked past myriad vender displays set up by people he assumed were his neighbors. They shouted for him to buy something, but he shook them off, feeling guilty that he had blown a new opportunity to make friends. At the train station, there were more vender booths and the people manning them were more difficult to avoid, so he put his head down and walked resolutely to the platform. On the platform, it was like a convention. There were so many people trying to sell things that fighting through the crowds, he almost missed his train. At the nearest cusp, he got off and immediately spotted the entertainment corridor below the elevated platform, lit up with marquees, signs, and flashing lights. He followed the crowd flow while eyeing a large contingent of armed security guards dressed in Hamilton's maize-yellow uniforms.

By late afternoon, except for having to resist salespeople who all but tackled him to get him into their stores, he had done no more than sightsee when he noticed a group of young people, his age, walking and laughing. The camaraderie was so unusual that he followed them, trying to stay close enough to hear what they were saying and why they were laughing. The street forked and forked again and listening proved difficult due to the incessant marketing by independent street entertainers and vendors.

Members of the group disengaged to enter various entertainment venues but Gil stayed with the five remaining people. He followed at a distance as they walked down a dim, lightly-traveled street and hid in the shadows to watch, curiously, as they stopped in a dark spot between streetlights and huddled together to smoke and laugh. The laughter increased and Gil was about to leave when two heavy-set older men appeared under a cone of illumination provided by the streetlights. Curious, Gil moved closer, but remained out of sight. One of the intruders walked up to the group and pushed one of the young men hard against an abandoned storefront. The young man dropped to the ground and tried to crawl away but the other bully kicked him hard enough to cause the young man to stop. Gil edged closer.

"Cry all you want you fucking techie crybaby," one of the bullies growled. "You're all pieces of shit; the whole lot of you. You don't pull your own damn weight. You schedule for shit and then you shut down our fucking lines. It's because of you that we got laid off and evicted. We're going to die out there because of your damn sorry asses." With that, he leveled another kick at the guy on the ground.

"We're going to die but you couldn't care less you arrogant little sons of poverty. We're goners and you're partying. What the fuck is that? Life for you assholes is living large on drugs and music. You don't care about working stiffs. All you creeps want is to burn your wages having fun. You don't give a rat's ass whose career you ruin.

"Well I care and it's time for you to pay up. What's happening to us isn't simulation, you shits. Good people disappear because you, you . . ." With that, he bent down and slugged the fallen young man in the gut. After another whimper, the victim remained motionless while the others in the group looked around, helpless. One, with his voice quaking, tried to reason with the bullies.

"Misters, please, I don't . . . we don't want any trouble. I can't speak for my friends here, but I'm doing the best I can. This last layoff wasn't my fault. Someone at Franklin Town developed a better process, that's all, and they're making better products right now because of it. I know it's not your fault either; but think of the big picture. Your layoff is just part of the creative destruction process we all live better because of. Layoffs can't be helped. I'm sorry. We're sorry."

One of the girls added, "I'm on a committee to reverse engineer Franklin Town's products and in a couple of months, I'm sure we'll compete again, but in the meantime our customers are canceling orders. We'll win them back, I promise, you'll see. Please don't hurt us. This is no one's fault, it's a free market; there are always losers but just you wait; business in our sector will return as good as ever in a couple of months, a year, tops. I promise . . ."

Before she could finish, the other tough pushed her hard, forcing her against a shop window her head causing a hollow thud as the glass rippled.

She screamed, doubled over, and grasped her head before sliding to the ground.

"What are you a fucking orator, girl? Shut up. You got a cake job and you don't give a rat's ass about production people like Ed here and me. For Morgan's sake, life is time and money and we have neither now thanks to you. If you really want to help us, empty your goddamned Pids and transfer your funds into our accounts." When the young woman on the ground didn't respond, the tough kicked the prone young man beside her. "Not up for charity? I didn't think so you capitalist piglets."

The man mumbled something and then tried to kick the young man who remained standing. He missed and cursed as the young man cringed against the wall. "I'm speaking to you, you worthless, gutless piece of *Waster* crap. I work hard for everything I have and that's a big zero right now. You caused my fucking problem; *our* fucking problem and you will pay."

"Please don't hurt us," a young woman pleaded. "We're late for our show."

The other tough, Ed, towered over the girl as he backed her against the wall.

"I'm going to disappear because of you and all you care about is your fucking show. You want a show?" The girl nodded. "How about you and me put on a show? What do you say?"

"No, you don't understand," the third woman whimpered. "It's Dyllon Tomas. She's performing tonight for the first time in a long while and the tickets are real expensive and hard to get. We spent a great deal to sit stage side . . ."

"I don't give a fuck."

"But we really won't be able to resolve anything here so please let us go. After the show, we can resolve this if you want."

"What's your name, sweet lips?"

"Vicki," the girl stammered. "I'm . . . I'm sorry about the production problems, but we're just *Conducers* too. I know you're mad but this isn't my fault."

"Well, Vicki, I'm Phil and I'm sorry it's no one's fault and I do appreciate how important your fucking show is. Permit me to apologize for troubling you and wasting your time." He bowed and turned to his partner. "Ed, we're sorry aren't we?"

Ed nodded. "Damn right, Phil. All we really wanted was a fucking sincere apology." The girl quickly offered one.

"Thank you, Vicki," Ed said politely as he moved closer, hiding her from Gil's view. "Say, sweetie, being so reasonable and friendly like, maybe you can make it up to us. We need friendly. We need you to be real fucking friendly, Ed and me, we'd appreciate it, wouldn't we Phil? Kind of like a send off, if you know what I mean."

Phil nodded. "Vicki, darling, we're sad and need you to be good to us, me first, of course, and if you are, we won't beat the living crap out of you and your friends and then steal your assets before we leave. Well, we might steal them anyway because where we're going we're going to need funds."

Frightened, Vicki tried to move away but Phil reached out, grabbed her, and gently lifted her chin. She appeared to be crying. "Crying? God, Morgan, I love crying, sweetheart. Ed and I always say that for all the intensity around here, there isn't nearly enough crying. Keep it up, darling; you are making this real special."

"Phil, look at those tears, I'm getting hard."

One of the young men staggered to his feet. "Listen mister, you know the law. You're going to incur a significant financial penalty if you do anything to us. You don't want that."

Phil turned and slapped the kid hard across the face. "You're a fucking smartass, huh, big fellow?" He took an aggressive step forward and as a group, the others backed away. "Next week, me and Ed are goners, fucking *Wasters*, so what more can the law do to us? And out there we won't have much to look forward to, so before we go, we're going to take some well-earned credit-free loving from one of you. Which one will it be?" No one volunteered. "With all her sobbing, pretty little Vicki is my preference. Ed, what do you think?"

"Don't!" the young man on the ground shouted. "If you do anything, the mayor will deny your work petition when more work comes in and you'll die out there for sure. Leave us alone. We won't say anything and maybe we can work out a loan for you at regular prime plus rates. What do you say, guys?"

From his place hidden in the shadows, Gil watched as one of the toughs, Ed, put his arm around Vicki who struggled to get away. When her friends moved to help, Phil stepped forward.

"I'll tell you what we're doing here," Ed said as stared down the group while rubbing Vicki's breasts through her heavy winter coat. "We're taking this little cutie down below and you can do whatever you like until we're done. The concert's obviously important to you so come back for her when it's over, or you can wait here as long as you stay quiet and don't cause any problems. What do you say?"

One of the guys responded, trying to sound calm. "Vicki, come here."

She tried to break free but Ed held her tight while Phil shoved the others away. "Who wants a piece of me?" he yelled. "Do you really want to give up forever to fight a couple of *Wasters* over a piece of tail? Well, do you?"

No one answered.

"I thought so," Ed said, holding the terrified and struggling Vicki in his arms. "Vicki, doll baby, it's time for some sweet, loving. We'll be good to you if you're good to us, but don't be too good if you know what I mean." He laughed.

"If we see your faces down below," Phil said, pointing a finger at the group, "she'll regret it and so will you. The town can't afford broken schedulers so you'll be out on your asses along with Ed and me and I wouldn't want that if I were you. Take her, Ed." Ed covered Vicki's mouth and though she struggled, he dragged her to the stairs that led down below the street.

Gil stared horrified, remembering how Bree was almost raped on the road to Profit, but he was unsure how he could help. As the young men and young woman stood by meekly, while the girl's muffled screams turned to sobs that faded as she disappeared below. Gil decided he had to act. He looked for help but in the distance, the crowds were busy partying and oblivious so he approached the remaining men and the woman.

"Should we go to the show or wait until they're done with Vicki?" one of them asked. While they were deciding, Gil popped out of the shadows, and frightened them. Slowly, they backed against the wall. "What . . . what do you want? Are you with them?" one of the young men said while striking a silly defensive pose.

"Your friend is going to get hurt. We can't let that happen. Five of us can handle those two."

"No we can't and why would we want to anyway? We have our careers to think about. Who are you? Do you owe Vicki something?"

"I don't owe her anything, I'm new in town. We have to do something."

"Why?" The girl responded. "That makes no sense. The cost to do something could be expensive."

"How does that matter? She'll get hurt. That isn't right."

"Look, you're new in town," one of the young men offered. "We don't earn extra credits for helping and helping, Vicki could be worse off if we cause damage, or those guys have value and we hurt them or more likely, they kill us. For Morgan's sake, the fines will be enormous and we don't have the insurance—or the time to get any—but if you have insurance, be our guest, knock yourself out."

Gil didn't understand what they were talking about or how they could abandon a friend. "I don't have insurance, whatever that is, but it isn't about that. She's going to get hurt."

"Of course and it's a shame," the girl said. "Say, you have an angle, don't you? What is it and how much does it pay? And if we agree to help, how do we benefit?"

Gil heard a muffled scream and turned toward the sound. When he looked back, the group was backing away toward the crowds in the distance.

"Where are you going?" Gil shouted. "This isn't right. I'm going after her and I sure could use some help." When they kept walking, he yelled, "at least call for help."

"You don't have a money-making angle, do you?"

There was another scream and with it, he ran to the steps. When he turned, the group had moved a safer distance away.

Gil bolted down the steps. When he reached the river level street below, he made his way cautiously in the dark. Somewhere, he heard the sounds of struggling. The street was filthy, dimly-lit with an occasional light that wasn't broken, and it was littered with refuse. Staying in the shadows, he maneuvered silently toward the noise using the girders to hide his movements as he carefully avoided stepping on piles of trash and waste. The muffled sobs of the girl got louder.

The men had thrown Vicki onto a pile of trash and were roughly disrobing her while she tried ineffectively to fight them off. He heard a slap and her cries turned to sad, pathetic, breathless mewling. Gil looked for something, anything that would help against these two brutes and found a long, thick rusty pipe that was propped against a girder. He grabbed it and slowly worked his way behind them. They were so intent on their prey that they didn't notice him. The girl's feeble resistance continued until one of the men slapped her again and she quieted as the other, Ed, crawled on top of her.

Gil stepped out from behind, closed the distance quickly, and swung his pipe hard at the man watching, Phil, hitting him with a glancing blow to his shoulder that deflected upwards to strike his skull. The man dropped to the ground as the pipe made a loud pinging sound and the unexpectedly intense vibration shook the pipe from Gil's now numb grip and with a musical chime, it hit the ground beside the now unconscious offender.

With his right arm numb and useless at his side, and without taking his eyes off the other man, he felt for the pipe with his left hand. He found it and grabbed it as the man on top of Vickie looked up startled. Before Ed could react, Gil swung the pipe again, this time hitting the man flush on the side of his head, creating a surreally loud pinging sound and causing yet another vibration that shook the pipe from his grasp once again. With both hands now numb, Gil looked frantically for another way to ward the men off.

He felt a tug at his pants and stifled a scream. It was Vicki. She had crawled to him and grabbed at his leg. He searched for the most immediate danger only to find that one offender's body was shaking violently, his head crushed and bloody, while the other had curled on the ground, moaning, while holding a severely broken arm. The girl looked at her attackers and screamed, screaming louder when the quivering body jerked spasmodically one last time and then stopped moving. That's when Gil noticed that he was trembling, too.

As the numbness wore off and feeling, in the form of pain, returned to his hands, he bent to take a closer look at the men. One, his skull crushed, was staring blankly into his future, clearly beyond anyone's care. The other was moaning quietly with blood seeping through his coat. Seeing that the girl was putting her clothes back on, Gil turned his back but kept a careful watch over the men, although neither moved. When Vicki was dressed, she grabbed Gil.

"Please, let's get out of here." With pain in his hands and with his legs wobbly, he allowed her to pull him up the steps. At the top, without saying anything to Gil, she ran over to her group of friends who had been waiting a safe distance away, and together they walked away, leaving Gil alone.

"What do I do about them?" he yelled.

"Are they dead?" one of the young men shouted back.

"One, I think. I hope not. The other might be without medical attention."

But they kept walking. "What's your name," Vicki shouted back.

"Um, Ron Cooper," Gil said offering the alias given to him when he entered Hamilton. "I work in the *Pharma* technology warehouse section."

She nodded but continued to walk away with her friends.

"What should I do?" Gil yelled.

Someone yelled back. "Security should be here soon. We're late for our concert."

"What about me?"

"Do you have tickets?"

"No."

"Sorry, the concert's sold out. Maybe you can get tickets for a later performance." With that, they merged into the crowd, leaving Gil alone at the crime scene.

He considered going back down the stairs to help the man who might still be alive but then he heard the sirens. His first instinct was to run, but he didn't know where to run to. And there was an injured man to consider. When the security team arrived, he walked to them, stopping when they pointed their weapons at him. He started to say something, but before he could speak, he felt a burning sensation in his thigh, and fell.

Chapter 12

Hamilton, MI.—2070

Once again, Gil awoke in a jail cell, but this time without the full-body tremors and nausea. He was disoriented, but as he sat up, the realization that he had killed someone sickened him and once again, he vomited on the cell floor. It didn't help that he had killed a bad man; he had ended a precious life and, locked up in a cell, he had time to obsess over it. Would the courts know that he was only trying to help an innocent person? And would they find his true identity during discovery? He worried away the hours with no one to talk to and without a satisfying rationalization for murder.

He felt worse about the man's death when he discovered that, technically, murder wasn't why he was in jail. His avatar, Joe, was representing him in court and Joe explained that there were no laws against murder; he was incarcerated to ensure that he wouldn't flee before damages could be assessed.

Joe assured him that the legal process was simple and brief and required no witnesses. This was purely a financial matter, cut and dried, and restitution would be assessed quickly. Joe expressed concern that, not having risk-mitigating, entertainment cusp insurance, Gil wouldn't be able to pay for his crime in the defined payback period, but he refused to discuss what that meant until a ruling was handed down.

So Gil sat in his cell worrying about moral relativism and whether his identity would finally be compromised. At any moment he expected HomeSec to haul him away to the Chairwoman to be tried for treason, a capital crime far worse than the economic crime that he had committed in Hamilton. Fear and guilt caused him sleepless nights and restless days so to pass the time until his hearing—or as it was called officially, a *Make Good*, or *Post Mortem*—he watched the comings and goings of other prisoners. Most were gone within a day although he didn't know where they were taken or why. Finally, at the end of a difficult week, he felt a vibration and jumped from his cot to grab his communicator.

"Mr. Cooper, I have great news," Avatar Joe announced.

"What, what is it?" he stammered.

"First, we found a replacement for the work you missed. Because your ill-conceived actions caused that expense, you will be assessed all incremental costs incurred by your employer during your absence—adjusted, of course, for efficiencies gained or lost by your replacement. After my usual thorough investigation, I discovered the victims were to disappear at the end of the week."

"I told you that."

"Of course you did, but your words have no bearing in these proceedings. That the victims were at the end of their employment cycle is good news. It limits damages to the date of separation."

"How are they the victims? And is the guy with the broken arm okay?"

"Alas, there is a bit of irony here. It turns out the object of your unbridled fury had a record of inefficiency as long and misshapen as the arm you mangled. That too is very good because it limits damages. Due to his poor performance history and the extensive damage you inflicted, the city solicitor—using a methodology provided by our Chief Actuarial Avatar—determined repair and recovery as well as the physical therapy required afterward, would generate an inadequate payback to Hamilton. So, rather than incur further expense, Phil Jones—that's the plaintiff's name if you're interested—was terminated. The financial outcome of that resolution is most fortunate for you as you are only being assessed the cost of the legal process, the cost to terminate the fool, and all fees necessary for selling his body parts, offset by the revenue generated from the sale of said parts."

Gil was horrified. "No," he moaned. "But his wounds weren't fatal. Why did they kill him?"

"I thought I explained this very clearly. You should be pleased. If the legal findings had gone differently, the financial penalties could have been very difficult for you to satisfy. Considering everything, you faired well. Phil Jones's deviant economic lifestyle put him at risk, and so he wasn't deemed worthy of forever. The court found that you were simply the instrument of his demise and the ruling is that you appeared at the confluence of events that led to the elimination of Mr. Jones's counterproductive nature. From your standpoint, this is a most satisfactory disposition."

"But he's a person, a bad person but . . . killing him, it's not right."

"Who is talking about blame? It doesn't exist, only restitution does. And right and wrong are unknowable. That's why we keep score with money; that is what advanced civilizations do. There are only economic consequences so I am disappointed with how you are taking this. On a personal note, everyone was impressed with my presentation and I earned a great deal of power points from this case, thank you very much. And while it was true in a general sense that Phil Jones was a person; that is no longer true or relevant. But wait, I am not done. Concerning the other *Conducer*, Ed Rains—the one you almost beheaded with an exuberance sorely lacking in your everyday job—compared to Mr. Jones, Mr. Rains was a model citizen, ergo your problem. Mr. Rains had ten years of productive work experience and projected possible supervisory capability."

"He was going to rape her. He wasn't a good man."

"Good man, bad man, who really knows or cares? The only fair justice is economic justice. A replacement was hired temporarily into Mr. Rains' position on the line for the remainder of his workweek until his layoff took affect. That required training costs and production inefficiencies until the replacement got up to speed. Then there was lost housing revenue, and profits on food and entertainment to consider. It turned out the cadaver, Mr. Rains, was quite a partier and an imbiber of great report. Tavern owners at every cusp have sued for lost revenue, but due to my stout defense, the cost is manageable. Much of the rest of the opportunity revenue lost with the demise of said Mr. Rains, I was able to offset due to certain profits he incurred in previous dealings. These factors were considered and your penalty was adjusted using a standard, complex economic multiplier."

"A what?"

"A multiplier," the avatar explained. "You're a rocket scientist. If you were an economist you would understand. A multiplier is a sophisticated algorithm that considers the downstream economic ripple effect as commercial transactions work their way through the system. It is one of the great and glorious foundations of capitalism, that and compound interest although consideration in legal issues is important also. It is so hard to choose just one. Anyway, let's say you, Ron Cooper, buy from someone who uses the revenue to buy from someone who uses the revenue to buy from someone else, it is all classic economics, one unit of value purchasing many, many things. Anyway, all that matters to you is that the multiplier effect sustains Hamilton's economy and our actuarial avatars have a well-established formula to calculate the economic effects to an extraordinary degree of precision. Bottom line, your wages for the next three years will be garnished by seven percent to repay the city for the economic loss of Mr. Rains."

Gil was too confused and appalled to respond. When he did, he struggled.

"Joe, this is . . . crazy. I killed . . . jeez, two men. Who cares about the economic loss and how to pay it back?" It sounded strange to voice that insanity. He had killed and had only debts to show for it. His mind flashed to that day more than five long years ago when his great-grandfather Bernie had confessed to murder. It seemed so terrible then. Joe's voice brought him back.

"You should be pleased by this outcome. As always, it is a perfectly fair settlement made better by my performance. The League of Avatars has commended me and certified the verdict, so once you are released from jail and begin work again; seven percent of your wages will be diverted to the city. Did I mention that includes interest? You are free to return to work and put your career back on track."

"I know but I killed a man and another died because of me," Gil said, his mind still unable to comprehend the scenario.

"While that is accurate, it is not productive to dwell on it, Mr. Cooper. It was foolish of those men to put their economic lives at risk by undertaking a dangerously unproductive venture. The result of which was, they paid the ultimate cost for their miscalculation. It was equally foolish for you to go off as you did, unpremeditated. As in most crimes, you are all guilty of poor decision making, and only you can make amends. You are new and that was taken into consideration. That and my sophisticated presentation are the only reasons your obligation is only seven percent. Justice has been served. At its best, economics is both fair and cruel."

"Will this affect my meeting with the mayor?"

"Not that again, Mr. Cooper. If the last time wasn't advantageous for a meeting, now it is even less likely. I did not want to mention it so soon after the ruling but, as is typical in these situations, your economic vitality is now in question, and so you have been re-classified as a potential economic liability. You must see this is reasonable. At this stage of your economic life, our mayor must consider the effect on the media that any involvement with someone like you might have, and simply, it just is not in his Honor's best interest. Frankly, unless you perform some superlative economic act, you will never have even a photo opportunity with the mayor, let alone talk to him."

"But . . ."

"But nothing, Mr. Cooper," Avatar Joe said. "Time is money and it is time to move on to productive efforts. You will be released shortly. Sign the waiver and return to your housing unit. After that, steel yourself for your new level of indebtedness because at seven percent, you must redouble your efforts so you can earn a promotion and a raise. Unclutter your mind; there is nothing more important than your work because your margin for error has been severely narrowed. As a preliminary warning, any attempts to reduce spending to cover for your increased fixed expenses will be frowned upon as cynical and bad for our economy. If you are uncertain how to generate more income, I can assist you, for a fee, and it would not be considered out of order here to thank me in the form of some substantial recompense."

Gil sat on the cot and covered his face with his hands. Frustrated, he forced himself to breathe slowly, allowing the warm air captured to relax him.

"Joe, thank you for your help," he said as sincerely as he could. When he offered nothing more, Joe signed off.

Later, Gil signed the dunning letter and was released. He returned to his apartment, he had nowhere else to go, and sat, alone, contemplating his role in the deaths. The silence in his tiny apartment only made everything worse.

Gil began to appreciate the solitary nature of his job in the weeks following the murders, as he tried to sort out his life and his need to increase his value. With the return of *Chrisnukkah* season, work became hectic and everywhere, there were signs exhorting *Conducers* to work harder and more productively. He tried. With Joe providing constant reminders that a boost in his performance meant profits that were food for everyone. As a way of not dwelling on his dreary life, he tried to find a rhythm in his work, but staring at small green and white boxes was too uninspiring to provide the kinetics he needed.

As was the *Chrisnukkah* custom, happy, up-tempo music was pumped throughout the city, along with short bursts of song to make the season bright. It may have worked for others but not for him. If, as advertised, *Chrisnukkah* somehow brought joy and personal satisfaction, it was lost on warehousemen Gil Rose.

One night after work, he arrived at his apartment as the last light of the winter sun dropped below heavy, snow-laden clouds announcing an approaching late-winter storm. The smell of snow brought back visions of Bree. He thought of her often, but constantly busy during the holiday season, he hadn't dwelled on her much lately. The snow also brought back memories of Profit and a need he fought hard to suppress. Bree had brought vibrancy to his life that living in Hamilton for the last few months had drained. He pictured her disappointment at what his life had become and shook his head. He was disappointing himself, too.

Gil dragged himself through the front door of the apartment building and walked up to his apartment. As soon as he opened his door, the fireplace monitor turned on and the glow provided heat and the hint of fragrance from the choices provided; tonight, it was evergreen, a reminder of Angel Falls. Famished, he selected a meal from the monitor on the door of his refrigerator-freezer-microwave and the meal appeared piping hot at the delivery window. Before eating, he paused to consider what he had to be thankful for. He was still anonymous and safe, and that was what he'd sought, if not all he'd sought. He hated to admit it but this small space was home and the anonymity hiding among the *Conducer* masses provided sanctuary. He wasn't dead or in prison, and he wasn't hungry. Loneliness he could handle, if it kept him safe. Maybe this was as happy as anyone deserved.

He ate the high fructose-sweetened synthetic food that was labeled dinner and stared at the business news on the holo without interest. Before more unremarkable time past, he noticed a message on his communicator. He pressed the button.

"Mister . . . Cooper, my name is . . . Vicki. We kind of met a . . . a few months ago, you know at . . . at the . . . river."

There was a long pause.

"Me . . . me and my friends heard about your court case, that it was settled and everything is okay. I'm glad. Anyway, I, we want to thank you for . . . you know, helping and if you're interested, we'll be at Rock World where, you know, tonight Dyllon Tomas is performing again. I . . . we want you to join us . . . if you can. Your ticket will be waiting at the club office. If you can, be there by ten. If you don't feel like it, I understand. I can sell the ticket and not take a loss. But try, thanks."

He had tried to put that night behind him, but the message made him think about it, in all its sad detail. That someone else felt something about what had happened made him hopeful. He posted his itinerary with Joe and prepared to spend the evening out.

By the time he left for the concert, it was snowing. He considered taking the train but decided to save money and walk. Even in the snow, his neighbors were busy manning the booths and kiosks that lined the sidewalks to sell to the few who were still out and about. It was a long, straight walk to the entertainment cusp and as he approached, the crowds made him feel even more isolated and out of touch. He pushed through, searching for the theater. Unable to find it on his own, Gil reluctantly contacted Joe who provided directions for a small fee.

Chrisnukkah revelers streamed in and out of stores, congregating at street kiosks and in front of strategically placed computer terminals, selecting gifts. Indifferent to the holiday, yet curious, he stared at their serious faces and wondered why they bothered.

When he located the club, he fought through more kiosks where tickets were available but not for the Dyllon Tomas show. When he reached the box office, above it, prominently displayed, was the life size picture of a coffee-skinned woman on stage in front of adoring fans, wearing a beret made from green currency and a yellow strapless evening gown with large gold coins sewn into the fabric. Below was the caption,

Dyllon Tomas©™®, Our Astonishing Butterfly of Truth in the Golden Age of Deceit

He had no idea what that meant.

Once his PID confirmed his identity, he was allowed inside the crowded, darkened theater. Vicki was waiting at the top of the main aisle and though her eyes showed panic, when she recognized him, she smiled, looking prettier than he remembered. After an awkward greeting, she walked him down the aisle to the front row of tables by the stage where her friends were jammed around a too small, round table. He remembered their faces, but not their names.

"Thanks again for coming, Ron," Vicki said. Then, she turned to the others, all around Gil's age. Vicki introduced everyone, but with the noise of the crowd, he had trouble hearing their names.

"James?" he asked one of the men.

"No, Janes. Janes Hallis," Janes said gruffly. "We'll do it again. This is Kyle, Kyle Drier and his asset partner, Dorothea Martinez. You've met Vicki. The quiet one is Kurt, Kurt Hemerling, he's our investment councilor."

Gil nodded to each. "Thanks for inviting me. I'm sorry we met the way . . ."

Janes put a finger to his lips. "There is no profit in remembering. We're here to have fun. So you know, Vicki and I share investment strategies but nothing more and she insisted we should thank you so this is it. Enough said. Let's enjoy the concert."

Gil stared at Vicki who looked down, sadly. "That's fine with me," he responded.

Janes eyed the crowd. "Do you like her music?" he asked.

"Dyllon Tomas? I never heard of her before . . . you know, before."

They all looked stunned by his confession.

"First of all, Miss Dyllon is real," Dorothea gushed. "And she's on message, she tells the powerful to fuck off, and she's so brave and brazen. If she didn't represent one of the most profitable artist franchises in the world, she'd be disappeared for sure for what she sings about."

"Disappeared?"

"Disappeared," Kurt clarified. "Is what happens to the unproductive, which Dyllon is most definitely not. She has great name recognition and with her aggressive cross branding, she's too strong a marketing presence for even HomeSec to fuck with. Some of her songs are about the mayor, but he doesn't do anything except invest in her. Wait until you hear what she has to say and how she says it. She's a commercial radical who gives it to people in power; even the Chairwoman, if you can believe that."

Dorothea added excitedly. "She's our muse. Because of her insight and her passion, we're able to struggle through our work life. She's our voice, our soul. She understands all the bullshit we put up with and she won't have any of it. Miss Dyllon is why our world will change."

"Does it need changing?" Gil asked, innocently.

They laughed again and this time Kyle responded.

"How do we know? But work is annoying a lot of the time and Dyllon tells us that it's all right to be pissed off, and to dream of more rewarding days. She's not like all the other artists, she has zero ties to Morgan and she's so intuitive." Kyle looked down at the table briefly. "She knows how we think and what our economic troubles are. She sings about the unforgiving market and unrelenting work that is boring and pointless, even cruel and . . . how incredibly hard it all is. And it is hard, it's real hard. There's so much stuff I want but it's so difficult to earn enough to buy it all and still save for forever and she knows the pressure we're under and she appreciates it. No one else appreciates it but her. She sings about the conflicted *Conducer,* the one who spends and saves, the sad *Conducer* who has to make hard economic choices every day, someone who wants to have fun while he can but doesn't want to die, either."

Kyle seemed frightened but he just shrugged and everyone at the table waited politely for him to continue. "She knows that unlike entrepreneurs, we're on our own and I guess it's good to know that important people like her recognize our financial problems and are willing to help with songs. I'm twenty-two and I've been working for almost fifteen years chasing dreams that won't pay off for another hundred years or more, and I get tired sometimes . . . tired . . . I'm just saying-."

"I feel that way, too, we all do, sometimes," Janes added dejectedly. Before he could say more, a clear plastic cart about the size of a vending machine rolled to a stop beside their table. It had four clear plastic shelves, each adorned with the ANGS corporate logo. Immediately, Janes jumped up smiling and motioned to the cart.

"The goodie wagon has arrived, folks," shouted Dorothea, happily. "It's time to party. What'll it be, Ron? It's time to get out of our *producer* mode and into our *consumer* mode."

Gil hesitated, unsure what they wanted and what was the right answer.

"Miss Dyllon's music is so much more understandable when you're relaxed and receptive," Dorothea explained. "The goodie wagon here has the best stuff in town and there's something for everyone. The stuff on the bottom shelf, they're downers; I don't recommend them until you're ready to go home and even then, you should clear it with one of us. You need good self-worth when you're bottoming out on them. The other shelves have varying degrees of attention expanders, rally boosters, and hallucinogens."

Vicki grabbed Gil's arm. "I forgot to mention it in my message. You do carry your inhalator with you at all times, don't you?"

"My what?"

"I'm sorry, it's my fault. You can use mine, tonight. Pick a cartridge from the shelf and pop it into my inhalator, put it up to your mouth, push the red button and breathe deeply. It only takes a second and you'll feel exactly like the label describes or you get half your money back. That's the guarantee, anyway. You have to fill out a long form correctly and that's a hard thing to do after inhaling. You never really get your money back, at least I never have. Don't worry, most times its money well spent."

Kyle spoke his order into the cart microphone and a cartridge fell from the third shelf into an open tray in the center. He snapped it into his inhalator, pushed the red button, and sucked hard on the mouthpiece. When he was done, it took him two tries to get his thumb working enough to finally remove the now-empty cartridge and put it in the recycle bin of the cart. His words slurred and Gil had to concentrate.

"See, each cartridge has this little bitty graph, down here on the bottom that shows what gets heightened, depressed, or enhanced. I love enhanced." Kyle started to laugh until tears formed. "Sorry, where was I? Oh, yes, the graph, you can track your high, except at level three, or two sometimes where . . . did I say you can check your high? Did I say that?" He began to laugh again.

Unsure what Kyle thought was funny, Gil smiled and nodded.

Kyle shook his head rapidly and forced himself to stop laughing. "The intensity and duration shows on the graph, too. That's, so you can plan your evening or at least think you can. It's Ron, right?"

Gil nodded again.

"Of course they're only general guidelines, but in my experience, pretty damn accurate." Kyle's body relaxed as if he had just completed an arduous task and he stared at the cartridge on the table with a happy smile on his face.

"I'll take it from here," Dorothea began. "Kyle's going to be busy relaxing for a while. Avoid the short cycle stuff. It's annoying at concerts because it makes you kind of frenetic and you'll find yourself constantly searching for the wagon to smooth out your mood. I guarantee you won't be bored, but if you have a chance during the concert, watch people in the audience who are fidgeting, turning, and searching for the wagon because they're the ones in fear of crashing. That leaves the bottom shelf. If you know you want to party but you're just not sure how much, the bottom shelf stuff is for you. It's more pedestrian and the ramp up is slower and more pleasant and the ramp down comes with far less angst. And they're cheaper, too. Which do you want, Ron?"

Unsure, Gil said nothing so Dorothea continued.

"For future reference, the second shelf from the top is what the regulars like us call *NASCAR*. It's all speed and collision, all the time. You roar out, but if you're not careful it's crash and burn. Having a slow downer loaded and locked is *de rigueur*. So there you have it. It's all coded and priced based on potency and duration, and to use it, an implied—but legally enforceable company waiver is filed in your account to protect Pharma. Normally, you won't die or kill anyone with this stuff, but the actuaries insist because sometimes there are damages. If you have entertainment insurance, it helps. Don't be scared, though, because if you're scared, it dilutes the full promise of the *Pharma* and wastes money. So you know, me and Janes ride *Formula 1*."

"What is *Formula 1?*" Gil asked as he waited for Dorothea to finish inhaling.

"That's top drawer. I recommend that you stay away from it. It's pricey and only for the strongest egos. Don't use it unless you feel unrewarded by the other *Pharma*. But once you can afford it and you've developed a tolerance for the lower shelves, by all means, taste from the top shelf. But be very careful up there, because there's no place to tie your balloon, if you get my drift. These are truly designer *Pharma*, truly *haute couture* molecules, and not for the faint of heart, literally and figuratively, nor for the weak of credit—or is that weak of heart and faint of credit?" She laughed as did the others. "Or the tarts of credit and weak kneed farting?" Bewildered, even Gil laughed at that.

Janes pointed to one of the canisters on the cart. "If you try one of those powder blue canisters with an alcohol chaser, you'll have to practice blinking and it won't come easy. Drink plenty of fluids early because you won't be able to later. My advice is stay away from them for now, Ron. *Formula 1* and *NASCAR* are good for people like us. We're trained and we live for stress, we're not like you, no offense. So what'll it be?"

Gil stared at the cart but didn't want to choose.

"I'll pick first," Vicki said and spoke to the cart. Two small green-brown plastic canisters dropped from the second tray. She took them and looked at the price. "Wow, prices are up." She turned to Gil. "So what'll it be? It's your choice. Start with shelf one."

"No, thanks," he said, finally. "I've never done *Pharma*. I kind of promised . . ."

They looked surprised.

"Never?" Janes barked. "Not even preparing for the National Selection Tests?"

Gil shook his head.

"Wow, I've been using since I was six."

"Howard didn't approve," Gil answered and let the cart roll to another table.

"Who's Howard?" Vicki asked.

"My father. He didn't want me to use *Pharma*. I'll enjoy the concert without it."

Dorothea was impressed. "Wow, you're home-raised. I should have guessed."

Not knowing what that meant, Gil just nodded.

"I've heard of home-raising, but you're the first person I've met who did it. We're all free-range kids—we're raised by our sectors, sponsored and supported by *Mobile Global* and other corporations if we show economic promise. Like all parents, mine were far too involved creating wealth and building forever careers and besides, they had no training and child-raising has few economic rewards attached to it. Their time was far too valuable to waste developing liabilities. Say, Ron, did you have brothers or sisters? Were there any kids around when you grew up? Was it boring? Were you still allowed to form junior corporations so you could make money and all? Maybe you were part of the Junior Management program like Kyle or the Junior Executives like Janes or the Entrepreneurs of Tomorrow like me and Vicki." Janes put his hand on Dorothea and stopped her. She seemed startled but was soon just staring vacantly.

"It wasn't boring," Gil explained. "Howard's my only family but I wasn't bored."

"Howard must've been rich?"

"No, I don't think so."

"He must have been. How could he afford to spend time with you while furthering his career? Wouldn't it have been more productive for both of you if you had gone to an Archive Academy like everyone else?"

"Is that where you went?" He asked and all but Dorothea nodded. Janes nodded vigorously.

"I guess Howard didn't like me being away."

"It must have cost a bundle to access Archive courses at home."

"I never thought about it but I guess it did."

"What did you do for *Pharma*? I mean for fun, for friends."

"There was no *Pharma*, even though it's legal, Howard insisted. I had lots of friends but most of them were in *Virtuoso*."

"Wow," Vicki said, "and you seem reasonably productive. I've been earning my way since I was seven and I never would have survived without *Pharma* and I wouldn't have passed my final exams without it either." Just then, the hall lights flickered signaling that the show would begin soon.

"Before the concert starts, turn on your communicator and plug in your headphone," Vicki instructed him. "Then check the list of frequencies posted on the monitor at the back of the stage." She pointed. "If you're not sure which frequency to try, I can recommend one. We each like to listen to Ms. Dyllon differently."

"Someday, I'm going to be able to afford to upgrade my PID and receive these concerts directly into my head. That would be so cool," Dorothea added, smiling.

Kyle added his input. "I set my frequency preferences for *Crank*. It's my favorite music form. The words are hers but they're synthesized and come out, well, crank, the way I like it. Vicki likes to hear her in *Neo-Folk* with stuff like electro-harp and glockenspiel that I find overly sentimental. She sets her phone to a frequency and then modifies it with a special program app she downloaded at a nominal cost from the Dyllon Tomas franchise website."

"I set mine for *Old Style Rock n Roll*," Janes said. "What's your favorite, Rick?"

"My name's Ron, not Rick, and Vicki's style will be fine."

Vicki smiled at that. "You hear her words better and her words are everything."

"That's not true," Dorothea argued. "Her music adds so much intensity and the different variations on her themes keep it fresh, forever. Today I'm dialing in *Classical Rap* with violette and electro-pan flute. Try it, Ron; you'll like it better than Vicki's choice. It's not so old fashioned."

Janes added, "There are an infinite number of options, but each costs a different amount. If I were you, I'd try Dyllon on the basic settings before paying for extras."

"I'll stick with Vicki's, for now," Gil said, feeling good that he could make her smile. "Maybe I'll try the others later if that's permitted," he added diplomatically and Dorothea nodded.

"Suit yourself."

The house lights fell to darkness and the crowd erupted in pregnant anticipation.

"Here she comes!" Dorothea screamed and along with the others, inhaled a new round of *Pharma*.

The intro music began and in the darkness everyone stood and stomped their feet in rhythm as the cabaret filled with the lustful screams of enduring fans. Vicki tugged at his sleeve.

"The words appear on your communicator," she shouted, "and also on the large monitor." She pointed. "Sing along, everyone does, but keep your headphones on."

Gil nodded.

Minutes passed and the din began to fade in anticipation. Soon, the room was absolutely silent. From his headphones, Gil heard the singer's footsteps echo off the stage surface as she approached and then there was an explosion of lights and hysteria. In juxtaposition to the frenzy, Dyllon Tomas stood silent and alone at center stage, enveloped in light from follow spots nestled high in the auditorium's rafters. Dyllon Tomas was prettier, and maybe more vulnerable, than her posters had shown. She was average height with big, dark, expressive eyes and long, dark, dreadlocked hair that hung down her back, highlighted with multicolored extensions. But the feature that attracted him most was her mesmerizing, shy smile. She wore what looked like the bottom half of a loose fitting metallic space suit with a string bikini top made from the inedible parts of fruits. Crowning her ensemble, she wore a black stovepipe hat that was adorned with shiny legal tender. Imbedded in the center of her hat was a small monitor that displayed the audience as if from her eyes.

"Hello, *Pharma-Tech!*" she shouted. "Welcome to my second in a series of six concerts during the High Holy Productive Days of *Chrisnukkah*. I'm happy to be back in my favorite cusp, performing for my favorite *Conducer* audiences." The audience cheered. "Check our Dyllon Tomas website for deals and experiences that are well worth it. And please attend my franchise partners' concerts in nearby cusps.

"On the way here, I hitched in a *Toller's* truck driving down from Saptown, north of Chicago. I was talking to the driver about the holiday season. I don't know how many of you know this but originally, *Chrisnukkah* was a celebration of the birth of the baby Jesus Christ, whose life gave rise to the greatest and most profitable marketing enterprise in the history of the world, one that later morphed into what we all know today as Morgan. But in the beginning, the marketing enterprise was called simply Christianity, named after that very special baby." A few in the audience nodded, most simply waited for her to start singing.

"In the beginning, *Chrisnukkah* was a series of economic rituals that occurred quarterly and focused on simply gift giving. That seems funny today, I know, but it shows how much we've evolved from those simpler days. Today, the *Chrisnukkah* holiday is all about getting and taking. To be a quality citizen of value, Morgan requires that highly motivated people invest their valuable time in the search and acquisition of that one exquisitely perfect and appropriate gift for each and every one of their valued business relationships. In doing this, by spending our hard earned credits in the pursuit of approval that leads directly to economic gain, we honor the baby Jesus Christ and all the other fine entrepreneurs of western capitalist thought. The celebration is great fun and it is rewarding, too, but somewhere along the way, I believe that we've lost the fragile art of receiving gifts. I believe that happens because people no longer talk to one another directly about what they really want or need. Yes, I know that everyone makes lists but sometimes, successful business endeavors require spontaneity and even a little honesty."

With that, Vicki leaned over to him and whispered, "See what I mean?"

He didn't.

"We spend our time googling everyone's wants and needs on the Mesh. Now granted, if we do it correctly we earn gratitude and respect credits from the recipients of our gifts, which in most cases can be converted in future business dealings into more valuable assets. Still, I don't know about you, but I long for the good old days when people made their wishes known in non-electronic conversation. There were risks and misunderstandings but it simplified the buying process and made it more personal and challenging. It was a sad day when Chrisnukkah went all data base and I believe we lost something when it did. Now don't get me wrong, *Chrisnukkah* is a valued *quid pro quo*, but it's sad that most of us have taken the less entrepreneurial way and no longer share the experience that comes from unexpected results. I'm older than many of you here tonight and I tell you, when I was young, waking up *Chrisnukkah* morning and watching my family's expressions when I opened gifts is a memory I still cherish."

The lights dimmed and music began quietly in the background. Gil could sense the pent up excitement in the crowd.

"But," she added, "Like everything else, if we want to change the world, we have to do it . . ." She paused and the audience shouted along with her. ". . . one step at a time, Sweet Jesus, one step at a time." There was thunderous applause and screaming.

"Sing, Dyllon!" a voice from the back yelled. The crowd followed with an emphatic "Shhh."

Smiling at the interruption, Dyllon continued. "My heart goes out to a beautiful poet from those dark days of the First American Republic, a Mr. Phil Ochs."

The music got louder and the air filled with the strong fragrance of flowers. The *Pharma* had kicked in nicely and the expressions on the faces of Gil's new friends were slack, but blissful.

Vicki leaned toward him again and with slurred words, advised, "Put your communicator on frequency three-five and listen. You'll love it." He keyed in the sequence and put on his headphones. The music was softer and more melodic. And then Dyllon began to sing.

Her singing voice was a much higher pitched than her speaking voice, sounding almost like whale song he'd heard once in Archive. The sound was heartbreaking. Some in the audience swayed and sang along, others were up dancing, more contorting, to a different rhythm, but singing as well.

> Show me a *Waster*, show me a jail,
> Show me a *Waster* whose face has gone pale
> And I'll show you a *Conducer* with so many reasons why
> And there but for fortune may go you or I
> Show me the alley, show me the train,
> Show me a *Waster*, who sleeps out in the rain,
> And I'll show you a *Conducer* with so many reasons why
> There but for fortune, may go you or go I.

The music and the voice were all so pure that Gil closed his eyes and for the first time in too long, he relaxed. Everything felt so right, so true—as if an itch he'd never known was being scratched.

> Show me the famine, show me the frail
> Eyes with no future that show how we failed
> And I'll show you liabilities with so many reasons why
> There but for fortune go you or I . . .

When the music stopped, he felt sad and empty. He opened his eyes and looked around. His new friends were smiling but had a misty, far away look of epiphany. Kyle and Dorothea were actually sobbing. Dyllon, having finished her song, turned and walked behind the curtain and the audience began talking quietly among themselves. Confused, Gil looked to Vicki.

"Isn't she wonderful?" she cooed. "After each song, she leaves the stage so the audience can discuss it. She'll wait until we finish before singing again. She trusts us to transform her words into something relevant to us."

"It was beautiful, but what does it mean? Words like that, what do they mean?"

Kurt laughed. "The first time I heard her, I felt just like you. It's best to let it come to you. That's why the *Pharma*. Sometimes, it takes awhile to really get to know her because the world is so straightforward and she's so complex. Once you're familiar with her songs, you'll understand. She's for personal freedom—believe it or not—more than economic freedom. She believes in the individual, not the organization. She believes we should do what we want rather than what is economical. She's a radical progressive that way and she tightropes danger with every verse. And with all that, she's for taking responsibility for our lives and our society and contributing to Gross Domestic Product the best we can."

"Really, she's for all that?"

"She gives our lives perspective," Kyle added. "She only dwells on the negative to show what's possible and she's a true original, not influenced by anyone. She respects, though rejects the status quo, and doesn't believe we should be forced to earn by doing something we don't believe in. She wants us to be productive, but in our way, not theirs."

Vicki continued. "She's so beautiful and independent. She isn't tainted or influenced by commercial stuff, not really. And she's been arrested so many times, but her fans rally to bail her out every time. It's quite a spectacle. You can watch it tonight after the concert on her website, her fans and critics chanting outside the jail, the bid and ask on her bail moving up and down with the cheers and boos. If we didn't have to work tomorrow, we'd be there. A portion of tonight's revenue from *Pharma* sales goes to her legal defense fund, but some goes to fund her estate in the Cayman Islands where she flees to avoid prosecution. For all that, she expects us to abide by business laws while she risks everything to stand for us. Dyllon truly understands the implications of funding a better world. How can you not love her for that?"

"Everyone loves Dyllon," Dorothea cooed.

"But how . . ." Gil started to ask.

"To Miss Dyllon, the how isn't important. How is beyond our capability to process," Vicki interrupted. "It's about wanting things different. That's the only way things change. She teaches us to know what we don't want and talk about it until everyone feels the same. Only then will things change. It's the beauty of true freedom . . . or the freedom of true beauty. Shhh, she's ready to sing again."

A sweeter smell permeated the room and the audience quieted. Gil decided to turn off his communicator and listen to her music unmodified. Introducing yet another Phil Ochs song, Dyllon began singing.

> The man who tries to tell you that they'll take your job away,
> He's the same man who was scabbin' just the other day,
> And your union's not a union till he's thrown out of the way,
> And he's chokin' on your links of the chain, of the chain,
> And he's chokin' on your links of the chain

Gil tried to understand the meaning of the lyrics but without references, the song meant nothing to him. As she sang, he looked around; trying to understand why people were so enraptured because listening to her voice without technological enhancement, Dyllon was merely a pedestrian singer with little emotion or range, with an effect nothing like her first song. To make it even more bizarre, the plugged-in audience was singing or chanting the words to different tunes and groups were up and dancing, all to different beats. Unexpectedly, he laughed at the chaos.

Kyle noticed and motioned angrily, holding up fingers for Gil to read. It was Kyle's frequency and Gil put his headphones back on, keyed in Kyle's numbers, and listened to an incredible soprano supported by intense tribal drums and shrieking background vocals.

> For now the times are tellin' you the times are rollin' on,
> And you're fighting for the same thing, the jobs that will be gone,
> Now it's only fair to ask you boys, which side are you on?
> As you're buildin' all your links on the chain, on the chain,
> As you're buildin' all your links on the chain.

The song continued. Listening with headphones, Gil was amazed how eloquent she sounded. And she seemed right, although he didn't know why or what she wanted or wanted him to do about it. The harder he tried to understand, the harder it was as the arrangement drummed her words into his head. The music stopped suddenly and he felt alone and empty.

Kyle shouted above the screaming. "Wow. I love it! That was my favorite. It rocks. She's so intense."

Vicki wiped tears from her eyes. "Oh my gosh, that was so sweet and forceful."

Gil struggled to keep from smiling as each of his friends searched for words to describe totally different feelings from what they reported sounded like totally different performances. He had no idea why but he found it refreshing.

"If what she says is right about greed and poverty," he asked, "what are we supposed to do about it? Does she sing about the answers?"

They laughed.

"Was that funny?"

"No. Dyllon treats us with the respect all *Conducers* should have. She lets us decide on appropriate action ourselves." Vicki pointed to the stage where Dyllon was returning for another song. "We'll talk later; she's really into it now."

He listened closely to each song. With headphones, there was beauty in each song but he searched in vain for truth. The music was rapturous and ethereal but when each song ended, his thoughts triggered questions apparently no one at the table shared. After enough terse looks, he stopped asking questions and just listened. Finally, Dyllon announced the end of the concert with her signature piece "Desolation Ragtime Band." Once again, Gil chose Vicki's channel to listen.

> I'm a citizen of life, and a singer of songs
> And charter member of the Desolation Ragtime Band.
> I sing of destruction and leadership wrongs
> And I sing in Ragtime as I take my stand
> I sing it happy and I sing it strong
> Joyous desolation in a Ragtime land . . .

Chapter 13

Hamilton, MI.—2070

Pharma—Private enterprise with the support of significant government funding advanced brain sciences by constructing molecules and delivery systems that pinpointed specific receptors in the brain thus modifying behavior with predictable, desired results.

With that enormous success, the *Pharma* Industry in the Second Republic became profitable and so popular that agricultural drugs were soon priced out of the marketplace and illegal drug cartels were driven to acquire majority shares in Pharma corporations, reducing reportable crimes, prison populations, and thus federal and state taxing requirements. At the same time, this increased revenue was a boon not just to the Federal government but to those *Wharton Towns* that specialized in *Pharma* production and distribution, particularly Hamilton, Michigan which rose from the debris of fabled Detroit to become the largest employer in the Midwest owning distribution rights for its *Pharma* from the Ohio River to beyond the Rocky Mountains.

Pharma brain science drugs were the cash cow that allowed Hamilton to diversify to become the leading Production town in the Second Republic. But even in the best-planned scenarios, there are unintended consequences. The irony of Hamilton as the *Pharma* manufacturing and delivery capital of the world is that the inexpensive and readily available drugs produced there have created productivity and latent anxiety issues among Hamilton's youngest *Conducers.*—**Archive**

The concert ended with Dyllon Tomas making a plea.

"Thank you all for coming. Like always, I'll be going into the audience in a minute, but first, I'm obligated by my franchise contract to hawk certain items so bear with me." She pulled something from a box on the stage.

"This is the national Dyllon Tomas doll—it looks nothing like me but really, really young *Conducers* seem to like it. I think it was modeled after that Dyllon slut from *Investment Banking* outside San Diego." The audience laughed and she smiled. "For a reasonable—by some standards—monthly fee, including *Toller* shipping and fondling, this anatomically overstated she-doll can be yours to play with after a long, productive day at work or you can gift it to the working toddler of your choice. Plug the doll into your communicator and watch and listen to her entertain you just like you were at one of our concerts. The doll even has a hat like mine to show you listening to her. It's just like my hat here tonight. Of course, there is a large catalogue of wardrobe changes for future gifting possibilities.

"This unique Dyllon Tomas doll has settings that reflect every Dyllon franchise at every location so if you are interested in nuance, well, check it out. Of course, set it for me because I'm the best." The audience laughed again and applauded as Dyllon tossed the doll back in the box. I have a few more gadgets but what the hell-."

She kicked the box to the back and stepped off the stage to cheers. Gil watched her as she wandered from table to table talking to her fans, many of whom made a fuss, some crying, to be near her. When she came to Gil's table, Vicki was so excited that she too cried. She put her head against Kyle's shoulder and pointed to the singer. Kyle begged her to say something, but all Vicki could do was bury her head and sob.

The singer stared at Gil with her dark, expressive eyes. Unsure what to say, he nodded. "Hey, good looking, did you like my concert?" Dyllon asked. The others stared at him, jealous.

"With all the fragrances and headphones, it was really enjoyable."

"But without them . . . ?" she asked smiling, her eyes never wavering from his.

Vicki slapped him on the arm. "I told you not to listen without the headphones. It ruins everything."

"Without them?" Dyllon coaxed.

Vicki grabbed his sleeve and tugged. "Don't dare say anything bad to her or . . ."

"Without them?" Dyllon persisted.

"It was less so," he managed. Vicki groaned.

"Less so?" the singer laughed.

"Don't take it the wrong way, I enjoyed the concert. I really did. Thank you."

"I'm glad you liked it. Do you have any thoughts about our songs?"

"I don't think so. Well maybe, what were they about?"

"Ouch," Dyllon said, still smiling. "I guess that means the rebel in me didn't connect with the rebel in you. That's on me, sorry."

Vicki elbowed Gil hard in the stomach making him grunt. "Be nice to her."

"What did you find lacking?" the singer pressed on.

"Ron, don't you dare," Vicki wailed. "Please, don't. We love you, Dyllon." She shouted, blushing bright red as she held out her arms to the singer. "Don't listen to him, we're your fans."

Dorothea added, "He never even heard of you before tonight. He's new here and he can't appreciate what you're singing about."

The singer smiled and returned her eyes to Gil.

"It's okay, I can handle criticism. I'm more concerned that you never heard of me, though." Her eyes stayed riveted on him. "Were you expecting . . . more?"

"I wasn't expecting anything," he said. "Don't get me wrong, I'm impressed. The production values were incredible. I'm sorry if I sound disappointed. Vicki's right, I'm new and I don't get out much. That's why I've never heard your music before. But I'd like to hear more. You're very good."

"Damned by faint praise," she said. "This is what I do. I won't be better the next time. Where are you from?"

"Back east. My friends here are your real fans. You should talk to them."

Dyllon smiled, her head cocked to the side as if trying to remember something. Finally, she bent over and whispered to him, her breath making him tingle.

"Maybe I'll sing about you someday. I will definitely see you again, soon. Bye-bye." Before Gil could consider a reply, she patted him softly on his cheek and then hugged everyone at the table before taking her leave to greet her other fans.

"What was all that about?" Kurt asked.

"I have no idea. She seems nice, though," Gil said.

"What did she whisper to you?"

"She said she hoped to see me again."

They stared at him with something like respect. Janes asked, "What did she mean?"

"She wants to see me at another concert. What else?"

"Well don't let it go to your head," Dorothea said. "Dyllon is friendly like that. I was at a concert last year in the Agra Sector cusp where she said the same thing to some of the people in the audience. Don't think you're special."

"Thanks for reminding me."

After the singer went backstage, Kyle and Dorothea suggested they continue the evening at a local dance hall. As they started to leave, Vicki looked back and invited Gil to come along.

It was still snowing when they left the theater. The dance hall was only a few streets away and as they walked toward the more populated part of the cusp, his friends, still high on inhalants, wandered down the center of the street playing in the snow, joking and laughing. He felt like an outsider but less so than earlier in the evening. When Kyle hit him with a snowball, he laughed and joined in. Soon, they were covered in snow and everyone was laughing.

"Hey," Janes shouted, "I lost my communicator." No one could find it so they carefully retraced their steps, kicking the snow to unearth the lost electronic. Gil was out ahead when he spied something lying in the snow. He reached for it just as a shadow appeared from an alley and someone sped across his path, grabbed the communicator and was gone.

"Yo!" Gil yelled and ran after the thief.

"What is it?" Kyle yelled.

"Someone grabbed your communicator," he shouted back. "I'm going after him." Gil kept his eye on the thief, briefly turning to see if his friends were following. He ran through an alley, almost slipping when he tried to stop at a small fence. The thief was on the other side, looking for a place to hide. Gil jumped the fence and found himself face to face with a very young boy.

"I'm not going to hurt you," Gil said. "Just give me back the communicator."

The boy ran to his left then cut to his right. Gil lunged, coming up empty and falling face down in the snow. He hurried to give chase when he saw Kyle and Janes holding the struggling boy against the fence that the boy had just climbed back over. Kyle grabbed the communicator and the boy struggled to take it back. Gil climbed back to join them.

"What have we here, people," Kyle said, "is a teeny tiny *Bayer*?"

"What's a *Bayer*?" Gil asked, brushing loose snow from his clothes.

"A *Bayer* is a scrounger, a ferret, a robber. They prowl the streets looking for stuff to steal so they can sell it on Mesh auction sites to make money."

"I'm no damn *Bayer*," the boy said as he wrestled to free himself. "Gimme back my communicator. My papa gave it to me for my birthday."

"It's not yours, kid, it's his," Kyle said pointing to Janes. "You're ruining an expensive high so don't piss me off."

"It's not yours," the boy insisted sullenly as Kyle handed the communicator to Janes, who inspected it. "He's right, it's not mine."

Gil began to search him. He reached into the boy's pocket and pulled out another communicator and lobbed it to Janes.

"Not mine, either," Janes said. "Keep searching."

Gil found two more, a ski mask, and a pair of hand warmers before finally pulling out the communicator that belonged to Janes, who nodded and took it.

"That's not your communicator," the boy insisted.

"What do we do with him?" Dorothea asked. "He ruined a good time."

"Should we turn him over to the authorities?" Gil asked.

"They won't do anything except take his stuff, sell it, and set him free," Vicki said. "We should post this stuff ourselves and earn some extra credits."

"Great," Kyle said. "Take his jacket too. Someone can always use a boy's jacket."

That concerned Gil. "You can't be serious? He's just a kid." He crouched down until he was eye-to-eye with the boy. "What's your name?"

The boy spit at him. Gil flinched but caught it on his cheek. He used his sleeve to wipe the spittle while Janes shook the boy hard.

"No, don't hurt him. Leave him alone." Gil turned back to the boy who was unapologetic. "Why were you stealing?"

"I'm not stealing. Just redistributing, a little, maybe, that's all. Papa doesn't make much and my mama and the rest are turning transparents."

Gil turned to his new friends. "Transparents?"

"He means transparent," Kyle explained. "When your value is barely positive, you spend all your time fighting off the heat and figuring out how to survive. You know, worrying about where to find more credits or how to get free things, or you steal. People like that don't interface well because any more transparent is disappearance."

Gil turned to his new friends. "He's just a little guy."

"Hamilton's full of little guys with no viable skills in families with no value. They're vermin and cost true *Conducers* like us hard earned credits."

"Why doesn't the city do something to help them?" Gil asked.

"The mayor tried but his efforts were declared unconstitutional. If it costs more to get rid of them than to keep them, you can't do anything. It makes no sense to throw good money after bad. But as soon as its cost justified, you eradicate them. Our only recourse is street justice and hope the economics means only a small fine."

"But . . ." Gil tried to find a way to save the boy.

"Kurt's right, Ron," Kyle added. "You're new here. We see this all the time. The kid's from a family of thieves. Why should we have to get up every morning and work hard at mind-numbing, stressful jobs while these lazy ferrets prey on us and our wealth? Everyone fears disappearing. That's why we work so damn hard. And frankly, some mornings it's the only thing that drives me to get up and go to work. They should have to live with the same pressure."

Gil shook his head. "It seems to me they do. If this kid's out late on a cold winter night stealing our stuff, we must be living a whole lot better than he is. I wouldn't want to change places with him, would you?"

"How the fuck does that matter? He knows the rules and no one will miss him. It's time these people act like Americans and honor property. As it is, they just take what they want. We can't allow his type to have it too easy when we have to work so hard for the stuff we have. It's not fair and by God, it's not right."

They all agreed, even Vicki who seemed to be the most compassionate. "But he's just a kid," Gil implored. "Janes, you have your communicator back. You're no worse off than you started."

"Hell no, Ron," Janes said. "You think you're being nice. Let the kid go and in ten minutes he'll steal something from you or he'll do it to someone else and it'll be your fault. I'm not sure that the city won't hold you responsible."

He considered his previous experiences in jail. "You have a point," Gil agreed. He looked at the boy. "Kid, if we let you go, will you stop stealing?"

Dorothea threw up her hands. "What do you expect him to say?"

"Let him speak. Well?"

"Mister, if I don't bring stuff home, my family is gone. We have to eat."

"See, unrepentant, let's take all his stuff, it'll be a good lesson," Kurt said. "And we can sell it easy."

Vicki agreed. "Ron, Janes is right. I worked hard for the credits I spent on this high. After everything that happened . . . you know, this was supposed to be a fun night. This little ferret ruined it and this is America and everything you do has a cost; he knows that. The kid must pay."

"But he's a kid. It's not right."

"Who cares about right? It is economically justifiable," Dorothea said, not allowing Gil to respond. "No, really, what does right have to do with anything? Life is nothing but costs and benefits and if you're going to prosper in Hamilton, you have to stop acting different. It was cute at first, but it's really annoying as hell right now."

"I'm not trying to be annoying. How about you take your communicator and I'll treat everyone to *Pharma* at the dance hall?"

"Treat? What does treat mean?" Dorothea asked, suspiciously.

"I'll buy you a round, a canister, or whatever. I can't afford much but I'll buy. Just leave the kid alone."

"Why are you doing this?" Janes asked. "He's nobody and you'll never see him again, or if you do, you'll be chasing him to get something he stole."

"You're probably right, but it doesn't feel right. Take your communicator and let me buy you your next high and you'll be better off than you were before the boy came along. Is it a deal?"

Janes stared at all the stolen property laying on a cleared part of the alley. "Fine, kid, take your stuff." He pushed the kid away but as he reached for his stuff, Janes stopped him. "Not these," he said as he pocketed a couple of items. "Ron, you owe us a second-drawer high. Now, boy, get out of here." He pushed the young ferret into the snow and he slid face first to a stop against the fence and then catlike, he scampered to his feet and scurried to pick up the rest of the stuff before someone else pocketed it.

"Get lost or you'll be sorry," Kyle said as he stepped toward the kid with his fists ready. The boy made one last grab and then turned and ran.

As Kyle bent to pick up the few things that were left, he looked at Gil. "Don't forget, you owe us a high." Gil nodded and followed them down the snowy street to the dance hall.

When they arrived at the dance hall entrance, a large crowd had gathered. Dorothea walked over to an attendant, kissed him and whispered something in his ear. He smiled when she put something in his shirt pocket and then waved them through as the waiting crowd booed.

They walked down a long, narrow, darkened corridor that bent to the right and opened onto a huge, high-ceilinged dance hall blanketed with smoke. Gil stared through the haze and hesitated. Lining the walls were hundreds of small *Virtuoso* kiosks. "Where did they . . . ?"

Vicki put her arm on his shoulder. "Amazing, isn't it? If you're a member, you can use them during the day, but it's extraordinarily expensive. At night, it's open to the public for a fee."

"What do we do?"

"We head to the bar for that taste you promised us," Kyle interrupted, grabbing him and walking him in that direction. Everyone ordered except Gil. While the Pharmacist was preparing the *Pharma* cartridges for use, Gil watched and was surprised when the woman opened a number of small green boxes that looked exactly like the ones he monitored at his warehouse job.

"You need to try it." Kyle said but Gil just shook his head. "Okay, but you're missing an opportunity to have a great time—one you'll remember."

As Vicki inhaled her choice *Pharma*, her eyes rolled back into her head. Gil leaned toward her and had to ask multiple times, "What now?"

She didn't respond until the flush left her face. "Get a kiosk, big boy," she slurred.

Gil looked at the machines, but didn't move. Vicki explained. "Enter the kiosk, it scans your identity. You're new so register, answer a questionnaire about social preferences, and modify your icon to look like whatever you want your dance partner to see. Be creative, it's fun. Earn more experience points and higher dance value points and you can adjust your dance moves, improve your rhythm, enhance your athletics, even modify gravity, anything you want to appear like a better dancer so you can draw a better dance partner and earn more points. When you're done registering, review the inventory of available wallflowers—that's what they call people who don't have a partner—or you can wait until someone finds you on their wallflower list. Then, be a dancing fool and have fun. It's that simple, but for you, I'd guess, having fun may be the hard part."

Everyone laughed but Gil.

"But I don't know how to dance."

"Why doesn't that surprise me?" Kyle said and they all laughed again.

Vicki tried to make him feel better. "Who does in the beginning? Don't feel self-conscious, remember, you'll be virtual. Just listen to the music and move to what you hear. If that doesn't work, there's always *Pharma*. Remember, your partner only sees you in virtual so trust me; you'll be dancing up a storm in no time. If you want, you can communicate to your dance partners through your headgear. The music is lowered so it will sound like it's just you two and there's no one else in the place. It's a great way to meet new friends. Though it's hard to believe, some say people discover partners on the dance floor, maybe short term partners."

Gil looked at the kiosks and the crowds. "Everyone goes into a kiosk?"

Vicki laughed. "No, silly, enter your information and wait. The kiosks support the virtual experience, but see all the people on the dance floor; they're connected. When you put on the headgear, you each see the other's chosen icon. Don't be scared, some people pick animals or monsters for the fun of it. When you dance, you dance to any music you want, it doesn't have to be the same music your partner is dancing to, either. The system seamlessly integrates the choreography. You don't even have to talk to your partner if you don't want to. You can pay to have an avatar do that while you talk to anyone else on any other frequency, pick a conversational avatar for yourself, or just read a book if that's what gets you off. The system keeps up a conversation, but some friends tell me the computer isn't capable of moving relationships along so, if you choose that option, you can only hope to get lucky. Whenever you get bored, move on to another partner. No one's disappointed, this is dancing. It's that simple."

"So you wait for a response."

"For a few credits more, you can rent virtual partners. If you really like the one you rent, you can lease, though it can happen, it rarely develops into a fulfilling relationship." Vicki laughed but stopped when she noticed, once again, Gil hadn't found that funny.

"Sometimes, if you're lucky, the media picks up your feed as a reality broadcast and sends it to homes that subscribe. You can become famous and maybe even rich. Keep that in mind when you're searching for the motivation to dance."

He didn't want media attention. "Do they use your real identity?"

"It's only your virtual persona until you're lucky enough to sign a professional contract, then you can pick any stage name you want. Why?"

Not wanting to explain, Gil just shrugged.

"Ron, this is supposed to be fun but you're acting way too serious. Here I'll show you." She dragged him to an empty kiosk. "You're scanned, now answer these questions." When he just stared at her, she pushed him to the microphone and stepped outside. "I won't listen, I promise."

Feeling awkward and embarrassed, he answered the questions, some very personal and others obscure. He participated but he didn't want to give away anything important about himself. When he completed the questionnaire, he put on his headgear and Vicki walked him out to the dance floor.

"Wait until someone contacts you. I have to go. I have a bunch of dance partners waiting in the queue. Good luck and have fun."

"Thanks, maybe I'll see you on the dance floor."

"Not likely," she said. "Sorry, I'm a high rated dancer; I can't afford to dance with just anyone. Have fun." She walked away, blending into the throng of dancers moving on the dance floor.

Alone in the crowd, he watched what looked like a syncopated comedy of smiling, happy people dancing, or more accurately, cavorting with no apparent unifying theme on a silent dance floor.

He wondered how something that looks this foolish made them happy.

Along one wall, he noticed a cluster of people sitting in wheelchairs also moving spastically to some unknown beat. That was one advantage. His thoughts were interrupted when his communicator vibrated. Nervous, he looked around for Vicki but she was gone. He wanted to ignore the call, but his communicator kept vibrating, tickling his ears so he answered.

"CooperRocket?"

"Yes, who is this?" he spoke.

"Bumpsie Agonweye. Want to dance? Say yes."

Nervous, he nodded and a tall and extraordinarily good-looking and colossally well-built brunette appeared on his visor. "You almost took too long. I had other offers but I'm curious. You said you're new and enjoy rocketry. I don't know what that is but it sounds sexy."

"I . . . I don't do that anymore," he not quite lied. "I work in warehousing."

"You don't rocket anymore."

"No, nothing, not really, not anymore."

"Oh, you said that was an interest."

"I did," he lied again, "but there's not much call for rocketry in Hamilton."

She laughed. "You're cute CooperRocket. I like that in a partner. Dance?"

He nodded. "What do I do?"

"For starters, do not step on my feet."

"I'll try not to."

She laughed aloud. "That's a joke. We are virtual, remember?"

"Right. So how do we do this? It's my first time."

"Rocket man, you're a virgin, I'm honored. It's simple. Listen and move." He listened to the music and moved. "You're getting it. You're a dancing fool!"

"I guess that's better than just being a fool? What kind of music is this?"

"If you're listening to my choice, it's called the blues. If you don't like it, try something else."

He stayed with the blues and concentrated on moving with the sounds. There was extended silence before he heard Bumpsie's voice again. "Are you from like Mars or something, or is this the only personality you can afford? Spend some ducats, sweetie. You will never get lucky with me otherwise."

Gil felt self-conscious, finding it difficult to move with the music, listen, think, and talk. "Thanks," was all he could think to say. A heavy, fruity fragrance emanated from his headgear and soon he found himself relaxing and enjoying dancing.

"That's better. You're doing great. You have a nice way about you."

"How can you tell?"

"Virtual is a form of real and I'm having fun so who cares. What about you?"

"It's okay, kind of fun."

"What do you mean kind of fun?"

"I'm enjoying it. You're a good dancer."

"How good?"

"I don't know, very good?"

"People say I am the best."

"They must know."

"What does that mean?"

"Nothing. If they say you're a great dancer, you must be a great dancer."

"What do you think?"

He concentrated on her. "I like to watch you dance."

"Thanks. So do I."

"You like watching me dance?"

"No, why would I watch you when I'm the better dancer? I watch myself, of course. I'm really good."

When the music stopped, Bumpsie's image evaporated. He looked around, knowing he'd never recognize her and if he did, he didn't really want to meet her. A message appeared on his gear notifying him that he was being charged more to continue. To avoid the charge, he removed his gear and hung it back on the kiosk wall. He was about to walk away to search for Vicki when he felt a tap on his shoulder and turned. A guard scanned him and pointed to the kiosk.

"Mr. Cooper, we don't put used gear back. Keep it for your next dance or turn it in at Hygiene, if you're done. You've paid for more time so you may want to use it some more. See, your light's green. Be careful, some of the less well-endowed will try to steal your time."

"No, that's okay." With that, the green light started to blink.

"You have another partner lined up," the guard said, helpfully.

Reluctantly, he put his headgear back on and answered, hoping it was Vicki so he could leave. It turned out to be a girl named PattEKake.

"CooperRocket?"

"Yes?"

"I would love to dance with you."

"I'm not very good."

"You're a lot better than you think you are. Say okay, please."

He agreed and as the music began a whiff of vanilla and then a hint of magnolia caused him to shiver.

From a distance, PattEKake looked very appealing. Closer, she was perfect.

"How are you?" she asked.

PattEKake was too perfect.

Chapter 14

Hamilton, MI.—2070

Stunned, he whispered. "Is it safe?" It might have been due to the quality of his headgear, or maybe it was the time that had passed, or maybe she was just older, but to Gil, she was the same person he had created all those years ago and ultimately fell in love with. And yet she was different, different in the way time and distance causes memory to diverge from reality. It seemed so long ago and so far away.

"I wouldn't be here if you were safe."

"I'm safe enough."

"There is never that kind of safe for you, but yes, for now, it is safe enough. How are you?"

"I don't know how to answer that because I don't know who I'm talking to?"

"Look at me. I'm Andrea. You know me. I missed you. It's been a long time."

In spite of his rising anger, her voice and all it represented snuck past his defenses and caused his heart to ache.

"Not long enough," he insisted. "I know it's you, Andrea, I just don't know who you are."

"You don't understand. Maybe you never did. I've always been Andrea, only Andrea, and I'm here for you."

"That's a lie!" he shouted. He quieted when his headgear showed alarm on the faces of the nearby dancers. "Don't lie to me," he growled. And then he said more quietly, "not again."

"I have never lied to you and I never will. What can I do to convince you?"

"There is nothing you can do to get what you want and still make it what I want, too. We're past that. I'm tired of being used by you. I don't want you anymore and I don't want to need you either." Resigned to the reality of her, he stared sorrowfully. "But it seems I can't stay alive without your help so what choice do I have?"

She remained silent.

"I beg you, if you ever liked me or respected me even a little, please leave me alone. This is my life and my problem and I will solve it without you."

"Gil, it's so much more than that and I can help. I want to help. Tell me what I can do to make you believe in me like you once did."

"We're past that and there's no going back." Her eyes were sad but he couldn't tell if he was seeing her sadness or his. "I would give anything to have never known you," he said. "Look what you've done to me. Please go away."

Andrea looked down, broken hearted, and though she was older now, her voice was that of the girl he remembered.

"I'm sad that you think that of me," she said. "You made me—no one else—you did it. And in spite of what you think, I will always be what you created me to be." Her hands reached out for him and like a magnet, his hands were drawn to her but he resisted and she nodded dejectedly. "Please believe that."

He smiled ruefully. "That's simply not true and if it was, it doesn't matter any more."

As if praying, she folded her hands in front of her, spreading the opening in her blouse just enough to reveal a hint of the freckles he had placed there during her creation.

"In our years together, Gil, did it ever feel like I was anything but true to you? Was I playing some role? Think. When you needed me, I was there. When you wanted advice, I listened and gave you the best I had. I can't hurt you, not ever, and I'm sad that you no longer trust me."

"Stop it. Stop it right now. It's too late. You don't get to be sad, not with all you've done." He remembered that day long ago when her tear fell on him and made him sad. Now, that memory made him angry. "I'm just a pawn to you in some master plan I can't possibly understand. Your words carry so many meanings that they're worthless to me." He fought to avoid remembering moments that would make him love her again. He turned away to avoid her but she was still in front of him.

"Gil, I want you to be certain of one thing. I'm yours more than you are mine. I'm nothing without you."

She was maddening and he wanted to rip his headgear off and put an end to it but he hesitated. "How do I compete with you? You know me so well and you never forget anything. You know what I want and you know what words work." He moved away but stopped. "If I had my glove, would there be two of you?"

"Stop it," she said, tearfully. In the background slow music played and the hall filled once again with smoke. Couples danced slow and close so he and Andrea became a stationary island in a rolling sea of bodies. She put her hand up to touch him.

"You promised me a dance."

Reluctantly, he reached for her, forcing himself to believe it was the music or the smoke that made him feel like crying. They touched and she molded herself to him. He couldn't resist the stirring and they moved as one to the music.

"How is it that I can feel you?" he asked.

"It is haptic response from the smoke," she explained. "I missed you."

"I've been so many places since the last time. Why here?"

"Because you need me."

"I'll always need you, it seems, but I don't want you, Andrea, not anymore. To survive, I'm doing my best to not need anyone, least of all you."

"I haven't done anything but love you."

Hurt by her words, he responded in anger.

"That's not an answer." He stared into her eyes and was taken in by that look. Fearful of enchantment, he stepped away and slowly unfastened the top buttons on her blouse. She didn't resist. He pulled her collar back until he could see the full freckled constellation of Orion appear above her breast. He was angry at the comfort it offered.

"You're a construct," he said defiantly, "a construct made long ago by an innocent boy. I'm not innocent or a boy anymore so I don't need you and I don't want you. Find another prepubescent pup to love; you're very good at it." She stared at him in that close-to-tears way that wounded him more.

"Thank you," she said simply. "I want to be very good for you. I don't know what you think I am, but you're wrong if this is how you feel. You built me but it was your love that made me who I am. How could I ever hurt you when you gave me something so vital, something no one else could? I love you and I wouldn't have it any other way."

"I'm sorry, Andrea. I appreciate what you did for me and I don't want to be angry with you but what I'm angry about can't be separated from you. I wish I didn't need you so much." He was upset for making that sound like a cry. "Don't you see? I can't want you anymore."

"You don't mean that."

"I have a daughter, I think. I ran away from my responsibility so I don't know for sure. I've seen men die, I've caused deaths. I'm not who you knew. I've grown up—badly—and our time is over."

"I wish I could have made it easier."

"You can't, not anymore. You made things easier, better, for me for a long time, maybe too long, and probably too easy. You were good for me until real people showed me the real world. It couldn't be helped. I've grown past you. Maybe I don't deserve you anymore because I'm not the person you say you love. I've done things, bad things. I wouldn't be here hiding if I hadn't. Don't you see I can't need you anymore? I don't want to hurt you, if I really can, but a construct isn't what I need in my life."

As they danced, she laid her head on his shoulder and cried. The headgear began displaying memories, his and hers, virtual memories of beaches, and surf, and beautiful sailboats, images of her standing at the window in the room that they had shared high up in the mountain resort where they made love that first time, that first beautiful time. They were in the resort with the enormous waterfall and a small village in the distance. Memories were of long ago when innocence was palpable and her first tears had touched him. But he was older now and more experienced so he fought against his emotions because he knew there was great harm in caring.

"Andrea, thanks for the dance, I have friends waiting for me. I have to go."

Her eyes were red and she was clearly distressed. He turned from her but once again she was facing him.

"Run from me if you have to, I understand, but not from your destiny." He wanted to argue but she was so intense, all he could feel was fatigue so he just stared and listened. "You want to escape to Canada," she accused him. "Don't. There's nothing in Canada that will save you from what's here. You can't run away."

"Bernie's dead, Angel Falls is gone and it's my fault. I'm a fugitive and I have no one I can trust."

"Then trust me. Now is your time. You have nothing to lose and you will regret it if you make your life about what others allow you to be. Run to Canada and you have the same chance of being caught as here. The difference is you will know you ran away. Stay and find your purpose. You'll never find it running away."

He put his hands on her shoulders and gently pushed her away. "Andrea, this is over. Respect what we had once and don't try to manipulate me any more. Stop trying to use my memories of young love against me. I'll respect you more if you stop."

"Love and respect only comes to those who care honestly and intensely. Gil, in your heart, you know that Joad and I are the same; not two but one."

He walked away. Again, she faced him, wiping tears from her eyes.

"Please listen to me," she said, the earnestness in her voice cracking with sadness. "Everyone has a place in their heart reserved for someone they love, someone who is truly special. I am that place in Joad's heart reserved for you."

With that, she turned and disappeared into the crowd. He watched her until the smoke and gyrating couples erased her patterns. Off in the distance, he caught the hint of a door opening and someone leaving. Ripping off his headgear he ran to the door while in the silent dancehall everyone contorted to his or her own beat. When he opened the door, outside, the street was empty and the snow was free of footprints.

Chapter 15

Hamilton, MI.—2070

Alone and disconsolate, Gil shut the door and wandered back into the dance hall to wait for his friends. It was late, the dance hall had mostly cleared, and the cleaning staff was preparing for the next shift when he realized his new friends weren't coming for him so he left the hall and plodded slowly through the deep, heavy snow to the train station. At the gray outskirts of the entertainment cusp, even the silence offered no respite from his troubled thoughts but he was too depressed to want anything but peace. Head down, he concentrated on the sensation of crushing snow under his boots and soldiered on. At the far end of the train station, he waited away from the crowds, and when the train finally arrived, he forced his way past the fresh merrymakers arriving at the cusp to party.

As the train spiraled through the various sectors of the city towards home, he stared forlornly out at his desolate surroundings. When the train finally arrived at his stop, he trailed the few revelers through the snow back to his apartment. By the time he reached his building, he was alone in body and mind. Inside his apartment, without turning on the lights, he threw his coat and gloves on the heater and plopped onto his bed. As soon as his head hit the pillow, he was alert. Something didn't feel right. He jumped up, snapped on the light and stared. As if this nightmare would never end, sitting on a corner of his bed was Dyllon Tomas.

"I'm glad you didn't scream or try to hurt me," she laughed. "I wasn't sure how you'd react."

"What . . . what are you doing here?"

"I told you I'd see you again."

"Yes, but why . . . and so soon?"

"Hey, you're an attractive guy," she explained. "And a girl who travels like I do can't be particular."

"You don't know me, you don't want me, and I've had a really bad night. Hell, I don't want me either. You are way too important for a slug like me."

"Thanks, it costs a great many credits to have people believe I'm important. I'll tell my public relations consulting group its money well spent. The reality, Gil, is your friends significantly overstated my reputation."

He was immediately alert at the sound of his name, but said nothing.

"I am a two-hit-wonder in a world that worships one-hit wonders but I have talent so I invested in a Dyllon Tomas franchise when the price was a lot lower than it is today and I created value touring the upper Midwest region. Some of the other Dyllons may have more talent, most have less. When our recording company releases nationally, we each get a piece of the profit for promoting the release while doing what we do best, locally."

"Why do I care?"

She smiled and continued. "In these days, you can't make a living unless you're incorporated. It's no different in singing, it's a business and because of that, my art suffers. It's a tough market that we compete in and that market includes *Virtuoso*, which eliminates a great many of my, of our prospective customers, and for people like me who don't do anything else particularly good, the choices are limited. The advantage of a Dyllon Tomas franchise is we pool our reputations and eke out a decent living doing something we like."

"I'm happy for you but it's late and I'm tired. If you're here for sex . . ."

"I was kidding about that but I hope you're disappointed." She smiled but he refused to.

"Can this wait until maybe my next day off?"

"What? You don't find me attractive."

Gil ignored her question. "If you won't leave, please get to the point."

"Do you have anything to drink?"

He pointed to the refrigerator. She checked inventory and accessed a cup of warm tea, which she took to the only chair in his apartment and sat facing him. "I'm ready."

"Why did you call me that?"

"You mean Gil?"

He nodded.

"It's your name. I was a friend of Laurence Hilliard."

He didn't know whether to be concerned or elated. "What does that mean?"

"I'm kind of a family member."

That surprised him. "You? How? Then you know . . ."

"Yes, Hilly kept us informed. Each of us values our life in the Mesh more, but we work in real because being a *Waster* is far too dangerous and it's impossible to generate enough wealth under any Wharton Town charter so we network in the Mesh to survive. Hilly told me that if you arrived here I should look after you—kind of like he did—staying in the background, you know. When we didn't hear from Hilly, we knew something was wrong. For economic reasons Profit tried to hide his death but we know. We have connections." She was silent for a few moments. "Hilly had a lot of faith in you."

"I don't know why he did and I'm sorry for your loss. I don't know why he gambled on me, either, but he lost."

"Hilly was no gambler. He was doing the right thing. That's why I'm here."

"Dyllon, or whoever you are, now is not the time."

"Dyllon is fine. My real name is irrelevant."

"Fine, but this isn't the time. I'm having a bad night and I'm tired of feeling sorry for myself. Besides, I have to work in a few hours."

"I understand about the timing, but I'm an entertainer and I'm on a completely different schedule. I can't sleep before dawn. What time do you get off work tomorrow?"

"It doesn't matter. You don't want to be seen with me."

She considered it. "You're right, with all the media gossip I pay for, pictures and stories about you and I will hit all the gossip blogs and that's too big a risk for both of us. Can we get together, say, in your warehouse at ten tomorrow?"

"My avatar watches me too closely."

"I'm open to suggestions?"

"Can't you just explain how you're going to do it and let me get some sleep?"

"Do what?"

"You're here to get me out of Hamilton and across to Canada, aren't you?"

For the second time that night, that statement made someone unhappy. "You're not running away? You can't."

It was clear to him. Joad was employing any and every resource to convince him to stay and fight. Andrea was merely the first option. Dyllon was a backup. He stood and angrily opened the door.

"Ms. Tomas, it was nice to meet you, and I liked your show, but we have nothing to discuss. I need some sleep. I appreciate you looking after me but once I meet the mayor, he'll help me get to Canada." He took her arm gently and guided her to the door.

"But the mayor won't—" she tried to explain.

"Good night," he said and closed the door on her. He punched his pillow into a comfortable position and turned the light out. Angry at being played once more, he tossed and turned until, too early in the morning and with too little sleep, Joe woke him.

Predictably, his bad night became a miserable day. With the *Chrisnukkah* season fast approaching, shipments and deliveries increased and because he was tired, he was slow responding to Joe, who spent the day haranguing him. It felt like he was back in Profit with Bon-Bon.

When his shift ended, he entered his apartment in a stupor. Disappointed that the mayor still hadn't responded to his request for a meeting, he contacted Joe.

"How long does this take?" Gil asked.

"What? Wasn't it bad enough at work? Do I still detect attitude? You had to know that playing the hero and getting arrested was a foolhardy and completely misguided way to attract the mayor's attention. He respects people who deliver the goods, not people who get arrested and sued."

"That girl would've been raped and maybe killed."

"It is wasteful to speculate, but one thing is certain, if you had not been involved, your disposable income would have been higher. Do not get your hopes up about seeing our mayor, of that, you can also be certain. Carny Dan is responsible for millions of *Conducers*, thousands of managers, and tens of entrepreneurs and you are one of the puny and ill-fated many that have a greater need to see him than you have the capacity. *Chutzpah* only counts for something if you've done something. You cannot help our mayor in any significant way, so rest assured he will not help you. How does he benefit?"

Frustrated, but too tired to argue, he disconnected from Joe, put a pillow over his head and fell asleep.

He awoke the next morning feeling no better but had a better day at work. He came home and sent a message to Vicki asking if they could get together, but she didn't respond. Too soon, the days blurred into a ritual of waking, working, and sleeping, a ritual unending. And there were no replies from either the mayor or Vicki. The few alternatives he had hoped for had all been eliminated. He was desperate and out of ideas. He couldn't return to the dance hall fearing Andrea and Joad and he couldn't go to the theater because of Dyllon. His new friends wouldn't return his messages and the mayor had become less than a remote possibility. He'd arrived in Hamilton expecting a way out and instead, like millions of local workers and millions more in Wharton Towns around the country, he was trapped in his job. He shuddered to think that this was his future.

Early one morning, he made a decision. Unsure of his destination, but with the intention of escaping, he grabbed Bernie's glove that he'd hidden in his tiny apartment, stuffed it in his pocket, and headed out of the city.

It was a foolish, stillborn plan, because as soon as his shift began, Joe contacted him on his communicator.

"You're late."

He hesitated. "I quit. This isn't the career that I want, so I'm leaving."

"This is not what I want either, whatever that means, but you can not go."

"Try to stop me."

"Please. Stopping you is too simple to dignify. City patrols are nearby and could pick you up within . . . thirty seconds. Are you sure this is the way you want it?"

"Why do you care? I just want to leave."

"Mr. Cooper, you are a disappointingly strange young man. Personally, I do not care what you do but each of us has a job. Let us suppose you actually do leave. Someone must be found to replace you. There is training and, of course, the learning curve to consider, all during *Chrisnukkah*. As poorly as you perform, your leaving will have a detrimental effect on Hamilton's economy and my career. But it is fantasy, you cannot leave."

"I've earned credits, take them. I don't want them."

Joe was silent for a moment. "Checking worth . . . no, according to the records, you cannot possibly leave before . . . I am sorry; the timeframe is so ridiculously far out that it will only cause more friction between us and I am working very hard to reduce said friction. Entertaining any thought of leaving is not a valid discussion point."

"Hamilton is a nice town. It's me, I can't stand it. I have to leave now."

"You should have considered that before you played the hero. You have debts now that must be repaid. But there is more. The joyous and profitable *Chrisnukkah* season is upon us and little outside help is expected for another month. If you leave, you will be considered subverting *Chrisnukkah* and anyone who wars on a glorious commercial high holy day is automatically considered a felon."

"Have someone downsized from another sector cover for me."

"That decision is at least two grade levels above anything I can work with."

"This is a free country. I want to quit."

"Your statement is wrong on so many levels that I won't honor it with an answer other than to correct you. America is bought and paid for. I am sorry, Mr. Cooper, remarkably, you provide value, such as it is, during this our critical commercial period. Return to work immediately and you will be docked only your morning wages. If you persist, I will charge you for this conversation and you will be put under room arrest until such time as your debt is satisfied plus the cost of retrieving you and monitoring to prevent more occurrences of this infantile behavior."

"Room arrest seems like my lifestyle choice."

"Return to work now," Avatar Joe said calmly. "This can only end badly for you."

He reconsidered his options as Joe continued to reason with him. "There is a patrol car two streets away with a Reverend Sergeant who could readily use some power points about now. Do you really want to challenge me? The cost of the patrol car and the wages lost, as well as overhead and the cost to you of simply ignoring a clear threat from a recognized superior, you would not be worth enough to be put to death. You have heard the rumors. You will live the remainder of your short, dreary life as a physical laborer with your only reward; a generally distasteful death. A career like that is not for everybody and most likely not for a rocket scientist from back East. You may shudder and beg for forgiveness whenever you wish, Mr. Cooper; however, if you do not report for work, immediately, this will be my last offer of help." With no better solution evident and bitterly irresolute, Gil returned to work.

When he punched in, Joe continued the discussion. "This must not happen again and you will do what I say from now on. Because of this irrational outburst, your performance rating has been downgraded. Yes, believe it or not, there's a performance level below what little you've achieved. You are reclassified as one who performs at a marginally low success rate—a pre-*Waster*, as it were. As you should be able to guess, that is not good. You must improve that rating to one who is marginally successful or just successful by the end of this *Chrisnukkah* season or you will find yourself without work or prospects and without value. Working harder in order to achieve high marginal success would be my recommendation to create some slack, but that, I think is unattainable. Failing that, you will be flushed from the city at the minimum out of pocket cost to Hamilton."

"If it gets me out of here, flush me."

"Believe me, Mr. Cooper, you don't want that. I don't know what your former town of Mellon accepts, nor do I know how they treat *Wasters*, but once outside our city, you are still subject to national laws and they are quite severe when it comes to negative worth and the handling of refuse."

He listened, silently.

"If you understand, please acknowledge."

He remained silent.

"If we cannot communicate effectively, the efficiency of this operation, our segment, and sector, is at risk. You are not permitted to sulk."

"I'll work harder," Gil said without conviction.

"Better. Now tell me why you will work harder?"

"If I don't, I'll disappear."

"It is not for you to use that word. Again, why will you work harder?"

"I don't want anything to happen to me."

"I have researched rocket science and I know how essential physics is to the financial industry so I say this advisedly. Are all Pittsburgh rocket scientists as dense as you? Of course the correct answer is, you work harder to satisfy your customers both internally and externally."

"Like I care?" he whispered. But he didn't want to prolong this discussion so he said, louder, "Okay, I want to satisfy my customers."

"And why do you want to do that?"

"A happy customer is a repeat customer which means more work and more profits for everyone. That is what I live for."

"In fact, that is precisely what you live for."

In the following weeks, work was an unrelenting series of bad days and Joe made certain Gil knew why. Whenever he complained, Joe humiliated him with his rapier wit. Reluctantly, Gil showed the requisite enthusiasm, but his heart wasn't in it so sustaining the effort was exhausting. Each night, depressed and fatigued, he returned home to sleep.

Finally, Nineteenth Eve arrived. It was an important commercial holiday, a time when everyone shipped gifts to recipients prior to the intense Christmas Day gift-giving evaluation that ended the quarterly *Chrisnukkah* shopping season. Due to his low seniority and even lower net worth, Gil was scheduled to cover a double shift that day.

"Good morning," Joe woke him with an annoyingly happy trill. "It's off to work we go on this most auspicious of days."

"I'll be there in about twenty minutes."

"As our joyous season begins, I wish to congratulate you. You have worked an almost exemplary two weeks. Finish with a flourish and we can all be proud."

"Almost exemplary?" he asked with trepidation.

"Yes, you have provided positive effort at the warehouse and your worth has appreciated. However, there is still something lacking. You have failed to demonstrate the requisite world-famous Hamilton *Chrisnukkah* spirit. As proof, your purchasing activity is far below the acceptable norm. You have been a negligent shopper. This has a deleterious effect on your overall evaluation."

"I didn't know . . ."

"Really, has that comment ever worked for you? You are fortunate to have me. I am such a diligent avatar, an avatar who—hint, hint—should be rewarded substantially during this holy gifting season. And once again I have rescued you from the commercial abyss by providing a list of people you must gift and gift now before it's too late. Belated presents have a reduced economic effect. Most provide no value whatsoever. Feel free to add to the list, but by no means must you delete any people. I do this one time as a service, but next *Chrisnukkah*, you must to do it yourself or pay my standard fee."

"Thank you," he said, dreading the consequences.

"You have been given time off with no pay to log onto the Mesh to acquire such gifts as required from your recipient's registries. Your account will be charged so I took the liberty of preparing the list sorted, high-to-low, from those who can benefit your career most with an effective gift that has a high value-to-value ratio, all the way to those more marginally desperate and dependent who require less demanding gifts but still count in the evaluation."

He reviewed the list. Vicki and her friends were on it as was Dyllon Tomas. In addition, there were many petty officials he'd never heard of and, to his surprise, even Mayor Burghe.

"Does a good gift mean I can get an interview?"

"Heavens no, a gift to the mayor is strictly *de rigueur*. There are no favors accrued here. Now is the time. Show the world your *Chrisnukkah* spirit."

"I don't know most of the other people on this list."

"And you never will if you continue to be such a humbug."

For the next few of hours, Gil assigned gifts and watched his minimal net worth decline. After assigning the final gift, sincere thank you notes appeared on his monitor from everyone on his list.

"What do I do with these?"

"Read them or delete them, but consider this. Each chose their message with precision; much like you chose their gift. You can learn a great deal about how people feel about you by their gift choices, their greetings, and their thank you cards. It is appropriate to complete the cycle by responding to their thank you notes with thank you notes of your own. Pre-validated thank you notes are available on the Mesh at a reasonable cost but they are quite passé."

He ordered what he felt were appropriate and affordable thank you notes and sent them to those he gifted. With the assignment complete, he stared at his net worth lamenting how all his hard work had come to nothing.

Joe wasn't buying it. "It's all about supply and demand. The later into the holiday season you participate, the higher the cost of gifting. Tonight being the last night is the preferred shopping night only for those who don't plan ahead or those who enjoy risk because buying tonight is expensive as you now know. If you had waited just a little longer, there would have been discounts but you would have scored fewer points with those you gifted. Of course, there were bonus points if you had demonstrated a competence in the fine micro art of supply and demand by purchasing certain valued gifts at reduced prices but you didn't do that. Most *Chrisnukkah* winners do it but they are our most entrepreneurial *Conducers* and they enjoy the privilege of inside information."

"But I didn't . . ."

"Yes, you didn't, but consider this a learning moment. Once the season is over, we will see what benefits accrue for waiting as long as you did. You might be surprised. For now, because of your low seniority and value, you will be required to pick up additional work during the holy days. This will allow you to borrow to get by; as long as you pay it back between holy seasons. No one is ever allowed to be in debt going into a holiday season. It is another wonderful *Chrisnukkah* tradition. The time between holidays, when commerce is generally slow, is the period when the economically viable diversify, while the debt-ridden work off their liens. During this period, you should work harder and longer and with greater purpose. From the personal security standpoint, the extent of your debt is factored into our ongoing downsizing evaluation so a careful balancing is required. Too much debt or too little and you're at risk of being jettisoned. A rocket scientist like you will learn the physics of just how much debt you can survive with. Having the right amount at the appropriate times is the difference between a productive life and a short one."

"Why did I have to put myself at risk by gifting people I don't know?"

"Alas, this is your *eureka* moment. The sacred, commercial act of gift giving is one of the holy, economic mysteries of *Chrisnukkah* and our faith, and it is a big step toward finding your comfort level with God. I have talked long enough, you must work now." On his monitor, a graph of his net worth appeared and he watched as it slowly declined. Gil got the point and ran to his station.

On the morning of the Nineteenth holiday, he arrived at the warehouse to find a stack of wrapped packages waiting. He moved them out of his way and worked his shift. Late that afternoon, as his shift was ending, Mayor Burghe appeared on Gil's monitor to deliver his quarterly holiday message. It was Gil's first opportunity to actually see the mayor. He was a vigorous, well-dressed, dark-haired man of maybe ninety. Gil listened carefully trying not to be distracted by the mayor's business suit that seemed to gradually change colors.

"My fellow citizens, as Mayor of Hamilton, I declare an economic holiday that will commence with the second and third shifts today and end with the first shift tomorrow. As is our tradition when profits allow, everyone will be credited with a full day's pay, less any garnishments, and everyone is free to spend their time off in whatever economic endeavor they choose. Entertainment centers are open for your enjoyment and there will be special holiday prayer sales throughout the day but since the gift giving scorekeeping has ended, purchasing today must be between you and God.

"This has been a momentous year for Hamilton. We broke revenue and net income records that have stood for ten years. Further, we have created the largest group of high-end net worth *Conducers* in our history. That's why, today, I'm proud to announce that Chairwoman Brandt has awarded Hamilton the Medal of Freedom, the highest award in the land and I, as Mayor, will receive the prestigious Medal of Honor. I am proud as punch to represent the most prosperous production town in our beloved country." The camera panned to show a cheering throng in the courtyard of the mayor's mansion.

"I accept these honors as irrefutable proof that passion, properly focused, generates superior economics. Hamiltonians, please enjoy the next twenty-four hours as your reward for living and working with passion. Your hard work, my fellow citizens, has caused our great city to be recognized as the economic paradise we all know it to be." Once again, the camera scanned the joyous crowd.

"Through each *Chrisnukkah*," the mayor continued, "we have continued our superior effort and I look forward to rewarding everyone again next quarter. On behalf of my administration, I wish every *Conducer* and his or her family a *Merry Chrisnukkah*. To every manager and entrepreneur, well, you already have your reward. Now everyone, work hard and be smart, spend freely, and party on."

Gil could now put a face on his challenge to see the mayor. The rest of his shift was uneventful. He arrived home and went immediately to bed. Too soon, his vibrating communicator woke him. He considered ignoring it but answered reluctantly.

"Hey, sleepyhead, this is Dyllon Tomas. Merry *Chrisnukkah*. I've been waiting for your call. Are you mad at me?"

"What do you want?" he asked, groggily.

"Are you coming?"

"Where?" Had he made an appointment he'd forgotten about?

"You didn't get my message."

"I was working. When I got off I took a nap."

"You can't nap, it's the holidays. It's time to be with friends, celebrating."

"I don't have friends."

"Well then, I'm here to prove you wrong. It's time for some fun. Come to my theatre, there's a party. All the performers and their friends are attending. Please."

"Thanks, but not today, I don't feel like it."

"I take it your life is so rewarding that nothing fun should interfere with it?"

All he wanted to do was lie down and sleep forever.

"Please. Come celebrate with me. It's the holidays. They only come around once a quarter. Have some fun. You need it more, I think, than anyone I've ever met."

"It was a long day and I'm tired. I need to catch up on my sleep."

"You're dying, you know?"

"What?" he asked.

"You're not tired," she explained. "You're depressed. It's the same malaise that gets every *Conducer* eventually. You've finally realized that you have nothing to live for so your mind has begun to shut down. Soon, it will affect your body, which will waste away. It's your choice, fight it or disappear. Sleep is the trap. It seems to help but it doesn't. It's the beginning of a lethargy that ends with a net worth below survival level. I know. I sing about it all the time. Frightened *Conducers* try to overcome that feeling with a rush of high fructose drinks or fudgie, pasty, carbohydrate rushes because they're more affordable than *Pharma* and in an otherwise uncaring world, eating is the only thing that feels good that you can afford. Do something or this will kill you. You'll get fat, dumb, and become so resigned and lethargic trying to feel good on the cheap that it will sap your will and your worth. Fight it. You can't shut down. Resist the unrelenting emptiness. This is a *Conducer's* life it's not yours. You can't succumb to it. You're better than that."

"Why do you care and why am I better? Leave me alone. I'm tired."

"Okay, you owe it to Hilly. How's that? He always said, 'it's how we navigate difficult, uncharted territory that makes us who we are.'"

"Stop! That bullshit won't work on me. I've heard it all before from the best." He tried to go back to sleep but Dyllon persisted.

"If you've heard it, you heard it from someone who cares. Get out of bed this minute and come down here. You're allowed to have a good time. You need a good time. Forget gifts and greed until tomorrow. For all its flaws, there's energy in *Chrisnukkah* that businesses can't squeeze into more profits. Please don't waste it. Come to my theater. Just off the alley, there's a door for the cast. Tell the guard you're here to see me then come to my dressing room upstairs in the back. Do it. If you don't . . . no, just do it." Before he hung up, she made him agree.

He closed his eyes and dreamed of snow and then a truck and shots in the night. He awoke soaked in perspiration with the memory of Hilly's body curled in a pool of blood. He didn't know how long he'd slept but he awoke certain that Dyllon was right and Hilly had died for him. That needed to be respected. Gil staggered out of bed, showered, dressed, and headed to the theater.

Chapter 16
Hamilton, MI.—2070

Christmas Tradition—Hanukkah is one of the earliest gift-giving occasions in human history. It was a simplistic Hebrew celebration that played out over an eight day period of gifting. It celebrated a people's God-given right to free enterprise millennia prior to the invention of currency and credit.

In the early days of the American economy, before the national corporation was invented, with the harvest in, produce sold and paid for, Christmas was a time to reward the family and business partners for their efforts during the work year and to provide incentives for the upcoming year. The late autumn holiday has provided the American economy with a significant boost during what would otherwise have been a slow commercial period.

By the mid-twentieth century, with the development of shopping malls and credit cards which provided economic concentration and convenience and then again with television which provided seven by twenty-four advertising to *Conducers,* American entrepreneurs modernized and expanded these two commercial high holy days to make them more efficient and productive. Commercial advantages were extended further with the development of home shopping networks on television and global shopping networks on the Internet, and the invention of sophisticated, rapid delivery capability as offered by various companies of which Federal Express and Mobile Global are good examples.

Since, the bandwidth for celebrating has expanded through *Virtuoso,* Archive, and the use of PIDs which advance convenience in the acquisition of things and stuff (in the loosest definition of those terms), along with various laws (See Circle of Life) that require a certain standard for economic activity from every *Conducer*.

In 2066, the two holy events were combined by Chairwoman Tanya Brandt and were extended first to occur twice, and then four times each year, during the historically slower commercial times in the American economy, early winter and summer, and then again, before the professional baseball and football seasons began.

Antiquity records many recreational activities played during the holiday seasons, but the one that survives and has become a staple in every religious economic unit is the Re-gifting game. It is great fun and totally into the true spirit of the holidays.

The basics are as follows (See: So This is Chrisnukkah: ANGS Press): Everyone at an economic party is required to bring a special gift and place it in the center of the room in a pile hereafter called the *crèche*. The excitement of fraudulent conversion begins with when all gifts have been offered to the baby Jesus. The first person, called the *Magus*, chooses and opens a gift from the *crèche* that they must keep for now. A second *Magus* then decides whether to take another gift from the *crèche* or steal from the first *Magus*. This continues on with everyone receiving an opportunity to steal with the host of the party playing God and deciding all disputes and thus preventing fisticuffs that are aberrant to the spirit of Chrisnukkah. The rules may vary. It can be played in multiple rounds with the host introducing gifts at different times to reorient the game and to add to the overall excitement.

Expect Re-gifting events to last hours and occasionally end in a brawl but the symbolism of this Capitalist inspired religious activity is essential as it is a microcosm of our Capitalist faith in competition, the joy of winning and the agony of defeat. Our fair, but cruel faith in capitalism, after all, requires winners and losers.

With the plotting involved, Re-gifting is a great fun game for the entire partnership and works across industries, too. It provides great insight into the nature of those involved and that can be a real boon during real commercial transactions.

Re-gifting is the perfect way to worship, concurrently, our Lord Jesus Christ and Saint Adam Smith. As a bonus, if Regifting is done well, it can improve personal worth.—**Archive**

The guard on duty at the theatre scanned Gil for access and he waited uncomfortably, as always, until his personal data was evaluated. Once cleared, the guard waved him in, wishing him a prosperous *Chrisnukkah*. He followed a long, narrow marble corridor but when he turned a corner, he bumped into a couple of inebriated young women who were laughing and embracing as they walked.

One of the girls stared at him, smiling. "Hey good-looking, how about we swap data?" she slurred. She leaned into her friend and laughed. Not knowing what to say, he just nodded. The girl frowned and turned to her girlfriend. "Mabel, I hate it when guys play hard to get but it's so much more frustrating when they don't have a clue."

The girls must have like that because while laughing, they embraced, and kissed. They laughed even harder when they realized Gil was truly clueless.

"I think we have here a future *Waster*. Look, *Conducer* boy, pass me your contact information or tell me to go fuck myself—which I don't have to do because I have Mabel—but do something. I'm wet, what about you?"

"Oh?" It was all he could muster.

"Gracie, honey," Mabel said, "He's cute but do you really want to go slumming with a *Waster*?"

"Maybe he's transparent or he's a ghost." They bent over laughing.

"Are you a ghost?" Mabel asked.

"No, I'm new here, that's all."

"God of Money, honey, open the fuck up. You're nice looking but it's not like I'm looking for a partner or trying to steal your worth or anything."

"I don't have much to steal." When that didn't seem to help, he made it worse by adding, "I don't want to get hurt or hurt someone."

The girls looked alarmed. "Did you steal or did someone steal from you?"

"No, I'm just not ready for a relationship, that's all."

"What relationship? I'm not looking for financial support. I just want to get laid. It's *Chrisnukkah*." Gracie said, giggling. "Anyway, if you've been hurt in a financial relationship, you're only good for fucking anyway. You're cute but you have way too much overhead for a simple girl like me, particularly during the holy fucking season. If you can't have fun today, I'd hate to have to rely on you the rest of the year."

When he didn't react, the girls strutted past him. As she went by, Mabel reached out and rubbed his groin playfully. "You can't say we didn't try, big fella," she said. "Maybe we'll swap spit later." Laughing, Mabel dragged her friend away.

As they disappeared around the corner he mumbled, "*Happy Chrisnukkah.*"

"Prosper," the girls shouted back, their laughter echoing down the corridor. Shaking his head, he walked down the hall toward a door and another guard.

Before Gil reached the guard, a man greeted him and pulled him into a room and shut the door. "Welcome, my fine spender and *Happy Chrisnukkah* to you. The food and beverages are sponsored by CEREBRAL SELECTIONS, a subsidiary of U.S. ANGS. Help yourself to the free stuff including various *Pharma* sample formulations that are intended for market next year. It's all safe if used responsibly, but we're asking everyone to sign a waiver just in case, for your protection." The man handed Gil a form. He signed it and handed it back.

"We're interested in your comments concerning our new marketing campaign. This year, we're not selling our *Pharma* through normal distribution channels. Instead, we've hired actors and formed them into old-time street gangs. We send them into target neighborhoods to find old dilapidated houses where they will set up and sell our *Pharma* like it was done, illegally, a hundred years ago—only of course, it's perfectly legal today. Get it? Pretty cool marketing, huh. We're really excited about the possibilities."

"I'm sorry, I don't understand?"

"Once you try the products all will come clear, although it may be fuzzy for a while," the man said, winking. "Have a profitable holiday."

"Thank you. I'm looking for Dyllon Tomas."

"She's probably in the *Crèche* Room participating in a traditional Regifting. It's at the end of the hall and up the steps near the stage. The Regifting is in the first room."

Gil started to leave but the man grabbed his arm.

"Hey, after you try our CEREBRAL SELECTIONS; remember the color of the container. Then, tomorrow, visit our Mesh site and answer some questions about the experience. Also, knowing the color will be important if you need medical attention. And hey, we're having a drawing. We're offering some cool prizes for a fee. Some lucky *Conducer* in each sector could double their current net worth. Yep, you heard me right. Double. Care to register?"

Gil declined and continued on in his way to find Dyllon.

At the top of the stairs a small, very old man stood watch by a door. Inside, people were sitting quietly in a circle on large comfortable chairs surrounding piles of gifts, each wrapped in decorative paper. The man asked him his name, nodded and pointed to the only empty chair remaining.

"Hurry and take your seat so we can begin." The man announced his name, "Ron Cooper, our last magus, has arrived." There was applause.

"What's going on here?"

"It's our traditional *Chrisnukkah* gift theft."

"But I came to see Ms. Tomas."

"You're not here for the Re-gifting?" Gil shook his head. "I should have known. You didn't bring a gift after all. Ms. Tomas is upstairs in her room. The theft began and as Gil was leaving vulgar insults began to fly among the *Magi*. He hustled upstairs and found Dyllon waiting in her room.

"It took you long enough. Did you get hooked into the Re-gifting?"

"It's a really silly custom."

She nodded and motioned for him to sit. He chose a chair near her bed.

"You said there's a party. What happens now?"

"Forget the party. Have you had any luck convincing the mayor to let you go?"

He shook his head. "So you agree it's what I have to do."

"No, I don't agree but no one can force you to stay and fight against your will. Only you know how much it will cost—how much it has already cost." After having thrown her out of his room, he was surprised that she was so reasonable.

"It's not that I don't want to help but I don't know what I can do and there's too much to fight against. After I've escaped to Canada, I'll figure it out and then I'll be more help to everyone. I came to Hamilton because Hilly told me the mayor would help me. How can he help if he doesn't know who I am?"

"Okay, who are you?"

"Not that again. I'm tired of being lied to and pursued for no reason. And I'm scared, too. I need space and time to figure it out. I need to be me, and as you say, I don't know who that is right now."

"If that's your sales pitch to the mayor, you'll have to work on it if you want his help. All Carny Dan will want to know is how helping you will help him more."

"Then I'm in trouble. I have nothing he wants."

"Dan is one of the few people to have worked with Crelli, Brandt, the rebels, and Omar Smith and is still alive and prospering. Do you have any idea how difficult that is?"

Gil shrugged.

"The mayor is an extraordinary entrepreneur and a true capitalist and you're on his turf. That means there's no direction you can choose that he couldn't help you or turn against you in a heartbeat if it benefited him."

"What choice do I have?"

"Besides running?"

He nodded.

"You can stay and fight."

He shook his head. "I can't. It's hopeless and I'm burnt out. I need . . . I don't know what I need." He shrugged and wandered over to the window.

"You'd best figure it out. What I'm hearing here won't help with Dan. This is important so get a grip. You're in a bad situation, but if you're ever going to get out of it, you need to take control."

"Super advice but how do I do that? Everyone wants a piece of me. I'm fleeing so I can clear my head."

"Gil, let me explain something. Regardless of what you think, this isn't a conspiracy. We all loved Hilly. He was a founding member of our Singularity Gang. Did you know that?"

"I barely knew Hilly. We talked a few times, he didn't know me either, he couldn't have, yet he gave up his life, his future for me."

"Hilly was a good man. He and twenty others were part of a private industrial design team that commercialized the first imbedded computer chip to work seamlessly with the human brain, replacing damaged natural brain functions. His team enhanced the functionality so it would boost brain function, and to test the breakthrough, each member of the Singularity Gang had the chip implanted in their brains. Based on the results, Crelli realized the power it had. He purchased Hilly's company in what can only be described as an extremely hostile takeover. Four of Hilly's partners died in the acquisition. Hilly fled and Crelli rolled the company in with his Crelli Enterprises and invested heavily in it. After some remarkable breakthroughs, rather than commercializing the process so humanity could benefit, Crelli held onto the technology so only the super rich could afford to utilize it.

"In order to protect his investment, Crelli had most of the Singularity Gang murdered except for Hilly and four other experts. So they couldn't communicate with each other, they were dispersed to *Wharton Towns* around the country where they lived under tight security. But, they were enhanced so they managed to find each other in the Mesh where they built a virtual refuge more real to them than this world.

"Crelli spent millions refining the technology using funds he diverted from the Defense Department budget. The commercial benefit was inexpensive PIDS that the government uses to help business control everything commercial. The wealthy and powerful got an internal communication device that gave insider trading new meaning and it was the beginning of the promise of immortality, while the rest of us had PIDS that branded us as *Conducers* to be controlled and discarded when we're no longer productive."

"I knew some of that."

"Hilly lived deep inside the Mesh and he believed you are the one who can stop the government but he was never clear to us how. Do you know?"

He shook his head. "I'm sorry, I've got nothing. I know this is important and I want to see the government overthrown as much as you. I just don't understand how I fit in. Believe me, I'm nothing special, really, and I don't know what's going on so I have no idea how to stop it, whatever it is. I'm just trying to stay alive."

She looked down and shook her head. "I'm disappointed and hope is all we have. I don't know why Hilly felt you could help but he and others truly believe you can free us. If I knew more . . . like it or not, you're a rebel. Too many people believe it, so denying it or trying to pretend you're not is out of the question."

This discussion was maddening, just like all of Bernie's talks. "How can you know more about me than I know about myself? Rebel if you want, you don't need me or my approval. I can't tell you how many times my great-grandfather, Bernie, lectured me about the rebellion and my role in it, but what he wanted was so unlikely, I couldn't believe him." Gil paused to consider how to say what was next. "I would help you, Dyllon,

I would but I can't see how, so if you're waiting for me, it's going to be a long wait.

"I'm not your guy. If I am, your rebellion is in a sorry state. Look, you're a celebrity, why don't you lead the revolution? At least you'd have a following. My friends say so. They would follow you. And you travel the country so you must know others who want Brandt overthrown. Help me out here. Why aren't you more dangerous to Brandt than I am? Is it that you see the impossibility of it and all you can do is sing about it? Is that it? No, revolution is crazy and I don't want any part of it."

She responded with a tinge of anger in her voice. "You want to flee yet you criticize my involvement. Don't worry about me; I'm doing what I can. Just having you here is a big risk. You're right about revolution, it is daunting, but you've seen the suffering, you know that people have been, are being exterminated. And you've seen how *Conducers* live and work, and *Wasters*, you know about them, too. When you flee, you're not avoiding responsibility; you're just trying to avoid risk which you never can. You can never run from that. We're not rebels, we're people, Gil, and we're more than ciphers. If you flee, you won't be able to live with yourself, knowing its wrong?"

He searched his feelings but like every other time, he came up sad and empty.

She threw her hands up in the air. "Is there nothing important to you?" she asked.

His only response was to stare back at her.

"You know about Omar Smith and his terrorist groups?"

He nodded.

"Are you willing to leave the field to people like him? In his way, he's a rebel, too. But Smith lies and cheats and uses the poor only to acquire power for himself. To Smith, freedom is a marketing slogan for his schemes to take power from Brandt. He has no intention of restoring our freedom, yet our people join him out of desperation. You have to stand up so we finally have someone to rally around that has our back, someone with the right intentions, who wants to help us. I'm doing what I can, and right now that's trying to convince you to stay and fight because so many believe you're our solution. I know it was Hilly's hope and so it's mine. If it's not yours," her voice lowered, "I guess we'll find someone else."

"Help me out here. Explain why you believe it's me," Gil said. "I'm at a loss, so explain it in a way I can believe in, or just leave me alone and find someone who wants to be the face of your resistance."

Her face reddened and she remained silent for a long time. "Frankly," she said through clenched teeth, "Hilly was a great, good man; he has . . . had faith in you, but . . . with the little I know about you, I'm at a loss, too."

Gil let her words sink in. His time with Hilly was important and he owed Hilly so much, his life and Bree's life, but he just couldn't see it as she did. "I know I'm letting him down," he said finally, "but you still didn't answer my question. Why me? What can I do? What special powers do I have? I don't know powerful people and I don't have special abilities. I'm not brave, I only want to run and everything about Brandt scares the hell out of me. What you're asking, what everyone is asking, is ridiculous unless you know something I don't."

Dyllon stared, helpless. "You will never know unless you stay and figure it out."

"Stay? I'm buried in a dead end Joe job? How does that further revolution? And I'm a fugitive. I've been lucky so far, but if I stay in one place too long, they'll find me. What scares me most is that wherever I go, innocent people are hurt or killed because of me. My hope and maybe yours too, is that maybe in the future I'll be the kind of leader your revolution needs but if I stay, I'll never get older."

"Can't you just have faith?"

"Faith in what?" he asked, frustrated. "You're not listening to me. Even if I knew how to do it, I don't have the resources to succeed. I'm friendless, you said so yourself. It's *Chrisnukkah* and you had to beg me to go to a party. How pathetic is that?

"Maybe you're right. Maybe I am the one. But who said I had to be the one today, tomorrow, or even next year? At least, in Canada, I can stay alive until I know what I'm fighting for."

Dyllon began to argue.

"No! Please stop. I know who the bad people are. That's not what I'm saying. My problem is I don't know who the good people are. Where are they? What do they want? And what are they willing to do?"

"Come on, you've met good people," she countered. "Think about it. You see them every day. They're terrified and they can't do anything, so they wait for someone to lead them, to give them a reason to hope. Maybe it shouldn't be that way but it is. When they lost their freedom, all control they had over their lives was lost and they want it back, but like you, they don't know how to get it without someone to lead them so they live in quiet desperation. They live in despair, wanting—no, needing—something and someone to believe in."

"Or what?" Gil asked. "Good people become bad. They lie, cheat, steal, and kill innocent people to survive while they wait. Is that what you fear because if it is, you're too late, that has already happened."

Angrily, she moved toward him. "Jesus, you have a lot of growing up to do. Okay, go to Canada, I'll even help. But once you're there, you'll forget about us."

"I just want to stop being afraid—even if it's only briefly. The rest—what you want—I can't consider right now. Please, Dyllon, I need your help."

She grabbed his shoulders and forced him to stare into her dark brown eyes. "I understand. How old are you?"

"Twenty, I think."

"I'll do my best to help you escape but there's one last thing you need to hear and you won't like it. Gil, you're a nice guy, that's clear. In my world, that's unique and maybe it's why you can undo all this. I don't know, but as an adult, you seem to be missing something. This is a sad, sad world and it won't change easily. We need intensity, people who care about people, certainly, but just as important, we need people willing to take responsibility. At twenty, you should be an adult, but it seems you're still a boy, so maybe you're right, you need time. But the fear of growing up and accepting responsibility is what condemned all of us to live under this abhorrent adult supervision of Crelli and Brandt. As a people, we became so enamored with diversion, fun and games, anything to keep from growing up, becoming responsible, or maybe to keep from dying. There's nothing more frustrating than someone who, instead of maturing, holds onto narrow, self-serving, childish behavior as he gets older. It's a colossal waste of potential and it's . . . sad.

"Being a responsible adult is difficult and painful so I can understand why you want to slow down the process, to take your time. But maturing is a beautiful metamorphosis amplified by the situations you face, situations that are so challenging that they distill your essence until you become the man you were meant to be. Run if you have to but for your good and ours, someday you must face the things you're running from if you're going to grow up and make a difference."

"So I'm a self-serving child."

"Yes, you are. That shouldn't surprise you. Look, what you're facing, no one would wish on anybody but I don't know how you'll face these problems and mature if you run to Canada." She shrugged and though obviously disappointed, she continued. "I guess, before you can help us you need to find yourself, so I'll do what I can. Please don't make me regret it."

He was relieved. "Thank you."

"I can only pray that you're listening."

"I am and I'm sorry that I've disappointed you."

"Not as sorry as you will be if nothing comes of this. This Saturday, there's a banquet to honor a sales rep for one of the mayor's important clients. The mayor and I go way back so I'm invited. Come as my guest and I'll introduce you to him. I promise. After that, it's up to you."

"That's great." He was so pleased that he kissed her. "Thank you."

He was so excited about his meeting with the mayor that while rehearsing what he wanted to say he wasn't concentrating on his work in the days prior the meeting and thus was forced to spend additional time reworking his mistakes. What to say? That was his problem. He had an opportunity, but there wasn't anything he could think to say that was valuable enough to interest the mayor and the limited advice Joe provided didn't help.

"I am impressed you found a way to our mayor," the avatar said. "Had you been this enterprising at work, we would have earned significantly more power points and you would have achieved this audience the right way."

Rebukes didn't bother him. "Joe, I'm preparing what I'm going to say so if you want to criticize me, please do it after my meeting."

"I wish you luck."

"Thank you."

"And I would greatly appreciate it if you would put in a good word for me and if he promotes you, I would consider it an honor to assist you with your improved status."

"I'll do what I can. Do you know the mayor? How is he to talk to?"

"He is a world class listener, but quite a talker, too. Everyone loves Carny Dan."

"What are his interests?"

"Wealth, obviously, and commerce, of course," Joe explained. "He started his career as a booth operator in a circus and quickly grew. He consolidated the underutilized, undercapitalized small towns that were once Detroit and turned them into the world-class *Wharton Town* that is corporate Hamilton."

"So help me out. How do I impress a man who's done that?"

"What can you offer?"

"Nothing."

"Then you should not waste his time."

"But I must talk to him."

"Why must you talk to him?"

"I want to leave Hamilton."

"Not that again? There is no place on earth better than Hamilton."

"I know that," Gil said. "But I . . . I'm a rocket scientist and I want to pursue my profession in a more . . . in a city with more scientists."

"Mr. Cooper, before you say too much, you do recognize that Hamilton is in close proximity to our Canadian adversaries and the mayor will be dubious of your motives to expatriate. We are in a constant struggle with economic terrorists who want to end our glorious way of life and to prevent it, our mayor has assumed ongoing, special wartime powers which include the authority to detain anyone if he believes it enhances the security of our community."

"That's not what I mean. I'm a rocket scientist and I'm frustrated trying to prosper here. I have too many debts and too few business opportunities. I know it's my fault but this isn't what I had hoped it would be when I arrived."

"So you are disappointed with your performance, not ours."

"Yes," he said quietly.

"And you are economically lonely?"

"Okay."

"Well unfortunately, Mr. Cooper, those are the traits that correlate to a loser and that makes you susceptible to being turned by enemies. The mayor knows that."

"I'm a loyal American, you know that."

"Mr. Cooper, a loyal American you might be, but you are also needy in ways that are very un-American. Hamilton provides myriad opportunities for partnership and once you repair your net worth, you may invest in our social avatar network which provides anything from stimulating conversation to an orgasmic girlfriend experience, a non-committal tumble in the sack, if you get my drift. Keep this in mind. The mayor believes that with perseverance, passion, hard work and business savvy, anyone can create all of the satisfying rewards America's open and free society allows.

"But because you are unsatisfied, the mayor will believe that it is your own self-loathing that has inhibited you from receiving the full benefits of his Hamilton. He expects you to commit fully to our way of life and will be disappointed that you wish to extract yourself because it improves no entities worth, particularly his. He will perceive your wanting to leave as inhibiting your career productivity. You must understand one thing, Mr. Cooper, whatever you lack here; our mayor believes resolutely that you will lack it elsewhere as well, and he is right. You carry your flaws with you wherever you go. You will always be in the presence of your most grievous enemy, yourself.

"I have a question about the singer, Ms. Tomas. What has she charged you for the invitation to speak with the mayor?"

"Why nothing."

"Nothing? That is so unlikely that I suspect you or she are not being truthful."

"I barely know her," Gil offered. "She works when I sleep and sleeps when I work. And she travels a great deal so I can't speak to her motives."

"Yet she charges nothing for a service that should return a premium fee."

"Dyllon is an astute businesswoman. I don't know what angle she is working but she has offered to do this free. Why are you giving me all this free advice?"

"As with Ms. Tomas," Joe said. "Nothing is truly free, Mr. Cooper. You will see the mayor and he will request research on you and become aware that I am your avatar. If you can impress him, my opportunities will improve."

"So that means that you will help me."

"Of course, it's my job. I recommend that you be straightforward with him and do not ask to leave. Whatever you do request, make certain he understands why it is in his and Hamilton's best interest. Ideally, we can develop a financial presentation with a significant return on his investment but you must tell me your plan soon so I can work up the numbers. It won't be cheap but think of how beneficial the outcome will be. Attack this as you would a critical marketing campaign and sell it like you've never sold before. Now, if we had more time, I would recommend classes with Coco, a sales and marketing avatar I often partner with. She teaches the psychology of the sale and can instruct you in ways that will achieve your goals and improve your worth. Unfortunately, there is no time to enroll in her class, but it is imperative that you create a presentation that has the rock-solid illusion of truth and whatever else you do, do not get caught lying. Lie, strategically, but don't get caught. The mayor can be won over by an airtight presentation that is indicative of the presenter's passion, productivity, and attention to detail."

Gil took Joe's advice and spent the rest of the week working on a detailed presentation to win Carny Dan over. And though he rehearsed it over and over in his apartment, it seemed lame but it was all he had.

The day of the banquet arrived and Gil dressed in a professional business suit that he had permitted Joe to purchase for him. He'd never worn anything like it before and felt awkward and uncomfortable with his shirt buttoned up to his neck, a tie constricting his breathing, and his feet compressed into narrow tied shoes but he persevered as he boarded the train to Dyllon's theater apartment.

She was waiting below the marquee in front of the theater and when he saw her, he felt better. Though she dressed evocatively on stage, today she was appropriately clad in a simple yet elegant light coral lace strapless top and beige metallic slacks that accentuated her skin tone. Her face radiated with a touch of nano-cosmetics and even through that, she appeared nervous. Soon they were in a limo and off in style to the mayor's banquet.

Feeling awkward on this "date", he stared at the passing storefronts.

She tapped his arm and smiled reassuringly. "It's all set up. The mayor has agreed to speak with you before the dinner. Don't worry, you'll do fine."

He wasn't reassured. "If I mess this up, I don't know what—"

"You won't mess it up, relax," she laughed. "Say what you feel. Don't force the conversation and don't make it sound like it's a presentation.

Carny Dan's a smart guy. He'll know if you're trying to work him so you may as well be yourself."

"So much depends on this."

"No, not so much," she teased. "It's not like you've been successful so far?"

He didn't smile. "Do you want to hear what I'm going to say?"

"Don't, Gil. You're not a salesman and he'll see right through you. Even if you were, you're not in Dan's class so just talk, man-to-man, no guile or anything."

Disheartened and unsure, he stared out at the passing scenery searching for courage while beads of perspiration dripped down his back.

"You can't have it both ways," she added. "You say you don't want to be special." She was trying to help. "Don't try to be. You're not and you'll really blow it. And don't pump yourself up or you'll overplay your hand. The best thing is to let him guide the conversation. It's a good sign if he talks about his circus days."

"His circus days, okay. Explain again why he wants to see me."

"Carny Dan has a soft spot for long odds."

"Great. That's comforting."

"You wanted to see him and today's your chance. Face it. You have to grow up sometimes. Enjoy it, have some fun—professional fun—it's time. We're almost there."

The limo slowed as it reached the administrative center of Hamilton. It was an oasis in the midst of desolation. In all directions, the land was carpeted with the decaying detritus like a long gone city that had been flattened by a high-yield nuclear bomb.

Gil tried to picture how the town might have looked when it was alive with people, but he shuddered when he thought of Angel Falls and realized what these residents must have endured for this place to look like what he saw now.

They passed rows of tall evergreens strategically planted to block the view of the wasteland from the administrative windows. The limo pulled onto a ramp and then under an enormous, windowless white marble cube that was the mayor's mansion and stopped under a canopy behind a great many other luxury vehicles that were in the process of disgorging well-dressed and important guests.

When their limo's door opened, Dyllon finished answering his question.

"Oh yes, and the mayor is very curious to see if you have what it takes to lead a successful revolution against Chairwoman Brandt." Deflated, Gil fell back against the car seat as Dyllon left. His legs were numb and he was too terrified to follow her.

"What?" he screamed, finally. But she was gone, escorted by a man wearing an ornate brocade uniform with silver medals and ribbons and a long, jeweled sword.

A similarly dressed man stuck his head inside the limo. "Sir, we have other guests arriving. Please join your companion." Gil struggled to get out of the limo and then jogged on wobbly legs to catch up to her. He grabbed her arm.

"The mayor knows?" he asked breathlessly. "Why are you doing this? Are you crazy? Do you know what he'll do to me? I can't go in there." She grabbed his hand and pulled him inside past security guards armed with pulse rifles.

Then it dawned on him. Of course, she was joking. It wasn't until they completed the security screening that he could call her on it.

She pulled him close and whispered. "Dan asked me what was in it for him and I thought it best not to lie. I didn't tell you until now because if you knew that the mayor knew, you wouldn't have come. Dan's a good guy, you'll see."

"But—"

She released his arm and offered it to a large, tuxedoed gentleman who escorted her to a grand waiting room. Once inside the room, a large group of well-dressed men and women, all seemingly more comfortable in their surroundings than Gil, made it impossible for them to further their discussion. The escort pointed to a large, very elaborate cart filled with various *Pharma* cartridges and alcohol.

"Enjoy, there is everything but hallucinogens, for obvious reasons." The guard added, "The mayor will call for you shortly." The escort then helped Dyllon remove her sequined half-jacket and left. She walked to a group and joined in conversation.

Gil tried to get her attention but she ignored him, so he sat in a corner indulging in an assortment of hors dourves, seething at what had transpired. During a lull in the conversation, she came over. He pulled her close and whispered.

"You were kidding back there about the mayor knowing. Right?"

She didn't reply.

"Please don't do this," he whispered. "He'll turn me over to Brandt and she'll kill me. Is that what you want?"

"Don't be silly. Why would he do that? You're not planning to fleece him."

"No, but the Chairwoman is searching for me. She destroyed an entire village and killed innocent people to get me. This isn't a joke. Tell me you're kidding."

She looked around to be sure no one was staring and kissed his cheek.

"It's time to take sides. Besides, no one is allowed to leave Hamilton without Carny Dan's permission and even with that, the exit excise tax is all but extortion. You wanted this meeting. Here it is. Before he agreed to it, Dan needed to know about you. He won't give his approval to let you go unless you're worth it to him because he'll be in deep trouble with the Chairwoman if he does. Those are the stakes; be worth it to him. If you have an A game, now is the time to bring it, tiger." She brought her hand up and gently touched his cheek. Before he could respond, she was off to join another group of guests leaving him to sag back into his chair to contemplate the mess he was in.

Too soon, another uniformed guard entered and nodded toward Dyllon. She turned to Gil and he grabbed the arms of his chair in a death grip.

"Ms. Tomas, you're most fortunate, the mayor has allowed you and your guest an additional time slot before the banquet. Please come with me."

The guard offered his arm and Dyllon walked out with him, without looking back at Gil. Briefly, he considered his options, of which he had none so he stood reluctantly and numbly followed her into the corridor. When he caught up, he put his elbow through hers and tried to slow her down so they could talk but the guard had her other arm and refused to alter his pace. Angry at being pulled, she extracted her arm from his and hapless, he walked quietly beside them. When they reached a set of large white double doors, the guard knocked. The doors opened and he gestured for them to enter. As the guard shut the doors, Gil turned back but Dyllon grabbed his hand and jerked him inside.

Gil recognized Carny Dan from his televised *Chrisnukkah* speech. Up close, he noticed the mayor's electric blue eyes. He had a broad, pleasant face with an appropriately infectious smile that he displayed as they entered. There was nothing about the man that should have caused Gil to feel the dread he was feeling.

The mayor's aide stepped forward to block their progress and announced them.

"Your Honor, Ms. Dyllon Tomas, cabaret singer, and her guest, Mr. Ronald Cooper, rocket scientist and warehouseman."

The mayor kissed Dyllon on both cheeks. "Dyl, my friend, it's been too many business cycles since we last conjured up profits together. You look fantastic as usual. How do you like my new suit? It's ANGS' latest nano-yarn construct. It's motion powered and mesh-enabled. I'm among the first to own one but soon all the mayors will be wearing it."

"You look amazing, Dan. I wish I could afford the technology. Does it come in colors?"

Carny Dan laughed. "Are there colors? Imbedded into the lining, there's a color wheel that allows you to change the color and shade to match the rest of your ensemble. In addition, it's weatherproof, stain proof, wrinkle resistant, with stealth capability and, of course, it's projectile and laser proof. Military corporations are using the technology as a one-size-fits-all uniform in whatever country they are being hired out to defend or rebel against. We're planning to market those advantages. With these as uniforms, our private military is always wearing the winning side's colors and being on the winning side means more profits."

She laughed. "Since I won't enlist to get one, I'll have to invest in one as a fashion statement for one of my concerts."

He showed her a button on an inside pocket that doubled as a transmitter. "In a few years, nano-wear will be all the rage. Look here, you take a picture of what you're planning to wear and, with access to the Mesh, it knows your schedule and everyone else's as well. It knows who'll be going where you're scheduled to be so the suit can change to coordinate the colors and even the style, for each given ambience—within limits that we are working to expand—without duplicating something someone else is wearing to the same event. This is version one, the technology will get better. My forensic accountants estimate that the commercial value will be through the roof once we get costs down. *Conducers* have little fashion sense but with this technology, they will dress in absolutely the most appropriate manner. There's even collaborative functionality. By coordinating with other guests there's zero chance you'll be embarrassed wearing something wrong or what someone else is wearing. It's an add-on at a very extravagant subscription price, as you can imagine. My woman's wear division is gearing up as I speak. Think what that will mean to profits."

"It sounds wonderful," Dyllon said.

"This is a ground floor opportunity and I control a great chunk of the media so I'll drive the *Conducer* flock to it *en masse*."

"How much more colossally wealthy do you need to be, Dan?"

He smiled. "Did I mention that the suit is self-sanitizing and self-cleaning? You'll never need another set of clothes, at least until release 1.1," he laughed. "Technology is a wonderful thing, isn't it?"

"Yes," Dyllon gushed. "But where's the revenue stream once everyone has one."

"The beauty is we're going to market as service providers with a lifetime subscription on the technology. It will require an annual maintenance fee and a paid monthly user license, as well as standard version release upgrade fees. I'm talking revenue in perpetuity. Soon, we'll be advertising for franchisees if you're interested. My Nanowear has been designated as the first product certified by the Morgan Church to provide a lifetime of value to its owners for all eternity." Carny Dan laughed, heartily. "And we're developing various templates with different end uses and we've back-burnered what we're calling integrated separates. I have my forensic sociologists developing marketing techniques to draw in the recalcitrant so we can ensure long term sales of our product line to everyone."

"Does your product have a name?"

"We're marketing it as 'Eternal Wear'. It's a term that has a far different meaning than in the old days. Once I link in the Morgan imprimatur, everyone will crave it."

"Where do I invest?"

"There's always room for your capital and name placement in my projects, Dyl. Discuss it with the other Dyllons and we'll talk about how, later. I have to apologize, I was hoping Queenie could join us before dinner but she's been delayed."

"I was looking forward to meeting her."

"She'll attend the dinner but she has to run right after. Maybe you'll meet her next time. Say, where are you performing this week?"

"I'm booked for three weeks rotating through the cusps. I've developed quite a fan base in this bucolic little borough of yours."

He laughed. "I know. My Entertainment Division Income Statement reflects your popularity. At our next board meeting, I'm thinking about recommending a larger region for you. Do you think the others will approve?"

"If it means more corporate profits, the girls will have no problem with it."

"Say," the mayor added, "my people tell me you're planning to open a virtual cabaret. Is it part of the franchise or are you going solo?"

"Solo if I can buy out of my contract. If not, I'll give the other ladies a negotiated cut. They were fair with me when I began so I'll reciprocate."

"Good business done well. If you need some leverage, you can count on me. I'm proud of where you're taking the franchise."

"Thanks. Between us, I'm contemplating expanding into the Virtual Spirituality market, too. They're looking for singer songwriters to re-impassion congregations."

"Here's some friendly advice, Morgans charge outrageous royalties to artists who want to tap their markets, and don't fall for their long term deal. Still, with your name recognition, there's great potential for cross branding so hang tough in negotiations. If there's anything I can do . . ."

"Thanks, Dan, I appreciate it. I'll let you know if something breaks so you can invest before the *Conducers* jump in and jack up stock prices. Hey, I'm being rude. I'd like to introduce you to—"

"Yes, I was wondering when you were going to get around to this fellow. So he's the one." She nodded and the mayor offered Gil his hand.

"Ron, I'm Dan Burghe and I'm pleased to meet you. Dyllon's a big fan. If you can impress her, you earn the right to try to impress me."

"Sir, it's . . . it's good of me to meet you. I . . . I hope I won't disappoint." He blushed.

Dan smiled and turned to Dyllon. "Do I detect sincere humility?" She nodded.

"Delightful, what a rare treat. Is he like this all the time?"

"He's the *Conducer* who saved that foolish girl from being raped a couple of *Chrisnukkahs* ago at the Tech entertainment cusp. I'm sure it got your attention."

"It did." The mayor stepped closer to Gil. "That was an interesting response. I can't think of anyone who'd hurt, let alone kill someone to prevent a simple gang rape. It's a straightforward act with a lone victim so the legal fines have been clearly established and they are very beneficial to the victim. So why'd you do it?"

"Sir, I . . . they were going to hurt her and nobody wanted to help."

"You should have asked why they didn't offer to help. Now that you've been through our legal system, you understand."

Gil nodded. "Yes, sir, I know now. And two people died because of me."

"Don't flatter yourself. People die because they don't plan; every other reason for dying is just an excuse. The important thing is you won't do it again."

"I'm sorry, sir, I don't know that. I think I'd help, regardless of the law. What they tried to do wasn't right. Still, I can't be sure what I'll do unless it happens again."

The mayor smiled. "Do I detect an honest response? You do understand that there are few benefits and a great many penalties to outing honest views." The mayor looked at his watch. "My time is valuable. We're meeting because I expect you to be worth it."

"I'll try, sir." With that, Carny Dan stared at him until he was certain that Gil was uncomfortable. As moments went by, Gil hoped for Dyllon's intervention but she seemed unwilling to interrupt as the awkward silence stretched interminably. Finally, the mayor spoke again.

"The beauty of our legal system is its objectivity. Declaring something right or wrong is a false claim on the truth when it's really only perspective so, son, if being right is what drives you to act then you've given yourself a hell of a lot of latitude."

"Isn't right just right?"

Carny Dan laughed. "Dyllon, where'd you find this guy? He's a riot. So you're saying that when others act badly, they know they're doing wrong but do it anyway?"

"I hadn't thought about that, sir."

"If you make it about universal truth," the mayor explained. "You'll never figure it out. The goal is to know with as much certainty as possible why people act as they do so you can profit from it. Once you know, the world slows down, everything becomes clearer, and your investment portfolio appreciates. Good luck to you if your search is for universal truth."

"But there are universal truths."

The mayor looked at Dyllon and winked. "I have time for a fool, but not much. Right isn't just right, Ron. You should know that by now. You seek universal truth as a way to unlock everyone's personal code so they do what you expect. That key isn't truth, its money. It's always been money, in all its forms. If you don't understand why people do what they do, follow the money and you will see their motivation, right as rain and clear as day. The pursuit of money is the physics that explains everything in our universe; particularly what is right and wrong. Money doesn't just identify the truth, money is the truth. What happens after that depends where the money is invested."

"If that's true, then what you do should feel right even when there's no law to say you're wrong," Gil said.

"Dyl, I had expected that you were bringing a man to see me. What I see here is just an unsure, idealistic boy. Ron, or should I call you Ronnie, there isn't right or wrong. People are selfish and stubborn and some may be bad to the bone. You can't legislate that and the American Judicial System no longer even tries. It doesn't trouble itself with right and wrong. Produce or waste or contribute anything in between, and your rewards are commensurate with results. Play by the rules or don't, it's all about productivity and money. If you do it correctly, you will be emulated, if you do not, you will, sure as hell, soon be a dead *Waster*. You've lived it. You were punished for your economic indiscretions, as were the men you killed. Forget right and wrong, its old world thinking.

"And say you were right, Ron, and in a way, I admire your misdirected deed, you were punished for actions that were detrimental to my society, actions I don't want perpetuated. Everyone understands that and there is no wiggle room. The law this way is far easier to act on and a lot more defensible than some obscure Judeo-Christian concept of right and wrong. Most of us share the same God, so what makes those who you think are wrong, less pure? Society has progressed beyond that. In modern times, a legal system based on right and wrong is just naïve and far too complicated to manage successfully for any length of time. Life is commerce. It really is and all the right and wrong in the world counts for nothing except for its financial affects.

"By the way, you are Morgan?"

Gil nodded but thought better of it and shook his head.

"That figures, too. Before it's too late for you, you should commit to Morgan because forever is enough time to grow up and change your outdated views. Commit and then pray that you're a quick learner because if you aren't, you'll become everyone's financial prey and you will be destined for a short and unrewarding life.

"That's all I have to say on that matter, Ronnie boy. Forget right and wrong, capitalist laws are formulated in simple, standardized English so that anyone—even the dimmest, dull LED—can understand and obey at every decision point in their lowly worm-brained existence—and still prosper enough to survive."

Gil knew that he was in way over his head. "I appreciate the advice, sir."

"Christ Morgan, that wasn't even a nice try. How do you ever expect to win support to overthrow Brandt's government agreeing with shit like that? I know Tanya. She isn't inclined to give up power, particularly to a pup like you."

"I'm not planning to overthrow the government."

Obviously disappointed, the mayor turned to Dyllon. "He's conning me, right. I can accept a little humility but terminal naiveté? I'm not feeling all warm and fuzzy right now, Dyl."

She nodded but refused to defend him. Carny Dan then put his arm around Gil's shoulders.

"Ronnie, or whatever your name is, few know this but when I took my circus virtual, it was Larry Hilliard who helped me. Dyllon tells me Hilly spoke highly of you, although why, I can't say."

"Hilly's gone."

"Yes, sad news. It forced me to pull funding from Profit when I heard. They won't survive without him but from my perspective, Hilly's death was beneficial because Profit had a stranglehold on some of my former customers. This is where you can help me. According to Dyllon, Hilly gave his life for you and normally that would be enough for me. But you're showing me nothing. Hell, less than nothing. You work in a warehouse and your wages are being garnished putting you at risk of dissolution. Hilly was a great man and I want to know what will you do to justify his great sacrifice. Right now, you're showing a severe lack of respect for a man that I valued highly."

"I'm sorry. I don't know—"

"Sorry? What does sorry mean? This meeting is a waste of my time. I see nothing in you that I should invest in. Still, I respect Hilly too much. Go, intrigue me."

"Yes, Sir."

"You're what, twenty one?"

Gil nodded. "Almost, I think."

"Do you have any idea why I granted this audience?" Gil shook his head and by so doing, caused Carny Dan to shake his. "By all outward appearances, you have nothing going for you except maybe good looks and that little-boy-lost ambience you throw off that, trust me, is fucking useless in the real world. But I didn't become the number one mayor in the free world by looking for the obvious. I conjure up the faintest whispers and dissect the invisible eddies that subtly move markets toward greatness and this is where it has taken me." He waved at his surroundings.

"Here's what I think. You should be easy prey for Brandt and her minions. You should have been imprisoned, dead, or indentured long ago, but as we see, you're clearly not. I see many types come through Hamilton but rarely someone with potential. You see, our system supports the kinetic very well, but it is constrained to prevent true potential so when I find it, in places where no one is looking, I find a way to take advantage of it."

"Sir," Gil began. "I appreciate what you're saying and I appreciate this audience but I have no desire or ability, for that matter, to overthrow Hamilton, America, or any other place. I'm no risk to anybody. I just want safe passage to Canada."

"If I thought you were a risk, you'd be dead."

Gil swallowed hard. He needed to say something that mattered. "I . . . I had problems here. I've been arrested twice, but they were for minor things—well two deaths, maybe not so minor—but I promise you have nothing to fear from me."

The mayor waved his hands dismissively. "The deaths are no matter. I'm interested in far bigger things. America is in a funk—has been since Andy left office. Brandt, the *Tollers*, the mayors, and even Omar Smith are all in an uncomfortable stasis right now. That should be good, Smith is hunkered down near Toronto and no harm to anyone and the few local terrorists that remain are merely a nuisance. The rebels talk or sing tough—no offense Dyllon." She nodded. "But they don't have the technology or the leadership to move forward. You'd think equilibrium like that would allow me to work the middle and add to my fortune. I do, of course, but stasis concerns me because it's impossible to know what side will break through and that makes it a lot harder get big returns from an unclear future—and I see the future as unclear. I want the peace to hold a bit longer while I'm figuring out how to gain from the next big thing."

"I promise you, sir, I won't be the one to upset the status quo."

"You believe that but when the opportunity presents, I'd be pleased if you considered me an ally." The mayor smiled, almost laughed, as he read Gil's expression. "You're obviously not a gambler, tighten up that look." Gil nodded and closed his mouth. "I can't promise much but for now, Ron, you're safe in my city. What you can do is keep out of trouble while you hope and pray that Chairwoman Brandt doesn't locate you."

"Will you turn me over to her?"

It was the mayor's turn to laugh. "In a New York heartbeat, son, in a New York heartbeat."

"Then please let me leave Hamilton."

"I'd like to help but I can't. Tanya's too powerful for that. However, there could be a pass at the North Electronics exit gate if someone decided to leave on his own."

"Thank you, Mr. Mayor."

"Don't get ahead of yourself," the mayor paused. "Running gains nothing but time, which is worthless without inclination. Ronnie, my boy, the world changes and if you try to hold up change, or worse fight against it because you're scared, hell, you don't deserve the honor of being an entrepreneur. I win in this environment and will win in any environment because I'm that good. In my early carnival days, I sold ten minutes of simulated racecar entertainment to the public for four bucks and parlayed that into riches beyond imagining, enough to guarantee forever, at least as much forever as can be guaranteed and I command the heights of a major production metropolis. Not bad for an old slot car operator in a Carny."

The mayor paused and his eyes went blank before he spoke again. "Queenie's helicopter has just landed. I have to wrap this up because she'll be in the building in a few moments. Where was I? Oh yes, America is the greatest concept yet invented. Take my advice; this is no time to be ordinary."

"Thank you, Mr. Mayor, I appreciate the advise," Gil said.

"Nobody has figured out yet how to rule people who'll live forever. You won't find it in any Constitution, Adam Smith never conceived of it, and no crystal ball exists. Even our overly wordy financial gospels don't cover it. Forever means that any seemingly impossible or improbable event has likelihood. Entrepreneurs are long-term thinkers and forever means that a leader must dwell on risk mitigation, in perpetuity, and frankly that is unappealing to me and a great many others. That's why, if an alternative to our current leadership appears, I will be open to assessing the risks and considering the benefits of said new leader."

"Does the Chairwoman know?"

Carny Dan smiled. "Tanya is paranoid and that means she doesn't have to worry about risk mitigation because what she doesn't already know, she suspects in a billion fabricated plots. Tanya has developed sophisticated Artificial Intelligence software that makes it dangerous for anyone to consider a better alternative to her. Way back when, Hilly discovered this intelligence while working on my computerized, cloud-enabled racing system but rather than joining me in my enterprise, Hilly went off in search of the source of the AI and I believe that's when he lost his marbles. No one can escape Tanya's web and I suspect the AI was what brought Andy down."

"I heard rebels took him," Gil volunteered.

"If the rebels took him, I'm a commie insurgent. As a risk taker by nature, I look for any edge and any opportunity—something that will make my heart beat fast again. There's nothing Tanya doesn't know about—except you. That's why I'm interested."

With that, the mayor ended the meeting. "We're done, here. Enjoy the banquet. The speeches will be short and the dessert extraordinary. I don't want to keep Queenie waiting," he said as he left. "Don't forget that pass, Ron."

When the mayor left, a guard entered and took Dyllon's arm. She grabbed Gil's hand and together they were escorted into another corridor where they followed the crowd into a large banquet hall. Their seats were in the furthest corner of the hall.

When they were seated, Dyllon asked, "So how do you think it went?"

"Great. Tomorrow, I'll be in Canada."

"Ease up, Gil. Carny Dan won't help you."

"He said he'd leave a pass. That's all I need."

"He won't help you."

Gil wanted to argue but before he could, they were interrupted by a waiter serving the meal. They ate in silence and he enjoyed the best meal he'd ever eaten, each course tastier than the last. When the meal ended, the noise died down. Dyllon tapped him on the arm and pointed to the guest of honor who was arriving now with the mayor. Although far from the main table, Gil stared at her in disbelief. For the second time in his brief time in Hamilton, Gil Rose saw a ghost from his past.

Chapter 17
Hamilton, MI.—2071

Once inside a woman's heart; A man must keep his head.
Heaven opens up the door; Where angels fear to tread.
Some men go crazy; Some men go slow.
Some men go just where they want; Some men never go.

—Shame on the Moon, Bob Seger

His mind was playing tricks on him. She was dead. He saw the bombs and the rangers chasing and shooting at her from a distance. She couldn't be here and not like this, dressed like—dressed like a beautiful fashion model. This wasn't his Stacey, it couldn't be. But he continued to stare intently as she sat demurely on the stage at the far end of the banquet hall. Anxious, he sweated through the speeches that were thankfully brief and the dessert, which, true to Carny Dan's promise, was extraordinary. When she was introduced, she stood, elegant in a shimmering off-white, tight-fitting, full-length, one strap gown and spoke, briefly and self consciously, thanking everyone for their business support—whatever that meant—and she quickly sat down.

Hearing her voice, he was certain and he felt warm all over. He watched as the mayor whispered something to her and she laughed. It was a smile he could never forget. He calmed himself and leaned in and whispered to Dyllon. "I know her."

"Know who? Queenie?"

"Dyllon, help me. I need to talk with her away from the mayor."

"Oh, you do, do you?" Dyllon smiled. "She's pretty, maybe prettier than me."

"No, I'm serious. I'll wait outside in the hall. Before she leaves, introduce yourself and tell her an old friend of hers wants to see her."

"You're not serious?" The look on his face confirmed it. "You are serious."

"I really appreciate your help with the mayor but I need you to do this for me, too." Before he left to wait for Stacey outside the hall, he watched as Dyllon walked slowly down the main aisle toward the dais.

He went outside the hall to wait. He was leaning against a post watching for Dyllon when he saw the mayor and his entourage hurriedly leaving for a waiting limousine through another exit. Not seeing Dyllon, he ran to intercept them.

Queenie was being escorted through a crowd that had gathered to gawk at local dignitaries. As her limo door opened, fearing he'd loose the chance to see her, he yelled her name. As fate would have it, at that moment, the crowd quieted enough to allow his voice to carry. She turned, searching until she focused on him. Their eyes met. Expressionless before, her face lit up and she began to yell but he did his best to wave her to silence. The recognition in her eyes quickly evaporated and she whispered to the mayor who looked his way and smiled.

As they approached, Gil steeled himself, hoping she would do the same. Her stoic expression was a reward as the mayor slapped him on the back.

"Mr. Cooper, I have a great affinity for people who have a way of popping up. You should have told me you wanted to meet Queenie." He introduced them. "Ron Cooper, this is Queenie Smith. Queenie, Ron works for me and I now suspect has a promising future."

He had never lost hope, not really. Forcing himself not to react to her last name or the large diamond residing on her marriage finger, he took her hand. After all this time, he looked at her as a not-quite stranger. Time provided an honest perspective. If he had missed it before, there was no denying it now, she was beautiful. Once, back in Angel Falls, Bernie had told him that with enough credits, nano-cosmetic technology could make anyone attractive. Clearly she needed neither the credits, nor the technology.

She smiled politely. As much as he wished for more, in this situation, that pleased him. "Mr. Cooper," she said, accentuating his last name. "It's good to see you after so long. I hope you're well." Good, she was playing.

"Ms. Smith," he said, the word, 'Smith' sounding foreign on his tongue. "The pleasure is mine. How have you been?"

"Quite well, thanks." She turned to the mayor. "Dan, would you mind if Mr. Cooper and I took a few minutes to catch up? It's been a long time."

The mayor graciously stepped aside and pointed to his limo. She entered first, graceful in spite of her form-fitting gown. Gil followed. When the door closed, she put a finger to her lips and when she kissed him on the cheek whispered, "It's bugged. We can't talk here."

He nodded.

"You look great," she said conversationally. "How are the children?"

His smile wavered briefly. Did she know, he wondered.

"Fine, Queenie. Are you traveling much?"

"More than I'd like. Brampton is home. I'm married. You didn't know." It wasn't a question.

Aware that surveillance equipment could interpret nuance, he did his best to remain expressionless. "No, I didn't. Congratulations, your husband is a lucky man."

"And you, what have you been doing since we met last?"

"Mostly going from place to place as you'd expect. The mayor's been kind enough to hire me into his technology warehousing operation and I have an apartment near there. How long will you be in Hamilton?"

"Unfortunately, just through tomorrow morning. I'm to finalize a deal for my husband and then I'm off."

"If there's a change in plans, please contact me."

"I'd love to but I'm sorry, it's unlikely. Look at the time. I really must be going. I hope we can meet again, sometime."

"That would be nice," he said. She put her hand out and he took it in his. He held it briefly before she opened the door and climbed out of the limo. He followed her out. On emerging, the mayor confronted him with a smile, although his demeanor was serious.

"For a rocket scientist, Mr. Cooper, you have interesting friends. Enjoy your evening." He slid into the limo beside Queenie, who had already re-entered without as much as giving Gil a second look. He stared as the limo disappeared into the night.

"Ouch," he grunted as someone poked him in the ribs. He turned to face Dyllon's concerned stare.

"You do know her," she said, surprised.

He nodded.

"Do you know who she is?"

He nodded again.

"No, I mean, do you know who she is, not who she was?" He was confused. "Let's get out of here so we can talk." They moved to the line of people waiting for transportation. Once their limo arrived, they got in and headed back into town.

As they sat side by side, Dyllon pulled him close to her and whispered in his ear.

"We can't talk here," she said. "Because of that stunt back there, I'm sure the mayor's already given orders to have you bugged. Things have changed. Be careful."

They rode in silence until the limo stopped near the entertainment district.

"Let's walk," she said grabbing his hand and pulling him out. Arm-in-arm like lovers sharing an intimate moment, they walked toward her theater. "The mayor and Queenie left before I could reach their table," she whispered, "but I found out some interesting things. I don't know how you know her, but the Mr. Smith she is married to is the terrorist, Omar Smith."

If it was possible, he was more than stunned. "What? No, not to the terrorist. No, there's no way. You have bad information."

"Queenie has been here before. In fact, she's kind of a regular. She comes down from Canada to do whatever her husband can't. The way I hear it, the government knows about her but gives her latitude in hopes of catching him." She paused, thinking, "Or maybe catching you. Carny Dan and Omar Smith are involved in some financial deals so he treats her with a great deal of respect when she visits." She stared at him again. "Wow, you know her. That changes everything. Now that you two have been linked, it's only a matter of time before Brandt sends someone to take you away."

"How did you find all that out so quickly?"

"That's not important," she deflected. "Could this Queenie have come for you?"

"No, she had no idea I was here. It was a coincidence. The mayor will help me."

"The mayor will not help you. Dan says a great many things and that pass at the North gate, don't believe it. He's no fool. This thing has amped up far too quickly."

"He wouldn't lie to me. I'm getting out of here tomorrow."

"Yes you are, but if you go for that pass you'll leave by HomeSec helicopter and arrive in the Chairwoman's lap and that won't be good. Even if Dan really wanted to help, he has no choice now. He won't risk Brandt's wrath. My gig ends early tomorrow morning and I'll need a few hours to get ready. Pack your stuff. I'll meet you at your warehouse and we'll go from there. What time is your morning break?"

"Oh nine hundred."

"We'll leave then."

"The mayor will know you're helping me. You're going to get into trouble."

"I've been in trouble before. If we get through the security gate, we'll head north and east to a place called Presque Isle, it's on Lake Huron. It's an underground railway exit point. I'll drop you off there and I'll go west and take a sabbatical somewhere in the *Unincorporated Lands*. I'll try to sneak out to the Caymans from there. I haven't had time off in years."

"I can't go to Presque Isle there are *Tollers* there and they'll kill me."

She gave him a questioning look. "*Tollers*, no, I don't think so."

"Presque Isle is a *Toller* community," Gil explained. "If they see me . . ."

"There's no where else. Presque Isle is the closest exit point and I'm certain there are no *Tollers* there."

"But—"

"I'm certain." She seemed so sure that begrudgingly he acquiesced, realizing he could always change his mind once he escaped Hamilton. "Why can't we leave now?"

"The city only opens one way at night, to let supply trucks in. We can't leave until morning when loaded trucks head out."

"So you're finally okay with Canada."

"I'm not okay with it but it's your only chance." She paused and stared at him. "And don't try to see Queenie before we leave." He didn't respond. "Gil, I'm warning you, don't do it. She may be a good friend but her husband is dangerous. This meeting may have been a coincidence, but it's not *kismet* so if you do something foolish like see her again, even see her while you're in Canada once you escape, you'll regret it, probably you both will. Smith kills people and he's very powerful in Canada." She stopped at the door to her theatre. "Go home and sleep. Pack lightly and tomorrow we'll meet outside your warehouse."

"But she's my friend."

Dyllon grabbed his arms. "Listen to me. Get this through that thick, innocent skull, even if she is a friend, believe it or not, for whatever reason and however innocently it may have happened, your friend has chosen your enemy for her husband. She's poison to you now." Dyllon stared at him, as if deciding something. "Listen to me! You must avoid her," she reiterated and then went inside.

In spite of her warning he headed to the train station confident that somehow he and Stacey would find each other.

It was late when he arrived at his apartment. He walked in expecting her to be there, but he was disappointed. He put the few things he needed for his escape tomorrow into a sack and laid down on his bed. With the lights off, he wrestled with anticipation until he finally succumbed to sleep.

He woke sometime later to the sound of someone entering his apartment. The light went on and she was standing there in the same gown she had worn to the banquet with a bright yellow bolero jacket. They grabbed for each other in a desperate embrace.

"Is it safe to talk?" she whispered breathlessly.

Gil shrugged.

She stepped away and pulled out a tiny electronic device from her purse. "Don't ask but this thing blocks surveillance." She checked the meter. "It says we're okay." They embraced again each trembling with joy.

"The explosion, the rangers," he whispered in her ear. "I thought you were dead." Crying, she reached up to hold his face in her hands covered him with kisses. It was the most intimate she had ever been with him but though he reveled in it and it excited him, too, he needed to make her stop.

He squeezed her close. "I thought you were dead, but then I heard a rumor that Brandt might have you and I didn't know what was worse. I'm sorry I was so angry with you." She kissed him full on his lips and he pressed her face against him. She shrugged out of her jacket and he felt the heat of her body against him.

"No, Gil, what happened, it was my fault," she said. "I—we—"

"How did you escape?"

"They chased us, your grandfather and me. We hid in our grotto and then we crossed into Canada in the morning," she was so excited that she paused to kiss him again and again. "I contacted the Underground. Oh, Gil, we went to Dex's trailer but the *Federales* got their first and they killed him, just shot him and he was innocent like everyone." She sobbed.

It was horrible news. Yet another innocent person dying. "Not Dex, the poor guy, he never hurt anyone. What did you do?"

Her face was inches from him, with tears in her eyes, her green eyes were electrifying and her perfect skin glowed in the moonlight. "Clyde, Clyde, he helped us and then the Underground took us to Toronto where we would have escaped but a tiny, tough scar-faced lady caught us."

"Ginger Tucker, Brandt's principal goon. She almost caught me, too."

Stacey sighed, it came out like a moan, and she rested her head on his shoulder before telling him of her experiences in Canada. "The Federales took me to the Toronto airport, but I escaped again. Your grandfather couldn't. He's in Washington."

"He'll be okay. He's been there before. Why did they want you?"

"I thought they wanted Mr. Rose, but I think now that they were after me to get you but I don't know. Anyway, a local woman helped me. She introduced me to . . . to Omar." His shoulder was dampening with her tears.

"He's a terrorist." Gil tried not to sound heartbroken or accusatory. "Did you know?"

Tears continued to flow. "Oh, Gil, I thought you were dead, my parents, my friends, all were dead. I had nobody. I was desperate and alone and that scar-faced woman was after me. He . . . he helped me, he saved me." As he listened, Gil's throat ached at the sight of her beautiful eyes glistening with tears and he felt a sharp pain in his chest that he couldn't swallow away.

"Omar, he's a patriot and a nice man, really. He helps the poor and funds charities throughout Canada. It's why the government protects him from Brandt. People say he's bad, but Gil, he protects me, when no one else could, and someday he'll make Brandt pay for what she did to our family and friends. She has to pay. Someone has to pay for it."

He embraced her tighter. "Stace, Stace, there's nothing anyone can do."

"No!" She began crying anew. "It was a crime. Mom and dad never did anything to anyone. They were murdered for no reason? Why? Why did they do it?" He knew he was to blame, and remained silent.

"I lost everyone. I saw the explosion, I saw Meat, I saw Meat and I thought you die. I had no one, no one in the entire world. They had cycles and helicopters and they chased me to a strange country and I had no money, or friends, or anything. Fate sent me to Omar and he protects me. He'll hurt them for what they did." She was breathing hard as she fought tears. "But you're not dead. You're not," she said sucking in air between words to stop from sobbing.

He tried to remain calm. "Stace, hurting them won't help."

"Omar says it will. It's what I live for now."

"Don't say that," Gil said. "It's not you. I've heard about him. He's not who you think he is. I'm glad that he helped you but don't trust him and don't trust Mayor Burghe, either. Tomorrow, during my morning work break, I'm getting out of here. Come with me."

She pulled away and stared at the floor. "I can't. He's my husband, and don't you dare accuse him of anything!" She stared at him angrily. "He's the only one who's been good to me, better than I deserve. You and I, what did we have back then? Hiking and having fun together, we were kids, those days are over. There's no trusting anymore; we're adults and to survive in this mean world, we have to use people to get what we want. That's why Omar provides Carny Dan with . . . incentives and why Dan reciprocates by giving us access to things we can't get anywhere else. Dan won't dare turn me over to Brandt because Hamilton's too close to the Canadian border and too many of his workers support Omar. If he did anything to me, Omar would topple his little kingdom so fast."

"Be careful. The mayor is more scared of Brandt."

"I know, but I'm Omar's wife. I'm safe." She stared. "What will we do?"

He thought back to a better time, a time he missed and failed to appreciate. What he remembered was a carefree time of hiking and freedom, with her. He was happy thinking back on what they had once shared and what occurred next came naturally. In the intense heat of the moment, their lips met soft and easy but the shock of it caused each to back away briefly in discovery. Soon they were in each other's desperate embrace, lost in kisses that stopped all thought. In this most unlikely of places and situations, he ached with his love for her. They clawed at each other, each terrified to continue yet unable to stop. She pressed him onto his bed and rolled on top of him, her hands searching his body, pulling at his clothes. He wanted her. He wanted her so badly, but he'd been in this position before. Experience made him responsible and regret made him stop.

"No, Stace, we can't," he said breathlessly.

"Oh, Gil, we can." His rougher skin had turned her chin and cheeks red from their passionate kissing.

"But you're married."

She kissed him again, tongue and all and embraced him hard.

"But he's a killer."

"Stop talking," she said as her kisses became more urgent and their clothes peeled off. Even though it felt so right, he struggled, he had to pull away. But he couldn't convince himself to stop and her kisses urged him on.

Finally, almost, but not too late, he shouted. "No, we can't do this. Not here, not now. Too much has happened. You don't know. Stace, please . . ."

They were naked, staring into each other's eyes, dilated with passion, each lost and scared, yet eager, so eager. He wanted her, so much. Here, with her, he could finally feel, he could want, he could need, the empty places inside of him were filling up. He needed that and he needed her and her eyes told him she needed him, too. She rolled back on top of him, this time with nothing to encumber their lovemaking. With her beautiful face floating above him like an exquisite memory, he closed his eyes in bliss. If heaven existed, he was at its gates. She fumbled trying to help him and their ardor and inexperience caused her pain. She shrieked, ever so slightly and that broke his spell. They were so close but when he realized how close, and how much trouble he was about to get them both into, he pulled away. Yes, he pulled away.

He held her and tried to make her understand. "Stacey, Stace, I love you so much. I really do but we can't do this. It is beyond dangerous." He begged her to listen to reason but she kept trying to entice him to make love to her and he was afraid that he couldn't resist hard enough. He didn't have that much strength.

"We can," she said excitedly, as she fumbled. "We have to. I want you so much. I'm so lonely. Omar, we . . . he's so different. He's powerful, in control, and fierce, but he never . . . we never . . . Look, I'm a married woman and I'm trembling, see?" She placed his hands against her body. Sure enough, she was trembling. His hands slid across her breasts her ribcage, and down to her lean, muscular stomach. He felt rippling tremors there too. She planted small, intense kisses all over his face and he wrapped her in his tight embrace to stop the shivering.

"I missed you so much," she said. "I thought you were . . . I love you more than anything. Love me back. Please, love me now. Gil, you have to love me back."

Her plea broke his heart and he thought of all the reasons why he should, they should, but still, he fought it.

"It's not right," he said. "You'll regret it, we'll regret it. I love you, Stace, I do, more than anything. You must believe me. When I thought you were dead, I knew I had lost my best friend. You are the love of my life. But I've learned things. Important things about myself. I won't, I can't do this. I won't hurt you again and I won't do something that could cost me you, even if you're not mine. We have to stop." Somehow, he'd found the strength.

Teardrops fell onto his chest as she sobbed uncontrollably. Gently, he felt for a blanket, found it, and covered her. Rolling her on her side, he held her close. Even red faced, with tears swelling her eyes, she was still stunning to look at, to admire. He moved a lock of blond hair from her face and using a small corner of the blanket, he wiped her tears away. It hurt to speak.

"We've been through so much. I'll never stop loving you and I'll always be there for you if I can, but we can't do this. You know it too. It's insane."

As she silently sobbed, she nodded. They stared intently at each other in the dim light and her sobs slowed. This was it for them, he knew it and he etched every fine detail of her into his memory while his hands traced her body one last time, committing that to memory, too. In time, she fell asleep but he continued to stare until his eyes closed.

He couldn't recall the dream, but he couldn't breathe and it was raining and it woke him. His eyes fluttered open. Still naked, she was straddling him, staring down and crying. Unable to move, he felt something sharp against his neck. He looked down. She had a knife pressed against his carotid artery.

"What are you doing, Stace?" he asked, worriedly.

"I'm sorry. I'm so sorry. I promised him that I wouldn't let you hurt him."

He thought he was dreaming. "Promised who?"

"Omar."

"No, Stace, stop it, please. I'm just trying to survive, too. I can't hurt him. I don't want to hurt him. Put the knife away and we'll talk. We could always talk." She pressed the knife harder "Ouch, you're hurting me. Stace, stop it. I'm sorry, don't, please don't." The knife point twisted tenderly against his skin.

"Ouch, Stace, that's enough. Why are you doing this?" He struggled for the right words. "You said you loved me and I love you." She lifted the knife away and struck his head hard with the handle. Pain exploded from the blow. He tried to reach up to stop her but her legs had his arms trapped. "Why are you doing this? This isn't you."

She returned the business end of the knife to his neck. Her face was slack, her eyes were bloodshot and vacant, and she looked drained. "Me? The Stacey you remember, she's dead. There is nothing of her left. You died. Everyone died. Everyone including Stacey, she's dead now too. Omar gives me things, he makes me happy, and he protects me. If you hurt him I'll have nothing, no one. Don't you see? Without him, she'll come, that evil, mean, scar-faced woman, and she'll hurt me. She'll kill me, she will. I could see it in her eyes. He protects me and all he wants is my loyalty. I owe him that and so much more. If I don't do this, he won't stop her from hurting me again. You don't know. I'm so scared of her. He'll protect me. He will. I do love you, Gil, I really do but if I let you go, you'll hurt him and there will be no one to protect me. You died and Omar chose me. He married me. I'm his. I wanted it to be you but you died. Why did you have to die? You never seemed to care, but you knew I loved you. Why weren't you there for me like Omar is? You were never there and now it's too late."

"Stace, I'm so sorry, please . . ."

The blade pressed against his artery. "Omar hates Brandt, but you, he fears."

"How? I don't understand."

"You'll take what he loves most in the world."

"I won't. I promise. Doesn't tonight prove that? I love you; but we didn't do anything. See, he has nothing to fear from me. I've done bad things, but I won't do anything that would make him stop protecting you."

She groaned and twisted the knife, drawing blood. "I'm not what he loves most. He loves his revolution more than he loves me."

"I won't do anything to stop it. I promise. Don't do this, Stace, please."

He could feel her trembling through the blade. "You didn't care when it mattered. It wasn't your home, it was mine. I had friends before you arrived and you had none. You were distant, so distant, even when we were having fun you weren't there. I could feel it.

"You had your perfect girlfriend somewhere else so how could I compete against her? I tried, I really tried. I even thought you were beginning to like me, a little, but you never ever did. You walled yourself off and I could never get close. I tried. I tried so hard . . . but you were always thinking of her. And then . . . and then it was all gone, everything, everybody including Stacey Grant, everything died that day. If you'd never come, my parents would still be alive and I'd still be there playing with my friends and . . ." Her chin dropped and more tears flowed, dripping down and onto his chest.

What could he say? She was right. He was a bad person and worst of all, he was bad to her. The bad things he'd done hadn't started after Angel Falls; he was guilty of doing bad things while he was still there. He'd been inconsiderate; no, worse, he'd made her sad. He was a bad person who caused bad things to happen to people he should have loved and protected. Her knife at his throat made that clear. Alas, there was something far worse than having people disappoint you; he had disappointed people who loved him.

"Oh, God, Stace, you're right and I'm sorry. It is my fault, all of it. I know you can never forgive me, should never forgive me, for what I've done."

Her voice was meek but what she said made him cry. "Meat died saving you. Your great-grandfather, my family, everyone died saving you. Why can't you be worth it?"

It was the question he feared hearing most. Her knife offered absolution, but his death would destroy her, too. "I want so much to be worth it, but I'm not—"

"That's your answer?" She pressed the knife deeper and he felt a sweet pain. "Why do innocent people have to die?"

"That's what innocent people do," he whispered. "I never asked for any of this."

"And I did?" She removed the knife from his neck and stared at it. "Oh, God, look what I'm doing," she sobbed and her hands shook. Then she threw the knife away. It landed point first and stuck in the floor, quivering like her. When she spoke next, she sounded more determined. "If you truly love me—if you really, truly love me or ever did—make love to me now. Make me feel. Show me how much you love me. Do it now." She bent and kissed him hard, teeth biting his lips, tongue exploring.

He didn't know what to do. The knife was gone, but he didn't feel better or safer. He still wanted her desperately but it was more important to protect her, now, because he had failed to do so in Angel Falls.

"I—" he was sad and defeated. "We can't. I'm sorry. If things were different . . . I don't even know what that means. But things aren't. I love you so much it hurts, but . . . I can't, I won't. There are consequences. Please, please believe me."

She rolled off and curled away from him.

"This is so you," she said. Her voice sounded so crushed that it broke his heart. "Like there's something in this world that's right and makes sense. You're so damn committed to being uncommitted that you do nothing. If you loved me, you would have made love to me." She pressed her head face down beside on his pillow. "But you don't love me. No one does."

"You're wrong, Stace. When you return to Canada—and you must—you'll be thankful we didn't do anything. You know I'm right."

"You're just like him."

"Like who?" He turned her to face him and as punishment, he forced himself to stare into her wounded eyes. Ringed in red, her green eyes had an ethereal look. Her voice was full of disgust.

"Just like you, he says he loves me but he won't. I'm his prize, not his wife. The Rabbi said that people are what they do when it counts. I never knew what that meant until now. Now, when it counts, you run while my husband plots, but neither of you will love me, truly love me. What's wrong with me? I'm going crazy. I'm doomed to love unloving people. What is to become of me?" She turned away. "I hate you both."

"Stace, I'm so sorry."

"Don't give me that," she cringed. "Fuck you, fuck all men. Why is it so wrong to feel? To care? Life is nothing without intimacy. What's wrong with me that men shun me?"

"There's nothing wrong with you. He loves you the best he can."

"Is that him, or you?" She wept uncontrollably. He tried to comfort her but with each sob; the empty ache in her soul became his. Eventually, she fell asleep in his arms again. Trapped in so many ways and saddened in so many more, he lay awake disappointed with himself and this world. Why was it so easy to create so much sadness?

In the early hours of dawn, she awoke, stared briefly at him and then pulled away.

"Queenie's a mess," she said, in a small voice as she looked in a mirror. "There's no way the Prophet's wife can be seen like this. Can I use your bathroom?"

He nodded.

When she came back, she looked better although she couldn't hide the redness around her eyes and nose. What saddened him most was that her voice seemed lifeless.

"This will take a lot of explaining. I'll walk, maybe the cold will help." She fought to continue speaking "I'm sorry about last night and, and everything. It was good to see you, Gil. I won't ever mention this. I'd appreciate it if you didn't either."

He tried to hug her but she backed away. "No, you and I are going in different directions. If you get to Canada, I beg you; avoid me because he will kill you."

Regretfully, he nodded. "Where will you go?"

"I have to pick up something downtown and then I'll take Omar's stealth chopper across." He wanted to speak but she put a finger to his lips. "Don't tell me where you're going." She gathered the rest of her belongings, and faced him once more. "Thanks for . . . for being my friend, once. I'll always love you for that. Be safe." With that, she turned and left.

Depressed, he sat on the bed and stared, not realizing time was passing until he heard a familiar voice.

"Rise and shine, Ronnie boy, time to earn your keep." Joe's voice was cold reality. He wiped his eyes of their remaining tears and walked to the window. He stared out, hoping to catch one last glimpse of her but the streets were full of people heading to work and none were her. He grabbed his belongings and headed to the warehouse. Today was liberation day.

Late that evening, Carny Dan returned to his mansion after seeing Queenie to her apartment. He spent the remainder of evening trying to figure out how to take advantage of the evening's startling revelation, Ron Cooper and Queenie Smith, what a weird and wonderful world it was. There had to be something in that relationship that he could use to his advantage, he just needed to figure it out. How Omar Smith fit into it, the possibilities for profit seemed endless. Before retiring to bed, he called security and instructed them to hold Cooper if he should try to leave the city. He knew better than to hold Queenie and one of them should be enough. She would need watching, though.

The next morning, as soon as he arrived at his office, he discovered that he wasn't in control anymore, a situation he had worked hard to prevent. His secretary greeted him nervously. "Mr. Mayor, there's a woman, a Reverend General, she's waiting inside."

"I'm not seeing anyone this morning, Maybelle," he said before that information seeped into his mind. "A woman Reverend General? Shit." The color drained from his face. "Excuse my French, Maybelle."

"Sir, she was here when I unlocked the door."

"Cancel my morning appointments and take a break. Be back in an hour and on the way out, lock my door."

She was concerned. "Should I call security? Is everything alright, sir?"

"May, security didn't keep her out. Don't worry, everything is fine." After his secretary left, he waited as long as he dared before taking a deep breath, and slowly opening the door to his office.

"Don't you post something when you're going to be late?" Reverend General Ginger Tucker asked from the chair, behind his desk.

"Ginger, it's good to see you again. What's it been, a year?"

"A couple of hours ago we received information that a fugitive we've been seeking is here. We expect full cooperation."

"And by God you'll have it," he said. "I'm sorry, Ginger, I should have notified Madam Chairwoman, but you know how busy I get this time of year. It's on me. She came in late last night and left maybe an hour ago." He volunteered the news hoping Tucker would appreciate his cooperation. "If I'd known you were hot for her . . . she can't be far."

"Cut the crap," Tucker said. "We know who you do business with. We're not interested in Smith's whore just yet. By the way—just a suggestion—back off a bit with Smith. My boss is never happy when you two play nice."

He started to respond but she put her hand up to stop him.

"We know. You're just using him and he believes he's using you. Slow down the deals so we can unwind them when the time comes. But that's not why I'm here. There's bigger prey. Mark Rose's grandson is here and we want him."

"I didn't know Rose had a grandson. How do you know he's here?"

She stood and walked to him. Even though her head only came to his chin, he knew her by more than her reputation and her reputation was intimidating enough. He stepped back.

"I don't have time for bullshit." She took out a small device and projected a three dimensional image of Gil Rose on the Mayor's desk. His face went white.

"So you do know him?"

"I believe so. That image is old and it isn't quite accurate. He's matured, filled out, a bit more muscular, maybe, but that could be him."

"Stop fucking with me. We want him and I'll get him."

"Yes, he's here," the mayor said. "He calls himself Cooper, Ron Cooper. His records say he's from western Pennsylvania, a rocket scientist, I believe."

She moved closer, her nose almost touching his chin as she looked up at him. "You're wasting my time. Get to the fucking point."

"Right, I'm just trying to be helpful," he said, as he backed away without it looking like he was retreating. "How was I to know? Mark Rose's white and this kid isn't. He—this Ron Cooper—he attended a banquet last night. By the way, here's some information you should know. He knows Smith's wife. I have no idea how."

"Of course you have no idea. Both were in Angel Falls and they escaped. I caught up to her in Canada before Smith took her from me. I'll get him for that later. They're married, so he must have taken good care of her but it doesn't matter. The boy's been lost to us for a while—until yesterday. He's getting help from terrorists everywhere, including here in your town."

The mayor shook his head. "That's not possible. Everyone's loyal in Hamilton."

"Tanya wants him so here's your chance to earn some respect towards that retirement you've talked so fondly about. Right now, my assault team is outside the city. Tell me where Rose is and invite me in and we'll be out of your way within the hour."

"Why the big play? If you'd contacted me, the kid would be waiting for you in one of my jails, both him and the girl if you'd only said something. You're too melodramatic, why do things the hard way?"

She stuck her thumb hard into his throat and he lurched backward, choking.

"Fuck you. We send bulletins to every fucking town in the fucking country and we catch every fucking one we're after, even if some mayors choose to ignore us for their own reasons, we fucking catch everyone. Now where is he?"

He cleared his throat while wiping tears from his eyes. "I'll check . . ." He queried his computer and handed Tucker a small, clear plastic memory square. "Here's a map. He's working first shift in Warehouse 2048D, Sector L in Technology. My security people will be there in less than five minutes."

She brought her thumb to her throat in a threatening gesture. "He's not there. We checked. He's gone."

"You're wrong," the mayor whined. "He's there. His avatar checked him in. Maybe he's on a break."

"Someone tipped him off. I want your transmission records."

"It wasn't me. I didn't let him go. Jesus, Ginger, I stretch as much as any mayor but I'd never cross the boss. She knows that."

"Give me the fucking transmissions or I'll have Gecko rip them out and a whole lot more you don't want us to know about. You know how thorough Gecko can be."

This was getting troublesome. "That's not our agreement."

"You're wasting time. Someone is helping him. Lock down the security gates because if he's out—"

"Who would help him?"

"Your local Dyllon Tomas, Dale Allen, for one, her, and Queenie Smith."

"It's not the singer."

"It *is* the singer. We took her into custody earlier this morning."

"You did it without telling me. There will be a fine."

"Fuck you," Tucker said, her face growing redder with each delay. "Stop stalling or I'll report back that you slowed down my investigation. Tanya has me cleaning up loose ends and the Rose kid is definitely one,

Tomas is another, and we're working our way up to Smith and his whore. The world's changing again, Dan. You had better be very clear that you're on Tanya's side."

"She can't doubt I'm her man. I know I'm a bit extracurricular—but when she needs me, she knows I'm here for here."

He received a call on his private communicator and held up his hand to show her he was listening. When he was done, he put his hand down. "Queenie has left the city."

Chapter 18
Presque Isle, MI.—2072

They say everything can be replaced, yet every distance is not near.
So I remember every face of every man who put me here.
I see my light come shining from the west unto the east.
Any day now, any day now, I shall be released.

-I Shall Be Released, Bob Dylan

He usually dreaded morning shifts because they were so agonizingly boring. Today's shift, his last, would be even harder.

"Late again, Mr. Cooper," Joe began.

"Joe, this is when I usually arrive. Why not change my starting time instead of bitching?"

"Excuse noted. Did we have another bad night? Was the mayor not friendly enough? You would have been better served to have spent your time helping our economy because you are not going to help it much today with that attitude."

"I'm here. Stop harassing me or find someone else to humiliate."

"Is that the thanks I get? Harassment and humiliation, as you call it, are what allows you to be productive enough to remain a *Conducer*. Be grateful, not snippy."

"There are other ways of motivating people."

"And I suppose you have heard them all. I am curious. Have any of them worked? Now that we have had our usual start of the shift squabble, it is time to earn us some credits. Can I recommend an enhanced, caffeinated morning beverage as an option to counter your proclivity for sloth?"

"Proclivity for sloth?"

"I repeat; our social minute is over. I will not be goaded into a tiff. It is time to produce for your country, city, sector, segment, and, of course, for you, and for me. It is time to effort proudly for the glory of earned income."

Joe kept Gil busy and he didn't have time to worry until his break finally arrived. Tired, but nervous and excited, too, he left to wait for Dyllon. He considered saying goodbye to Joe but when he thought about it, he laughed. Outside, he leaned against the warehouse wall shielding his eyes from the bright sun while staring down the long alley between the enormous buildings, waiting for Dyllon. Time went by and he began to worry. His break was almost over and their margin for escape was dissipating.

A security van stopped at the main door to the warehouse and his concern increased. In the distance, two more vehicles approached. Unsure what to do, he panicked and climbed a nearby maintenance ladder to the roof, three stories above. When he was safely on the roof, he assessed the situation below. At both ends of the warehouse armed security guards bolted from their cars and began checking docks and doors. He knew he was in trouble, but he was worried about Dyllon, too. Fortunately, there were no helicopters visible but satellite surveillance could easily be focusing on him so he had to act quickly. He ran to the far end of the warehouse roof and stared down. More security guards were checking various access points from the building.

He found a skylight but it was locked so he searched for something to pry it open. All he could find on the roof was a large bucket filled with dried concrete so he picked it up and dropped it through the window. The sound of glass breaking and the bucket landing with a crash three stories below caused the security patrols to surge into the warehouse. He pulled the communicator from his belt and dropped it through the window, also, and turned to watch from above as the guards followed the sound. When the street was empty, he climbed rapidly down the ladder and ran across the alley to a nearby warehouse.

Once inside, he worked his way through the maze of racks until he reached a door leading to another alley. He looked out, saw no one and bolted down the block and away from the warehouses and guards.

He was committed now, but without Dyllon he had no plan. He ran, putting as much distance between him and the guards as he could, stopping whenever he saw someone on the street or a truck going by. Finally, he approached the North Hamilton departure gate. He hid behind a stack of pallets and surveyed the area for a way to escape. At the security gate, cars and trucks were being checked and there were so many guards he realized that leaving Hamilton would be harder than entering.

He worked his way as close to the security gate as he dared and waited. There was no easy way so he paused to build enough nerve to make a dash for it. Just then, from an alley out of sight of the guardhouse, a limo drove straight for him. Worried, he hunkered down and watched the vehicle pass. When it was out of his view, he decided to count to ten before running for the gate—not a good plan but it was all that was left to him. By the time he had counted to five, the limo had backed up and stopped in front of him.

The door opened and he heard a shout.

"Get in!"

It was Stacey.

He hesitated briefly then jumped in. She slid over to the far door. He couldn't help but stare as since she left him, she had applied nano-cosmetics that made her look phenomenal, and she was wearing another beautiful, sexy dress, bare midriff and cut very low in front. She pointed to the car floor and pulled a lever under her seat. A hidden compartment opened under her. She pulled out some bags and boxes to make room.

"Hurry, hide in here, now." He slid to the floor and wiggled under her seat coiling fetal in the limited space. "Be quiet," she said as she closed the secret door. "I have a pass so this should be easy, but you never know. If they find you, don't struggle, whatever you do. Guards are licensed to kill and they're free from economic consequences so they've been known to kill indiscriminately. It limits runners."

He curled tighter and held his breath as the limo drove to the security gate.

He heard a window open. "Miss, can we see your exit visa?" He heard it so clearly, it made him feel exposed. There was brief silence. "Everything's in order. Do you mind if we check those boxes and your trunk?" He heard the trunk lid open and then quickly close.

"Ma'am, we need to check inside."

"I have a special pass from the mayor and I'm not to be hassled. I'll show you the boxes. You can look at them through the window if you want." He heard another window open. "Say, could you do me a favor?" Her voice had changed to something he'd never heard from her before. It sounded . . . seductive. "My brooch came undone. Reverend Major, can you fasten it for me?"

He heard the excitement in the guards' voices as each gladly volunteered.

After a brief silence, he heard her laughing. "That's it; the clasp is so small and it's hard for me to work with my big, clumsy fingers. Can you feel it?" She laughed. "That tickles. Now don't get fresh." He heard subdued chortles from the guards. "That's it, you got it. Thank you very much. Here are a few credits each for your trouble." It sounded like she was purring.

He heard the satisfying sound of a window close and then the car moved forward.

"Stay down," she whispered. "You can climb out from under in a few minutes."

He waited patiently until she told him it was time. The door to his compartment opened, he blinked at the blinding daylight, and rolled out to sit beside her. He was about to speak but the look on her face stopped him.

"We said everything that can be said last night," her voice cracked with sadness. "It hurts. I hurt. I know you do too, so please . . . no more." He nodded. Aching in a shared way provided no relief.

He gave the driver directions and they drove north in silence. Finally, the limo pulled to the side of the road and stopped. She pointed to a dirt path that intersected the highway and disappeared into a mass of bushes. "Presque Isle road," was all she said.

"How do you—"

"Gil," she whispered then looked away to avoid his stare while struggling to find her voice. "When you get to Canada," she labored, "don't see me. It won't be safe and I can't, I won't . . ." She pointed at the door. "I couldn't live with myself if I caused your death."

"But . . ."

"No, don't, please," she pleaded. "Just say goodbye, please. I can't . . . just goodbye." She turned away.

He got out of the limo without looking at her. Outside, he weakened and turned to her one last time, but her hands were covering her face. Her tears caused his to flow. He needed to be strong for her so he forced a smile.

"Goodbye," he croaked. That was all, his one last favor to her. All too quickly, the limo disappeared and he was left to stare at the now-vacant dusty road until long after the car had gone. He had the sinking feeling of déjà vu.

He turned to the Presque Isle road. He had escaped. He should be elated but he wasn't so he plodded down the road, every step causing his heart to ache. After a while, the desolate path turned into little more than an overgrown trail. Finally, after walking all afternoon, he saw a sign for the town of Presque Isle. He continued on until the path opened onto a small, verdant valley. On a sugar loaf slope in the center of the valley, a single decrepit wooden house stood incongruously on stilts. Unsure, he carefully climbed the rotting wooden stairs and knocked.

An old man came to the door. He was gaunt with sparse gray hair and a long gray beard that was separated into two tight braids. The old man supported himself on two crooked legs with the aid of a shillelagh. His face seemed worn and pained, but he greeted Gil with a smile.

"Welcome, pilgrim."

"Pilgrim?"

"Sorry, it's a line from one of my favorite old movies. My name's Clarke Jackell. Come in. You must be hungry."

He held out his hand. "I'm Ron, Ron Cooper."

"It's nice to meet you, Mr. Cooper." The old man shook his hand. Gil should have been apprehensive, but something about the man made him feel safe. The house was little more than a shack with a wood stove in the center and a few chairs clustered around it. Clarke offered him a chair and he sat while the old man finished preparing some food. There was plenty and Gil ate until he was full. When he finished, he helped the old man wash the dishes. It wasn't until the last dish was dry that the old man sat and spoke. "I expect you're here to escape."

"I am, in the worst way. Is this Presque Isle?"

"This is what's left of it. Presque Isle is me, now."

"I thought it was a town?'

"Once, like a lot of places. Today, it's the right size for what's needed. It's too late to cross over today so you'll have to wait until morning. It's safer in daylight, though there'll still be risks. We have time so tell me why you need to cross 'in the worst way.'"

"It'll be safer for both of us if you didn't know."

"That's what most of them say. So how do we kill time until tomorrow?"

"I'm sorry, I can't tell you anything. I'm not trying to sound important, but there are people who would do really bad things to you if they knew you helped me."

"They say that, too. It's okay. If you'd like, I can tell you my story, the others seemed to appreciate it."

It was better than silence to Gil who was tired of stewing in his own morose juices. "I'd like to hear whatever it is you want to talk about, Mr. Jackell."

"They say that, too. It gets real cold at night so I need to bring in my wood first." Gil offered to help and soon there was pile of firewood in reserve, a good fire in the woodstove, and the house began to warm. Gil sat near the stove, rubbing his hands as the old man began his tale.

"My brother, Jake, and I were born and raised in Philadelphia back when we had a kind of republic, maybe the First Republic, or whatever the hell it was before everything changed. Jake and I, we had a typical childhood being in what was then called the middle class. We lived on safe streets and played with other kids who lived nearby. We went to schools that prepared us for college and in our free time we had the kind of unsupervised fun that kids today no longer enjoy."

"Like what?"

"Well, we played ball mostly. In the morning, we'd see how many kids we had before we decided what to play. If it was only my brother and me, it meant a catch or one-on-one basketball. Three, we played football with what we called a steady quarterback. Four and we could play team games. More than four and it was tag football or team basketball. In our neighborhood, there was an open, flat field at the end of a hilly street so our parents always knew where to find us.

"It's funny, looking back. Where you grew up, what kind of neighborhood you lived in, and what kind of jams you got into and out of as a kid, that pretty much determined what kind of adult you would be. My jams and Jakes were easily manageable and life was good. I graduated from college when college was a place you attended, and I worked for companies that no longer exist, but I never did well working for them so I started my own accounting practice. It was enough to feed me and allow me to live the carefree life I deserved.

"My older brother Jake was my polar opposite. He was outgoing and as he got older, he was a natural social climber in the great American tradition and a fast-talking ladies man. He never applied himself in school because he was too stupid, but he was born charming, really scary charming, shallow charming, the kind people love when they first meet and avoid ever after. As an adult, he blossomed into a selfish, boorish, ignorant, and shallow man, the kind who succeeds in this world, but God, Jake was personable as hell. I hated him but he had his moments. When he was on, he kind of glowed. It was his gift. He could make shallow, needy people feel wanted and was so naturally sycophantic that important people felt they needed him. If he felt you could help him and your approval was what he desired, he could make you love him, really love him. He knew better than anyone that he was a limited thinker, so there was nothing he wouldn't do to get ahead if it didn't take thinking—and he wanted desperately to be successful. Jake was a force of nature and never, ever let pride get in the way of his quest for self-importance. He could have been, hell, he was the poster child for America's shallow, despicable capitalist ways. If he'd been a tad smarter, he'd have been president. As it was, he wanted the presidency so badly that he got uncomfortably close to achieving it. I never understood it, but he managed to work for brilliant people in the rarified air of national politics and that permitted him to attain positions far beyond his intellectual capacity. Hell, anything was beyond his intellectual capacity. His career was about the perverse leading the amenable. He thrived because he was impervious to consequences and grasped instinctively at the first, best solution, untroubled by morality and ethics, which, at best, mystified him.

"That was Jake. Me, I never let anything get in the way of a good time. I was happy and healthy and unconcerned, playing ball, running, skiing, traveling, and dating beautiful women free from entanglements. It was enough to keep the real world at bay. Then everything changed. I didn't see it because, as I said, I didn't pay attention. Like millions of Americans back then, I was self-absorbed, but unlike most of them, I survived to tell about it.

"It was late 2035 and I was just beginning to work on my client's taxes for the coming season. The months of carefree living were once again diminishing with tax season approaching. It was the time to transition from play season to work season in my well-planned life.

"But that year was different. My revenue was diminishing along with my client base and change was on the horizon and rapidly accelerating toward me. The government announced the phasing out of the Internal Revenue Service and I only had another year to diversify, or find real work to support my social calendar. For me, work was an unforgiving master, particularly during my three month tax season when it was unavoidable. But I never truly taxed myself because I needed to be rested and available for my first love, me."

Gil listened intently, smiling when he thought appropriate, and nodding when the old man made a point. The fire crackled and Gil settled into a more comfortable position.

"At forty, I still had it," the old man continued. "I was good-looking in the healthy, athletic way that attracted mature, lonely, independent women of means of whom I had my pick. Because of my many interests and my purpose for dating, I never needed to plumb the depths of my relationships to enjoy them because they never lasted long enough. And though I regretted not being as good looking as Jake, my easy success with women soothed that lifetime injustice. And unlike Jake, down deep, I was sensitive, but that could get in the way; so I made it clear to my dates that they were important, but secondary to every one of my other pursuits and if they wanted to spend quality time with me, my pursuits should become theirs.

"To ensure that my active social life was manageable I practiced meticulous selective avoidance. Every call on my time underwent rigorous evaluation and had to pass a comparative utility threshold. Events, particularly family events such as visits to my brother's home, plummeted into the abyss of the unlikely. So when Angie, Jake's wife, persuaded me to attend her family Christmas dinner that year, it was a stark reminder that I was becoming too sensitive."

Chapter 19

Montgomery Country, Pennsylvania—2035

The Jackell family with all the relatives was in the living room, drinking and listening devotedly to Jake boasting of his latest career success. Taking a deep breath, Clarke entered to shouted greetings and obligatory handshakes, hugs, and quick kisses. After introducing his date to his brother, he extended a hand but Jake smiled and grabbed him in a great bear hug.

"Sweetie," Jake called everyone that as if it expressed emotion. "Glad you could come, baby bro." Clarke was six feet tall but Jake, at an intimidating six-four, always made him feel deficient, particularly with his annoying habit of standing so close you had to strain to stare up at him.

"What have we here?" Jake's smile widened to broadcast approval of Clarke's date. "So this is your latest squeeze." Next came the ladling of charm as Jake touched, pawed, flattered and otherwise worked over Clarke's date. Clarke scowled, not because he loved her, but because he hated Jake for trying to make her love him. But there were so many things he hated Jake for, his arrogance, his success in spite of abject stupidity, and countless other conceits his older brother heaped on Clarke to prove his dominance. And as always happened when their paths crossed, Clarke conceded the field, turned and walked away, allowing his brother the latitude to work his magic on the woman he was dating.

He found refuge from Jake with all of his annoying aunts, uncles, and cousins who pelted him with questions about his career to which he provided the only response possible, brief and unenlightening, all the while watching Jake winning over his date. Occasionally she blushed at some flattery Jake spewed from his vast arsenal of charm. He'd warned her, but she had willingly accepted the challenge and was giving it her all.

Finally, with Jake staring down at her, nose-to-nose, his large hands firmly placed on her hips, his thumbs touching and gently rubbing her upper pelvis, his fingers messaging her glutes, Clarke intervened. He grabbed her arm, turned her away from his brother and enveloped her in a deep, theatrical kiss.

When they unclenched, he turned to Jake who was smiling, "Way to go, Clarkie, this one's a sweetheart. Not like all those others." His brother insinuated himself between them, placing his hand under her chin and tilting her head back. As if in a daze, she allowed it.

"Sweetie, your eyes are so much prettier," he whispered to her, "after you've been kissed. They are, you know, sweetie. But be careful with my baby brother. Don't go too deep, that's not where you'll find him. He's a charmer but I can tell you're choice stock and you can do better. Don't expect old Clarkie to commit, you'll be disappointed. Trust me, doll, I've had too many of his ex's crying on my shoulder. I can tell you from experience, Clarkie doesn't know what to do with quality."

Her face turned red. Clarke was certain no one had ever talked to her that way. "Jake, cut it out," he growled, balling his fists.

That's when Angie entered the room and in spite of the situation, seeing her calmed him. She was why he bothered at all. His brother literally couldn't have done better. She was great looking in a very sexy yet conservative way and though she was short and appeared pudgy in clothes, in a bikini, it was clear why Jake had married her. She was smart; too smart for Jake and she knew his nature, yet was loyal to a fault. She was another good thing Jake failed to appreciate or deserve.

"It's been too long stranger. Is this your date?" Angie asked, hugging him and then his date. "I wish I knew you'd arrived so I could have apologized for my husband, sooner."

His date laughed.

"Jake is really harmless unless you take him seriously. He likes to sample, that's all." After introductions were made, Angie turned to Jake. "I asked you to be on your best behavior."

"I am, sweetie, but it would be a damn shame if this little cutie didn't experience real Jackell charm when she has the chance," Jake said winking at Clarke's date.

"If that's charm, it's a malignant form," Clarke responded, doubling over when Angie punched him lightly in the stomach.

"I didn't hit you that hard. Your folks are in the kitchen." She guided him there.

His parents sat wheel-to-wheel in matching assist chairs joined at the oxygen tank they shared. Theirs was a bad marriage that had come full circle. Clarke paused, steeling himself against the onslaught of excess gross hairs and malignant moles before hugging them. He wasn't prepared for the overpowering smell of tobacco that barely camouflaged the alcohol fumes. Except for being older and forced to be closer, they hadn't changed.

"Clarke, is this your girlfriend?" his mom asked.

"No, Mom, she's just a friend."

"Can I fuck her, Jake?" his dad roared loud enough for everyone to hear. There was no doubt he was imbibing again.

In the ensuing awkward silence, Clarke responded. "I'm Clarke, dad, and no, you can't."

"Have you fucked her yet?" his dad persisted. "Get me a scotch, will ya Jakie boy?"

He shrugged and turned to his date to apologize. She displayed a game smile. "It's Clarke, dad. Of course."

"I can see it in her eyes, you did fuck her. Way to go, boy. Score another for the Jackells. I remember when you were a teen, the old ball and chain and I thought you'd go in a different direction, sexually, I mean." His dad winked and Jake laughed at that.

"Thanks, Dad. I meant I'll get you your drink." He turned to Angie. "You let him drink?"

Angie scowled. "I'm kind of defenseless here, Clarke. When does Jake stop anyone from doing anything? How an old man in an assist chair coupled to someone who doesn't approve can acquire liquor, weed, and tobacco without us knowing, and then find a secure place to hide it is beyond me."

"Mom probably orders it so she can berate him for it when it arrives."

"At least while he's stoned or drunk, she gets some relief," Angie said.

"You mean he's worse than now? Poor Mom, she never learned. Dad denied her everything. Hell, he denied everyone everything except himself."

"Not now, Clarke," she said. "We don't see much of you. What have you been doing?"

"Where's the scotch?" his dad roared, interrupting them. "Jake, for a sales guy, you aren't much fun and you're way too slow pouring my drinks."

"I'm not Jake, Dad. I'm Clarke. I do tax returns for a living, remember?"

"What the fuck do I care. Get me my scotch."

Angie tried to help "Dad, this is Clarke, your accountant son."

"Accounting? Fuck accounting. Sales are where it's at. Sales is what gave you kids your lives."

"How would you know, Dad, you were drunk all the time."

With that, Mom spoke up. "Hush, Clarke. Don't talk to your father like that. Times were tough and jobs were hard to come by. You were too young to know, but the brown people stole all the good jobs. Being white wasn't easy, back then. Thank God for my boy Jake's success. You don't know. Your father's career was shortened because he had to fight prejudices you can't understand today. And he did it because he loved you boys and we had bills to pay."

"Mom, he couldn't hold a job because he drank so much," Clarke explained.

"I'm fucking sitting right here, fool. Speak to my face, not my asshole."

"That's enough, Dad," Angie interrupted. "It's Christmas. Come on everybody, let's enjoy it." She grabbed a hold of her in-laws' oxygen tank and pushed their chairs to the dinner table.

Clarke sat between his date and Angie while Jake sat at the head of the table where he dominated the conversation with more career talk, interrupted occasionally by Dad's outbursts.

Tell them about your charity walk, Jake," Angie cued.

"About two hundred of us walked in support of my current charity, Selfishness."

"Does that need a walk?" Clarke asked.

"Now that the Democrats are finally out of power, the selfish, an unrecognized minority, can finally come out and seek assistance until they're accepted again in society. I work to earn money for them in their time of need."

"Their what?"

"Their time of need," Jake explained. "People who create value have been looked down on for too long. Their incomes and their estates have been taxed to death. It's truly sad. A great many of them have lost great wealth that their parents bequeathed to them. They were taxed too heavily by bleeding heart socialist Democrats and they were made to apologize for that wealth. How un-American is that? To apologize for being rich when the rest of the country is poor, it's insane. This is America and no one should apologize for being rich, so we're collecting funds to restore selfishness so that these people and others can make America great again like their ancestors did. Part of the funds come from selling books by Ayn Rand and other objectivist philosophers that explain why everyone in America should be proud of selfish people and we're distributing pamphlets that will help them fight the socialists who controlled America's politics for so long. That's why the walk. It's a 3k and we have great cash prizes for the winners. What's left goes to the selfish."

Clarke could only stare in disbelief.

"What can I say? I do what I can," Jake said humbly.

"Oh." It was all Clarke could think to say. In the awkward silence, he mumbled, "So what else is new, Jake?" Almost immediately, he regretted it.

"I flew to London last week on a company jet that had a real water shower. When I arrived, Herman Stent, the leader of the Tory party—he's going to be the next PM, you know—he greeted me, personally, and took me to Soho for a private party." Jake gazed around to confirm he had everyone's attention. "There was this sherry—or was it a port? I'm not sure which one, except that legend has it Napoleon pissed in the bottle."

"Jake, no, I asked you not to tell that story."

Jake continued on, ignoring his wife. "A shot glass of that piss cost more than a two liter bottle of really good bourbon or a Reeperbahn whore, for that matter. Sir Herman said he liked the stuff so much; I bought him the bottle and he let me have another shot. It was too rank for me but I drank it just so I could tell everyone how good Napoleon's piss really is." Jake roared with laughter and the in-laws joined in. "It was kind of musty, you know what I mean, and way too sweet for my taste, but everyone at our table was impressed when I bought the bottle."

Jake then smiled at Clarke's date. "I visit New York regularly, sweetie. Have you ever been there?" She nodded, but rather than including her, he continued to work the table. "Hey, everyone, I received a personal invitation to visit Morgan headquarters."

"Did you see him?" An aunt asked, obviously impressed. "Did you? The new Holy Father, His Eminence, the Secretary of State?"

Jake laughed. "He's the Chief Spiritual Officer of the United States now. I call him Tom. What else? Tom Morgan was a co-worker of mine at ANGS; we used to go to meetings together all the time before he became Secretary and then founded the most relevant religion in the history of the world." The family oohed and ahhed. "And no, I didn't see him. No one is allowed to see him; he's far too busy overseeing heaven on Earth to invest time in mortal visitations. But I will next time."

"Jake, you're speaking blasphemy," Mom interjected, appalled.

"But that's what the Morgan religion is, Mom. And New York, what a town. The Morgan Church Headquarters twin towers reach to the stars and they are filled with palatial estates that take up multiple floors and are a city-block-long! New York is so much grander than Philly. Some of the mansions high up in the Towers have irrigated hanging gardens and their own airport runway."

"Wow," Clarke's date said in wonder. "That's so wasteful."

Jake smiled back. "Oh no, Clarkie, you're not dating an environmentalist. I thought you'd learn your lesson from the last one. Anyway, it's not waste, darling, if you can afford it. It's beautiful and owning gardens like that are a sure sign of success and class. As a Morgan, you need a great deal of money to live forever and an ostentatious lifestyle proves that you have the confidence and capability to qualify for everlasting status. One of my customers explained that his Tower gardens rival the ones in Cairo, which, years ago, were once the greatest wonder of the entire world."

Clarke couldn't stand it. "It's Babylon, you moron."

"Have you been there, smarty pants?"

"Of course not. But the Hanging Gardens were destroyed millennia ago. They were in Babylon, not Cairo."

"No, dipshit, have you ever been to New York?"

Angie interrupted. "Did you notice our 'For Sale' sign in the yard, Clarke?"

Jake took the bait. "Pro-mo-tion!" he yelled. "We're moving to the new ANGS regional headquarters. I found a mansion in Merion with an indoor and outdoor pool. It's worth a fortune, and our plans to renovate will shame the neighborhood."

"We're getting a place at the shore, too," Angie gushed.

"Drinks for everyone!" Dad shouted, "The Jackells are living large."

As her husband continued to rant about their move, Angie put her hand on Clarke's leg and asked quietly, "So really, how've you been?"

"Really good, Angie. Last triathlon season, I finished first in my age group."

"Talking about domination, Sweetie," Jake bellowed turning from another conversation toward Clarke's date, "I'll show you my triathlon ribbons after dinner."

"How does he hear anything when he talks so much?" Clarke whispered to Angie.

She laughed. "It's one of his gifts. Jake, tell everyone the really exciting news."

"Angs finally figured out that he's a worthless piece of—"

"Clarke, stop it," Mom pleaded. "Don't be rude. He's your brother and not everything's a joke. Why can't you enjoy his success like everyone else?"

"Mom, do you really want me to answer that?"

"Pay attention, Sweetie," Jake interrupted, smugly. "Clarkie, this will absolutely destroy you. The president approved a special program that is so secret; all I can tell you is its name. It's called the *Circle of Life* and I'm going to be appointed to run the whole damn thing. This is it. This is a homerun. We're living top shelf after this."

Clarke was flabbergasted. "The president of what?"

"Shush," Mom scolded. "Jake means the President of the United States, dear. Jake, honey, that's wonderful. Dad is so proud of you." With that, Mom reached for her husband's hand, but he moved it away.

Jake put his big hands around his mom's head and planted a wet kiss on her forehead. "Are you proud of your big boy, Mama?" She laughed and struggled in her wheel chair to escape the attention. "Are you proud of me, big girl?"

"You'll be hiring," Dad said. "I can sell anything, you know that. What do you say, Jake-O? I've always wanted to work for the president."

"No can do, Dad. If I told you anymore about this project, I'd have to kill you, really. Sorry, Dad."

Dad roared with laughter. "Then get it over with. Tell me and kill me, but first, let's celebrate. Where's my drink?"

Clarke made a mental note never to attend another family dinner.

"Jake, how can you trust President Crelli?" Clarke asked. "No one with a brain does. Oh, I guess that's my answer." Angie gave Clarke a nasty look as Jake deftly avoided the critique.

"Spoken like the child you are. You don't like Andy because he's a hard worker, a straight shooter, a man who cherishes family values, and he knows what he wants, goes after and gets it. And he's successful which is so different from you."

"Dear, does the president allow you to call him by his first name?" Mom asked.

Jake smiled. "Before the election, I met Andy in D.C. and bought him dinner at a gourmet restaurant that actually serves human meat over pasta with an incredibly rich organ sauce. They even have a veal-like—"

"What the—" Clarke sputtered.

"Gotcha, it's a joke." Jake said laughing hysterically. "You Democrats have no sense of humor. Actually we ate at an exclusive restaurant that flies in whatever you want from any restaurant in the world. *Eight with Us*, it's called. You call your order in and give their logistics chef eight hours to ship dinner in. When I invited him, Andy said to me, he says, 'Mr. Jackell', he calls me that. He says, 'Mr. Jackell; I love the Coral Islands Paella so I had it shipped in. It cost a mint and arrived just in time. He was impressed. Let me tell you. Doing stuff like that is one of the reasons he offered me the job. I get things done other people won't even think to do. To make sure everything was perfect, I wired a fabulous tip to the owner of the Coral Islands restaurant, the pilot, the express delivery guy, the port authority, the owner of the restaurant, and the waiter, but it was all worth it, I got the job. As soon as the Circle of Life bill is passed by the next Congress, I'll be the second most important person in the government."

"Explain how important, Jake," Angie prodded.

"Andy says the Circle of Life is the most important legislation in his administration and maybe in the history of the United States. It is very high-level stuff."

Angie hugged Clarke's arm. "This is our big one," she said, looking proudly at her husband. "Don't tell anyone, but Jake will be president someday. Isn't that exciting?"

"Scary is more like it," Clarke said. "Remind me to move to Canada if he gets the nomination."

"Sour grapes, Clarkie boy?" Jake bellowed. "When I'm on top, I won't forget family, or at least not all of it." He laughed.

"Is that a promise or a threat?"

"Boys, stop acting like children." Angie pleaded. "Think about it. In ten years, Jake and I could be living in the White House."

"Excuse me, but picturing that, I'm going to have trouble keeping dinner down."

"When I get there, little bro, don't embarrass me like other presidential brothers."

Before Clarke could rebut, the family bombarded Jake with questions and adulation. When even his own date offered Jake a rapturous stare, Clarke sat back infuriated and then angrily escaped into a nearby bedroom and closed the door. Feeling claustrophobic, he opened a window to breathe in the cold fresh air. He could still hear the conversation from the dining room, so he plopped onto the bed and covered his head with a pillow. Unfortunately, even with that, he suffered through Jake's bellowing voice.

It wasn't until Angie began discussing her future that he couldn't resist and lifted the pillow to listen to the conversation outside his door.

"We'll send Jenna and Clarice to private school, of course, probably somewhere in New England. We haven't decided yet. Jake wants to send them where all the right people send theirs. And we promised Jake Junior a new car if he starts passing courses and stops trying to impregnate his dates." There was laughter. "JJ's been bugging us for one of those new *NASCAR* series, grain-burning, sports convertibles." Angie paused and then shrieked. "And I'm on the list to receive one of the first nano-cosmetic surgeries." When all the women shrieked with Angie's news, Clarke grabbed a pillow and covered his head again. "Oh, it's only a touch up," she said, "I don't need more, don't you think? And we've applied to become Morgans. We've been assigned a Certified Eternal Financial Adviser from Forever Enterprises who'll help develop our infinite financial plan."

For the first time in Clarke's memory Mom raised her voice and scolded. "Angela Jackell, you're not leaving the church. You and Jake were married there and our grandchildren were baptized in it. Our family's been in the church since forever. I simply won't allow it. I won't be the last Catholic in our family."

"Clarke hasn't changed religions," Angie offered hopefully. "Has he?"

Jake turned to Clarke's date and smiled. "We should ask his pretty little lady if she wants to raise little papists with Clarkie."

"Jake, don't be disgusting," Angie said. "Mother Jackell," she contended, "times change. The Catholic Church was fine for your generation, but given the times, the catholic view of life is just too narrow and unyielding and their moral and ethical stances are so medieval. That and the price of sacraments have become so expensive that the parishes are charging a la carte for them now. We may as well go to a church that has a robust revenue stream to defray their costs.

"Mother Jackell, the Catholic Church won't change its views so Jake and I have found a religion that's more accommodative of today's realities. What sold us was that Morgan has a bona fide plan for everlasting life right here on earth. We don't have to die and that's a significant advantage and it makes a hell of a lot more sense than that silly heaven thing."

"God forgive you, Angela Jackell, you must never say such vile things again."

"I'm sorry, Mother. I know it sounds insensitive but that's the way it is. All of Jake's business associates are Morgans and so are their wives. Just you wait, Morgan will spread throughout the world and Jake and I want to be early adopters, it's cheaper and there will be more benefits down the road. In Jake's new position, he can't ignore his social responsibilities."

"Dad will be so disappointed, won't you dear?"

"If it'll get me a job with Jake and away from you, darling, where do I sign up to be a fucking Morgan?"

"I'm sorry, Dad, to qualify for life everlasting, Angie and I had to clear a wealth accumulation hurdle that you won't qualify for."

"If you're so god damned important, square things for me with your church. I worked too damn hard to get you to this point. Why should I have to die? When do I get my reward? Jake-O, it's time to show your father the love. You owe me. I want to live forever, too."

"I'm sorry, Dad," Jake said, intervening. "You should have thought about that sooner and started building your wealth instead of spending it on frivolous things. You just don't have enough to qualify."

"Frivolous things?" Dad shouted. "You stupid asshole. You mean the money I wasted on your food, clothes, putting a roof over your head, and getting your dumb-ass educated? You never complained when I spent the money, so now that you're going to be rich and important, show me the love, god damn it. Fuck that, show me the money."

"You'll only blow it on scotch," Clarke added from the now open bedroom door.

Dad turned, scowling. "Done pouting are we? Good scotch is never blown money. You would know that if you were a real man."

"Touché, Dad. Jake, help our dear father out with his future why don't you?"

"I can't and Dad knows I would if I could, but we've already been pre-qualified. If we drag Mom and Dad's finances into the equation with all their medical bills and liabilities it would sink our net worth below Morgan standards and we'd be disqualified for sure. If this was a social club, sure, I'd help them. But this is life or death for Angie, me, and the kids. I'm willing to make life easier until you pass, Dad, but that's it. Hell, the way you take care of yourself, I never expected you to live this long. If you love me, you won't begrudge me the opportunity to live forever. Angie, me, and your grandkids, we'll keep your memory alive, forever. We'll light candles. How many of your friends can say that?"

Dad continued to plead. "You were my favorite. This is how you treat me?"

"Dad," Clarke contributed, "if I was in Jake's position, I'd do whatever it took to keep you alive, happy, and in scotch forever."

Jake scowled. "Shut up, Clarke. Dad, there's nothing I can do. Technology makes forever possible, but consider the logistics and the overcrowding. Because of that, Morgan can only include the truly qualified, and like always, the riff-raff must be kept out for a forever economy like ours to work efficiently. Let's look at it realistically; Morgan is a self-funding perpetual life assurance policy you just can't afford. Maybe someday, when it gets cheaper . . . If you're still, you know . . ."

Dad lifted his empty glass. "To my fucking ingrate of a favorite son."

With that, Angie stood and motioned everyone to the Christmas tree. "It's time to open presents."

Chapter 20
Philadelphia, PA.—2036

Consumer Spending—During the ongoing recessions of the early twenty-first century, corporations ceased much of their spending on research and development and kept inventory low until they were certain consumers would return to the marketplace. It often took too long for consumer confidence to build and the cash reserves that corporations held back built up, often providing more profit in the financial markets than could be derived in their core business. As this provided more value at less risk for shareholders, the commercial economy began to spiral toward failure.

In 2025, the Progressive Parrington Congress voted to provide a tax credit to consumers for money spent on commercial products and services. It wasn't enough and the depression lasted long enough to prevent President Vernon Parrington from winning his bid for re-election in 2032.

The depression lingered well into President Crelli's first term as spending declined to the lowest levels in a hundred years and everyone suffered. With the passage of Circle of Life legislation, taxes were eliminated, the Internal Revenue Service was disbanded, and the consumer tax holiday was declared null and void. Since that monumental legislation, depressions are more frequent, deeper, and longer but only *Conducer's* have been affected.—**Archive**

It was a year of rapidly declining lifestyle that passed too quickly. Even though Clarke hadn't talked to his sister-in-law since the last Christmas dinner, Angie had insisted that he look presentable for this year's dinner. He left his home wearing his only remaining suit and tie having sold much of his other clothing to help pay the rent and utilities. Badly underdressed for the weather, he leaned into the winter wind as he headed for the market to purchase the appetizer Angie insisted he contribute. It had been a difficult year in which, along with most of his funds, his social life had evaporated, so this year he decided not to burden himself with a date.

The co-op down the street from his condo was crowded with late Christmas shoppers looking for deals. He looked through the window at the mob inside and berated himself for agreeing to another Christmas dinner at Jake's. Last Christmas had been a mistake, but this visit would make Christmas dinner seem like a tradition, one he wanted no part of. But Angie insisted that he come, and he couldn't remember the last time he'd eaten a satisfying meal. He hadn't earned income in so long that his life's savings had become life threatening, and he had just heard from the lender that his mortgage was underwater. Without equity, he was officially worthless and he had reached the depths his father had predicted for him.

He rarely shopped, getting by on bulk foods with long shelf lives purchased at discount stores or off the backs of trucks. Those outlets were slowly being phased out so he was forced to go to the market for Angie's request. He hesitated before entering, watching others going, one-by-one, through a scanner. If they were merely shopping for food, he wondered, why the security? Finally, he was cleared by two weapons-carrying, thug-like security people and he entered. Inside, one counter was jammed while the other had a short, orderly line. He went to that counter where a man scanned him for his PID.

"Sorry, sir, your PID isn't active."

Clarke was confused. "I haven't been getting mail so I may have missed it. Do you have any extras?"

"PIDs? You don't understand, it's a device the government has mandated to improve commercial efficiency. Everyone is required to register at the closest hospital or with their physician and have a PID installed. It's quick and relatively painless."

"And that's the only way I can get in this line?" The man nodded. Clarke turned to the chaos of the other line and shrugged. "But I have money."

"Yes, you would. With a PID, you don't need currency. Everything is electronic. That line," the man pointed, "they will take your money although things will cost more. They want everyone using a Pɪᴅ by spring. Now move along, we have other customers."

Clarke moved to the back of the crowd and waited. Behind the counter, a very old man and woman wearing dirty, blood-smeared white aprons were frantically responding to everybody's shouting of last minute orders. When a man behind him tried to squeeze in front, another man standing beside Clarke blocked him. Then another tried to squeeze past and someone took a swing but hit a lady who was standing beside Clarke. She dropped to the ground and just lay at Clarke's feet, moaning. But before another fist could be thrown, an undercover guard tasered one man into submission and two others were carried out and flung into the street by another set of security men.

"The crowd's really unruly," Clarke said to one of the guards nearby.

"You mustn't get out much. It's like this everywhere, every minute of the day."

"I don't and I didn't think the economy was this strong, even at Christmas."

"The economy's fine for the wealthy and the technology-enabled. When it's not good for them, that's when everyone pays attention. I'm just working here temporarily as a guard but hey, if you're buying, you must be one of the lucky few with a job. Is your employer looking for a hard worker, someone with experience? I'm your guy and I'll work cheap. I'm even willing to work for nothing as a trial but I have to be paid sometime. Here, take my business card." He handed Clarke a small piece of translucent plastic, no bigger than a fingernail. When Clarke looked confused, the man explained, "Your phone, put it in your phone and it will transfer my *Bona Fides*."

Clarke shook his head. "Sorry, no phone and no job. I wish," Clarke admitted. "I have cash."

The guard stared at him. "Being out here with so little, aren't you concerned about the wagons?"

Clarke didn't know what wagons were and didn't want to ask. "I'm bringing something to my brother's Christmas dinner. My brother has a great job. He's loaded. They live in a mansion in Merion." The man said nothing. "My brother's an asshole who doesn't deserve anything he has, but if I can get a good meal, I don't care. I'll be fine once I find some new clients, but it seems everyone is cutting back."

While looking over the crowd, the guard replied, "You should be worried because President Crelli delivered a speech this week and said it's time to clean house, whatever that means. That group that elected him has been trying to starve the beast, that's our government, for generations and this time they may have succeeded. The debt topped what is it, thirty trillion, and welfare is gone and there are rumors that Medicare and even Social Security will end real soon. That means that there will be hell to pay for all those people depending on those funds, but those are the rumors."

Clarke stared at the man, curiously. "Starving the beast?"

"The beast is what conservatives—Republicans, Libertarians and other radicals call government programs that don't directly help their business profits; government programs that help people like us who they think are just plain lazy and unproductive fuckoffs. Crelli says he's going to wipe out all the damn lazy welfare queens and dope addicts, too, the ones who take tax money that was confiscated from the wealthy, the money the government redistributes to the needy. Good for him if he does, but he talks like everyone is a welfare queen or an addict or a dependent lazy and he's going at it so relentlessly that half the time I'm scared shitless of what he'll do.

"I'm a music teacher. I took this security job because it's the only one I could find. The storeowner is my uncle and he almost didn't hire me. He's scared shitless, too. Mark my words, Crelli is all about money and doesn't care about folks like us or these in here. He'll finish me off along with the rest of the lower class and the bottom half of the middle class before he's done and I voted for that son of a bitch. All my life I thought what Libertarians had been promising made sense. I never realized that when someone else chooses who the pests are, I would be included on their list. Hell, after President Parrington's last term fiasco, we needed change we could believe in and Crelli is that. He isn't fucking around. He knows that if he doesn't succeed, he'll be a one-term president, too, or worse, we'll never see the next president. Mark my words. Everything's insane."

"I knew it was kind of bad but I don't get out and I can't afford to communicate much. What's that have to do with these lines? If the economy's so bad and no one's buying, I should be able to just walk in, purchase what I want, and leave."

"If you want to avoid lines, stop purchasing necessities." The man pointed to the raucous crowd. "I'm not an economist, but if you don't have a PID, buying will never be easy again."

"I guess I'll get one."

"Do that. But then they'll know where you are and what you're doing every minute of the day, but at least you buy conveniently. They'll know if you're productive but more important, they'll know if you're not and if you're not, they'll send *Waster Wagons* for you. PIDs are a great convenience, but if you believe in freedom, it's not worth it."

The man put his arm around Clarke's shoulder and leaned in to whisper over the crowd noise. "Aren't you tired of assholes like that brother of yours getting rich when good people like you and me struggle?" Clarke nodded. "Have you ever wanted to drown them in their own shit?" Clarke nodded again, this time less sure. "The system allows assholes like your brother to get all the breaks and it squeezes everything from good folks like us."

Clarke smiled and nodded again. "You don't know my brother Jake but you're dead on. I'm tired of his gloating and story telling about how much money he makes and spends, and on whom and where. He makes it sound like that's the only measure of a person and it makes me sick."

The man hit him softly in the chest. "Exactly. That's why there's a crowd here and not over there. You ever hear of Omar Smith?"

Clarke shook his head.

"Smith," the man explained, "is a former Congressman who campaigned for the poor until Crelli and his people tried to kill him. He fled the country ahead of the FBI and CIA but eventually returned to America as a certified professional Prophet dedicated to helping the poor. His first name is Omar, but he's not Arab; he's white and he believes in compassionate capitalism. He's rallying the desperate to him and when he has a big enough army, he'll overthrow Crelli and take care of all of us working poor. He's going to take our country back and allow hard working people like us to have a chance again."

"How's he going to do that? The president has a lot of power."

The man pointed to the crowded store. "For starters, chaos. He preaches that armed rebellion in America is hopeless. Even fragmented insurgencies don't have a chance because of government technology, the police, and FBI. The only way to make the government work for us is to bring more and more people over to the Prophet's side—our side. That's what we're doing. The movement is a kind of civil and economic disobedience, no felonies, only misdemeanors, and it's designed to bring down the country's commercial capability so that everyone loses faith in Crelli and what he stands for. Hey, if it brings another depression, who cares? The poor don't. We're fucked anyway and it'll give Smith a better chance to change things. He says it's kind of how villagers in Africa brought down elephants before rifles were invented. They'd inflict hundreds of lesser wounds until finally, weakened; the elephant would fall to its knees where their knives and spears could finish the job—and they'd eat."

"That seems violent. Do you think that will work in America?"

"The Prophet is against violence. He's working on a commercial solution and he'll support anything that achieves his goal. As long as President Crelli is willing to throw the baby out with the bathwater, you and I have everything to gain by following Smith. Hey, you seem like a sharp guy, are you interested in joining us?"

"Sorry, I'm not a joiner. I don't like my brother or what the president is doing, but I try not to get involved. Good luck all the same."

"Sooner or later, things are going to get worse for you. When that happens, you won't notice us but you will find us everywhere." With that, the guard returned to his station.

Clarke waited patiently. When he reached the counter, he ordered. "I'll take a pound of goose liver pate," he shouted to the old man behind the counter.

"Fuck you, too," the old man responded.

"No, I mean it. I'm a paying customer." Some people in the crowd booed and shouted obscenities when he offered to pay.

"Let's see your script," the suspicious old man asked.

Clarke reached into his pocket and pulled out the remaining currency from his last withdrawal from his bank before it had crashed last year. He'd hidden it under his floorboard for an emergency, and he was desperate now. He was hoping to convince Angie to help him. "Do I have enough?"

The man shook his head. "Ever since the terrorists took down the financial system, paper money costs more. The government says everything is okay now, but they enforce a surcharge on hard dollar currency. Everything is an extra twenty percent."

"Do I have enough?" he repeated, unhappily.

The man counted Clarke's currency, nodded, carefully double wrapped the pate and, to a chorus of boos, handed the package to Clarke. He pushed through the crowd but once outside, he realized he couldn't afford a cab, if he could even find one, so he began the long walk to the affluent suburb of Merion where Jake and Angie lived. As he walked, he noticed the many homes that were darkened and seemingly empty, this being the holiday season. As he got closer to Jake's, more lights appeared; mostly what was displayed were the dollar sign and lemniscate, the symbol of the Morgan Christian Church, although occasionally he saw a reindeer or a Santa. The Dollar Sign was prominent in so many places that it seemed to have replaced the crèche and the baby Jesus on the lawns of America that he remembered from his youth.

There were more patrol cars, too. Most had the markings of private corporations and they prowled the streets where he walked, subjecting him to targeting by high intensity beams until he was beyond their checkpoint. Finally, after a very long, worrisome walk, he arrived, shivering, at the community that housed the first great mansion ever owned by a Jackell.

At the gate to the community, he was accosted by two heavily-armed guards who forced him to wait outside their guardhouse while they confirmed his invitation. They didn't so much clear him as push him toward Angie's house. When he reached it, he followed the long circular driveway up past a fountain containing marine-based marble figurines and on to the front door. He rang the bell and was greeted by a tuxedoed black man wearing white gloves who offered to take his jacket. Still shivering, Clarke declined and was shown into the main dining hall, where he noticed all the servants among a great throng of guests. Some of them were serving drinks, others distributing appetizers but all were dressed in silly glittery red, white and blue Uncle Sam uniforms with American flag matching ties and handkerchiefs.

Angie ran to him. In spite of all he had put up with to get here, he stared at her and laughed. She was so out of character in an ice blue princess gown with a sapphire studded tiara, that even she looked embarrassed. "Where's your wand, Princess?"

She blushed. "Please don't, Clarke. Don't make fun. This is for Jake, although he's going to owe me big time for it. We're entertaining his political bosses. See, over there, that's Perry Mannix and his wife Beryl talking with Senator Burnham of South Carolina."

"I've heard of Senator Burnham. Who's Mannix?"

"He's President Crelli's Press Secretary."

"Oh. Say Angie, your home is incredible. How'd you qualify for the mortgage?"

"It's Jake's doing. He found the place. The owners couldn't afford the payments so we took them over. It turns out they were quite reasonable on Jake's new salary."

"What happened to the owners?"

"I don't ask, you know that Clarke. Please, you shouldn't either."

"Why are you dressed like a fairy tale princess?"

She blushed. "I'd feel better if you said I was dressed for a prom. Well, maybe not even that." She smiled nervously.

"Maybe you should be wearing a mask."

"That's enough, Clarke!"

He smiled. "I meant for a costume party."

"Is it that bad?"

"On someone else, definitely, but nothing looks bad on you, you know that. Where are the folks?"

"They're downstairs. Jake insisted. We're having separate parties. The better food is up here, so try some before you go down, but before you do, you should head to the powder room and clean up. You're a bit disheveled and everyone is staring. Did you bring the pate?"

He nodded.

"Good, give it to any of our servants. After you grab some food, Clarke, you know, could you please stay downstairs with the family." Though she looked embarrassed, she kissed him on the cheek and pointed to the stairs. "These are important people and Jake doesn't want the family to . . . well, you know."

"Yes, I know."

She shrugged and spread her arms. "Don't be tough on him. Look at all this. He's on the fast track and when you're on that track everything you do counts."

"If that's the case, Angie, I hope you have a Plan B. Where did you get all this stuff? It must have cost a fortune."

"I don't think so. Jake's job gives him access to things people no longer need or want. They're repossessed or something. Anyway, I access this online catalog and order whatever I want. I've always liked to decorate and this is a decorator's dream come true. It's crazy, Clarke, I even have an etiquette coach. She instructs me and comes to my parties to grade me.

"Really?"

"Really. And afterward, we go over and over the party films, so she can correct my mistakes. It takes all night but I'm getting more comfortable with my superiors."

"You're kidding? Now that's funny."

"Shhh. She's standing right over there, see?" Angie pointed to a corner of the hall where a tall thin woman wearing a formal gown in what only could be described as pumpkin colored with lace, was staring back balefully while speaking into her telephone.

"This is Philly. You shouldn't have to put on airs."

"Au contraire, mon ami, any misstep could cost Jake the presidency."

"You've got to be kidding, Angie? He doesn't really think . . ." She nodded. "As I recall, our boy is a dimly lit bulb. Have they found a cure for that?"

She smiled politely. "Maybe you're right, Clarke, I don't know. But, he's good at something these people want him to be good at, and that has him on the fast track. I know the president loves him. And I've never had so much of so much. It's incredible. You saw the servants?"

"Yeah, what's all that about?"

"It's a big house and we entertain constantly." She paused, looking around the room. "Elena, that's my etiquette coach, she looks concerned. I'd love to talk more but I have to work the room. I'll be down later if I have a chance. Most of these guests leave early and family always stays too long so we'll catch up later."

"I take it you're not going to introduce me to your A-list guests."

She shook her head, squeezed his hand, and walked away.

He stepped into the closest bathroom and cleaned up the best he could. He then wandered downstairs to a cavernous basement where the family had been relegated. The men were watching football on a 3D screen wearing virtual headgear while the women sat in front of another screen watching reality shows. One of the women noticed him and they all yelled greetings but the men ignored him until he sat to watch the game.

When dinner was served, everyone sat at a long dinner table and waited until Mom and Dad were rolled out of a side room to their places at the table. When he saw them, he was surprised and turned to a cousin. "They're not drunk."

His cousin smiled. "They'd better not be. They recently returned from a rehab boot camp. They're clean about three months. As I understand it, if they drink again, they're gone."

"Gone?"

"Don't ask."

"I never remember them not drinking. I hate to think how Dad's taking it."

"Even with medication, he's still way too testy to have a conversation with."

"How does Mom take that?"

"She gets plenty of *Pharma* to bolster her. If anything, she's more . . . mellow."

"I can't put it off any longer," Clarke said as he put his napkin on the table and went to his parents.

"About fucking time you stopped by."

"Sorry, Dad. How're you doing?"

"I'm fucking miserable. My own seed sends me to prison. It proves what I've been saying for years, the best part of that boy ran down your mother's leg."

Mom blushed and covered her mouth with a napkin before whispering. "John Jacob Jackell, you are a certifiable cretin. Please shut your pie hole," she said softly in a weirdly pleasant voice.

"Up yours, Mary Catherine. I'm not long for the world so I'll say whatever I damn well please. That prick of a son is holding me here against my will. He's doing it for spite. He wants to watch me suffer, the son of a bitch. He keeps me away from a decent drink and he's hired all these uppity blacks to make sure. God damn it, Mary C, if you had any gumption, you'd make them treat me like the lord of the manor I am."

"I don't want to get involved," Mom sighed. "I'm sorry, honey."

"At least show me respect, bitch."

Instinctively, Clarke tried to defend her. "Stop talking to her that way, Dad. Apologize, Christ, give her a hug."

"Fuck you. The only way that bitch gets a hug is if she gives me some of her damn *Pharma*. If I could get it up, I'd have her blow me as a sign of respect now that her teeth are gone."

Repulsed as usual by his dad, Clarke turned and gave his mother a hug. She put her hand up to his face. "Where's my honey, Jake? Is he coming down?"

The Christmas meal was served and the though the food was great, the best part of it was that it ended quickly, without incident, and without Jake. As dessert was served, Angie came down to visit.

"Where's Jake?" Dad shouted. "I need to discuss business with that ingrate."

"Father Jackell, he's in a meeting. He has a great deal on his plate, so much, I rarely see him anymore."

"So that's why you look so happy," Clarke interjected.

She looked at him, sadly, and shook her head. "Clarke, please don't. Be happy for us. He's under a lot of pressure. We both are."

"If you're happy, Angie, I'm happy. It's just that, well, he's such a pig."

"Clarke Jackell, stop it at once," Mom said. Then she blushed and looked away.

"Calm down you cow and take a pill," Dad yelled. "Or better yet, give it to me."

"Stop it, all of you," Angie said firmly. She took Clarke's hand and together they walked away from the table. "You look like you've been having tough times or maybe taking things too easy, even for you."

He put his hands to his new belly. "You mean this?"

She nodded.

"It's not taking it easy. It's the damnedest thing, Angie, when I was making money, I ate nutritious food and it was cheap. Now that I'm cutting back, the only food I can afford is loaded with sugar and carbs and it's doing this to me." He grabbed his paunch with his hands and squeezed. "Sometimes an hour after eating, I get this shaky feeling I never felt before. I'm stuffed, but I'm still hungry and my teeth ache all the time. The only thing that keeps me from getting more depressed is more food."

"Poor dear. The Secretary of Health Services says Americans are the most undernourished obese people in the world. Have you tried vitamins?"

"I can only afford cheap ones and they are made up mostly of corn syrup, starch and food dye. Angie, I need to talk to you. I need help. Maybe you can talk to Jake about getting me some work."

She squeezed his hand. "Maybe, Clarke, but I don't think Jake would listen. Then she turned to the family. "Say, everyone, I have a great idea how to liven up the party. This is so fun. We did it at our Thanksgiving *soiree*. I ask the servants to tell us what they have to be thankful for and they tell such wonderful, sad stories. It's great fun and it gets everyone in the spirit of the holidays. You'll see, it's so fun."

Angie called two servants into the room. "This seems really insensitive, Angie," Clarke whispered.

Angie ignored him and walked up to them so she could read their name tags. "Barbara, Roger, would you both be kind and to tell us what you're most thankful for on this beautiful Christmas day. Don't be shy. My family will appreciate whatever you have to say. Before you start, briefly tell us your background and then how you came to be here. This will be great fun." While Angie clapped her hands in anticipation, Clarke felt embarrassed for the servants.

"You start." Angie pointed to Roger who was obviously uncomfortable.

Roger, a barrel-chested Latino stepped forward, timidly. "My name is really Ramón Tejada and I was chief chef for U. S. Angst's executive kitchens in King of Prussia, Pennsylvania."

"I believe that's Angs, dear," Angie corrected, "and I didn't know that we had a retail food company."

"I'm sorry, Mrs. Jackell, you're correct. I was chef for the Angs executives who worked at the King of Prussia office. Before I was employed there, my wife and I were both head chefs in New York City. My wife didn't want to move but the compensation package was so good and they assured her she'd find work in Philly. She tried but the economy was so bad, she never found a job. A few years ago, Angs closed their manufacturing facilities in northern Maine and in Missouri and laid-off a whole bunch of people, including me. Instead of the pension I'd contracted for, I received a small stipend and an even smaller separation check. My wife still hadn't found work so we lived on that check and my unemployment. But then Mr. Crelli got elected and unemployment and welfare just stopped. My money ran out and we couldn't afford our home but we couldn't sell it either, no buyers, so we put some stuff in my car and I moved my wife and . . . my beautiful daughter, Holly, to an empty row house in Olney."

"Olney? Not that horrid place? How awful for you."

"Yes, it was horrible. My wife and I were suburban folks, unequipped to fight with hardened, desperate city people for food scraps. We couldn't fit in, the neighbors and squatters thought we were uppity. I wasn't and I wasn't able to protect my family. The first year, I lost my wife." Eyes moist,

Ramon paused. "She was beaten and then raped so many times that one day she just left. I couldn't stop her and I never saw her again." He wiped his eyes with his sleeve.

Angie turned to the family. "See; let that be a lesson to you all. No matter how bad you think our economy is, you must persevere because someone else is suffering more. You may continue, Reuben."

"It's Ramón, ma'am. Our daughter, Holly, she was my gem, our joy, she was beautiful and an honor student. She was going to be a physician." Ramón paused to gain control of his emotions but Angie urged him to continue. "One . . . one of the local bosses took a liking to her and . . . and he kept her. He just kept her." Ramón was clearly struggling to continue. "He compensated me, but when he was done . . . with her . . . he passed her to his subordinates and the money stopped coming in. I lost track . . . I was two years from a nice life in a great neighborhood with a good salary and my family and now everyone was dead to me. I was forced to live . . . to eat things I would have never have thought to cook. Then, one day I gave up and left Olney. I headed back to my old home. I won't lie, I was going to kill myself there but before I arrived, I was arrested by HomeSec for looting. I wasn't, honestly; I had nothing to live for so why would I steal? Frankly, I was hopeful that I was going to be executed but Mr. Jackell's secretary saw my name in the database. She came for me. I remember it. She joked about how Master Jake's career and mine had diverged so much since Angs." Tears poured from the man's eyes. "Now I cook here for you."

Angie wiped tears from her eyes. "What a beautiful story of salvation. Thank Morgan you had skills to fall back on. It's like President Crelli says, 'skill and passion make everything possible'. Thank you, Ray, for sharing that. Barbara, what about you? Tell everyone your story of glorious redemption."

Barbara was a pleasant looking woman in her mid forties with blond curly hair and gray roots, glasses, and wide, unblinking blue eyes. She attempted a curtsy but the silly patriotic costume she wore wouldn't allow much of a bend.

"Yes, ma'am. There isn't much to tell. My name is Barbara Rohrbaugh and I was raised in Perkasie, just north of here. Me and my husband, Bruce, who was a very successful dentist; we lived there and raised three beautiful children. Fortunately, I've lost track of the twins, Dane and Willie, but my daughter, Paige, she was our special project. Paige was a great student and a cheerleader when schools were doing things like that. Two years ago, right after she graduated, Paige and her boyfriend, Rob Baier, decided to marry. Bruce and I had been saving for years and planned a big party at the Fire Hall next to the Church. Everything we had went into it.

Paige had picked out her wedding dress, it was frightfully expensive, we had the flowers and everything, it was much more than we thought it would cost but she was our only daughter and this is what parents do . . . did. The week before the wedding . . ." Barbara's chin began to tremble and then her upper lip followed suit. She looked down and tears fell. "Please ma'am, may I have some water?"

Angie nodded. "Certainly, Barb, take a moment. Is everyone getting this?" Clarke looked around at his family who, at Angie's prodding, had gathered closer to listen.

When Barbara had recovered sufficiently, she continued in a small, pained voice. "Well, we had sent out invitations and everyone was coming, even my in-laws from Pennsauken who Bruce hadn't seen since the depression began. Can I use that term?" Angie nodded. "So everything was ready. We met with the Preacher and we were preparing for the rehearsal dinner. My Paige was beaming, her future assured."

"It sounds lovely. What happened?" Angie asked, excited.

Shaking, Barb brought the glass of water to her mouth, spilling some. "It was at the dinner . . . at the rehearsal dinner . . . that the trucks came."

"What trucks?" Mother Jackell asked.

"I . . . I didn't know. I had never seen them before. They were unmarked, black; shiny trucks the size of Greyhound busses. There were two of them and they pulled up, I could hear the sound of them approaching and sometimes, even now, I wake from a deep sleep crying at the sound of the air brakes. Anyway, men, men armed with rifles and wearing riot gear, they broke into our dinner, just as the radicchio salad with almonds and tarragon was being served. They . . . they read a list of names, Paige wasn't on it, thank God, but Bruce and I and a great many others were. I don't know about the others, but Bruce and I had overspent on the wedding and were pretty deep in debt. Bruce's practice had been deteriorating, so many of our neighbors had just up and left town for some reason and he wasn't able to keep his usually busy schedule of cleanings and fillings. Anyway, we had this debt. The bank was okay but we broke the law. It was a new law."

"Yes," Angie interrupted. "The Circle of Life laws. They're what Jake manages. They got us this wonderful home."

Barb seemed terrified. "I'm sorry, I . . . didn't mean anything. We . . . we didn't know we were breaking the law. My wedding cost more, but my parents must have had more than Bruce. We didn't know. If we had, we would have told Paige to elope or something. She was our only daughter, she deserved . . . we wanted . . . everyone was doing it."

"So what happened? I'm too old for the suspense." Dad interjected.

"They . . . the men in the trucks, they took us away for processing, at least some of us. I . . . I never saw my family again. My Bruce, he . . . I don't know. They said he died. He tried to run, they said, and he died. He was a dentist, such a good dentist. And it was just a wedding, a wedding for my only daughter." Barb looked down and sobbed silently.

Once again, Angie wiped the tears from her eyes. "Yes, well, thank you, Barb. That was fun and enlightening. Once again, family, this is an example of how ignorance of the law is no excuse. We simply must live within our means. Sure it's nice to have good things like Jake and I have but we can afford it so it's okay. We don't overspend because we know the consequences. Jake always tells me when I come back from a shopping spree that if America was allowed to overspend its budget, it would die just like families do. Thank God for the balanced budget amendment and the Circle of Life that requires that each and every citizen live within their means." With that, Angie draped her arms around the servants, Barb and Ramón. "Thank you both very much for your service and have a Merry Christmas."

"Merry Christmas to you." The servants responded quickly and just like that, they scurried out of the room and upstairs.

With the farce finally over, Clarke excused himself, vowing once again never to set foot back in Jake's house. At the gate, he stared back at the mansion, shook his head, and shouted, "Thank you, Massa Jake." And under his breath, he whispered, "Give me a break." He pulled his coat tight against the wind and began the long trek home.

Chapter 21
Philadelphia, PA.—2037

The days of his life passed so slowly that when another Christmas arrived, it felt like a reprieve from his life as a troglodyte. Clarke struggled awake to the dying sounds of a wind up alarm clock. He rolled out of his sleeping bag and onto the frigid wood floor where he stared at his frozen breath while trying to remember why he'd set the alarm.

Of course, it was Christmas day. His savings were gone, but he had managed to make it through another year even though he had failed to generate any income. He had reduced his lifestyle to a level he never thought anyone could subsist on. It hadn't been easy because he had always lived frugally. Surprisingly, even with a severely restricted food budget, his weight had increased on a diet of bread and cheap, flavored soft drinks that made him jittery, yet listless. If he hadn't traded his scale for food, he would have been embarrassed by his weight gain. He had stopped exercising long ago.

The diet and inactivity made him anxious and irritable as well. Earlier in the year, he had managed to unearth work opportunities, but during interviews he fidgeted like a *Pharma* junkie and failed to get hired. Wherever he went—and he didn't go out often for fear of the rumors that folks were disappearing—there was an ever-decreasing presence of the unemployed. In the end, the risk of death wasn't worth getting rejected by employers so he stopped applying. In fact, he suspected that some employers were in cahoots with the government to attract the unemployed, but he had no one to ask about it and no way to confirm it so he just stayed away. It wasn't long before the inactivity, the rejection, and the paranoia turned him into a recluse. Since most real estate was in default in his neighborhood, the banks had stopped hounding him and he was thankful that he had no other debts and that no creditors were searching for him.

There were no women in his life because he could no longer afford to show them a good time and frankly because of his diet and the way he looked, he had simply lost his libido. And since he was never able to sustain a serious relationship, there was no one to call him for companionship or for him to call on for help. Even if there had been someone, without a phone—which he couldn't afford—he had no way to communicate.

For all that, he feared this Christmas because his brother had become his only hope. Angie and Jake were surely hosting another stupendous party and at least there would be food so he would go. He had to. The last of his pride had withered away with the less than epic realization that his only choice was to beg Jake for help. He washed the best he could in preparation by holding old paper under the cold-water spigot in his kitchen and wiping his face and body with it. Shivering, he dressed in layers of dirty, smelly clothes augmented with cardboard and paper packing, whatever he could place between his body and the cold for insulation. He wished he hadn't been forced to pawn his most prized possession, his twenty-speed bike, because even though he lacked the riding stamina, it would have made the trip manageable.

He started his trek in the windy, bitter cold. On the sidewalks, the homeless lay frozen dead, their faces blue and contorted in frightening agony and yet there was tranquility as they waited to be hauled away by the trucks. But the trucks that picked up the dead weren't the trucks he feared most. It was the other trucks, the *Waster Wagons*, the sleek black trucks that came for the living that he needed to avoid. Lacking proof of value, if a wagon passed, he'd have to hide and quickly. But even this fear wasn't his worst nightmare. He'd heard they were knocking on doors. Jake was his last resort.

He walked north, into the wind, toward his brother's mansion and even though it was Christmas, the streets were deserted; the wisps of driven snow drifting on the same side of the frozen bodies in what from a distance looked like a pretty pattern. He progressed slowly, hiding as he checked the roads for wagons before moving on. With little protection from the unforgiving wind, he walked in zigzag patterns as he worked his way up the main road to his brother's gated community. Along the way, he noticed the homes—grand and ordinary—that were abandoned; some even burned to the ground and although they sometimes protected him from the biting wind, their locked doors and barred windows seemed to mock him. When cars drove by, he resisted the desire to hitch a ride because drivers were just as scared of the *Waster Wagons* and besides, the Waster Wagon LLC offered bounties.

It was midday when he reached a small bridge over a frozen creek. Below, he heard voices. Concerned but curious, he walked to the middle of the bridge and stared down. On the banks, atop the frozen mud, a small group huddled beside a fire burning in an industrial drum.

Teeth chattering, he yelled to them. "Hello. I've been walking for hours. Can I come down to get warm?" No one responded so he yelled again. Finally, a young woman looked up and yelled back.

"Come down but don't try anything. We have a gun."

When he got closer, a woman pointed her gun at him. His knees started to buckle as he held his hands up. There were five young women, alone, faces bright pink in the cold, trying to get warm.

"What, what are you doing here?" he asked.

"We should ask you the same thing." A girl motioned him forward. "Is there anywhere we can we go to get out of the cold, that's safe? We'll take suggestions. We've been out of work for months and they kicked us out of our apartment. We're trying to avoid the wagons."

Panicked, he looked around. "Do, do the wagons c . . . come here?"

"They're everywhere."

"Where do they t . . . t . . . take you?"

"Where do you think?"

He shook his head.

"It doesn't matter. No one comes back."

"That's . . . that's not legal."

"So you're a lawyer?"

He shook his head. "No, an accountant, or was. C . . . Can't your parents help?"

The girl with the gun cocked it. With that sound, he felt a warm spot in his pants that turned cold, immediately. He tried to cover up when another girl, short with short straight dark hair and circles under her eyes, pressed the gun down. "Why don't our parents help? They can't even help themselves. I haven't heard from my dad in a year."

"Where are they?"

"Are you from Mars? Life today is simple. Have a job, live, no job, don't. I majored in Sociology at Villanova and studied poverty. This isn't poverty, this is death."

"It always was in America," another girl added.

"I'm not getting into another philosophical argument, Ann."

"Are we . . . we safe here?" he asked.

She shook the gun at him. "What do you think? Everyone is trying to survive so they keep trying to take advantage of us. They've stolen our stuff and . . . well, and worse. We avoid people with obvious money because even if they can help, they think of us as criminals or whores and they call the cops or the wagons."

"I won't hurt you, I promise. You can put the gun away?" As the girls huddled by the fire to discuss it, the gun stayed visible.

The girl named Missy, a large, cute girl with bruises on her face and neck put the gun in her pocket. "Last night, some HomeSec goons searched the area so we hid. God, it was so cold in all this water, ice and mud. Where are you headed?"

"I'm visiting my brother for Christmas."

As one, the girls stared at him.

"Is it Christmas already?" Missy asked. "There are no decorations anywhere. There used to be lights. Does your brother live near here?"

"He lives a few miles north, in one of Merion's gated communities."

The girls looked envious. "You're lucky to know someone who's working. He must be doing well if he is having people over for dinner. What's he charging you?"

"It's free," he hoped. "Jake is a successful businessman who is big in the government. He and I haven't spoken since last Christmas, though."

"Are you sure he's still there? People are disappearing everywhere. About the only safe places left are executive communities, resort homes, and townhouses in protected parts of the city, and maybe some farms, I don't know. We lived in a nice place off Rittenhouse Square when we worked for a local Angs *Pharma* but they moved operations to Pakistan and we were part of a massive layoff. That's why we're . . . here."

The girls were very young and although they were filthy and wore many layers of torn, soiled clothing, much like he did, under the layers of filth, a couple of them appeared to be quite pretty. He offered his hand but the girl's didn't respond.

"My name's Clarke Jackell. Maybe I can help. Come with me to my brother's for dinner. He's very rich, you can eat there. What do you say?" Cautiously, they made room for him by the fire as they whispered among themselves. When he stepped too close, Missy raised her gun.

"Whoa," he said nervously. "What's wrong?"

"People offer to help all the time but they always turn on us. You had better not. We have other weapons too, and I'll shoot you dead, I swear to God."

"There are five of you and one of me, why would I do that?"

"You're desperate and desperate people do desperate things. I'm warning you. I'll kill you without thinking twice about it."

"But I want to help you. I have no one, either . . ." He considered how bad that sounded. ". . . except my brother." He whispered it, knowing how sad that truly was.

"So you say," Missy continued to point the gun. "There could be a pack of desperate old men like you on the other side of the bridge and you're trying to lure us there. They'll overwhelm us and make us do things . . ." She lowered her head to her chest and sobbed.

"Empty your pockets," one of the girls demanded.

He reached in and turned them inside out. "See, I have nothing."

"Take off your clothes."

"What? No way. It's too cold." She waved the gun, motioning him to begin. "I'm not going to hurt you. Please don't hurt me."

"The clothes."

Reluctantly, he removed layers of his clothing carefully laying the paper and cardboard where they wouldn't blow away. Finally, shivering and down to his underwear, Missy walked closer and aimed her gun at his groin. "Now, where are they?"

"Who?"

"Your friends."

"I . . . I don't have any friends." It sounded as pathetic as he felt. "It's j . . . just me."

"Take them off," she commanded, pointing at his underwear. Reluctantly, he pulled his shorts down. "He's got a small one," Missy said, giggling.

"It's . . . cold."

"Where are your friends hiding?"

"There are no friends, nearby or anywhere. Please I'm so freaking cold."

"I shot the last guy who said that." Her hand was shaking.

"Who, who said what?" Weak from lack of food, he shivered uncontrollably until his legs buckled. He hit the frozen ground and screamed as the ice was even colder. He clawed at it, searching for purchase, too feeble to get up and fearing if he didn't he would die. He groveled and sobbed. Then, beyond caring, he closed his eyes and prepared to give up and die on this spot in the unbearable cold. One of the girls intervened. "Missy, I don't think anybody's near. They'd have rescued him by now."

"It could still be a trap."

"Open your eyes, mister. We're sorry. Put your clothes on and come here by the fire." She tossed him his clothes, but he was shivering too much to put them on so two of the girls had to dress him while tears rolled down his numb cheeks. When he was dressed, they helped him to the fire where he sat sobbing quietly until the trembling finally stopped.

"I know you're scared," he said, finally. "Me, too." He told his tale.

Sue, the very tall, good-looking girl who spoke up for him first put her arm around him when he finished.

"We understand how you feel without any friends, but it may be for the best. My folks had lots of friends. Every weekend they'd have, I don't know, like a hundred people over for a barbecue, or a swimming party, or something. But when the jobs disappeared, their friends, like began disappearing, too. My parents became frantic. At first they thought they were being shunned, no one showed for their parties but soon enough, they knew. So having friends doesn't help. When Mom and Dad . . . disappeared last summer and there was, like nobody in the community who knew what happened and no one was willing to help. Everyone was afraid of HomeSec and I'd never even heard of it before. The few friends of my Mom and Dad who remained wouldn't even open their doors and didn't talk to me or do anything." She paused. "I miss Mom and Dad so much." She sobbed on the shoulder of another girl, who patted her as she cried.

"We have similar stories," another girl added. "I was a marketing rep for Angs *Pharma* when the government passed a law requiring health care corporations to consolidate their practices and it allowed non-certified practitioners to deliver services over the Internet. It got too expensive for Angs to market the way they once did so they downsized their domestic sales reps and added representatives overseas to support growth opportunities in India, Brazil and even Iran and Turkey.

"Like the rest, I was laid off, too." She too began to cry. "My parents had guaranteed all of my student loans which didn't seem like an issue because I had a good job. Then one day, I called to see how they were doing but their phone service was cancelled, so was their Internet service. I tried to see them but I didn't have the money for fuel so I just worried for a while until Maryanne," she pointed to another of the girls, "gave me a ride. My parent's house, my home, it was empty. I still don't know what happened or where they are."

All the girls were crying now. In his previous life their misery would have made him feel awkward or opportunistic, but that life was over and he was genuinely sorry for them. Finally, to comfort them, he attempted to embrace the two girls closest to him but Missy jerked her gun in his direction and he backed away fast. He offered, once again, to take them to Jake's. This time, they agreed.

As the six of them walked, more and more homes looked lived in and all of them were impressive. It was in these neighborhoods that, for the first time, he smelled fires in fireplaces and the briefest whiff of home cooking propelled by the frigid winds. Occasionally, they passed a house that was decorated and even less frequently, there was a car in the driveway. Whatever calamity was occurring elsewhere, it seemed to have bypassed this section of suburbia. To pass the time, silence begat awkward conversation that drifted into a shallow kind of flirting they seemed to appreciate and he was most proficient at. As the sun was setting, they reached Jake's gated community. The main security gate was well lit, but locked. The girls stared at him hopefully. At a loss, he looked futilely for a guard or an intercom but there was nothing. Frustrated, he suggested that they split up and look for a way in.

He worked it out so that Sue, the tall attractive one, joined him while the other girls followed the gate and circled the community in the opposite direction. As he walked, he tried to picture, from last year, where Jake's house was so at least he could yell or throw something to attract attention when they got near. He was still searching when Sue shrieked and began sobbing, hysterically.

He put his arm around her and whispered in her ear. "What is it?"

"They're gone. They're gone. We've walked all the way around. See, there's the gate. And we didn't pass them. Something bad happened to them."

He was concerned, too, but tried not to show it. "They got lost or found a way in that we missed. That's all. We'll wait here. They'll be back soon."

Frightened, Sue continued to sob. He hugged her close and walked her to a large tree that blocked the wind but was still in full view of the main gate. They sat, nestled in the exposed tree roots and to keep warm, he pulled her close so her head rested on his shoulder. She continued to sob so he massaged her neck until she finally stopped, if only briefly.

"They should be back by now," she whimpered like a child. "They're gone. We never should have come here."

"No, no, we should wait. Everything will be okay. You'll see. We'll stay here. They'll be here shortly, laughing and ready to tell us a funny story."

"That . . . that doesn't happen anymore. There aren't any funny stories. What happens to me if they don't come back?"

"They'll be back. I promise it won't be long before we'll be in a warm home eating hot turkey and cranberry sauce."

She forced a smile. "I like turkey. Mom and Dad made it every Thanksgiving."

"There, you see." Even though she was dirty, her big, innocent blue eyes drew him in and he kissed her. That was all it took. She moaned, sadly, and clung to him desperately and they kissed and fondled in the coming darkness. He worked his hands under layers of clothing, quickly unbuttoning her blouse and pants allowing him access. He felt a hard jolt on his shoulder and his invading fingers went numb. They both screamed and he tried to stand but something pressed him back down.

"Both of you get up very slowly," a woman said.

Confused, he stood awkwardly, favoring his numb arm. Two armed men immediately grabbed him. He looked at Sue who was red-faced and crying hysterically, her coat and blouse open as she frantically worked to button her jeans with cold, un-cooperating fingers. An officer helped her to stand. Clarke tried to help too strong arms restrained him.

"Miss, take a minute to straighten up. Sir, what are you doing here? You're not allowed outside these gates."

He looked at the uniforms—light green jackets and black pants, each with a winged insignia with the word HomeSec above it. "Officers . . ." he pleaded desperately.

"Sir, please do not cause us any problems," one of them said as he searched Clarke. "We are licensed to kill if we must." When the officer found nothing, he continued. "It's good that you have no weapons."

With that, Sue screamed. Her friends were carrying. The female officer grabbed her shoulders. "Please miss, calm down."

"What . . . what would have happened if we had . . . had a weapon?"

"We're permitted to kill anyone wandering the streets with a weapon whether they have a license not. It's the law."

Sue's wailing increased. "But what about a trial . . . or prison?"

"Prison, miss, that's the old days. The government is no longer in the hotel business; can't afford it. Hell, if we sent people to prison today for breaking the law, there'd be lines forming around the block waiting to commit crimes so they could have a protected place to live and three squares. No, miss, prisoner coddling days are over." The officer turned to Clarke. "Remain calm or we will neutralize you. A van will arrive, momentarily. I trust I'm being clear."

With head down and shoulders heaving, Sue continued to sob as a woman officer helped her dress. When she tried to speak she was trembling so hard she could barely make herself understood.

"I . . . I'm s-s-s-sorry, ossifer," she rasped. "I'm so, so embarrassed. I didn't . . . didn't I mean I didn't . . . Please let me go. I promise I'll go straight home. Ossifer, please," she begged.

"Will you confirm that your PID has been disabled, miss?"

Sue shrieked again. "I didn't do that. They made me. I know it's wrong, but I'll get it fixed, I promise. It was a mistake. I'm sorry. I'm a good girl, I really am. I won't do it again."

"Miss, will you confirm that your PID has been disabled?" Bawling loudly, she nodded.

The officer turned from her and nudged him. "What about you? Why don't you have a PID?"

He shrugged.

"Everyone who works is required to have a PID. Are you aware that without it, you are considered a rebel and a *Waster*? Do you know the penalty for terrorism?"

"No!" Sue screamed. "I don't know him. We just met. I'm not a terrorist. I'm Catholic, not Muslim, and I'm studying to become Morgan. I am. I was employed . . . I'm still . . ."

"Miss, don't cause problems, please. I'm talking to this fellow. Sir, why no PID?"

He looked at the man's badge. "Officer Klottz, I don't need much money to live on. I own a home and only go out to buy food. I didn't think I needed a PID to do that until . . . well I just didn't."

"Ignorance of the law is not a defense. What you say may be true but it's not my job to interpret. Sit beside that tree and don't move or speak. We're waiting on the van."

Hearing that, Sue screamed again. "Officer, he kidnapped me. Please, I'll give you anything. I beg you, officer, I don't want to die."

The officer took the prod from his belt and pointed it at her. She stopped screaming and covered her mouth, drool running down her fingers. She slipped to the ground, head between her legs and sobbed quietly.

Clarke tried to be reasonable. "Officer, this is a mistake. My brother lives behind these gates. Maybe you know him? Jake Jackell, he's big in the government. This girl and I are invited to the annual Jackell Christmas dinner. It's a big party and I'm sure you've seen others arriving. Call Jake. You'll see its okay."

"Very good, sir. Now please be quiet, sit and don't do anything foolish."

"Damn it, you're not listening. I'm the brother of an important government official." The officer frowned. "It's true. Don't be a damned stooge. When my brother finds out, you'll regret it. Call, he'll vouch for me." Before he could regret the remarks, Clarke saw a club leave the officer's belt. It seemed like slow motion until it crashed against his shoulder. The rest occurred in real time. The pain flashed as light from his shoulder to his brain. He screamed and fell to the ground rolling in pain and gasping loudly for air. Tears froze on his cheeks and he screamed.

"Shut the fuck up, asshole," the officer sneered. "This is a damn long holiday shift and I'm not in any fucking mood for your shit." Just then, a large van turned the corner and headed toward them. From the ground he stared up at the van with its circular logo of black water and a deep red setting sun. Below was the name, *Darkwater, Incorporated, a Limited Liability Security Enterprise.*

When the officer turned to open the van door, Clarke panicked. He pushed a guard and tried to escape. He pictured his body, trim like the tri-athlete he was, badly outrunning these younger men but the years hadn't been kind and his legs felt leaden. He stumbled almost immediately and felt a shock in his calf so intense that he wet himself and fell immediately to the ground. Whimpering, he rolled into a fetal position and held his throbbing leg while being warmed once again by his own urine that was melting the urine that had frozen from earlier. This time he didn't dare move. His heart was thumping and once again, Sue was screaming. The officer bent down to him and—what had to be just for fun—poked him again with the prod. Intense, painful tremors coursed through him causing him to shake violently. Urine burned as it was forced out of him before it's time. Limp and through moist eyes, he watched the guards take their time putting on rubber protective gloves before hoisting him into the van. Once he was secure, they guided the girl to a seat across from him and handcuffed her to the wall. The officer secured the door, tapped it, and the van pulled away.

When her sobbing subsided, Sue looked at him. "You were going to run away and leave me. You're nothing but a coward." Even if he felt like speaking, he couldn't think of anything to say. She looked sorrowfully at the officer. "Did you . . . did you pick up four girls near here?"

He shook his head. "That's none of your business, miss."

"Please, they're my friends," she wailed.

Fighting through the bile in his throat, Clarke rasped, "We'll find them."

Before the officer could stop her she kicked Clarke hard. "You pig. You seduce me, but as soon as we're caught, you run. You're a slug like all men."

"I'm sorry. I—"

She kicked him again. The officer smiled and looked away.

"Officer," Clarke croaked, struggling to speak, the bile still burning his throat, "my brother really is Jake Jackell."

"Then you're a lucky man. When we get to the processing center, you become my chief's problem. Maybe you can interest him in your story. For now, be quiet, or . . ." He touched his prod. "You're giving me a headache."

It was a long drive to the processing center that was located in an ancient two-story gray stone building just off the Delaware River and directly under the Benjamin Franklin Bridge. It was more of a fortress with a reinforced metal gate to limit street access and a series of docks. The gate opened slowly and the van drove in. When it stopped, the back door opened.

Someone out of sight yelled, "Hey, Klottz, just two tonight? Doesn't seem worth coming in with just two."

"I pick 'em up, I don't count 'em. How many did you get?"

"Five on the way out and two on the way back—a good early Christmas haul."

Sue, who had been sobbing quietly, perked up when the door opened and yelled to the officer. "Did anyone pick up four girls about my age?"

The guard ignored her until he finished his paperwork. "There are always girls. That's a free market trade that never goes away." He laughed. "Everyone goes into the corral; you can check them out there before the six in the morning ship out."

"Ship out?" Sue asked.

"None of your fucking business." The guard walked away.

Officer Klottz explained the rules. "If you have anything on you, we confiscate it. Don't fight or create a disturbance because we're authorized to kill you with the prod or a gun. So keep that in mind." He stared at Clarke. "And don't assume you're dead and go rushing around. We will prod you as much as we need until you comply and from what doctors tell me, the nerves stay raw until the end. Those who've been through it tell us they wish we'd just killed them."

"What about my lawyer?" Clarke asked.

Officer Klottz laughed. "I'm sorry, who?"

"My lawyer."

He continued to smile. "No lawyer, you're not a criminal, you're a *Waster* and our actions are covered by the Patriot Act and amended by the *Circle of Life*. There's a copy in the cell but it's been through a lot so it's hard to read. Trust me, you have no legal rights."

"But that isn't legal."

"Oh, so you're a lawyer, now. Well, we get plenty of them here, too. They bitch a lot—quote chapter and verse from old laws that no longer apply—but the prod here shuts them up soon enough. Shows how good legal expertise is these days. Before going out, you should have read the fine print in the Patriot Act, or the *Circle of Life* legislation so you'd know how few rights—as you call them—still exist or that you no longer qualify for. The easier you make this, the easier it is."

"But my brother . . ."

"Fuck your brother. Who did you say he is?"

"Jake Jackell. He works for the president."

"Which president?"

"The one who runs the country, you . . . he works for President Crelli."

The officer pointed the prod at Clarke. "Cut the attitude. Sorry I asked." With that, he walked away.

Even though Sue was angry with him, when they were separated and she was being pulled into another room, she screamed and tried to fight her way back to him. When the door shut and he was all alone, Clarke was escorted into another room, told to strip, and forced to sit on the solitary metal chair anchored to the concrete floor in the center of an otherwise empty room. Before he left, Klottz pulled a switch and warned Clarke about leaving the seat. As soon as Klottz left, Clarke started to rise but received a shock so severe that he screamed as urine spurted out from him.

Trembling on the cold, uncomfortable chair, he responded to every question from a computer voice that warned him to tell the truth on threat of additional shocks. When the questioning was complete, exhausted, he fell asleep sitting up. Some time later, Officer Klottz entered and threw Clarke's foul clothing onto his lap, waking him.

"Mr. Jackell, you're a very lucky man. Get dressed. The chief checked your story. Your brother is who you said he is. He's sending a servant to pick you up."

"Thanks a fucking lot. Wait until I tell him what goes on here."

"Sir, Mr. Jackell is my commanding officer's superior and while I'm sure he'd love to hear your view of what goes on here, I'm quite certain it won't surprise him. We're on the frontlines and it's our job to defend America against terrorists, *Wasters*, and other crazies out there who hate us for our freedom. Mistakes are unavoidable but believe me, it is better if you just accept an apology. We're sorry to have inconvenienced you this evening but what we do here is an essential part of the critical effort to save our republic and if that is a hassle, you had better get used to it and find a good job or a different country. It is because of people like you that the terrorists win."

"Officer, I appreciate your position, but I'm still going to complain."

"Do your worst."

"What about the girl?"

"Mr. Jackell said nothing about a girl."

"What happens to her?"

"She will learn a bitter lesson about lack of productivity and once it is determined how she can best contribute to the economy, the appropriate action will be taken. Don't worry about her."

"I kind of promised her Christmas dinner at my brother's. Is it too late to call her back for it? My brother will vouch for her safety."

"I'm no pimp. If it was up to me—with your economic standing and the way you treated that poor girl—I'd have sent you where all America-haters go."

"I'm not like that. It's been a really bad year."

"Bad? While your luck has changed, that young girl's luck has gotten worse."

"But—"

"Forget her, she's gone. I'm sure a cretin with your connections can find others. Just like I'm sure we'll see you again and hopefully without your brother running interference." The officer left and Clarke waited in the cold cell until a guard entered.

"Mr. Jackell?"

Before Clarke raised himself from the chair, he had the presence to wait for the guard to disable it. Then, using the chair to steady him, he stretched and stood. "I haven't eaten all day."

"Like I care. Follow me."

He shuffled along behind the guard. When they reached an office a heavy set old woman was waiting. She introduced herself as his brother's servant and led him to a waiting limo. On the drive, he fell asleep and woke when the car door opened and Angie poked her head inside.

"Jesus, Clarke, it stinks in here and you're a fright. What happened?"

She struggled to avoid it, but he hugged her like she was his only friend. With a weak, gravelly voice, he thanked her. "Angie, thank you, thank you, you saved my life."

She peeled his arms from around her neck. "I accept your thanks but let go, you smell horrid and look worse. You need a long, hot shower and something less . . . foul to wear and you're probably hungry, too." He nodded and was helped by her servants to a guest room where he cleaned up and put on some of Jake's oversized clothes. When he was done, he sat at Angie's large kitchen table while another servant served him a meal.

Angie watched as he ate it ravenously. "Thanks," he said between mouthfuls. "What about Christmas dinner? Where is everyone?"

She shrugged. "Why'd you get involved with HomeSec?"

"I had no choice, Angie. I've been down on my luck since they closed the IRS."

"Do you want to talk about it?"

"Not really." Tired, he finished his meal and put his head on the table.

It was daylight when he awoke. He was in a strange room wearing pajamas that were two sizes to large. Set out on a valet stand were some of his brother's clothes. With his added weight, they fit except he had to roll up the sleeves and pant legs. When he was ready, he went downstairs where Angie was waiting.

"Angie, thanks for being there for me. I don't know what I would have done."

She smiled. "Clarke, we're family. Now what's going on with you?"

He discussed his situation and she listened patiently.

"So what have you been living on?"

"Savings. I sold everything but my condo which is worthless. Then I went to food kitchens, but patrol cars were parked outside so I had to be careful. At the end of summer, the kitchens closed and since, my diet has consisted of unsweetened lemonade that I buy in vats and stale bread, when I can find some."

"That's horrible, Clarke. You know better than to eat like that. You need to eat from all the food groups."

"I'll try, Angie. What's happening here? Where's Jake?"

Her smile disappeared. "The job's changed him, Clarke."

"That's a good thing, right."

She shook her head. "We rarely talked, now, even less."

"Hell, Angie, Jake never speaks unless he can own the conversation."

"You think you're disparaging him but you're really directing your anger at me."

"I'm sorry, but you two never talked like we did."

She looked down for a moment. "Please, we agreed not to discuss it."

"I never actually agreed to that."

"Clarke."

"I'm sorry."

"You don't understand. Jake is under tremendous pressure. Don't get me wrong, the president is pleased and the program is going great but he's on duty constantly."

"I'm sorry your social life isn't all you expect. I'd change places in a heartbeat."

"Stop it. Our parties are great even though we haven't had one in a while. The problems in America are so great that they have caused everyone in the administration to become so focused and secretive. It's understandable, I guess. They're doing important work to save the country from those who hate us for our freedoms and Jake is the point man for much of it. When he does come home, he doesn't say much."

"There are some who would take his absence as good news."

"For God's sake, let it go. What does talking like that get you?"

He put his hands up to deflect her anger. "Okay, I'll stop. It was your choice and I accepted it and I have far too much to worry about, now, anyway."

"What will you do?" she asked jumping at an opportunity to change the subject.

"Can I stay here for a while until I find work?"

"It will be too awkward with Jake not around. He's still sensitive about us."

"Angie, it's not like you don't have the space here, the place is mammoth. It'll be real easy to avoid me and you have all these servants."

She shrugged.

"I've put us in the past, why can't he? Right now I could use some sensitivity."

"I can't do it. You being here would be . . . impossible." She looked like she was going to cry.

"You've discussed it?"

She nodded.

"Jake refused? Why that son of a bitch . . ."

"I know you think he's bulletproof but he's not. He believes he can be president and you know how the media is. They find everything and everything matters. He can't harbor a *Waster*, even if it's his brother."

Clarke had thought he'd effectively insulated himself from Jake but that hurt. "What about you, Angie? How can you live with a man who does this to family? How long do you think it'll be before he reevaluates you, Ang? You're family, too."

"There are the kids to think about. No, I'm not going to do this. He's my husband. The servants will pack some food and I'll give you warm clothes, but you have to leave."

"Angie, our time is past; I didn't come here to revisit it. I'm here because I have nowhere else to go. Jake can't be that big of an asshole to turn me out and you can't let him. I need you to stand up for what's right, regardless how he sees it. Don't send me away. Angie, please, I won't survive out there. I promise, I won't threaten Jake—in any way, not his marriage or his career. For God's sake, I need your help."

"I'm sorry, Clarke, he insisted."

"You won't fight him on this. I don't understand. What does my presence do?"

"Let it go, please, he won't have you here."

"But it was so long ago. Why did you have to tell him, anyway?"

"I didn't tell him, he just knew, somehow. It was so unlike him but he waited until I knew that he knew."

"You two deserve each other."

"I wish you meant it."

"I do, Angie, I do."

"I know you're having a tough time but so are we. There are reasons why you can't stay. You haven't asked about Mom and Dad."

"Have they started drinking again?"

"They're dead, Clarke."

"They're what?"

"We buried them over a month ago—just before Thanksgiving."

"Why didn't you—they died together?"

She nodded.

"How?"

"Everyone's having economic problems. The government stopped paying health benefits and insurance companies have filed for bankruptcy protection, its chaos."

"What's that have to do with my parents?"

"I don't know all the details, but Jake said Congress has passed a law that allows certain service industries to renege on obligations if providing them will have a deleterious effect on their business and the country's economy."

"Weird, but, so?"

"So nearly everyone defaulted on healthcare benefits and retirement obligations."

"They can do that?"

"They can now."

"And Mom and Dad?"

"The new legislation requires everyone to be responsible for their own lives and their own debts. There is no such thing as government help anymore. Families are allowed to take on the debts of other family members but they must have the means to pay them down. Mom and Dad never took good care of themselves and with high medical bills due to their drinking and the emphysema from smoking; Jake and I had to pay their premiums, deductibles, co-pays, and kickbacks for years."

"Are you still angry that I never helped? I'm sorry but it's a little late now. Besides, Jake made ten times what I made when I was working and today . . ."

"That's in the past, Clarke. It would have been nice for you to help your parents but obviously in the past year you were kind of useless."

"Thanks."

"You know what I mean. Anyway, with Jenna at Bryn Mawr and Jake Jr. preparing to enter Dartmouth, with house payments, cars, and our busy social schedule, we didn't have as much disposable income as you'd think and what we do have is tied up in a potentially lucrative new venture Jake got in on the ground floor. It's a business called *Waster Wagons,* or something like that. Maybe you heard of it."

He nodded, dourly.

"I don't know much about it but Jake says the wagons help the poor and he expects the stock appreciation will be extraordinary. Anyway, until this venture turns a profit, we had to cut some things out."

"Are you saying you cut my parents out? You stopped supporting them to protect your lifestyle?"

"It wasn't like that. We cut back, sure, but their health was declining anyway and their medical expenses had soared in the past year. You don't know. When the IRS disbanded, there were financial timing issues so salaries were frozen and compensation delayed. These are tough times as you know. Jake didn't get the raise he was expecting and we were forced to make some tough—and I mean really tough decisions. Don't look at me that way, Clarke. You weren't here. We all sacrificed. Jenna's working part time now for a local congresswoman, while JJ plans to enter a public university here in town until we get a handle on our expenses. We even had to forego putting the cabana in until things get better. You don't know but it's hard to have a good pool party without a cabana. But even all that didn't put our economic value where it needed to be. As Morgans, it's vital to our future that we maintain our worth so we had no choice but to move Mom and Dad into an unassisted living facility."

"A what?"

"It's a new facility program for seniors. It's a place where people can live real, real cheap until they die."

"You sent them away to die?"

"They were fading anyway, Clarke. The doctors said it was only a matter of time. I have friends who made the same decision with their parents in order to make ends meet. Believe me, it was the right thing to do. Mom and Dad were old and sick. There was no purpose in spending more . . ."

"But—"

"It doesn't matter. They died shortly after they arrived at the facility."

"Shortly after? When did they die? What did they die of?"

She was silent.

"Angie?"

She looked down and started to cry. "Okay, they died the day they arrived."

"Oh Jesus, Angie, what have you and Jake done?"

She said nothing.

"Why wasn't I notified of the funeral?"

"There wasn't time. There are so many now at these facilities that they have efficient, inexpensive, just-in-time mass cremations and they don't allow spectators. The Morgan Church owns the process and we were provided with a certificate and an amber encased facsimile of their remains. Do you want to see it?"

He shook his head.

"We held a brief ceremony, here at the house. I'm sorry, Clarke, but be happy for them. They've gone to a happier place and Jake finally got his raise and Junior is enrolling at Dartmouth in the spring."

"You two are out of your fucking minds. You don't even believe in a happier place, for God's sake."

"There was nothing anyone could have done."

"My nothing was better than what the hell you did."

"Who are you kidding? If I had found a way to contact you, you would have found a way to avoid responsibility. You always do. And like now, you'd have found someone else to blame."

"Are you kidding? You and my asshole brother ARE to blame."

Angie cried silently. "I'm sorry. It shouldn't have ended this way. Jake and I are on top, I should feel better than I do. Why don't I, Clarke?"

He tried to feel sad for her but couldn't find that switch so he moved on. "Do you have any money?"

"Currency? We don't use currency. In Jake's position, we have to support Crelli's policies so what we buy, we charge electronically using our PID. I may have some currency in a drawer upstairs in my room. I'll get it and you can have all of it." She went upstairs and after a few minutes, she returned with a handful of paper money. "It's not much. What will you do?"

"I heard there may be work in St. Louis, or maybe Denver."

"That far away? How'll you get there?"

"I don't know. Is your neighborhood patrolled regularly?"

She nodded.

"And Jake won't help?"

She nodded again. He walked to her. She looked fearful and stepped back but he reached out. She resisted but then her body remembered and she folded comfortably into his embrace, tears continuing to spill. He bent to kiss her. She responded, but only briefly, and then she shook free.

"Clarke, take care. If we find work opportunities here, we'll let you know."

"Angie, who are you kidding? This is goodbye. If Jake actually found something, you won't be able to contact me. Be careful with him. Even after all these years, he's not one for constancy."

"As we both know, that's a trait that runs strong in your family. Be well." He took the money and left.

Outside, he realized how difficult this was going to be. He decided to head generally west, while avoiding HomeSec any way he could. Fortunately, a few days later in the far western suburb of Philadelphia he found an old green clunker of a car with the keys still in it abandoned in a driveway of an empty house. He walked to a nearby station, purchased fuel at a premium with cash and filled it. Then, he drove west without eating to conserve his meager funds until he reached St. Louis.

Once in St. Louis, the preponderance of HomeSec patrols worried him so he drove cautiously through and reached Denver a few days later. Without money, he drove the car until it ran out of gas in a remote part of town and sat in the car, contemplating his next move. Without a clue, he simply fell asleep, awakening before dawn, shivering in the cold. He abandoned the car and walked in search of information and hopefully a job.

He noticed a crowd gathering in a nearby park. According to the banners, there was a rally sponsored by the Prophet Omar Smith. He didn't care for the terrorist agenda but he was very interested in the food that was laid out on tables near the stage. Like the rest of the starving crowd, as he listened to a white-haired prophet preaching anarchy, he had one eye on the food. When the speeches ended, he and the rest of the crowd raced for the buffet tables. Completely enveloped, he forced his way to the front and grabbed for a box. A small man grabbed his arm.

"Take this and run," the man said, handing him a box. "HomeSec will be arriving any minute and we have to get out of here."

"But I'm starving," Clarke yelled back. "One box isn't enough." He wasn't able to grab another before the crowd pushed them from the food. The small, wiry man dressed in a weathered leather jacket scanned the area nervously and then ducked in and grabbed a second box from someone in the crowd. Before that person could react, the little man disappeared into the crowd, reappearing next to Clarke. He handed the second box to Clarke and steered him away.

Clarke followed the man until he heard the sirens and then everyone ran in terror. Those yet unfed rushed the tables knocking them over and spreading food onto the grass as they tried to grab for a meal before the patrols arrived. Clarke and his new friend ran to the top of a nearby hill and looked back as the first HomeSec patrols began corralling the people below.

"Fortunately for us, they're only capable of processing so many people at a time so if we stay low and wait them out, we'll be safe," his new friend informed him as they ran further away. They waited and watched as the patrols rounded up the poor throughout the park. When it seemed like it was ending, he followed the small man as he darted through the park. Just then another set of sirens blasted.

"Let's get out of here," the man yelled as others hiding near them fled, too.

He had no choice but to follow. In the distance two patrol cars drove toward them on the road above. The cars bounced over the curb and headed in their direction but just when he thought they were going to be cut-off and captured, another group bolted from a hiding place and the officers jumped from their cars and chased them down, nightsticks in hand.

Relieved at not being captured, Clarke and his friend worked their way to the edge of the park and as soon as it was clear, jumped out onto the sidewalk and began walking slowly.

"We're surrounded. The only way to avoid capture is to act like we're not concerned and hope they've reached their quota."

With patrolmen running around beating frightened people with their nightsticks and prods, it wasn't easy to act nonchalant, but they did their best as they meandered as far away from the action as possible. When they reached the top of another hill, a patrolman who was leaning against his car pointed at them and began chasing after them.

Exhausted, Clarke ran but his new friend stopped him. "If it's over, it's over."

As the patrolman approached, in the distance, a loud siren sounded and the patrolman struck the palm of his hand angrily with his prod and pointed at them. "Next time," he shouted before returning to his car.

"Wow, that was lucky," Clarke said, breathing heavily.

"You won't need luck, not when you're with the master. Pay attention and learn and you'll live a hell of a lot longer. I've been avoiding these goons for months, ever since the laws changed. I'm the only one in my socioeconomic bracket I know who's been safe that long." He offered his hand. "By the way, the name's Whittaker Coski, my friends—all of whom I suspect are dead now—call me Whit. What's yours?"

"Clarke Jackell. Where're you from?"

"It doesn't matter. Former lives are as irrelevant as current ones."

"What do we do now?"

"There's an underpass nearby where we can rest in relative safety, unless, of course, you have a reservation at a nearby hotel." Whit untied his leather coat and pulled two more box lunches from the inside pocket and gave Clarke one. "If you're curious, I chose you," he said, simply, "because it's easier to survive in pairs and I lost my partner earlier today."

"I'm sorry. What do partners do?"

"You could blow me." Clarke backed away and Whit laughed. "Just kidding. If a local overheard that, tough, we'd be dead."

"Are you . . . ?"

"Gay. Actually, yes. But don't worry. As perverse as it is to the powers that be, I'm a strong believer in monogamy and besides, I'd never let sex stand in the way of survival."

"Good because I'm straight."

"Good to know. We'll eat at the underpass. By the way, those clothes are almost useless here. Find someone dead or almost dead with a good jacket that has a belt and take it."

"What's wrong with these clothes?"

"They're not nearly warm enough and you'll need a jacket with a belt so when someone tries to steal it from you while you're sleeping you'll feel it and be able to protect yourself."

They walked to the underpass and ate in silence. He remained awake and watchful while Whit slept and Whit returned the favor. It was late evening when Whit woke him.

"We're heading out. Remember; look for a trench coat or a heavy jacket with a belt. With the wagons patrolling, there are fewer bodies around these days but we'll find something. There are always dead bodies lying around. Don't be timid."

They walked toward the tall buildings in the center of town. On the way, he noticed people sitting on park benches and under trees.

"How do you know if they're dead?" Clarke asked.

"Try to steal something from them, if they move, they're not dead."

"Whoa, that's dangerous?"

"No more than freezing to death or waiting to be captured by HomeSec."

"They're going to get us eventually so why fight so hard to survive?"

"Not true, my friend, salvation lies at the Last Chance Saloon."

Chapter 22

Denver, CO.—2037

They entered downtown Denver on a cold, blustery afternoon. As they walked, Whit explained the rules of survival to Clarke. "I've been in a few cities but Denver's by far the best. That's why I came back. Even though HomeSec has a headquarters here, there are so many homeless and out-of-work folks that it improves our odds. Bigger cities are generally safer because the smaller ones—and the towns—are closer knit, and strangers, particularly poor ones, are easier to spot. Local law enforcement is afraid of the *Federales* and willingly herd strangers into their jails until HomeSec sends transports. But more important, there are almost no money making opportunities in the towns because they keep any opportunities for their own."

"It sounds like you travel a lot."

"I've been as far away as Dallas and Wichita, Kansas and all the towns in between. After Crelli was elected, it was easy to see what was happening so I started looking around for a way to protect myself. Along the way, I met a guy who told me about an Underground Railroad connection near Abilene where they help people escape to Canada. That's where I was headed, but Wichita was as far as I got. I found a money-making opportunity there and thought I was out of the woods."

"What happened?"

"I got stupid and greedy and some hayseed husband went and got jealous and turned me in to local law enforcement. I escaped but it cost me everything I had made and I've been on the run ever since, looking for my next payday. One night, I literally stepped on a dying man who told me with his dying breath about the Last Chance Saloon. Ever hear of it?"

"No," Clarke responded. "What is it?"

"The old man said—and I've confirmed it—it's a very, very secret and secure gambling casino, where a private contractor gives the poor like you and me a fighting chance to earn our lives back so we can reenter the economy and live forever. I was looking for leads as to where it's located when I lost my partner. The way I see it, freedom and money here in the states is a lot better than freedom and no money in Canada. If I can't find the saloon, and I'm trying like hell to find it, the Underground Railway is my last resort."

"So it's some saloon or the Underground Railway, those are our choices?"

"Unless you can find another way to create value," Whit said.

"I'm looking. How did your partner die?"

"I didn't say he died."

"Was he caught by HomeSec?"

"He was tired of it all so he joined Smith's terrorists, if that's what they are. If you ask me, they should be called 'Smith's pains-in-the-ass' because all they do is annoying shit. In my book, they give terrorism a bad name. They piss people off applying the theory that Americans are so overwrought that petty annoyances will push them over the brink into rebellion. It's stupid and if it wasn't pathetic, it would almost be funny. Only in America are terrorists merely annoying although I have to give it to them because when the government doesn't fix whatever Smith's people break, everyone does get more pissed off. Maybe this Smith guy is on to something, I don't know, I'm just trying to survive long enough to hit the jackpot."

"What kinds of things do these terrorists do?"

"Silly stuff like stopping rush hour traffic at key spots in key cities by setting fire to beaters and other transportation, or they park hoopties on roads or bridges and leave them there. Sometimes they bomb or set fire to some obscure out-of-the-way property just to prove no one's safe, but they try to stay in the field of misdemeanor to avoid actually killing or hurting people and they never do enough to change anything. What a Mindfuck. We desperately need a revolution but the only one America gets is people being annoying."

"Why did your partner go if it's so pathetic?"

Whit shrugged. "I told him they'll never win or even prove anything, but he was tired of running. If you're ever confronted with that choice, do yourself a favor and keep running."

"I'm not the terrorist type but I guess I won't know until I have to face it. I'd prefer to find work. There must be someone hiring?"

"Sure, but I don't have the airfare to Caracas or Mumbai, do you?"

"That's it?"

"You could try the economic parks outside L.A., Boston, or New York but I doubt you'll find work there. Besides, having a job isn't the final answer because you can still starve to death or get disappeared with the subsistence wages American businesses are paying and calling it wages. I read last week that one in three workers can't hold a job long enough to build enough equity to survive. I don't like those odds."

"Is it that bad all over?"

"All over," Whit confirmed. "Shit, President Crelli and his Libertarian hypocrites didn't need much time. Word is they've been planning this for years. And don't be confused; disappearance isn't incarceration. Christ, I'd welcome prison for the comfort and the regular meals. It would be a holiday after what I've been through. But the government is no longer in the business of providing accommodations to lawbreakers. It's more cost effective to just disappear them. The private prisons are being converted into processing centers. If you ever have some extra money, invest, disappearance is the next profitable private industry in America."

"This is all new to me. Until last year, I was economically viable."

"We're all new to this. I've owned a few businesses, including a real estate venture. Like most American workers, my career is dotted with regular stops in the latest bubble industries and I've lived through more popping than a popcorn factory. I worked in chemicals, food, technology, hotel services, and healthcare, I even wrote software for phones. I followed the money everywhere and I can tell you, following never let's you get ahead. Who'd have thunk it. The last big bubble to pop turned out to be the American dream."

As they walked, Whit pointed to a tall building. "Over there, the second to fifth floors, that's our parking garage, our destination for tonight. We ride out the cold there, but only for a few days at most."

They had been bothered by HomeSec vehicles all day and Clarke saw another turn the corner. "Run!" he yelled and they took off. He followed Whit to the building he'd pointed to earlier and they raced up two flights of stairs before Whit stopped and peered over the wall. The vehicle had slowed down at the building but kept moving. When it was gone, he pointed to something else.

"Clarke, look over there. There's a guy lying in the doorway wearing a leather trench coat with a belt. It's perfect. I'd jump at it but we're partners and you need it."

"What? You want me to take it from him?"

"By the looks of him, he won't put up much of a fight."

"I can't do that."

"Why the hell not?"

"It's cold. If I take it, he'll die. Besides, I'm an accountant, not a thief." Whit wasn't buying it. "I can't. He'll fight me for it and I don't know if I'm that desperate. Maybe I can find someone who is already dead."

"Trust me, if they're dead, they won't be wearing a useful coat."

"Whit, there must be another way."

"Do it or you're no partner of mine. With what you're wearing, you'll freeze to death in a couple of nights. The guy's a goner anyway and someone else will get it. I'd really prefer not to look for another partner so soon so take the damn coat. Let's see how much you value your life."

"But . . ."

"Don't look at me. I'm not doing your work for you. Dead is dead. If you really want to live, start behaving like it. It's your call. I'll find another partner. I can do it in a heartbeat. Come on, rookie, show me your stones."

"Is this how we live now?"

"Fuck you, man, what choice do we have?"

"But . . ."

"Go."

Reluctantly, he went down the stairs to the street. When he opened the door, Whit was staring down at him from above, smiling. When he didn't move immediately, Whit waved him on. Cautiously, he moved toward the slumped figure. When he got close, he stopped. The man was resting on the cold ground, his back against a vacant store window, his hands tucked deep into the pockets of a long, heavy duty brown leather winter coat. Cautiously, he bent down and checked the belt, which was knotted securely around the man's waist. He coughed quietly but the man didn't move. He turned and shrugged. Whit waved him to continue.

He gently prodded the man who stirred briefly; his eyes fluttered but remained closed. Slowly, carefully, he untied the belt and unfastened the buttons. When the coat fell open, he pulled gently at one of the leather sleeves, removing it from the man's arm. He moved to the other side to work on the other sleeve. As he grabbed it, from the corner of his eye, he saw a blur and felt a blow from a club on the back of his leg. He screamed as his knees buckled and he rolled away from the second blow. The man shouted, crawled over to him and swung again. Frantically, Clarke crab walked away, kicking the man and looking anxiously toward Whit who was smiling and goading him on. He dodged another blow and grabbed the man's sleeve again, pulling harder until it spun the man, his face slamming hard on the concrete. As the man struggled to turn, he swung his club wildly. The momentum from the swing freed the jacket all the way to the club head. Clarke rolled the jacket over the club and held it, tying up the man.

"Hurry up, Clarke, I'm freezing here!" Whit yelled jumping up and down.

Clarke turned back to the victim who was frantically trying to free his club. Not knowing what else to do, he kicked him hard in the side causing him to wheeze. He continued to kick him until finally, the man lay still, blood and mucous dripping from his mouth and nose. Clarke bent down for a closer look. Too late, he saw the jacket unroll and the head of the club whiz by his head hitting something with a loud thud. He kicked again, this time hitting the man in the throat and he continued to kick until the man stopped moving. Exhausted and breathing hard in the light, cold air, he turned the man over carefully only to see a wide-eyed, unblinking stare. He stepped back, horrified at what he'd won.

"Atta boy. That's it," Whit yelled, "grab the coat and run."

Avoiding the collar, which was coated in blood, he yanked the coat off and tried to wipe the blood off on the sidewalk. It left a brick colored stain on the leather and a burgundy stain on the ground.

With Whit applauding, he climbed the steps three at a time with his prize. Wheezing and trembling, he reached Whit and looked over the wall at the victim who lay motionless in a pool of blood. He backed against the wall and vomited.

"It's good to see you haven't lost your vestigial survival instincts. Welcome aboard partner. Don't worry about the stains. Where we're going, people consider them merit badges."

"What . . . what now?"

"Put it on, tie it tight, and let's go." Whit climbed the stairs and Clarke followed.

"What'll happen to him?"

"He'll be cleaned by the next wagon that comes by. Don't worry; he was never your problem. Don't blame yourself. By the looks of him, what you did was a blessing. Someone else would have taken that coat if you hadn't. It's not your fault. Blame the damn political system and what they force us to do to survive. And be proud because you'll live another day. As long as you can say that, you can still hope to get lucky. You and me, we'll do fine."

He felt miserable—but warm and miserable as he double knotted the belt tightly around his waist, knowing he too would die before he lost it.

When they reached the fifth floor, he saw men wearing heavy winter jackets milling around a fire.

Whit explained as he held the door open. "They're watchdogs. If there's trouble, their job is to create a disturbance so everyone else can get away."

"What's in it for them?"

"They get a free place to sleep until they're caught. We'll be asked to watchdog but I know the leader so I think I can buy us a night or two before we stand duty—at least I hope so. Let's go."

They walked by the watchdogs who ignored them and went into the parking garage. Near the elevator, huddled beside a drum of burning scrap, several warmly dressed men with various types of clubs eyed them, warily. Whit waved at one who pointed to an old jalopy where two men were sitting.

Whit explained the situation. "The fat guy in the driver's seat, he's Mambo. His real name is Sollie but he doesn't think it sounds tough enough. He's in charge. Before the *Circle of Life*, he was a partner at some local accounting firm. He's nice enough so be respectful. Without his support, we're toast."

Whit knocked on the window. The back door opened and they entered.

"Who do we have here?" the man in the passenger seat asked.

"Whit Coski and Clarke Jackell," Whit replied.

Mambo twisted and offered his hand. "Clarke, it's nice to meet you. Whit, you've been here before, right. You know the rules."

Whit worked his coat off and rolled up both sleeves. Then, he contorted his body until he was able to pull down his pants. He twisted to show his backside to the man. Mambo motioned for Clarke to do the same.

"What's this for?"

Mambo explained. "We have to be sure you don't have one of those new fangled PIDs or if you do, it's disabled. We don't want surveillance picking up your signal here."

Once they'd been checked, Whit began the negotiation. "You know me, Mambo, and I vouch for Clarke, here. He's my partner."

Mambo smiled. "If I remember right, you go through a lot of partners."

"I really found a good one this time, Mambo. See that coat? In broad daylight, he rips it from a big bruiser coming out of an office building. What a tussle. See the bloodstains? This man is one tough dude." Clarke felt uncomfortable. "Mambo, we can provide you some real value, but not if you put us on detail."

"Rules are rules," Mambo said.

"And exceptions are exceptions. We're going to rob a store."

"What good does that do me?"

"You know how HomeSec operates. They round up *Wasters*. We've got a solution. We're stealing briefcases." Mambo offered Whit a blank stare.

"Briefcases," Whit repeated. "We hand the briefcases to the better-dressed among your regulars." Mambo looked more interested. "They're props. The briefcases will make your lookouts invisible to the HomeSec patrols. They will look like value-adding businessmen, and the patrols will ignore them. It works. I've done it before. Who carries a briefcase if they don't have to?"

Mambo nodded. "Sounds like a plan. How many will you take?"

"It's a small job, just Clarke and me. We each grab four and bring them here. You distribute them any way you want."

"Sounds okay. What do you want for your efforts?"

"We keep two briefcases and you give us two days deferment before we stand watch."

"You keep one and you get a day."

"Two briefcases and one day. And I'll throw in a raid at your competition's garage around the corner just to shake things up."

"You've got yourself a deal." Whit shook on it. As they walked away, Mambo yelled at Clarke. "Did he say your name's Jackell? That sure sounds familiar."

Clarke continued walking. "I'm from out of town," he mumbled. "I don't know anyone here." On the ground floor, he asked Whit to explain the plan.

"When HOMESEC raids, Mambo loses assets—his men and his value to the community as a protected site. Until HOMESEC catches on, the briefcase thing will keep him from having his people identified so that saves him. And for us, it buys tomorrow. By then, we find a way to the Last Chance Saloon or we're on the street again dodging HOMESEC and wagons."

"The Saloon? Tell me again why we're searching for it?"

"Salvation, partner. Let's get the briefcases and I'll explain it once we have a choice set of sleeping accommodations for the evening. You're my lookout." They walked until Whit stopped at an alley between two tall buildings. He opened a gray plastic box fastened to the brick wall of one of the buildings and began to separate wires.

As he worked, he explained what he was doing. "This is a building that still hasn't been upgraded to wireless and connected to the national security protocol. Once I disengage the alarm—there, I got it—I'll break the front glass and grab the briefcases. The signal has to jump from old-style wired, through an analog to the new digital security system. That can take up to thirty seconds for the surveillance system to query and maybe another thirty seconds for the alarm to go off at the closest police station, which is another three minutes away. That gives us four minutes to get in and out. I want you to stand by the door and grab the first four briefcases I throw out and run like hell over to Mambo's. Be sure to go back the same way we came and I'll meet you. Got it?"

Clarke nodded.

"Here we go."

Whit severed the wires and then ran to the front of the building and crashed through the store's glass window. Seconds later, he tossed out four cardboard boxes with briefcases inside them. Clarke grabbed the boxes but hesitated. From inside the store he heard, "Get the hell out of here, now." With that, he retraced their steps back to the parking garage. People looked at him as he ran but no one moved toward him so he arrived at the garage and waited on the ground floor for Whit but he was nowhere to be seen. Worried and unsure what to do, he waited as long as he could then, fearing the worst he slowly climbed the stairs to meet with Mambo. While he climbed, he wondered what he was going to do next, without Whit. At least he had a place to stay when he traded the briefcases. He kicked open the door and headed for Mambo's car office. When he got closer, he saw Whit and Mambo talking.

"There he is now," he heard Whit yell through a rolled down window. "It took you long enough. Keep one and give Mambo the other briefcases. The deal is sealed."

Mambo nodded. "Good job, Clarke, you have tonight before you stand duty."

Whit smiled as he left the car. "We're sleeping in luxury tonight, partner."

Clarke kept one briefcase and followed Whit up to the sleeping floor. When they were out of sight of Mambo and his guards, Clarke asked, "How'd you get back so quickly?"

"I took you the long way so you'd run through the other garage on your way back. The police will have you on their surveillance tapes and will assume you went to that garage. They'll raid it as soon as they correlate your image with the robbery."

"But they'll know who I am. Wait, you said the police, not HomeSec."

"Crime is police work. The tapes will show you running into the garage where Mambo's competition hangs and the police will raid it. We've satisfied our bargain."

"But innocent people will get hurt."

"If there are any innocent people left. Everyone knows the rules, there's no blame anymore, only survival. Right now, you should thank God that you're not one of them."

"How'd you know about that store?"

"It's my father's."

"You stole from your father?"

"It wasn't an inside job, if that's what concerns you. When times got bad, my father chose to support my sister instead of me. I worked hard for that son of a bitch, but he never appreciated it, or my reputation as a local hustler. My sister, on the other hand, was a professional, a college grad with opportunities. She had nice tits and a great smile, which helped. She had a good job too. But when she lost that job—to protect her from getting disappeared—my fucking father fired me and hired her. This isn't just a family squabble; this is life and death we're talking about. You know where you really stand when your family chooses you to die. That bastard sentences me to death and all he says is, 'be a man.' Do you believe that? Be a man! Die like a man, he means, and die so my sister can live. Die and leave him the hell alone, that's what he wants. God I hate him.

"Before I left, the son of a bitch rationalized it that I was the type who'd find a way to survive and support myself. What type is that, expendable? He didn't want to take the chance that my sister wasn't that type, I guess. That's why the cheap bastard will never be accepted as a Morgan, he doesn't make high value choices. I had the best chance to prosper so I should have been given the best chance to survive. That's how it's stated in Morgan's Ten Commandments. In spite of all that, I'm still traditional enough to reduce the whole damn thing to one thing—he loves my sister more than me. This was payback."

"Whit, I'm sure he loves you."

"I know the way things are today. Families have to make tough choices all the time, whether they want to or not. If you can't afford someone, jettison them."

"So why blame your father?"

"Who is he to decide that my sister couldn't survive and I could? I was the one who could have grown his business and after all, that's the important thing."

"But you said you were the hustler."

"I don't want to discuss it. He made his choice. He could have kept both of us. We could have made sacrifices, even living together to save money. I don't know. Whatever he could have done, he didn't ask and chose her, not me, so fuck him and those briefcases. I'm going to get a good night's sleep tonight and dream, in warmth and comfort, of a day in the near future when he goes broke and he and my sister are forced to live like he sentenced me to live. Let's see how they like it trying to dodge wagons and collection teams." He smiled. "I picture my sister's big tits heaving as she struggles to outmaneuver the patrols and then, when she's caught, offering her double D's as a last defense. Who knows; maybe she'll end up a slut and live forever. She deserves it. Anyway, I'm going to sleep good tonight."

"What do we do now?"

"Pick an unoccupied car. I'll even let you sleep in the backseat where it's cozier. There won't be any heat but you can use the briefcase box for a pillow and that nice jacket of yours will keep you toasty. In the morning, whoever has food usually shares and if one of the cars has any fuel left, we'll cook it on the engine block."

They found a car and settled in. "About the Last Chance Saloon?" Clarke asked.

Whit's weary voice responded from the front seat. "Some say it's an urban legend but it isn't. A few years ago, when the poor and homeless began disappearing, everyone assumed the worst. Months after the first disappearances, rumor had it that there were at least some survivors, people who had gotten lucky in some televised reality contest that viewers needed an annual membership to watch. Don't ask me why but about that time, shows started appearing on the Internet, with the same subscription requirement, and they offered forever as a grand prize. It was set up like the old Roman coliseum where the poor fought various predators on live TV to survive. It became so competitive that the FCC had to suspend their rules and make it either forever or death—and there was a lot of death. The shows drew a huge audience share in their time slot and soon more shows appeared with more and more competitive themes. Competition among networks to acquire poor people willing to fight and die got so competitive that soon the networks were offering a great deal of money just to attract gladiators. That's when the government stepped in, outlawed the shows and calmed the networks down."

"The next generation of those shows and the most popular because they were a hell of a lot less grisly were called the Last Chance Saloon and for obvious reasons, it drove the competition away. Everyone assumed it was staged but I've done the research. In Wichita, I slipped into a Member's Only Bar and Grill and for a few minutes I watched the show. Based on the discussion in the restaurant, I'm certain it's for real, a chance to gamble, which everyone loves to watch, and to win a jackpot so you can start over."

"Do you know anyone who's won?"

"No," Whit admitted. "According to rumors, not many win, but those who do live like royalty."

"Why would the government allow that?" Clarke asked, in disbelief.

"The government sponsors it, I think, so it helps pay for things now that taxes are gone. But private enterprise pulls it off and they do it for the same reason they do everything; profits. Reality based media is low overhead and very profitable and for some perverse reason, watching desperate people vie for prize money in life and death situations is titillating enough to the subscribing populace to interest a hell of a lot of advertisers."

"So how do we find this saloon?"

"That's the difficult part. Nobody seems to know where it is or how to get selected for it, but I'm pretty sure there's a special pick up place here in Denver. Wherever it is, I'm going to find it because I'm not going to risk hiking to the Underground Railroad in Abilene in the middle of winter through all those patriotic little towns along the way."

"Isn't Abilene in Texas?"

"No, it's Kansas. You need to spruce up on your geography if you're going to survive. Abilene is the terminus and someone there helps you escape to Canada."

"Canada sounds safer. Why hope to get lucky?"

Whit laughed. "Why? It's the American way, that's why. Who wouldn't rather be alive, lucky and rich than dead or poor? Besides, I believe the saloons are regional and that improves the odds of finding one. People I've talked to hint at one in the east and another in the west."

"We're betting our lives on that? That's not a lot to go on."

"As things stand, we can only lose so how bad a bet is it? I've talked to some *Wasters* who swear it's outside Denver. Our job tomorrow is to find someone who can get us closer. Right now, I'm going to sleep." With that Whit stopped talking and minutes later he was snoring. Clarke covered himself with his hard-earned jacket and he too fell into an exhausted slumber.

He awoke to the sound of sirens. Through the car window he saw Whit peering over the parking garage wall yelling. Clarke put his coat on and walked over.

"What's happening?"

"Yeeha! They're raiding the other garage. Look at everyone emptying out. It'll take a couple of wagons at least. Grab your briefcase and let's go—and for god's sake, look business-like."

"Where to?"

"We walk through the crowd looking for anyone who isn't fleeing and we ask them about the saloon. Get as much information as you can."

"That'll work?"

"Shit, I don't know. Do you have a better idea?" He grabbed his briefcase and followed Whit. When they burst out of the parking garage, the street was bedlam.

Clarke shouted, "Are you sure we're safe?"

Whit shrugged.

"What are we looking for again?"

"Anyone who wants to be captured."

"And you're sure these briefcases will work."

Whit shrugged again and waded into the chaos of patrolmen chasing *Wasters* streaming from the parking garage. There was shouting and screaming everywhere as charged nightsticks immobilized the fleeing crowd. Whit paused at an alley and bent to talk to a man crumpled on the sidewalk, moaning.

"Friend, have you heard of the Last Chance Saloon?"

The man laughed. It came out as a high-pitched scream.

"It's over. There's no way out!" he shouted to a nearby patrolman, "Kill me!"

"The saloon exists." Whit yelled. The man sobbed as he was dragged away.

Clarke followed along reluctantly. Each time a patrolman ran past him, he flinched, expecting to be assaulted. He found a man hiding behind some boxes but before he could ask him anything, a patrolman stopped, looked at Clarke's briefcase and gave him some advice.

"Sir, you shouldn't be here right now, it's dangerous. Go back to work and forget what you see here. You don't want to be involved." He thanked the patrolman but when the man left to chase someone, Clarke continued on. The man behind the boxes, thinking he'd been exposed, started to run but Clarke grabbed him. "Do you know anything about the Last Chance Saloon?"

"Are you crazy?" the man asked. "Get the fuck away from me. Let me go. They're gonna kill me."

"What about the saloon?"

"It's just another of their fucking games. Now leave me the hell alone."

Behind the man, inside a larger dumpster, he heard another voice reverberate. "The stories are true, the saloon exists. I saw something about it in the media."

He bent down beside the dumpster to speak to the man when he heard another voice.

"Sir, this is a warning. You are interfering with law officers in pursuit of their duty. Move away. We cannot guarantee your safety."

He backed away as the patrolmen reached into the dumpster and pulled a man up by the hair and stuck him with his prod. Blood flowed as the man sank back into the dumpster.

"Climb out now and we will take you to a hospital." The man refused so the patrolman climbed into the dumpster. Just then, another man who was hiding behind the dumpster broke and ran. The patrolman swung and missed and then gave chase.

Clarke stared into the dumpster where the first man was laying on top of wet garbage, bleeding profusely from his ear and mouth, a long black and blue bruise running up his cheek from his chin to his ear.

"I'll help you get out. Clarke told him. "Where's the closest hospital?"

Without opening his eyes, the man slurred an answer. "Are you an idiot? Can't go to the hospital, they'll kill me."

"You'll be safe. You'll die if you stay here bleeding like that."

The man refused to move. When Clarke started to climb in, the man shouted. "Leave me the fuck alone. Don't you know? Hospitals get paid to kill the poor now."

Clarke was sure the man was wrong. "But doctors take an oath . . ."

"Get the fuck away or you'll draw more patrolmen. I'll take my chances here. The doctors have no choice. If they don't kill the ones who can't pay, they lose their license and then they become poor and that's not something a doctor wants, particularly during these times. Now get out of here and leave me alone."

Unsure, Clarke closed the dumpster and turned to see more bodies lying in the street, bleeding, moaning, and immobilized by the charged nightsticks. Some were being systematically dragged to nearby vans and trucks.

He grasped his briefcase tighter and walked purposefully away, trying not to stare at the carnage. An elderly woman peered out from under an abandoned car.

"Try the stadium, young man," she said as he walked by.

He moved closer and knelt. "I beg your pardon?"

She motioned frantically. "Go away. Try the stadium, but get out of here, now!"

He nodded as two patrolmen ran to the auto and reached under to pull her out, kicking and clawing. They beat her with their sticks until she stopped moving and her eyes rolled up, the whites showing as they dragged her to a corner and threw her onto a pile of bodies.

Clarke stared as blood flowed from her wispy white hair down across the bridge of her nose, past her mouth and onto her clothes in an expanding burgundy stain. Her eyes refocused briefly on him and she smiled, showing broken and yellowed teeth. She mouthed the word, stadium, and then her eyes lost focus and she was gone.

With all the pandemonium on the street, Clarke still managed to find Whit talking to a man who was climbing a light pole as patrolmen beat the man into submission. A patrolman pushed Whit rudely against a wall and put his nightstick against his throat.

"Stay here. Don't get involved or . . ." He pressed the nightstick harder into Whit's throat, causing him to gag. Clarke yelled and pointed to the garage. Whit nodded and followed him there as soon as the patrolman stopped.

"How'd it go?" Whit asked.

"Before she was beaten to death, an old lady told me to go to the stadium," Clarke revealed."

"Which stadium?"

"She didn't say. They were beating the crap out of her."

"So we'll find a stadium. It's the only lead we have."

They walked through the business district asking, but people were reticent to help. Briefcases worked on the police but with everyone carrying a briefcase, their unkempt look made people decidedly unfriendly. Even so, Whit persisted until someone gave him directions to a local stadium. It was a long walk and it was dark before they saw the fenced-in parking lots that surrounded the structure. Whit pointed to a dimly-lit underground garage where people seemed to be milling around. They approached and were eyed warily.

"We're looking for the Saloon," Whit said to an old man who was sitting alone.

"What saloon is that pray tell?"

"The Last Chance Saloon where we can win back our lives."

The man smiled showing a mouth full of bad teeth. "There's no such place."

Whit wouldn't be denied. "I know it exists. You do too. Why else are you here?"

"I'm here because I've been chased from everywhere else."

"Why are they doing this to us?" Clarke asked.

The old man cackled. "No one rightly knows. I was a stockbroker, a profitable profession in the good old days. The bastards who owned my firm were always posturing about how much more efficient our economy would be if we didn't have so many lazy unemployed dragging us down. Back then, I thought it was just bitching; you know how the rich complain that America is filled with crack heads, meth addicts, and welfare queens who live to steal from hard working people. I never could figure it out. What is there about wealth that makes those people hate the way they do? They work so damn hard to get it; you'd think money would make them happy."

"At least they should be content not to hurt others," Clarke interjected.

"Right, that's what I'm saying. I worked the market and I know these people. There aren't any Christians left because greed sucked the Christianity out of us. Those with money are perfectly willing to listen to other opinions about religion and god but you can't argue with them about capitalism or free markets, no siree, you can't, because you're immediately branded a god-loathing, autocratic socialist. There's no room for a differing opinions in the entire country, it's sick. Hell, the bosses I worked for, they felt like they've solved life's issues and are living as God intended winners to live and everyone else—the losers, those who aren't living in the best interest of the free market—the poor, the needy, the fucked, they should be shot and shipped off to Satan without passing go or collecting the two hundred dollars that you're supposed to get for passing go; no handouts. Anyway, I never thought my bosses had the balls and the influence to turn their bitching into reality. Boy was I was wrong.

"Look around. You gotta hand it to the rich; they don't just sit around and complain like everyone else, they do something about it, no matter how fucked it is. Look around, son. How was your day? Yep, this time they sure as hell did something about it. Hell, my former bosses advise President Crelli now, so draw whatever conclusions you want, but facts are facts. Everyday, there are fewer and fewer poor so I'm not waiting around because the poor sure as hell aren't going to Disneyland."

"The man's right, Clarke," Whit added. "Pay attention. Mister, you're waiting for your trip to the Last Chance Saloon, aren't you?" The man smiled but said nothing.

"How do you know they won't just kill you?" Clarke asked.

"Assuming that's what I'm here for," the man shook his head, "that's the question, isn't it?" He laughed. "My guess is, either way you need the faith of a gambler? So what do you think, young fellow, do you feel lucky?"

Whit nodded to the old man. "I'm betting on you, friend, and I feel lucky."

The old man looked first at Whit and then Clarke. He took a deep breath and let his breath out slowly watching it cloud in the cold night air. "You might be right and then again, you might not. My name's Herbert Vigorish, you may call me Vig."

They waited with the old man for a few days. The days were boring and the nights were cold and Clarke missed the comfort of sleeping in a car but he had hitched his wagon to Whit and this is where Whit wanted to be.

One day, Vig opened up. "I'm just guessing—like the rest of these folks—but a guy I met in St. Louis told me he knew a guy who lived in a mansion. The guy claimed he had been poor and homeless and was hanging out here when he was picked up by HomeSec. They put him on a special train on a special track that took him to a place in the high mountains north and west of Denver. It was the Last Chance Saloon and he won his future there."

"I knew it!" Whit hollered and slapped Clarke on the back. "Tell us more, Vig."

"The fellow claimed he and hundreds of others were taken to gamble in a glitzy saloon built into a mountainside and in the end, those who won the most were allowed to keep their winnings and more."

Whit was so happy, he knelt down and genuflected. "Thank you Jesus," he said with a big smile on his face. "See, Clarkie boy, I told you to stick with me."

Clarke smiled at Whit but he was also concerned.

"I don't understand why they do it?" Whit and the old man looked at him like the answer was obvious.

"There must be something in it for them is my guess," Whit explained.

"He's right," Vig said. "Why does the government and private enterprise do anything? All they care about are profits. There's a regular nightly broadcast, a kind of private pay reality show that ANGS and others sponsor. They pay for everything. Even the losers get a special surprise so there must be a shit load of money involved. Anyway, this fellow won and so did others. He's living large in St. Louis and I'm going to be the next one to take advantage of it and I don't care why they're doing it."

"How do they choose contestants? It's not like you can write away for tickets."

"Don't rightly know. The guy says there are regular pickups here and at other sites. According to him, there are casinos throughout the country—in the mountains, one in West Virginia, and possibly another in upstate New York but he told me not to quote him."

Whit was ecstatic. "This is it, Clarkie, our ticket to forever."

"Whit, please don't call me Clarkie." Whit looked hurt. "I'll do whatever you think is best, but I'm not a gambler so if either of you win, you'll need a good former CPA. I can help make your money work for you."

Vig shook his head. "I'll keep that in mind, but as a former stockbroker, I feel pretty good about my ability to grow money." Clarke hesitated to ask. If that was the case, why was he in this situation?

Whit was still gloating over this wonderful turn of events. "I'm buying my Dad's business and I'll kick him the hell out. Let's see how he likes it on the street. I might even take my sister in if she makes it worth my while."

"That's sick," Clarke said. "It sounds like it will be every man for himself."

"You're my partner, Clarke, but this is America," Whit replied.

On a cold, clear morning, a couple of days after Vig's revelation, surveillance drones flew overhead. Later in the day, four canvas-covered HOMESEC trucks pulled into the far side of the parking lot while above, helicopters hovered.

"This is it," Whit said excitedly. Then the HomeSec patrols arrived. Some of the people who had been waiting lost faith and fled, but most waited quiet and hopeful. Clarke stood nervously beside a smiling, happy Vig while Whit stared fearfully as the patrols began to herd everyone into the vans. Everything was orderly and efficient and soon all was ready.

Clarke, Whit, and Vig found seats in the back of a truck with about thirty other hopeful poor. All were underdressed and shivering in the cold air. Though they congratulated each other for their good fortune, Clarke remained concerned. Soon, they were in the foothills on the outskirts of Denver where the caravan turned off a main road and followed a rough dirt trail that meandered far up into the mountains to a deserted train depot. Guarded closely by HomeSec personnel, everyone was loaded onto several cars of a small, old-fashioned commuter train. Once inside the train, they found the seats to be plush, though worn and filthy. Clarke sat and relaxed for the first time. Stressed and exhausted, he fell asleep as the train pulled out and headed north to the cheers of the passengers.

At the first lurch to a higher altitude, Clarke woke. Although an avid skier, Vermont had always been Clarke's destination of choice because it was close and more affordable. This was his first opportunity to see high mountain country so he stared out at the snow-covered peaks wondering why he'd ever considered skiing anywhere else.

"God spent more time in Colorado than anywhere," Vig mused.

"It sure is beautiful," Whit responded. "Maybe I'll build a chalet over there." He pointed. "Clarke, you can visit me."

"Your wish is my command, my lord," he joked as he stared out at the wonders of the snow-covered peaks, frozen creeks, evergreens, and aspens as far as he could see.

It was dark when the train screeched to a stop and HomeSec workers shifted the tracks manually so the train could head northwest on what looked like a rickety old abandoned line. Soon they were heading toward the wonderfully promising unknown, a bit troubled by the creaking and swaying of the train.

The train continued up, stopping briefly at the brink of an abyss in the middle of nowhere. Everyone ran to the windows but there was nothing to see except a sheer drop into a bottomless ravine. Clarke looked down, yelped, and stepped back. Whit and the old man laughed. The train then lurched, screeched and labored up a precarious incline to the top of the mountain. Some who were standing fell over trying to get back to their seats, but soon the train leveled off and entered a majestic valley. On the narrow track, thousands of feet above the valley floor, the train chugged slowly upward again.

Clarke was thrilled by this unique experience. The flimsy track was all that stood between him and a frightful plummet and it felt like he was flying above the valley. Instinctively, he and others grasped their seats in fear.

Vig looked out and pointed. "We've made it. There's the saloon."

Sure enough, in the distance, there was a dome of white light and below it were bright yellow, red, blue, and green lights. Everyone scurried to the windows again, this time on the mountain side of the train. They had reached another plateau where a station had been carved into the mountain. They were so high now that Clarke's heart was beating hard and fast and he felt dizzy. A voice crackled to life over the speakers.

"Attention, may we have your attention?" Immediately, the car got quiet. "Welcome to all of you who are seeking your rightful share of the American dream. You have arrived at the great Colorado gold rush of the mid twenty-first century. For those who, through a combination of skill and luck, win your fortune today, the promise of a new tomorrow awaits. We congratulate you on your perseverance and deep belief in our great American ideals. Be proud for your luck has changed and your reward is near."

The car erupted with cheers. Clarke heard the muffled roar from the other cars. Then the speaker continued.

"For those who at the end of this adventure find yourself short of skill or luck, don't despair. Your efforts will be watched by a media audience of almost a billion people worldwide, and like others who came before you, you may be able to parlay that notoriety into fame and fortune and a uniquely American life of unbelievable economic possibility. And for those who reap nothing from this adventure other than the adventure itself, be comforted that America was willing to provide you with this opportunity and you did your best. When your journey is complete, all that we ask is that you spread the good word that great opportunity still exists in America for everybody—even for those who have quit on life or thought life had passed them by—because America is truly the greatest country on the face of the earth, bar none.

"For now, we ask that you remain in your seats until your local celebrity host escorts you inside to begin the registration process. This is very important. Our celebrities are all sweet, young lovelies from local high schools in the area so we insist that you treat them with respect and courtesy. We repeat, you must show restraint, do not accost them or you will lose your opportunity for fame and fortune forever. Good luck to all of you."

For a while, they waited in silence and, like everyone else, Clarke was nervous and impatient. A passenger, seated in the first row, kept everyone abreast on the progress of the other cars as passengers were escorted off the trains and through the revolving doors of the saloon.

Whit slapped him on the back. "Well, Clarke, we did it. We're almost inside. Good luck and thanks for your help."

"What do you think happens inside?"

"Poker, slots, stuff like that. They'll give us credit to gamble with and after I win, I'll live the life I deserve—the one my asshole father denied me."

"You wish, little man," Vig cackled. "I'm born for this. I've been gambling all my life, though usually with other people's money. This is my time. The worm has turned for me. I won't forget you guys, at least not until I win." He smiled.

Clarke remained silent and glum. He knew that he had no chance. He was no gambler—he didn't even know the rules to most games of chance. When he explained that to Whit, Whit tried to comfort him.

"Cheer up," Whit said, "sometimes, not often; lady luck overcomes skill."

"Whit, I think my luck was exhausted a long time ago."

"That's no way to think," Vig pointed out. "You'll ruin the karma for all of us. Think like a winner, be a winner. Think like a loser . . ."

Whit hugged Clarke. "Don't let him get to you. Games of chance are just that. Luck may be all you need. Believe and pray hard to whatever god you believe can help."

Clarke sighed and stared outside. From the train in front, an old woman with dried blood on her forehead staggered into the casino. "Is that the old lady from the garage?"

Whit stared. "I thought you said they killed her."

"She took quite a beating. What a tough old bird. I hope she gets lucky, but . . ."

In unison the three said, "Not too lucky," and they laughed.

A short, chubby, attractive and young blond girl entered their car wearing a one piece bathing suit under an open fur coat.

"Hello gamblers, I'm Stella, your celebrity hostess." Everyone cheered. "When I get to your row, please stand and get in line facing the front of the car. When everyone's ready, we'll go. Ouch!" She turned to the man who'd pinched her and she said out loud, "Seat 3d."

Immediately, guards entered with weapons drawn. Terrified, the man cowered in his seat. He claimed innocence but was dragged, crying, out of the train and through a side door into the saloon.

"What happens to him?" someone yelled.

The hostess replied. "I wish he hadn't done that. He's disqualified and will be shipped somewhere for redistribution and he'll lose his casino privileges, forever. Please, please, everyone, pay attention. When you get inside, each of you will be required to fill out a casino membership card. You will then receive an I.D. card worth five hundred thousand dollars." She had to raise her voice to be heard over the cheering.

"Quiet, please," she demanded. "This is not yours to keep. It's just a stake. Keep your I.D. card with you at all times. You will need it to play and we use it to keep track of your winnings. You will have two hours. At the end, the top two winners will be invited to the CEO Suite to receive their prize. Everyone else will continue gambling, however . . ." she signaled for silence as the cheers drowned her out. ". . . you continue gambling with a reduced stake which you will be allowed to keep when the train returns to take you away."

There were more cheers. "Do we go back to Denver?" someone yelled.

"No," the hostess replied. "You saw the tracks. The train can't turn around here so the next stop is Cheyenne, Wyoming where you may transfer to a train back to Denver if you have enough funds on your card. That brings us to an important point. You must have at least fifty dollars remaining if you want to return to Denver, otherwise, you will be living in Cheyenne until you earn enough to travel. Those are the rules and there are no exceptions. Come with me and remember, you will be on television so you must follow the rules and there must be no non-conformance or you will be disqualified."

Clarke, Whit, and Vig waited patiently. When their turn came, they got in line and entered the casino. Inside it was just like Clarke imagined a casino would look like. Everything was ornate with gold, glitter, and lights flashing everywhere. Loud music was playing and beautiful, scantily-clad women were serving drinks. On various open levels above and below the garish, well-lit casino entrance, hundreds of machines were flashing red, white, and blue. The hostess walked onto the saloon stage, grabbed the microphone, and pulled out a sheet of paper. She read further instructions to them.

"Quiet please. You will sign up at the tables to your left and right. Speak slowly and clearly into the monitors. When you're asked about your dreams and aspirations, be expansive and lie if you must, you are trying to win over an audience. Millions of avid fans are watching, ready to choose their favorite gambler and no one knows why they choose as they do. This is important and should be noted here. You will be participating in games of luck and skill but the odds of winning will improve relative to the votes you get from the national and international audiences. Smile now." She smiled.

"Therefore, it is in your best interest to do everything possible to sell yourself to your audience. I repeat, your chances of winning are based on a sophisticated mathematical formula that improves dramatically for those who become audience favorites. Slow down and read this carefully." She slowed down her reading.

"This is gambling but not gambling alone. This is also reality television, so you must play to the viewing public in ways that you think best and that will translate into votes that will enhance your chances of winning riches forever. In most cases, a good gambler will beat a poor one, everything being equal—just as in life—but a fan favorite has the best chance to win here so play smart but be as charismatic as you can possibly be. Remember, this amounts to competitive theatrics and that is the best chance for most of you to win here so do not constrain yourself. Make the audience love you. Repeat this." She repeated that part of the instructions as well.

"And if you exhibit any behavior that our advertisers believe is detrimental to the economics of their products, the show editors will see to it that you cannot win. So that you know, our audience is primarily made up of girls and women between the ages of twelve and seventy-five who have inherited their wealth or are working within their parent's corporations. They tend to be attention deprived and on the social spectrum from conservative to reactionary, they are the most left leaning, being moderately conservative. These are the people that you must become memorable to. Most of the older ladies have advanced high school degrees while the younger ones have received the equivalent of a middle school education. Still, they have the money to vote and they use it. Keep that in mind. You're not here to make friends; you're working to befriend lonely people who value their ability to spend money to change lives. Make it fun for them or make it pathetic, but make them want to send money to the network in your name. That is what our advertisers demand. How you do it is your choice. We provide no guidance except to say that past winners have done things that, if this wasn't life and death, their parents would be mortified to watch and that's good. You will see a meter on your gaming device that will provide feedback as to how well you are doing. Monitor it, work it, and change your methods accordingly." The hostess waited until everyone had completed the sign up phase before reading the final instructions.

"Everyone, it is time to find your gaming device. You must not push or fight for it will cause disqualification." Clarke rushed with everyone to find an unattended device. "Everyone begins when the last card is inserted into the gaming machine slot. Your cards work any device so the choice is yours. This is a one-hour show so we need about two hours of footage. At the end of two hours, the results will be tabulated and whichever device the winners are currently playing at—that device will flash and sound effects will explode from it. You'll know that you've won and unlike every other American who must work in anonymity to achieve forever, you will have achieved it during this two-hour period and in front of a vast, admiring audience. This will be the most memorable experience of your long life so treasure it. Smile broadly or cry pathetically, but play to your audience." The girl smiled and looked around the room. "Gamblers, good luck to you. Are you ready?" She put her hands up above her head as the crowd of hopefuls shouted, "YES!"

Before she dropped her arms, Clarke who was standing at a devise between Vig and Whit asked Vig, "What game should I play?" But Vig was preoccupied with his own thoughts. He muttered a response.

"Do you have any experience with *Donkey Kong*, or *Mario Brothers*, or maybe *Final Fantasy*? They require the least skill, but my guess is they also have the lowest payout."

Seeing Clarke's confusion, Whit tried to help.

"Do you remember any games from your childhood? Surely you were a game player."

Clarke shook his head. "I played sports."

"Sorry, it looks like your deprived childhood is going to cost you," Whit said. "It seems the games we played as children are the gambling games of today."

"I remember *Centipede*, when I was a kid," Clarke offered hopefully.

"Can't help you there. I never played it."

"What are you playing?"

"*MechWarrior*," Whit said, proudly. "It's really complex, but the bonuses should provide a good pay out. I've won a great deal of money playing it in the past."

"How do you play?"

"It's a . . ." Whit started to answer. "Now's not the time to learn."

"What other choices do I have?" Clarke asked.

The crowd was getting restive as the hostess kept her hands above her head, wavering. There was some cursing due to the delay.

"I don't know what to say, Clarke, pick something and try like hell. Good luck."

With that, they each inserted their cards in their devices and the hostess dropped her arms and screamed. "Let the games begin! Good luck and may forever be a chance worth taking."

Clarke chose the game, *Rome*. He clicked and read the directions. They were very detailed and as he read, he could hear others around him racking up points and cheering or wailing. It was distracting but he read on. The victory condition required that he build a financial army from the outnumbered stockholders in the city of Rome in order to defend against a hostile takeover by various barbaric, socialist Germanic tribes with each level increase in the Roman Stock Market adding to his reward points—while concurrently he had to provide the Holy Church with enough tax revenue so they wouldn't be forced to move to Constantinople. The longer Rome remained the capital of economic Christendom, the more reward points he would receive. Hoping his experience as a CPA would help, Clarke prepared for the barbarian onslaught.

As Clarke played, the man behind him screamed and cursed while banging the game console and demanding an audit while on one side, Whit was sobbing so hard that tears were pooling on the game monitor, blurring his results. He kept wailing something about a guy named 'Murray', and how desperate Whit was to be rich so they could join in a forever partnership.

Almost immediately, Clarke was losing. He wasn't a student of history and never realized how shrewd the Visigoths were with their investment portfolios. Romans seemed naïve or uncaring about barbarian market capabilities and never quite reacted like he expected, and thus his portfolio came up short of expectations. In fact, Roman stockholders seemed to only want to drink and make love and he was not going to watch that while his life went down the drain. To make it more difficult, he could never quite gain their attention. It looked so hopeless for him that at times he was forced to just stare helplessly as Roman citizens were bought out, or sold cheap or maintained inadequate coverage for their short positions and held on too stubbornly. A great many went bankrupt and Rome and Clark were falling. He bought new incentives to change behavior levels and that gave him more control, but as the market makers shifted their allegiance to the Barbarians, the odds of Rome surviving decreased forcing him to apply more leveraged financing as the hour progressed. Inexorably, the Roman Empire began to fail under the influence of the socialist Germanic hordes and he was helpless to turn the tide.

Clarke's despair deepened as he listened to the background noise, the joyous shrieks of victory and the miserable wails of defeat that reverberated off the casino walls. On the gaming device to his left, Vig was doing well, so well that he was delivering a monologue in a great, stentorian voice to his supporters explaining in great detail why and how he was investing his funds and what he would do for their lasting entertainment with the winnings.

Soon, Clarke was resigned to the inevitable defeat, and quiet and glum, he faced divestiture after forced divesture, as Roman landlord after Roman landlord renounced economic Christianity and accepted the Visigothic religion. He watched, forlorn as the streets of his empire turned from capitalist blue to socialist red. Defeat was imminent while all around him, the other contestants were beating on their machines, tearing at their clothes, dancing, singing, sobbing, and ripping their hair, anything to communicate ultimate pathos or joy, soaring confidence or abject defeat, in order to reel in the unseen audience and improve their odds for victory.

Despairing, Clarke remembered the one piece of advice his brother Jake had offered him that seemed sincere. "Clarkie, boy," Jake had often said when they were young, "the only thing a good loser really is, is a loser."

He turned from his monitor to look around. Some—the losers—stared vacant-eyed and morose as they played. Other had ceased to play at all and just stood there defeated. When he turned back, he focused on the reflection from his screen. He saw morose loser's eyes staring back at him.

With more Roman streets turning from blue to red and capitalism only remaining in the guarded bank vaults of the Holy See, Clarke tried valiantly to find a winning level of exuberance, though all he felt was despair. Slack jawed and down to his last proxy vote, he selected a retired CEO—a defrocked priest—to implement his last ditch management strategies and watched hopelessly until, somehow, the tide slowly turned. Street by street and corporation by corporation his free markets recovered. Hopeful now, Clarke put more of his winnings on the CEO-Priest who, at great odds, continued to bamboozle the Visigoths. Seeing his estate grow, he was incredulous, but elated, and he invested more and more and his economic power grew. The CEO-Priest was rolling the Visigoth's big government social programs back and the entrepreneurs were regaining capital. Rome was being saved from yet another communist onslaught.

Clarke was into it now, using CPA tricks to frustrate the barbarians, all the while jumping, spinning, tap-dancing and whooping his way to victory. Soon, as the total victory proposition appeared attainable, he shrieked and bellowed his orders, ruthlessly removing deadbeats, and sending merciless debt collectors after the fleeing Visigoths. For the first time in his life, his body was electric with job satisfaction as he worked. And then, as the clock was winding down, the Vatican Board of Directors cut a deal behind his back with the Ostrogoths and the Vandals, and though he had defeated the Visigoths, just like that, a socialist board was appointed and he was out. Just like that, the tide had turned and he had failed.

When the warning siren sounded signaling a minute remaining, the gates of Rome were thrown open and the socialist horde poured in, redistributing the wealth and diluting the city's assets until they were worthless and the great Roman entrepreneurs fled east to invest again another day in Constantinople.

But for Clarke, all was lost. Rome had fallen and taken his hopes with it.

The siren went off and his monitor went dark. Seventy dollars was the measly value that remained to him, just enough to return to Denver with a little extra to buy a sandwich. He watched as all the other monitors went dark followed by all the lights in the casino. With nothing to look at, he could only focus on his own misery.

He was startled when a monitor in a far dark corner exploded into loud, joyous celebratory sounds and flashing lights. The man whose device it was screamed and raised his hands to the heavens and danced his own special victory jig. Then Vig's monitor sprung to life. He didn't overreact. As a tear slowly rolled down his cheek, he touched his heart with his fist and then raised his fist to the heavens in triumph.

Brokenhearted, Clarke looked for Whit who stood beside him, disconsolate, holding his monitor in a death grip, his forehead leaning against it, tears flowing down where his winnings should have been.

"This is so fucking unfair," Whit said to nobody in particular while choking back tears. "When will I ever get a break? I'm great at this. I should have won. He slammed his fist hard against the monitor, causing it to twist out of alignment. Immediately, a guard moved toward him but Clarke stepped in to prevent a confrontation. A quick kick to the chest thwarted any chance Clarke had to save Whit who collapsed to the floor where the butt of the guard's rifle bludgeoned him. Whit tried to protect himself but when the guard finally left, all Whit could do was sob.

Even battered and sobbing on the floor, Whit complained. "What were the winning scores?" He shouted. Another rifle butt made contact and Whit screamed and quieted. Clarke dropped to the floor and cradled Whit's head in his lap and wiped the blood away. Whit's concerns were picked up by the rest of the gamblers. They chanted. "Show us the winning scores. Show us the winning scores." The cost of losing was so great that in spite of what happened to poor Whit, each participant braved the consequences to stand up for their rights and make sure there were no mistakes.

Lights throughout the casino began to flash and on the floor above them, a man in a business suit and tie stepped out of an office. Illuminated by a spotlight, he spoke to the crowd of indignant indigent.

"People, may I have your attention! People, these machines have been audited by the firm of *Sanderson and Sons of Chicago*. There can be no mistakes. Let's have no hard feelings. The crowd booed and began shaking the gambling devices until guards appeared above with their weapons at the ready. In the now quieted crowd, Clarke watched in envy as Vig and the other winner, pumping their fists in victory, smiling and elated, were escorted up to the offices above.

"There are two winners, today," the man in charge continued. "That is irrefutable, the public has decided. Each of these fortunate people will receive their fortune per the rules and each will be relocated to the location of their desire."

There was more booing on the floor.

"Quiet please. I have good news for all of you. It has been determined that this performance, today, is the episode with the highest call in dollar ratings in the history of the game show, The Last Chance Saloon. Because each of you contributed to this new record, you will all receive another opportunity to increase your wealth. We must clear this floor for the next contestants but on the floor below the one you are standing on, there is another gambling room. The stakes aren't as high, nor are the rewards, but for many it will be enough. And even if you don't win downstairs, don't despair. Our advertisers are good, kind people and because you have entertained a record audience, and by so doing, provided our advertisers with a economic boost, they have agreed to stake each of you to an additional five hundred dollar stipend as you leave. You see, you can't lose."

Though falling far short of his hopes, Clarke was pleased because any money would help. He stared at his friend. The blood from Whit's wound had slowed and he had a smile on his face.

"Whit, did you hear?" They slapped hands. There was another announcement.

"Everyone, please follow the blinking lights. Move in an orderly fashion to the freight elevator that will take you to your future."

Whit was groggy but insisted on continuing so Clarke helped him to the elevator. They were the last of the losers to get on and it was tightly packed. They squeezed onto the chicken-wire-enclosed elevator and when the door closed, they were squeezed even more. As he wiped blood off on his sleeve, Whit looked at a sign on the far side of the elevator, which stated, "Exit this way", and he complained.

"My fucking luck won't quit. We're on the wrong side of this damn thing and by the time it unloads, I'll have lost valuable gambling time." Clarke smiled. His friend was recovering.

The lights went out and the cage lurched downward in total darkness. There was a screech and a sudden stop and someone inside screamed, causing some nervous laughter. The descent continued, smoother now, and everyone in the confined cage remained silent so all that could be heard was the whir of the elevator's motor. When the elevator stopped again, abruptly, and the lights didn't go on, there was some laughter but more complaining. Clarke heard the motor restart but the elevator didn't move. Growing concerned, he grabbed the chicken wire. Indiscernible in the darkness, his hand was being forced, slowly across the wire. Something was moving, but moving where? He felt pressure on his back. The reinforced chicken wire wall was pressing him forward, pushing the people in the already crowded cage tighter. Then he heard the wall on the other side of the elevator spring open and there were screams that seemed to echo throughout the cavern.

"What the fuck? What do you see, Clarke?" Whit yelled above the bedlam.

Clarke could see nothing. "It's too dark," he yelled over the screaming, "What's going on." No one responded. In panic, the occupants kept screaming while the cage rocked dangerously as the people in front tried to push back. The pressure from the cage door behind him forced him to press against the people in front and there were even more screams. The screams were long as the abyss was deep and they created an eerie Doppler effect as people disappeared into the depths below with continuous horrible echoes that extended beyond their lives.

Clarke was frantic. *What had gone wrong? Where was the saloon security team? Why wasn't anyone helping them?* Inexorably, the wall pressed on him, forcing him against those in front who were desperately pressing back. Clarke thought to turn and push against the encroaching wall but he was too constricted to move.

"They're falling," Whit yelled. "Push harder, Clarke, push harder."

In the chilled darkness, Clarke couldn't see, but he leaned his back against the slowly advancing wall to no avail. Even with everyone pressing against him, the wall moved inexorably forward. At this altitude, his breath was coming in gasps, but still he pushed. Then his feet slipped and he was being scraped against the wire by the moving wall with only his jacket protecting him from being ripped and torn. Suddenly, the pushing stopped and real panic set in. Hysterical people began climbing and jumping onto the people behind them, screaming as they tried to save themselves.

"Is there anywhere to go?" he yelled to Whit.

"No," Whit yelled back. "It's too dark and we're packed too tight." The screams were getting louder as he and Whit were pushed closer and closer to the open front and the abyss. He found traction by digging his heels in against the wire and he tried, with all his strength to push back against the invading wall but he gave up because he wasn't making a difference. Suddenly, there were a great number of screams and the pressure seemed to ease. There were fewer people in the elevator now. But still the screams of those falling into the abyss continued to echo, each stopping abruptly to be replaced by yet another blood-curdling scream. Those few remaining in the cage scrambled and shrieked, fighting for purchase and their lives. He punched at the elevator wall hoping to find a weak spot but the wire wall was reinforced with two-by-fours on the outside and so it would only bend.

And still he was pushed into those in front, which sent them over the edge to a horrible death below. When the last few in front of him were scraped into the abyss, it was only Clarke and Whit remaining on a narrow ledge. In the unearthly quiet and with no time to think, each balanced precariously, looking down into the dark death below. Clarke kept himself from falling by grasping the chicken wire, but the moving wall cut into his fingers and forced him to let go before his fingers were amputated. His feet felt the unseen edge and he was truly frightened. Whit's hands grabbed for Clarke's coat and in a death grip, held on, as they both fought against gravity to avoid the void that waited below.

"Hold tight, Clarke. Don't let go, I don't want to die!" Whit screamed as the wall invaded the last bit of floor space available and he fell. His hands slid down from Clarke's jacket to his pant legs and there was nothing Clarke could do to help as he held on for dear life. The added weight of his friend caused Clarke to teeter on the edge with Whit dangling out over the abyss, his weight dragging them both toward certain death.

When the last of the floor disappeared, Clarke screamed as his feet slipped off but instead of falling, his chest tightened and breathing became difficult. His coat belt had caught between the side of the cage and the moving wall and he was dangling above the darkness, with air slowly being squeezed from his lungs. In the pitch dark, as his belt slowly crushed him, pain generated bright flashes of blue-white light before his eyes. Below, Whit clawed at his pant leg, adding even more strain. Alive only by his coat, Clarke's body spun out over the abyss, his legs flailing with Whit attached as he struggled to remove his jacket so that he could breathe, knowing once it was off, he'd plunge to his death.

From below, he felt blessed release and brief joy before realizing as the weight suddenly lifted and the strain on his arms lightened that the agonizing scream that followed was that of his friend. Whit's grip had slipped and his scream went on and on, and the echo lingered in his mind as if it would last forever.

Without the added weight of his friend, he worked his belt loose and unfastened his coat. Holding it as tightly as he could, he spun out of one sleeve and swung out precariously below the cage, dangling by the coat sleeve alone. Frantically, he reached out with his free hand for something to grab. In the dark, his hand contacted with something. It was tantalizing but he couldn't quite grasp it before swinging away.

As he dangled, he noticed that the screaming had stopped. In absolute darkness, there was total silence. His arms were burning with fatigue as he swung back and felt for whatever it was he touched the first time. He grasped it and held on, but only briefly. Losing his grip, he screamed as he swung away again. He was losing the feeling in his arms but willed himself to hold on for one last swing. This time, he grabbed with his hand, found purchase, and let go of his coat with his other hand. He took a deep breath and pressed himself up until both hands had a death grip on a bar. He held on for dear life in the dark, frigid, stench-filled cavern. His heart was beating rapidly and his breath was coming in spurts and the cold, the acrid smell of death was so strong in the thin air that he coughed and almost released his grip.

Chapter 23
Denver, CO.—2037

In the frigid darkness, Clarke clung to a metal rod that was vibrating now as the cage gears reset above him and the cage returned to the upper floor. When the gears stopped, all was silent once again. Fearing numbness and the loss of strength in his arms, he had no choice so he swung, like a gymnast, trying to hoist a leg up over the bar. When that failed, he fought through panic—and the pain in his arms and shoulders—and with his hands, he inched blindly along the bar praying that he was moving in a life-saving direction. He silently willed his hands forward and endured the pain. In the cold, the sweat on his palms froze his hands to the bar on contact forcing him to move quicker than he wanted so he wouldn't rip his skin off. It was tempting to hope that there was respite from this pain in a short drop below, but the memories of the duration of the echoed screams drove him onward.

In the dark, his mind detected subtle changes. There was a dim light source at a distance just below him so he continued to inch in that direction until his hands confronted an obstacle, a vertical post. He felt around it with his lead hand, grunted and swung that hand around to grab the rod on the other side of the post. In the cold damp cavern, the sweat that poured down his face caused his eyes to burn and he tried, unsuccessfully to blink it away. In the silence, he imagined moaning and pleas for help coming from below but he refused to be distracted as he continued working his way through the pain toward hopeless salvation.

Finally, his feet touched something. He inched closer until his entire body touched the cavern wall. Exhausted, his muscles screamed for lack of oxygen and his fingers begged for release. He fought it and walked his feet up the wall until they were level with the rod that supported him.

The increased pressure on his shoulders and the blood rushing to his head almost caused him to let go as he tried to wrap his feet around the rod to take pressure off his arms. His quivering muscles were becoming unresponsive so with his feet now encircling the rod, he tried to roll his body over the bar but lacked the strength. Stifling a scream, he made one last attempt and pressed his body until an elbow hooked around the bar and he rolled onto a precarious perch on top of the bar. Exhausted and holding on for dear life, he allowed himself only a groan and a shudder while his muscles spasmed. He tried to find a position that would allow him to relax enough to regain some strength, but after all the effort, he feared he would relax too much and roll off to his death. With another great effort, he wrapped his feet tightly around the rod, released his hands and arms and balanced on his chest. His arms shook uncontrollably and his numb fingers tingled painfully as he concentrated on not blacking out.

Physical relief brought the fear that he couldn't maintain his balance. He shook his fingers and his arms, trying to bring them back and then he surveyed his perch by patting around, evaluating. Finally, he held on and slowly sat up on the rod, his back against the rock wall, his lungs rasping for air, wondering how life could get worse. The chasm below was an immediate and effective reminder.

He lost track of time and twice he had to catch himself from rolling off his perch. Exhausted, he fought sleep, which was no easy matter in the darkness. Reality became nothing more than holding on. He didn't know how long he was there and when he first saw it, he thought he was dreaming. Just below his perch, a dim, yet blinding light flashed, causing him to unbalance briefly. A door opened up, and two men stepped through, silhouetted in the light.

"Two more to go, Jorge," one said to the other. "And then we can head to the slopes and the lodge for some brewskis."

"I can't wait, Dwight, I hate this part of the job. It stinks and it's fucking creepy."

"Barely worth the premium pay. Let's get out of here. They haven't dumped the chemicals yet." With that, the men left and the door closed.

In that brief light, he'd caught a glimpse of his escape. The light had dispersed quickly, but it left a burn spot in his retina and it accentuated the abject darkness of the abyss but it had illuminated a small maintenance platform cut into the cavern just a few yards below him. He had been fortunate to find the steel latticework supporting the elevator system that attached it to the cavern.

When he was certain the men were gone, he guessed at the height and jumped, landing awkwardly. He screamed, in pain, the cavern echoing the sound but he quickly stifled himself although the echo took a long time to dissipate. In the dim light emanating from a door at the top of the metal steps, he surveyed the platform and then silently limped up to the door on wobbly legs. By the time he reached the door at the top of the stairs, his ankle felt better. Cautiously, he opened the door. With misbehaving muscles, even the act of opening it was difficult.

On the other side was a narrow, empty corridor with a long flight of stairs that led to a locker room. He entered and searched it, finding a few towels that he used to dry his perspiration. He took what clothes he could that fit and whatever currency he could find and continued to search until he found a winter jacket. He put it on, stuffed the money into the pockets and headed out. By the door, he noticed a brass plaque hanging. Something on it caught his eye so he stopped to read it.

This plaque is awarded to members of the Federal Emergency Relief Administration Region L, (FERA-L) *for their outstanding quality, discipline, and loyalty, by the President of the United States. You have the thanks of a grateful President.*

The plaque was signed by Andrew M. Crelli, President of the United States and J. Jacob Jackell, Secretary, Federal Emergency Relief Administration, Region L (Fera-l).

Mesmerized by the signature yet unable to fully comprehend it, he started laughing. Then, with the intent of beating the plaque to death as a substitute for what he wanted to do to his brother, he grabbed a hammer that was lying nearby and swung. After the first loud ding and the reverberation it generated through the halls, he stopped for fear of being discovered. For all his charm, Jake wouldn't escape retribution for this, but this wasn't the way and now wasn't the time. Seething and frustrated, he put the hammer down and snuck out of the locker room and into the deserted hallway.

The fact that his brother was in charge of this hell was beyond contemplating, but to survive he had to put that behind him and focus on his current dilemma. At the end of the hall, he opened the door a crack.

Below, he saw the casino floor, and more unfortunate people who were being escorted inside. He thought back to when he had arrived. There had been another door, a revolving door. One of the men on the train, the one who'd broken the rules, was escorted through it. He had to find it.

He walked down another corridor until he saw a control room with a large monitor displaying the casino below. In a far corner, two men and a woman were sitting in a side room, eating and talking. He entered the control room and looked around. On a terminal were the instructions he had read and signed when he was getting ready to gamble. With the workers unaware of his presence, he typed new instructions, "Get out. They're going to kill you!"

He pressed the 'enter key' and left, scurrying down another corridor where he came to the revolving door near the front of the Casino. He tried to go through it but it only allowed people in. He took a deep breath and caught a whiff of the fresh cold mountain air rushing in, but he couldn't reach it. Suddenly, sounds of chaos emanated from the casino floor so he hid in the shadows as the main door opened and armed guards coursed through in full battle gear. For what little benefit it might do those poor souls, he was glad he'd left that message.

After the last guard ran in through the main door, he sprinted as fast as he could, hit the door with his shoulder before it closed, driving it wide open, and he tumbled outside. The cold air seared his parched throat as he searched frantically for a means of escape. At the far end of the station platform, a train was leaving, heading north. He gathered his remaining strength and staggered along the platform before jumping onto the final car as the train accelerated away from the station. Exhausted, he curled up against the biting cold wind as the Last Chance Saloon faded into the distance.

Even though freezing, he didn't enter the railcar in case guards were present. But when the sun slipped below the snow-capped peaks, it grew colder and shivering, he had no choice but to crawl into the car and hide. He found a place under a seat and slept until he felt the train slow as it approached Cheyenne and a new set of problems. He struggled to the door, opened it and jumped from the train. He rolled in the snow, stopping in some high reeds where, fatigued, he closed his eyes and listened to the mournful sound of the death train pausing to reload. Exhausted, he fell asleep.

When he awoke, it was morning. He checked his coat pockets and found a snack and some currency. Maybe his luck was changing. His entire body was sore but he was able to walk and it didn't take long to decide on a destination. He would head for Abilene, the Underground Railroad, and Canada. As he walked in the bitter cold, his hands deep in borrowed pockets, his body bent into the wind as he tried to remember enough geography to get him there. All he knew was east; he needed to go east, so he headed into a winter sun that provided light but no heat. He was free, or at least as free as he could hope to be. With memories of Whit still fresh in his mind, he trudged along in sorrow through the deep snow.

It was exhausting, working his way through the snow so fearing recapture even though most roads were sparsely traveled, he walked them anyway. His hands were numb and he couldn't protect them. He needed them to balance as he lurched forward. Still, he walked undisturbed for days and that was the important thing. And though it was frigid, fortunately there was no new snow to slow him down further. He avoided Fort Collins and other nearby towns remembering what Whit had said about his chances of receiving help or sustenance in these isolated, frightened villages. From time to time he heard the sound of a train but never saw one until he reached Holyoke.

It was past dusk and he was at a train crossing. When he stepped onto the track, he felt a vibration so he waited, hoping he could steal a ride. Finally, in the distance, a dim red light appeared and grew rapidly. He hid in nearby bushes, waiting as the reddish eye got larger but he couldn't see the train itself or hear it until suddenly, it flashed by, silent like the wind. He prepared to run and jump onboard but froze instead. It wasn't a train, not like any he'd ever seen. It was sleek and shiny black, like the exoskeleton of an insect. But there was more. From its streamlined segments, large, bent, black shiny metallic-like legs protruded, making it appear like immense locusts flashing by in a line. When it passed, Clarke ran onto the track to stare but the train had disappeared silently into the night. Only the slight hum of the track told of its existence.

He tried to sleep that night but he was kept awake by nightmares of a train coming alive, leaving the track to hunt him down.

The following morning, he found a train more to his liking and hopped aboard. Before entering the next town, the train slowed as guards checked each car. He jumped off and walked around the town to wait for another train. He continued this way heading generally east and the days and nights passed without him spotting the black train again though it remained to haunt his dreams.

Starving now, he hoped he was far enough away from the Last Chance Saloon to risk human contact. Finally, exhausted, he entered a small town on the Nebraska border. At the general store, he tried to purchase provisions but when he paid for them with his currency, he knew he was in trouble.

"Mister," the clerk said. "You think we're hicks here 'cause we're in the middle of nowhere? We have first-rate technology; the kind business says we need, so your currency's no good here anymore. You're required to pay through your PID."

Clarke shrugged and acted like he didn't understand so reluctantly the clerk allowed him a few things and took his currency.

He continued to walk and ride, skipping town after town until he ran out of supplies again at McCook. There, he headed to the bank.

"Can I help you?" the bank manager asked, clearly disgusted by the unkempt appearance of a stranger.

"I'd like to give a gift to a friend. Can I get a debit card?"

The bank manager smiled condescendingly. "Sir, nobody uses debit cards anymore. We prefer to transfer funds from PID to PID and there you are in luck. The bank is running a special on PID-to-PID transactions that will also qualify you for an adjustable rate mortgage. We have great rates right now and homes are not only cheaper, they're cheaper than ever before. Would you like to see some? I'm a realtor, too. This is a great time to invest in America and America is more than willing to invest in you."

"I'd prefer a debit card, please," Clarke said, obviously not interested.

"How about a savings account? You can earn a free ski trip to Colorado if you transfer fifteen hundred into your account." Again, Clarke declined and the bank manager acquiesced. "May I see identification, sir?"

Lacking any, he bolted from the bank—and the town—and continued east. This time he checked out abandoned farmhouses when he passed nearby, searching for identification that would help him to acquire a PID. It was dusk and he was in need of sleep when he surveyed a farmhouse from a distance. When he was sure it was empty, he entered and searched until he found a small bag with currency and an old work visa that would have to suffice if he could convince someone he was Cilveria Rodriguez, the name on the visa. That night, he wrapped himself in old towels and rags and slept in a bed for the first time since Philly. Even though it was just an old, stained, lumpy mattress, he didn't care. He slept, fitfully, once again dreaming of huge, sleek, jet-black locusts chasing after him.

Days of trudging through snow near starvation brought him to another bank, this one in Oberlin near the Kansas border. Here, he was allowed to open a savings account for which he received a coffee maker and managed to convince the branch manager to provide him with a debit card. After disposing of the coffee maker, he headed to the general store where he bought a backpack and supplies. Then, he was off again.

It was still winter and the nights were cold, but during the days, the sun began to do its job and he was warmed as he walked and rode trains through northern Kansas, heading in the general direction of Abilene. He passed the town of Minneapolis, near Salina, and the signs told him his long ordeal was almost over. As he continued east, sleep was still difficult as his nightmares continued, but none of the trains he saw were anything like the terrifying shiny black train of his dreams.

He was just south of Abilene and it was dark when he had jumped off a train before the local law enforcement could discover him. Far off, on the horizon, he saw his goal; the lights of Abilene were visible. He found a grove of trees near the train tracks, kicked the snow away to make a bed and settled in only to be awakened by another nightmare. With a sense of foreboding, he crawled to the edge of the grove and under a full moon, watched the tracks disappear into the distance. He turned to go back to sleep when he saw a red orb in the distance and he began to sweat. Approaching was the monster of his dreams.

The red light and the train got closer. It slowed, and then stopped without a sound. He crawled forward to get a better look. Even in the cold, he began to sweat. Now that he had a good look at it, the train truly looked like a series of large locusts with shiny black exoskeletons. He was startled and almost screamed when suddenly the elongated black legs on each segment unfolded and began to dig deep trenches perpendicular to the track. Then the legs finally retracted, the train lurched forward slowly. In the light of the moon, what happened next was so horrendous that Clarke forgot to breathe or even blink. It was a memory that rivaled the death screams from inside the darkened cavern and yet another memory seared into his brain that he would never forget. Segments of the railcars lifted off and then some kind of conveyer appeared, tilted and shot human bodies into the freshly dug trenches. The segments then returned to their original position and once again the train inched forward and the legs unfolded again, this time to bury the bodies by covering the trench. This continued throughout the night as Clarke watched, too stunned to move, until the last of the bodies had been covered over. Silently, the train lurched forward and then sped away leaving Clarke alone as a witness.

In disbelief, he ran down to the track to investigate. No sooner had he made contact with it than an alarm went off and the track around him illuminated. Scared, he bolted back toward the grove to hide while in the distance, a yellow light appeared far down the track and closed on him rapidly. Soon two more lights appeared from the area near the town. The light on the track stopped first and two vehicles roared out into the night cutting him off from the grove so he ran searching for a way to escape as the vehicles in the distance closed on him as well.

The lights converged and he could see them now, four all terrain vehicles, racing over the rough terrain to cut him off. Exhausted, he crossed a small bridge and stopped to consider where it was safe to flee. The cars had cut off his escape over the bridge leaving him only one choice. He jumped off the overpass into the blackness below. About ten feet down, his feet hit thin ice, and then broke through to water. He was up to his waist in freezing water, struggling to free himself before he was caught. He slogged his way close to the bank, breaking up the ice as he went, and pulled himself up onto the bank just as lights from the chasing vehicles' lamps lit up the creek. Fighting fatigue and trying not black out, he ducked behind a fallen tree, shivering from the cold water.

"Hey, Pigsy, do you see him?" someone shouted.

"I'm looking," said another. "Was one of them alive? That's really creepy. I mean someone digging out. They don't pay me enough to go after zombies and shit."

"Don't be stupid, Pigsy, they're not zombies. Everyone is certified dead before they get here. At least they've always been dead before."

"God, I hope so. I'll never sleep again if they're burying them alive now. I can't keep doing this. They never said I'd . . ."

"Shut up Pigsy, the pay's good and without it, remember, you'd be on that train. This is clearly an intruder, a *Waster*, no doubt. The bad news is that according to FERA rules, we're required to kill him if he resists. If he don't resist, Judge O. will have him killed after the trial for sure."

Clarke clenched the log tightly as the bright lights continued to span the creek.

"Pigsy, I called it in. The Reverend Major says we have to go in and find him."

"Boss, I'm not going in there. It's dark and cold . . . and besides, the people . . . I'll puke. Let's just stake it out and catch him in the morning."

"No can do, Pigsy. Orders are orders."

With that, Clarke heard the men open the trunk of their vehicle. Soon they were on the bank in odd-looking outerwear, looking for a way into the stream.

Clarke left the shelter of the log and ran, stumbling into the creek. Almost immediately, light beams located him. He dove into the frigid water, surfacing undetected and traipsed on. He didn't go far before the beams caught him again so he dove under the ice and moved toward the shore, where he lay, holding onto a branch, shivering in the icy muck on the bank. He looked up. The moonlight provided just enough illumination so that he could see his surroundings, and a scream escaped his lips before he could stifle it.

Above him on the eroding bank, were body parts. Appendages, bones, people. Dead people. Some still with flesh and markings, a tattooed anchor, brilliant white teeth, an earring, a crucifix. Mostly there were skeletons and it wasn't a branch that he was holding, but an elongated femur. The flashlights were on him now. Trembling, he stood and ran in terror along the narrow bank, trying to avoid the lights while trying to shake all memory from his mind. When the men started shooting, he plunged back into the water and tried to swim away. At that point, the creek forked. He chose the deeper fork and staggered, numbly through the frigid water. Behind him, he could hear the men chasing him. Above him he heard the cars that had been added to the chase.

The creek widened and the water became shallower. He slogged through until the beams of light reappeared. When the creek forked again, he took the narrower section and sank below the surface. He fought his way back, coughing and sputtering up foul-tasting water and then he grabbed at some branches, pulling himself out of the creek to rest on what appeared to be a beaver dam. Vomiting the acrid creek water as he lay there trembling, he looked up. Damn the moonlight! He screamed again and burrowed his head deep in the muck to avoid seeing what was all around him.

That was where the men found him. They pried his hands from the death grip he had on the decaying bones of a child, her body parts, even in the cold, crawling with maggots and larvae.

He woke in jail wearing someone's dirty clothes but he was warm under a thin blanket. At first, the warmth caused him to smile but then the visions of last night reappeared and once again, he tried to vomit but came up dry.

"What do we have here?" the sheriff smiled though the bars. "Cilveria Rodriguez. Well, Cilveria, good morning and welcome to America. It says you're from Guadalajara. Is that right?"

He struggled to explain. "No. I was . . . I was traveling with Cilveria. He took everything I had and cut out on me."

"Everything but her identification," the sheriff said, emphasizing the word 'her'.

"Yes, Mr. Sheriff, she did."

"That was foolish of her. So you aren't this Rodriguez girl?"

"No, sir. My name is Jack . . . son, Clarke Jackson. I'm sorry if I inconvenienced you and the others. I understand if I'm not welcome here and I'll leave immediately."

"I hope you don't think we're being unfriendly, but in these times, you can't be too careful."

"No, I understand completely. But you have nothing to worry about from me. I won't say anything or trouble you any longer."

"What would you say if you had to say something?"

"No, I didn't mean anything. I didn't see anything. I have nothing to say."

"And you don't have a PID."

"Cilveria and I ran out of gas a while back. It was late, I fell asleep. When I woke, I was alone in the car and everything was missing."

"So you want to report a crime and you don't have a PID."

"No, no crime," Clarke said. "She's long gone and I've been walking for days. She could be anywhere."

"If she's done something illegal, she won't be free very long. I'll contact HOMESEC."

"No, that won't be necessary. You folks shouldn't trouble yourselves. I'll leave and won't cause you any more problems."

"That's not possible."

"Why?" Clarke pleaded. After all he'd been through, he felt like crying.

"A stranger out here with no PID. There will be a trial, of course, so we can set the record legal. You understand."

"A trial? No, why? I was minding my own business. What'll happen to me?"

"This is America so don't be scared. If what you say is true, the trial will proceed by the book and it'll be fair—maybe cruel in the end, maybe—but always fair. Judge Ohmpere will be officiating but the trial itself is Web-based and collaborative. It's my job to read you your rights, limited though they may be. You choose your defense attorney from those who apply after reading your case on the Internet. Since you have no value, the pickings will be a bit sparse but, hey, you might get lucky. Sometimes, real good lawyers prowl the web searching for interesting cases. Mostly, avid gamers apply because with trials like yours, they earn power points towards prizes and more abilities. You won't get a JD, but many have acquired significant legal skills in previous trials while accumulating power points. Some put on remarkable defenses without formal training.

"That's the kind of stuff that makes America great. We have so much talent and opportunity. Now on the flip side, it's been known to happen that seven-year-olds playing around bid to become lawyers just for the fun of it but that's rare and Judge Ohmpere will insure you get a proper defense. The Judge chooses a prosecutor from the Internet. On our town's budget, we can't afford the best prosecutors but our regulars have a pretty good track record."

The sheriff thought he was being helpful. Clarke just stared through the bars.

"Web-based case research takes about an hour and each side presents evidence for maybe another fifteen minutes. Once both sides have had their say, Judge Ohmpere deliberates and writes his opinion, which he files on the Internet. Up to four randomly selected oversight judges, depending on the amount of funds involved—and these are professionals, not gamers—they review the proceedings and the Judge's decision and write their opinion of the Judge's decision. A consensus verdict is recorded and the Judge announces sentencing.

"We have one final control to ensure all is square. After sentencing, the decision is sanctioned by a jury of your Internet peers as determined randomly from anyone who happens to take an interest in your case. The votes are tabulated and sentencing is confirmed, usually within the hour. In rare circumstances, and I don't think it'll happen in your case, a mistrial can be declared and we start over."

"That sounds really complicated and expensive for what I've done," Clarke thought about it for a moment. "Sheriff, what have I done?"

"Until the case is decided, it is premature to identify the crime because, well, there might not have been a crime and you don't want it—whatever it was—on your permanent record. Anyway, freedom has its financial burdens, and everything will be determined at the trial. Keep in mind the service you will provide to the community. Whether you are found innocent or guilty, independent young legal minds receive experience points that qualify them for more complex cases and often some wonderful prizes. Their decisions tend to be fairer and it's a lot less expensive than back in the old days when progressive trial lawyers were destroying the American judicial system. As a side benefit to offset the legal costs of your trial, we accept advertising on your personal trial webpage. Believe me; except for your life, you have nothing to worry about."

"Except for my life? But I didn't do anything."

"May or may not be true, but I'm duty bound to tell you that death is an option."

"Can't I just go free?"

"I'm sorry, Mr. Jackson, there are many possibilities but freedom isn't one. Should you be exonerated, there is still your lack of wealth and PID to deal with."

Distraught, Clarke settled back on his cot as the Sheriff left. He spent the night worrying and slept little. The next morning Judge Gerald Ohmpere arrived at his cell. The Judge was a short, thin, well-dressed balding man with a pencil-thin mustache and he was all business. The proceedings moved along quickly and by lunch, the trial was over and by dinner, he was declared guilty by an Internet jury of his peers and sentenced to death, without appeal.

Facing execution without hope, anxious, and emotionally spent, Clarke was lying on his cot, staring up at the ceiling when Judge Ohmpere appeared again at his cell.

"Well, well, well, Mr. Jackson, how are you?" The judge was smiling. "At this point, you probably have no objection if I call you Clarke, Mr. Jackell?"

Incredulous he grasped at hope. Somehow his asshole brother had come through. He was being rescued. He sat up expectantly. "How did you . . . why did you withhold that at the trial?"

"It had no bearing," the Judge explained. "Frankly, if the jury knew who your brother is, you would have been drawn and quartered. Isn't it ironic, by his absence and exclusion, your brother may have saved your life?"

Confused, Clarke grabbed the cell bars and squeezed. The term 'saved your life' was promising. "I don't understand."

"According to government records, Mr. Jackell, you were captured in a raid in Denver and quite effectively disappeared. These are tough times but even in these times, dead men are outside my jurisdiction."

Clarke was mystified. What was the Judge saying? Was this a good thing?

"You're saying I'm not going to die?" The judge was silent on that matter. "Your Honor, I've been through so much. Have you heard of the Last Chance Saloon?"

The Judge smiled. "As a matter of fact, yes. Much like the Underground Railway, the stock market always appreciating, and free enterprise, it's an American myth—a story that provides a modicum of faith for those who best operate buttressed by fantasy."

"But it's no myth. I was there and I was lucky to survive. I don't want to die, not here, not now, and not for no reason. Why do I have to be a victim?"

"That's a great question that should have been asked generations ago. Mr. Jackell, there have to be victims. That's how Capitalism works."

"But . . . but what law did I break?"

"You broke no law, you broke the most important commandment of the rigid theology that drives America to excess, the religion that has always ruled America since it's inception, the religion of Capitalism—Thou shall not waste. You have and therefore you die."

"I could get a job," he said, hopefully.

"You say that yet like all *Wasters*, you didn't. It is the law, Mr. Jackell and the law is there to protect society from what it fears most."

"The law? Our government runs a killing operation in the Colorado Mountains—and in other places. Is that the law?" He told the judge his story.

The Judge seemed unconvinced. "Why should I believe a dead man?"

"Maybe in Kansas," Clarke said as he gripped the bars tightly, "nothing's wrong, but throughout the country, people are being rounded up and exterminated for no reason other than lack of productivity. What law is that? People are being murdered! If there was work available, they would be contributing assets."

"The law you ask about, my fine criminal, is the Circle of Life. There is no more to be said."

Confounded and exhausted his head ached. "I'm tired, your honor. I've been through too much. I don't want to die. I don't know why you're here but would you please just leave me alone."

"Mr. Jackell, I want to help you," the Judge said. "I do, sincerely. And I wish I could help more. Yes, there is something wrong in Kansas, just like in the rest of the country. As citizens, we allowed our government, no, we enabled our government; we acceded to the rich and powerful who made our government their government. We gave to them what we, the people, should have kept for ourselves—the power to make and enforce decisions. While we were busy raising our families and living our lives, having fun and facing responsibilities, we forgot one of the most important responsibilities of the governed and those who took power had only passing interest in us, because we didn't care to make them interested so they expended effort to confuse, diffuse, and divert our attention so they could do what they wanted. They brought forth sophisticated media which allowed our citizens to fantasize about a better or different life or to fritter away valuable time by playing games, as we let them raise our children for us, allowing them to give our children their standards while we endured each and every day working as if that, and not our lives and our future with our children, weren't our primary responsibilities. We took our eye off the prize—responsible freedom—and they took our prize away."

"I don't care . . . I . . ."

"No, Mr. Jackell, you do care you've just been trained not to. When our government went bad, few protested and nothing was rectified. At best, some of us took sides against the self-serving media and professional-politician-types, but we only used the words we were taught to rationalize or condemn their behavior feeling satisfied that we'd done our part to keep our republic strong. But government, Mr. Jackell, isn't some nuisance to endure while we live our lives; it's an essential part of that life and our future. We in Kansas and around the country, we allowed ourselves to be convinced that governance was a job for others so it became a place for graft and greed. What else could it be in a free market capitalist, win-lose society? The people created a vacuum and fools rushed in to profit from it and they became the professional politicians that the wealthy and powerful paid to do their bidding. Some railed against power, but none spoke truth to it, regardless what they claim, and we all did far, far too little.

"Mr. Jackell, are you a family man?"

Clarke shook his head.

"Maybe you'll understand this anyway. If we as parents never trust our children with strangers why then did we trust strangers to control our lives, and the lives of our children? Why did parents ignore that responsibility? Why did they allow strangers at all levels to teach our children what it means to be a responsible adult? I'll tell you why. Most Americans are required to work so relentlessly hard in order to survive and maybe prosper that we became lazy outside of work and too distracted. To gain time and to hide our embarrassment, we made a bargain with the devil using our children as payment. Now, our children are grown and they accept so much more than we should have and we live in fear and regret and worse, we live in denial."

Clarke was weary. "Sir, it doesn't matter. I'm going to die."

"Clarke, you're a decent man but you're asleep. You've also been selfish and you've wasted your life on yourself. Look around you. This is where that lifestyle has taken you. There is redemption. You have a story to tell. Tell it and make a difference in your life and in the lives of others. Tell what's happened to you and tell it true and fair and maybe someday you'll tell it to someone who'll be so outraged that he will do something about it."

"I don't understand," Clarke pleaded, "How?"

"There is good fortune here. HomeSec believes you are dead so they won't search for you. Go. Go now and don't waste this chance—consider it a gift that you have yet to earn. You've seen what the world is becoming. You've lived through something a great many formerly free American citizens have died from. It's time. It is time to do your part to correct the errors caused by your selfishness and inaction. I can save your life, but only you can give it meaning.

"The time has come, Clarke, for you to become necessary in other people's lives because only then will you give your life value. I set you free. Go and tell your story to everyone you meet. Help them understand. Learn from their experiences and pass that on as well. If they don't want to hear you, make them listen. It will not be easy and it will be dangerous, but you must make them believe or those who die while you live will remain unconsecrated and that will be on you. Think of those poor souls and help us put a stop to this. Freedom wasn't lost in a day and we must win it back a day at a time."

Chapter 24
Presque Isle, MI.—2072

Clarke finished his tale and stared off into some distant space. Appalled at yet another story of a victim, Gil sat quietly and allowed the old man time to recover. After a while he smiled wanly at Gil and then quietly went about stoking the fire. With a fire roaring again, he rubbed his stiff old legs and tried to bend them.

"You won't believe it by looking at me but I was in great shape once, a marathoner. Poverty has a way of forcing changes and I let myself go. After that ordeal, my legs were never the same. I barely hobble around now. I've told this story so many times to so many people and I still don't know if I've ever made a real difference, but I'll tell you one thing I'm sure about. The old Judge was right. I like myself a whole lot better now than I ever did before. I have too much time on my hands now so when I think back on it, it's sad and disappointing to think I managed to live so long with my eyes closed to the unfairness of life and the burdens of others. I was like so many. I thought happiness was the goal and I could be happy without depending on anyone and having no one depend on me. The Judge would say that's how they want it, but I'm not such a conspiracy theorist, unless you consider molding people's value systems is a form of conspiracy. It seems crazy now but I believed that being independent was the secret to a good life. I was wrong and it cost me so much but I'm doing something about it. And I feel better about myself."

Gil wanted to say something but it was difficult to find words so he hunkered down in his chair as Clarke sat quietly beside him. Finally, he just blurted it out. "I'm sorry."

Clarke worked the fire and didn't look at Gil. "It wasn't your fault, son, you weren't even born yet."

Anxious, he tried to find the right words. "No I mean . . . I'm sorry that . . ."

Clarke jammed a large stick into the stove, broke it off, and shut the door. He turned to Gil.

"For allowing this to continue, we're all guilty. We could all do more . . ."

"No, I'm just sorry. I'm happy for you if you've found your way. You're doing what you can. This is on me. I . . . I need to do more. I just . . ." He paused to mull that over. "I miss Bernie, terribly. Bernie was my great-grandfather. He died. I didn't know him long, or well. He was real old and feeble when I first met him."

Clarke wiped his short-cropped white hair and smiled. "Like me," he said while stretching, his stomach paunch visible under an old gray sweatshirt as he tried to straighten his impossibly skinny legs.

Gil continued. "You'd think with everyone supposedly living forever, there'd be more old people, but then again, Profit had a horrible way of getting rid of them. I never thought it through. Bernie tried to help but I was too caught up in myself to understand, maybe like you were. And I never thought it through.

"At Angel Falls, I thought Bernie was teaching me to be something, to do something and I thought that he wasn't very good at teaching, so I wanted no part of it. I was homesick and worried about Howard—Howard is my father. I felt trapped and sorry for myself. I didn't know anyone, well that's not true. I did. And she was terrific, great really; I just . . . I never let her know. I didn't want to depend on anyone and I felt sorry for anyone who needed to depend on me.

"Stace . . . she never knew, she still doesn't know how much . . . how much I care for her . . . I was too busy and then . . ."

Clarke smiled and gently poked Gil with his walking stick. "Regret, you sound like me, so maybe you'll find your way yet. Being too busy is always a great excuse for not committing. I worked that angle a lot."

"Clarke, I'm ashamed for what I've done and not done. I never thought my life would take me here."

"To Presque Isle? I never thought I'd end up here either," Clarke responded with a cackle.

"No, I mean I never went anywhere when I was young. I had *Virtuoso* so who needed to travel?" Gil thought back to what it was like in *Virtuoso* and his thoughts were mostly of Andrea but he fought those memories off and pictured Bernie, lying in bed, pleading with him—begging him. But begging him to do what? He struggled to remember.

What was Bernie trying to make him do back in the beginning, before he had aged too much, no, before Gil was ready to grow up? He strained to remember a relevant moment from the beginning. What had they talked about? He pictured their flight to Angel Falls. What had they talked about in the homes of Bernie's friends, people who put their lives at risk so Bernie and his teen ward could spend a night in safety? Why hadn't he seen what Bernie was doing? Why couldn't he remember what they discussed? All he remembered was the inconvenience and fractured parts of long forgotten conversations that made it hard to determine what was real and what was faulty memory. It wasn't history or politics they discussed, or anything about being the Messiah. That came later. He wouldn't have been able to stomach Bernie talking about that at that point, when he had choices. But what choices did he have back then? In the beginning, when he felt alone and isolated, missing Howard greatly but not showing it, what had they argued about? He missed Howard so much but he refused to let Bernie see it. But Bernie knew and Bernie wanted him to learn, of course, but Bernie . . . but Bernie . . . Bernie wanted him to feel, to care, to empathize, to sympathize, to become involved with other people's lives and feel things for them, but it was too hard, Bernie. It is so hard!

"Bernie knew that I couldn't feel," Gil said it out loud.

Clarke banged his walking stick against the stove, surprising Gil.

"Hell, you're an American, why should you be different? You feel, you feel but it's just short by degrees of what others need and what you need too. It's you and how can you feel any different? To feel more, that's the hard part, believe me, I know, I've been there. When people leave here after visiting, I beg them to talk about how good old Clarke Jackell spoke to them and how he was kind and generous and good looking as hell in a particularly manly way. But what I want most for them to say about old Clarkie Boy here, is that he was easy to talk to because he had learned, before it was too late, how important people are."

Gil stared at this old stranger and wished that he was Bernie. It had taken him too long to mature and senility had arrived to soon for Bernie and they had passed like two ships in the night and Bernie could never ever be there for him again.

"I let him down," Gil said. "He tried so hard and I failed him. I don't like how it feels when I think that he failed because of me. Stacey, too, she tried but I was so angry and mad that I couldn't be what they needed. I'm a fool, Clarke, and not worthy of any of the good people that I've met. I need to be worthy and it hurts that I'm not."

"Bernie was a smart guy, he knew. If we stick with it, we all get there, eventually. We're human and it takes the time it takes. Bernie realized that, I'm sure."

"Did you know my great-grandfather?"

Clarke smiled and his entire body seemed to awaken. "Everyone's heard of Berne Thau, the old man, the Rabbi, Bernie Rosenthal. I knew some people who knew him. They worked with him in his *Greenhouse* operation. Your great-grandfather would help *Wasters*, give them a place to live, food, and then he'd pay them and train them and give them work so they'd have experience and a reference for getting another job so they wouldn't die. He taught them how to be productive, but more, he taught them to be, you know, human, as much as possible while still surviving. Thousands passed through his *Greenhouses*, thousands of helpless souls that Berne Thau, your great-grandfather, kept alive. These people needed to learn how to breathe in this toxic environment and he was their incubator."

"I wish I knew him like you do," Gil said, saddened by the realization of the time he had wasted with his great-grandfather.

"Don't get down on yourself, maturing is about how we adapt to the stages of comprehension that we all go through in life."

"I should have paid attention. But I never know what expression to put on my face and what to say, mostly, what to say."

Clarke kicked the stove, causing embers to bounce around inside. "Say what you feel and feel what you say?"

Gil's heart ached and he needed to change the subject. "Would you give that same advice to your brother?"

"Jake? Hell no. I wouldn't try to advise Jake on what to do, but then again, I can't. When the *Circle of Life* project disbanded, years later, I lost track of him. The media no longer covers him and Archive has been adjusted to reflect the best possible story line to promote patriotism among the masses so I'll never find any links to him, there, that's if I was looking. No, Jake just disappeared and that's fine." Clarke made a funny face. "It would be ironic if he was disappeared like the millions he caused to die."

"So you don't forgive him?"

"Forgive? I've changed a great deal but forgive him, no, that might just be one bridge too far. I have the time and I pray everyday for the strength to stop hating what he stood for and hating him for all the cruelty inflicted on his watch, but I'm not naive. Jake was a fool, but Crelli could have chosen from thousands, maybe millions of fools like him who would have gladly done what Jake did. I want to love everyone like a brother, so hating my real brother has to be impossible, doesn't it?"

"I think I understand."

"I can't guess what it was like for Jake. We become who we will be by growing through things and he would have had an awful lot to grow through for us to put aside our differences. But you never know. Look, it's late and I'm tired and talk of Jake makes me sleepy. You've been a good listener, thanks." With that, he curled up facing the stove and covered himself in a light blanket.

Gil couldn't let it go. "Clarke, what would you say to your brother if you saw him again?"

Clarke didn't move and let the question hang in the air for a bit before answering.

"You're asking a question I can't answer for certain until faced with it, so it's not important," Clarke pleaded. "What's important, I think, is being as honest and as caring as I can be. Those traits haven't made me the steadfast friends and fellow travelers that everyone deserves in this life, but at least I'm easy to know. How else will the people I have that in common with recognize me?"

"I appreciate this, thanks," Gil said. "Is there anything I can do to help you?"

"You're a hard man to read. You're so closed and you don't seem to react."

"In the past fifteen minutes I've been as free and open as I've ever been. Showing and telling people how I feel, it has never been a part of me. If I let down my guard, even for a minute, it could cost me my life and I'll take innocent people with me. That doesn't mean I don't have feelings."

"That's precisely what it does mean," Clarke offered. "Everyone believes they have feelings, but only those who show them and act on them truly do. The rest are just having an internal conversation. We have a busy morning and I'm going to sleep."

"Thanks for tomorrow and Canada." Gil settled on the floor, pulled a blanket over his head and slept.

Gil woke refreshed and excited to be off to freedom. After breakfast, he packed his communicator glove into his sack. He considered turning it on but thought better of it.

Clarke handed Gil a map and explained how to find the hidden submersible that would take him across the lake to Canada.

"I wish I could go with you but my legs don't do well confined in the sub, even on short trips. It's easy though. Follow the path outside my lodge. In a mile or so, you'll see a series of deserted old wooden cabins that form a semicircle. Go into the middle cabin where you'll find a plastic key taped to the underside of the table. Take it and follow the path to the water's edge. You'll find the submersible under some dense trees in a small cove to your right. Climb inside and seal the hatch. After it's properly sealed, it will start automatically and the craft will submerge and resurface at a preprogrammed location on the Canadian side. The hatch will open automatically when everything is secured. Wait there. Someone will be there to take you to the closest rebel headquarters. The rest, as they say, is up to you."

They shook hands and Gil turned to jog down the trail. "Thanks again for that story and your advice. And good luck." He was off.

Gil jogged happily past a broken gate, and then followed the path along the green-brown water of Lake Huron. Between two small, lightly-wooded hills, he saw the cottages Clarke had described and breathed a sigh of relief. He was almost free. His relief was short lived as the air began to rumble and the nearby water developed ripples. He heard the sound of approaching engines.

Frantically, he searched for a place to hide and noticed a rock formation nearby. He found a crevice and squeezed in to wait and hope. Almost immediately, helicopters and *SurveilEagles* were hovering near him. When the assault troopers descended, he knew he was in trouble. He hunkered down, hoping the patrols would pass him by.

Frightened, he hid and waited as patrols combed the hills nearby but didn't discover his hiding place. When the troops left and some of the aircraft took off, the area quieted. Afraid to move, he was startled by the crackle of static from his glove. He grabbed for it, turned the speaker volume lower, and put the glove to his ear.

"Gil, Joad," a female voice whispered. "I can block your signal, but you need to get out of there now. You may have to stay stateside for a while longer."

He whispered, frantically. "I can't. I have to go. I'm dead if I stay. Can you block the rangers a little longer so I can get to the shore?"

"Your problems are here, not in Canada," was her reply. "I can help. Have faith and face your issues. There are people who will help. Canada is not your only choice."

Would this never end? Even while he was at great risk, Joad was still playing games with his life.

"I'm done with this. I know what you want, but it isn't going to happen now. Before I can save others, I need to save myself. Please, help me." There was silence. "Joad, I'm sorry . . . about everything."

There was more silence, then, "I'm sorry, too. There is a path down the far side of the hill. I will keep it open to the shore. After that you are on your own."

Before he crawled out, he thought back to that night he freed his grandfather. He had been so frightened waiting among the troopers, but Joad had confused them and he and his grandfather had slipped away, safely, because of it. Could Joad do it again? As he ran, he searched for stray patrols but the area was deserted. Cautiously, he ran through a small ravine where he found the path. He turned and ran as fast as he could down a dirt trail into another small valley. He was approaching the submarine and freedom.

As soon as he entered the valley, he stopped so fast, he almost fell over. Deployed around him were armed HomeSec troops. He turned to flee but before he could move, a small woman in military gear stepped out and blocked his path.

He stared at his glove in disbelief as she kicked him hard in the stomach. He doubled over in pain and fell to the ground.

"Gil Rose," she said, her boot firmly on his neck, "Please resist. You are under arrest for treason and I'm allowed all necessary force to bring you in."

He looked up at the General.

"It's Tucker, isn't it?" he groaned. "It's been a long time. Nice to see you again."

She kicked him hard and a blinding light flashed across his eyes. Instinctively, he curled up, his hands, including his glove hand, protecting his face.

The Reverend General kicked him again and again, and then ordered him dragged onto an aircraft. Once inside, his arms and legs were shackled and, helpless, he stared through tears of pain as Tucker boarded the plane.

Had Gecko won? Why else would Joad turn on him? Tucker's boot accelerated toward his head and then . . . nothing.

The reflecting light of the aquarium calmed Chairwoman Brandt as she reclined on her divan waiting expectantly for the news.

"Madame Chairwoman?" the pleasing female voice in her head called out.

"What good news do you have for *Us*, Joad?"

"As I promised, Gil Rose has been secured. Ginger's patrol is flying him here."

With her fist in the air, she let out a yelp of glee at her long-delayed triumph.

"Good! The world is a little easier to manage thanks to you. You kept your promise and I appreciate that."

"One more thing, Madame Chairwoman."

"Yes?"

"I expect that you will keep your promise as well. Gil Rose must not be harmed."

Tanya laughed.

"Madame Chairwoman, you promised?"

"Madame Chairwoman . . . ?"

Thus ends Book 3: Circle of Life

The story of Gil Rose concludes as does the Joad Cycle in Book 4: The Rightness of Things